ILLE[GAL ALIEN]

"Robert J. Sawyer skill[...] [...]h first-contact science fiction—[...] [...], [...] John Grisham. Sawyer displays an impressive depth and breadth of both legal and scientific research—his aliens and his lawyers are equally credible. *Illegal Alien* admirably combines the hard side of science, law, and order with the softer side of compassion and idealism."
—*The New York Review of Science Fiction*

"Innovative, imaginative, and pioneering—not just excellent science fiction but also excellent popular literature. A fast-paced, exciting book that shows the imaginative heights to which science-fiction writers can climb when they combine SF with something else."
—*The Washington Post*

"As gripping as anything encountered by Perry Mason."
—James Gunn, Hugo Award–winning author

"Sawyer mixes tongue-in-cheek humor with courtroom drama and impending doom for humanity. The result is a tightly written page-turner that satisfies from the start."   —*Rocky Mountain News*

"Few novels (science fiction or otherwise) can match *Illegal Alien* for imagination and intelligence. Sawyer has created a smart and satisfying mystery, and we're caught looking the other way when he springs his big surprise at novel's end. After we've shaken our heads a few times, and caught our breath, we're left thinking not about a writer's cleverness, but about ourselves."   —*Mystery News*

"This is one fine courtroom drama, with enough twists in the plot to keep any mystery fan flipping the pages; it puts Perry Mason and John Grisham to shame. The novel is far too good to attempt to summarize; let's just say that Sawyer delves into all sorts of strange and wonderful conflicts, including the war between science and belief, and just what God may or may not be. *Illegal Alien* is the best Canadian mystery of the year."
—*The Globe and Mail* (Toronto)

continued . . .

"An intriguing mix of science fiction, mystery, and courtroom drama."
—*Hartford Courant*

"Some of the best trial scenes in SF, an intriguing mystery, interesting aliens, and a sinister back-plot, all excellently balanced. Add another hit to Sawyer's string." —*Science Fiction Chronicle*

"A tour de force of intricate, puzzle-like complexity. Well worth reading for its cleverness, its portrayal of a fascinating alien race, and its thematic consideration of the role of philosophical and religious beliefs among rational beings." —*Science Fiction Age*

"So many science-fiction accolades have been showered on Robert J. Sawyer that it's all too easy to forget his prizes include an Arthur Ellis Award from the Crime Writers of Canada. Sawyer's *Illegal Alien* embraces clues, criminals, and cross-examination in an immensely satisfying whodunit."
—*The Toronto Star*

"An enjoyable thriller where legal points and jury psychology matter more than astrophysics. The trial is fascinating, the ending satisfying, and lawyer Dale Rice, who is both principled and unscrupulous, is a fine character."
—*Starlog*

"Sawyer deals metaphorically with the issue of racism in the courts, but entertains the reader with sharp wit along with the heavier themes."
—*The Nashville Tennessean*

"Blends the world of John Grisham with that of Frederik Pohl or Larry Niven. Sawyer's skillful use of dialogue moves the case and the novel briskly along. *Illegal Alien* has a lot to offer those who enjoy sophisticated morality plays." —*Winnipeg Free Press*

Praise for the WWW trilogy

"Unforgettable. Impossible to put down."
—Jack McDevitt, Nebula Award–winning author of *Firebird*

"A superb work of day-after-tomorrow science fiction; I enjoyed every page." —Allen Steele, Hugo Award–winning author of *Hex*

"Cracking open a new Robert J. Sawyer book is like getting a gift from a friend who visits all the strange and undiscovered places in the world. You can't wait to see what he's going to amaze you with this time."

—John Scalzi, John W. Campbell Award–winning author of *Fuzzy Nation*

"Once again, Robert J. Sawyer explores the intersection between big ideas and real people. Here the subject is consciousness and perception—who we are and how we see one another, both literally and figuratively. Thoughtful and engaging, and a great beginning to a fascinating trilogy."

—Robert Charles Wilson, Hugo Award–winning author of *Vortex*

"The thought-provoking first installment of Sawyer's WWW trilogy explores the origins and emergence of consciousness. The thematic diversity—and profundity—makes this one of Sawyer's strongest works to date." —*Publishers Weekly* (starred review)

"*Wonder* is not only a superb conclusion to a tremendous trilogy, but stands alone as one of the best books that Sawyer has ever written." —*Winnipeg Free Press*

"Fun . . . [an] intelligent and compassionate approach . . . to the nature of consciousness." —*Sacramento News & Review*

"Caitlin is a very likable protagonist, and well drawn, as are Sawyer's other characters. *WWW: Wake* is a very promising start to what could turn out to be a very thoughtful and compelling science fiction trilogy." —*Blastr*

"Sawyer's take on theories about the origins of consciousness, generated within the framework of an engaging story, is fascinating, and his approach to machine consciousness and the Internet is surprisingly fresh." —*Booklist*

"*Wake* is about as good as it gets when it comes to science fiction." —*The Maine Edge*

"Sawyer continues to push the boundaries with his stories of the future made credible. His erudition, eclecticism, and masterly storytelling make this trilogy opener a choice selection." —*Library Journal*

Books by Robert J. Sawyer

Novels

GOLDEN FLEECE
END OF AN ERA
THE TERMINAL EXPERIMENT
STARPLEX
FRAMESHIFT
ILLEGAL ALIEN
FACTORING HUMANITY
FLASHFORWARD
CALCULATING GOD
MINDSCAN
ROLLBACK

The Quintaglio Ascension Trilogy

FAR-SEER
FOSSIL HUNTER
FOREIGNER

The Neanderthal Parallax Trilogy

HOMINIDS
HUMANS
HYBRIDS

The WWW Trilogy

WAKE
WATCH
WONDER

Collections

ITERATIONS
(introduction by James Alan Gardner)
RELATIVITY
(introduction by Mike Resnick)
IDENTITY THEFT
(introduction by Robert Charles Wilson)

For book-club discussion guides, visit sfwriter.com.

ILLEGAL ALIEN

ROBERT J. SAWYER

ACE BOOKS, NEW YORK

THE BERKLEY PUBLISHING GROUP
Published by the Penguin Group
Penguin Group (USA) Inc.
375 Hudson Street, New York, New York 10014, USA
Penguin Group (Canada), 90 Eglinton Avenue East, Suite 700, Toronto, Ontario M4P 2Y3, Canada
(a division of Pearson Penguin Canada Inc.)
Penguin Books Ltd., 80 Strand, London WC2R 0RL, England
Penguin Group Ireland, 25 St. Stephen's Green, Dublin 2, Ireland (a division of Penguin Books Ltd.)
Penguin Group (Australia), 250 Camberwell Road, Camberwell, Victoria 3124, Australia
(a division of Pearson Australia Group Pty. Ltd.)
Penguin Books India Pvt. Ltd., 11 Community Centre, Panchsheel Park, New Delhi—110 017, India
Penguin Group (NZ), 67 Apollo Drive, Rosedale, Auckland 0632, New Zealand
(a division of Pearson New Zealand Ltd.)
Penguin Books (South Africa) (Pty.) Ltd., 24 Sturdee Avenue, Rosebank, Johannesburg 2196,
South Africa

Penguin Books Ltd., Registered Offices: 80 Strand, London WC2R 0RL, England

This is a work of fiction. Names, characters, places, and incidents either are the product of the author's
imagination or are used fictitiously, and any resemblance to actual persons, living or dead, business
establishments, events, or locales is entirely coincidental. The publisher does not have any control
over and does not assume any responsibility for author or third-party websites or their content.

ILLEGAL ALIEN

An Ace Book / published by arrangement with SFWriter.com, Inc.

PRINTING HISTORY
Ace hardcover edition / December 1997
First Ace mass-market edition / January 1999
Penguin Canada premium edition / December 2009
Second Ace mass-market edition / January 2012

Copyright © 1997 by Robert J. Sawyer.
Cover art by Paul Cooklin / Getty Images.
Cover design by Rita Frangie.
Interior text design by Laura K. Corless.

ISBN: 978-1-937007-21-8

ACE
Ace Books are published by The Berkley Publishing Group,
a division of Penguin Group (USA) Inc.,
375 Hudson Street, New York, New York 10014.
ACE and the "A" design are trademarks of Penguin Group (USA) Inc.

PRINTED IN THE UNITED STATES OF AMERICA

10 9 8 7 6 5 4 3 2 1

For Edo and Roberta van Belkom,
with thanks and friendship

ACKNOWLEDGMENTS

Amici curiae in the creation of this novel include my wife Carolyn Clink; my editors Susan Allison and Ginjer Buchanan; Asbed Bedrossian, who was my host during my visit to Los Angeles; Richard M. Gotlib, barrister and solicitor, sessional lecturer at Osgoode Hall Law School, Toronto; Professor Edward F. Guinan, Department of Astronomy and Astrophysics, Villanova University, Villanova, Pennsylvania; Dr. Ariel Reich, Esq., of the Silicon Valley office of the firm Weil, Gotshal & Manges, LLP; Dena Rosenberg Thaler, J.D.; Ted Bleaney; Linda C. Carson; David Livingstone Clink; Richard Curtis; Paul Fayter; Karl Fuss; James Alan Gardner; Terence M. Green; Howard Miller; John-Allen Price; Alan B. Sawyer; Jean-Louis Trudel; and Ralph Vincinanza. If any errors remain in the text, *mea culpa*.

For Justice, though she's painted blind,
Is to the weaker side inclined.

—Samuel Butler (1612–1680)

ONE

The Navy lieutenant poked his close-cropped head into the aircraft carrier's wardroom. "It's going to be another two hours, gentlemen. You should really get some sleep."

Francis Nobilio, a short white man of fifty with wavy hair mixed evenly between brown and gray, was sitting in a vinyl-upholstered metal chair. He was wearing a two-piece dark-blue business suit and a pale blue shirt. His tie was undone and hung loosely around his neck. "What's the latest?" he said.

"As expected, sir, a Russian sub will beat us to the location. And a Brazilian cruise ship has changed course to have a look-see."

"A cruise ship!" said Frank, throwing his arms up in exasperation. He turned to Clete, who was leaning back in a similar chair, giant tennis-shoed feet up on the table in front of him.

Clete lifted his narrow shoulders and grinned broadly. "Sounds like a big ol' party, don't it?" he said, his voice rich with that famous Tennessee accent—Dana Carvey did a devastating Cletus Calhoun.

"Can't we cordon off the area?" said Frank to the Navy man.

The lieutenant shrugged. "It's in the middle of the Atlantic, sir—international waters. The cruise ship has as much right to be there as anyone else."

The Love Boat meets *Lost in Space*," muttered Frank. He looked up at the Navy man. "All right. Thanks."

The lieutenant left, doing a neat step over the raised lip at the bottom of the door.

"They must be aquatic," said Frank, looking at Clete.

"Mebbe," said Clete. "Mebbe not. We ain't aquatic, and we used to land our ships at sea. This very aircraft carrier picked up an *Apollo* command module once, didn't it?"

"My point exactly," said Frank. "We *used* to land our ships at sea, because that was easier than landing them on land, and—"

"I thought it was because we launched out over the ocean from Canaveral, so—"

"The Shuttle goes up from Canaveral; we bring it down on land. If you've got the technology, you come down on land—if that's where you live; the Russians came down on land from day one."

Clete was shaking his head. "I think you're missing the obvious, Frankie. What was it that boy said a moment ago? 'International waters.' I think they've been watching long enough to figger it'd be a peck o' trouble landin' in any particular country. Only place on Earth you can land that ain't nobody's turf is in the ocean."

"Oh, come on. I doubt they've been able to decipher our radio or TV, and—"

"Don't need to do none o' that," said Clete. He was forty years old, pale, thin, gangly, jug-eared, and redheaded—not quite Ichabod Crane, but close. "You can deduce it from first principles. Earth's got seven continents; that implies regional evolution, and *that* implies territorial conflict once the technology reaches a level that lets you travel freely between the continents."

Frank blew out air, conceding the point. He looked at his watch for the third time in the last few minutes. "Damn, I wish we could get there faster. This is—"

"Hang on a minute, Frankie," said Clete. He used one of his long arms to aim the remote at the seventeen-inch color TV mounted on the wall, turning off the mute. The aircraft carrier was picking up CNN's satellite feed.

". . . more now on that story," said white-haired Lou Waters. "Civilian and military observers worldwide were stunned late yesterday when what was at first taken to be a giant meteor skimmed through Earth's atmosphere over Brazil." Waters's face was replaced with grainy amateur video of something streaking through a cloudless blue sky. "But the object flew right around the Earth well inside our atmosphere, and soon almost every public and private telescope and radar dish on the planet was trained on it. Even the U.S. government has now conceded that the object is, in all likelihood, a spacecraft—and not one of ours. Karen Hunt has more. Karen?"

The picture changed to show a pretty African-American woman, standing outside the Griffith Park Observatory. "Lou, for decades human beings have wondered if we are alone in the universe. Well, now we know. Although the U.S. and Russian military aircraft that flew over the splashdown site earlier today failed to make public the videos they shot, a Moroccan Airlines 747 *en route* to Brasilia passed directly over the area about three hours ago. That plane has now safely landed, and we've obtained this exclusive footage, taken by passenger Juan Rubenstein with his home-video equipment."

The image was coarse, but it clearly showed a large object shaped like a shield or a broad arrowhead floating atop gray water. The object seemed capable of changing colors—one moment it was red; the next, orange; then yellow. It cycled through the hues of the rainbow, over and over again, but with a considerable period of pure black between being violet and red.

Cut to a dour, middle-aged man with an unkempt beard. The title "Arnold Hammermill, Ph.D., Scripps Institute," appeared beneath him. "It's difficult to gauge the size of the spaceship," said Hammermill, "given we don't know the precise altitude of the plane or the zoom setting used at the time the video was taken, but judging by the height of the waves, and taking into account today's maritime forecast for that part of the Atlantic, I'd say the ship is between ten and fifteen meters long."

A graphic appeared, showing the vessel to be about half the size of a Space Shuttle orbiter. The reporter's voice, over this: "The United States aircraft carrier *Kitty Hawk* is on its way now to the splashdown site. Earlier today, the president's science advisor, Francis Nobilio" (black-and-white still of Frank, a few years out of date, showing his hair as mostly brown) "and astronomer Cletus Calhoun, best known as the host of PBS's popular *Great Balls of Fire!* astronomy series" (silent clip of Clete at the rim of Arizona's Barringer crater) "were flown by military jet to the *Kitty Hawk,* and are now on their way to rendezvous with the alien ship. The *Kitty Hawk* should reach its destination in just over one hundred minutes from now. Bobbie and Lou?"

Back to CNN Center in Atlanta and a two-shot of Lou Waters and Bobbie Battista. "Thanks, Karen," said Battista. "Before Dr. Calhoun left the U.S., our science correspondent Miles O'Brien managed to interview him and University of Toronto exobiology professor Packwood Smathers about what this all means. Let's have another look at that tape."

The image changed to show O'Brien in front of two giant wall monitors. The one on the left was labeled Toronto and showed Smathers; the one on the right was labeled Los Angeles and showed Clete.

"Dr. Smathers, Dr. Calhoun, thanks for joining us on such short notice," said O'Brien. "Well, it looks like the incredible has happened, doesn't it? An alien spaceship has apparently landed in the middle of the Atlantic. Dr. Smathers, what can we expect to see when this ship opens up?"

Smathers had a square head, thick white hair, and a neatly trimmed white beard. He was wearing a brown sports jacket with leather patches on the elbows—the quintessential professorial look. "Well, of course, we first have to suspect that this ship is unmanned—that it's a probe, like the *Viking* landers, rather than carrying a crew, and—"

"Look at the size of the thing," said Clete, interrupting. "Pete's sake, Woody, ain't no need for the thing to be that big, 'less it's got somebody aboard. 'Sides, it looks like it's got windows, and—"

"Dr. Calhoun is famous for jumping to conclusions," said Smathers sharply. O'Brien was grinning from ear to ear—he evidently hadn't expected to get an impromptu Siskel and Ebert of science. "But, as I was about to say, *if* there are alien beings aboard, then I expect them to be at least vaguely familiar in body plan, and—"

"You're hedging now, Woody," said Clete. "Couple years ago, I heard you give a talk arguing that the humanoid body plan would be adopted by purty near any form of intelligent life, and—"

Smathers was growing red in the face. "Well, yes, I did say that then, but—"

"But now that we're actually goin' to meet aliens," said Clete, clearly enjoying himself, "you ain't so sure no more."

"Well," said Smathers, "the human body plan might indeed represent an ideal for an intelligent lifeform. Start with the sense organs: two eyes are much better than one, since two give stereoscopic vision—but a third eye adds hardly any value over two. Two ears likewise give stereophonic hearing, and they'll obviously be on opposite sides of the body, to give the best possible separation. You can go right down the human body from head to toe, and make a case why each part of it is ideal. When that spaceship opens up, yes, I'll stand by my contention that we'll probably see humanoids inside."

The Clete on the TV set looked positively pained. The one sitting next to Frank aboard the *Kitty Hawk* shook his head. "Peckerwood Smathers," he said under his breath.

"That's hooey, Woody," said the TV Calhoun. "Ain't nothin' optimized about our form—y'all only get optimization when you've got an ultimate design goal in mind, and there wasn't one. Evolution takes advantage of what's handy, that's all. You know, five hundred million years ago, durin' the Cambrian explosion, dozens o' different body plans appeared simultaneously in the fossil record. The one that gave rise to us—the ancestor of modern vertebrates— weren't no better than any of the others; it was just plum lucky, is all. If a different one had survived, nothin' on this planet would look the way it does today. No, I bet there's some critter inside unlike anything we've ever seen before."

"Clearly we have some differing points of view here," said O'Brien. "But—"

"Well, that's the whole point, ain't it?" said Clete. "For decades, guys like Woody been getting grants to think about alien life. It was all a good game till today. It wasn't *real* science—you could never test a one of their propositions. But now, today, it all goes from being a theoretical science to an empirical one. Gonna be pretty embarrassing if every-thing they've been saying turns out to be wrong."

"Now, hang on, Clete," said Smathers. "I'm at least will-ing to put my cards on the table, and—"

"Well, if you want to hear my—What? Crying out loud, hon, can't you see I'm on TV?"

A muffled female voice, off camera; Frank recognized it as Clete's secretary, Bonnie: "Clete, it's the White House."

"White House?" He looked directly into the camera and lifted his red eyebrows. The shot widened, showing more of Clete's cluttered study. Bonnie crossed into the frame, holding a cordless phone. Clete took it from her. "Calhoun here. What—Frankie! How good to—no, no. Sure, yeah, I can do that. Sure, sure. I'll be ready. Bye." Clete put down the phone and looked into the camera again. "I gotta go, Miles—sorry 'bout this. They're sending a car for me. I'm off to rendezvous with the alien ship." He unclipped his microphone and moved out of the shot.

Cut back to O'Brien. "Well, obviously we've lost Dr. Calhoun. We'll continue our conversation with Dr. Smathers. Doctor, can you—"

Clete hit the remote, and the TV went dead.

TWO

There was indeed a Russian submarine present by the time the U.S.S. *Kitty Hawk* reached the splashdown site, and the Brazilian cruise ship was visible on the horizon, coming closer. The *Kitty Hawk* held station one kilometer from the alien ship, the hull of which was still flashing through the colors of the rainbow. The Russian sub was slightly farther away on the opposite side.

The alien ship seemed to be about two-thirds submerged in the water, but it was bobbing enough that intermittently most of its upper surface was visible. Frank, Clete, and a young Navy pilot boarded one of the *Kitty Hawk*'s SH-60F Seahawk helicopters and took off from the aircraft carrier for a flight over the vessel.

"It sure is streamlined," shouted Clete, over the noise of the chopper's rotor.

Frank nodded. "It *must* be just a landing craft," he shouted back. Since the ship had first been spotted entering Earth's atmosphere, NORAD had been scanning the heavens, looking for any sign of the mothership. Meanwhile, Canaveral was readying *Atlantis* for flight. No American or

Russian Shuttle was currently in orbit; *Atlantis* was the next one scheduled to fly, but it wasn't supposed to go up for another eighteen days.

The alien ship's hull seemed to be one continuous piece. It had neither the riveted metal plates that made up the *Kitty Hawk*'s exterior nor the ceramic tiles that covered a Space Shuttle. There were four mirrored surfaces that might have been windows across the pointed end of the shield, and there was something in grayish green that might have been writing going down one side of the upper hull, but it was difficult to make out, especially with the background constantly changing color.

"I bet they see into the infrared," shouted Clete. "It's probably still changin' colors while it seems to be black before turning red, but we just can't see it."

"Perhaps," said Frank, "but—"

"Look at that!" shouted the chopper's crew chief.

A narrow cylinder was rising out of the center of the spaceship's hull. At its apex was a bright yellow light that was winking on and off. *Blink,* pause, *blink-blink,* pause, *blink-blink-blink*.

"Counting," said Clete.

But the next sequence was *five* blinks, not four, and the one after that was seven blinks. And then the sequence started cycling over and over again: one, two, three, five, seven; one, two, three, five, seven.

"Prime numbers!" said Frank. He shouted at the pilot, "Does this copter have a searchlight?"

The man shook his head.

"Get us back to the aircraft carrier as fast as possible. Hurry!"

The pilot nodded and took the chopper through a wide, banking turn.

Frank looked over at the Russian sub. It was already returning the signal: the first five prime numbers in sequence, cycling repeatedly.

The pilot was wearing a radio headset. Frank shouted at him. "Get the *Kitty Hawk* to use its searchlights. Tell it to blink out a reply at the ship. The first five prime numbers, over and over."

The pilot relayed the message. It seemed to take forever—with Frank fidgeting through each second—but eventually a large searchlight just below the carrier's radar antenna started flashing out the sequence.

The yellow beacon sticking up from the lander went dark.

"Could we have said the wrong thing?" asked Clete.

The Seahawk touched down on the flight deck. As the rotor was twirling down, Frank got out, the wind from the blades whipping his hair. Clete followed a moment later. Hunching over, they hustled away from the chopper. The captain, a bald-headed black man of about fifty, was waiting for them just inside the base of the conning tower. "The Russians are still signaling the same thing, too," he said.

Frank frowned, thinking. Why had the aliens shut up? They'd replied exactly as the aliens had, showing that humans understood prime numbers, and—

No. All they'd shown is that humans can parrot things back at them. "Try continuing the sequence," said Frank.

Clete nodded, immediately seeing it as well. "They gave us the first five primes; give 'em the next five."

The captain nodded and lifted a small intercom handset off the wall, pulling it close to him. "Signaling room—continue the sequence. Give them the next five prime numbers."

"Sir, yes sir," said a staticky voice, "but, ah, sir, what *are* the next five?"

The captain looked at Frank, eyebrows lifted. Frank made a disgusted frown. Clete rolled his eyes. "Eleven, thirteen, seventeen, nineteen, and twenty-three," Frank said.

The captain repeated the numbers into the microphone. "Sir, yes sir," said the seaman's voice.

"We better get up there," said Clete.

Frank nodded. "How do we get from here to where the controls for the searchlight are?"

"Come with me," said the captain. He led them to a circular metal stairwell and took them up to the radio room. As they entered, Frank saw the seaman who had been operating the light. He was a young white fellow, maybe nineteen, with a half centimeter of blond hair. "The aliens have started flashing again," he said.

"What was the sequence?" said Clete.

"They repeated back all ten prime numbers," the seaman said.

A wide grin spread across Frank's face. "Contact."

The captain was looking out the window. "The Russian sub is signaling the ten numbers, too."

Frank pointed. "And here comes that damned cruise ship."

The yellow beacon started flashing again. One. Four. Nine. And then so many flashes that Frank lost track.

"It's gotta be squares," said Clete. "One squared; two squared; three squared; four squared."

"Give them five-squared as a response," said Frank, looking at the young fellow. "That's twenty-five."

The seaman started clicking the trigger button for the searchlight as he counted out loud.

"God," said Clete, pointing out the window. "God."

The alien craft was lifting out of the ocean. It rose about twenty meters above the waves, water streaming off it. Its hull had stopped changing colors; it was now a uniform dark green. There seemed to be four jets of some sort positioned on its underbelly. They churned up the ocean surface beneath. The ship started moving slowly horizontally. It flew in the direction of the Russian submarine, but stopped just short of the vessel, apparently to prevent its jet exhaust from blasting down on the sub. The lander then flew over to near the cruise ship. With binoculars, Frank could see people on its deck taking photographs and home videos. Then the spaceship changed direction and headed toward the *Kitty Hawk*. It stopped about five meters off the projecting bow of the flight deck, and just hovered there.

"What's it doing?" shouted Frank.

Clete shrugged.

But the seaman spoke up. "Sir, I believe it's waiting for permission to land, sir."

Frank looked at the young man. Perhaps he'd dismissed him too quickly.

"I believe the boy is right, Frankie," said Clete. "They know this is an aircraft carrier. They've seen our helicopter take off and land from it, and they can probably tell just by looking at the planes out on the flight deck what they are— they're clearly designed according to aerodynamic principles."

"By all means they can land," said Frank. "But how do we tell them that?"

"Well, if the question is obvious, the answer must be, too," said Clete. "Give 'em the prime numbers again. Do it correctly, and that's 'yes.' Do it incorrectly—say, one, two, three, five, eight—and that's 'no.'"

Frank nodded. "Signal the first five primes," he said.

The seaman looked at his captain for confirmation. The captain nodded, and the seaman used his thumb to operate the light trigger. In the window, Frank could see the alien ship moving over the flight deck.

The intercom whistled. The captain picked up the hand unit. "Raintree here."

"Sir," said a husky voice, "the Russian sub has radioed us, asking that we send a helicopter to bring three observers over here immediately, sir."

The captain looked at Frank, who frowned. "Christ, I don't want—"

Clete interrupted. "Now, Frankie, they *chose* international waters. You can't really—"

"No, no, I suppose not. Okay, Captain."

"Take care of it, Mr. Coltrane," said the captain, and he replaced the hand unit in its clip.

"I want video equipment set up on the flight deck," said Frank. "I want everything recorded."

The captain nodded, and spoke into the intercom again.

"Let's get down there," said Clete.

Captain Raintree, Frank, and Clete went back down the circular staircase they'd gone up earlier, and emerged from the same door at the base of the conning tower, exiting onto the flight deck. There wasn't much wind, and the sky was mostly clear. The lander was still in the process of lowering itself.

"Damn," said the captain.

"What's wrong?" asked Frank, over the roar of the lander's exhaust.

"It's setting down in the middle of the runway. No way we can launch a fighter with it there."

Frank shrugged. "It's the biggest clear area."

In the distance, another Navy Seahawk was now hovering over the conning tower of the Russian sub. A rope ladder had been lowered, and a man was climbing up into the chopper.

Captain Raintree looked at Frank. "We do have recorded music, sir. We could play the national anthem."

"Is there a United Nations anthem?" asked Frank.

"Not as far as I know, sir," said the captain.

"Anybody got the theme from *Star Trek* on tape?" said Clete.

The captain looked at him.

Clete shrugged. "Just a thought."

"I could assemble an honor guard," said the captain.

"With rifles?" said Frank. "Not on your life."

The lander came to rest. Frank could feel vibration in the deck plates beneath his feet as it clanged against them.

"Shall we go have a look?" said Clete.

"Sir," said the captain, "the lander could be radioactive.

I suggest you let one of my people check it over with a Geiger counter first."

Frank nodded. The captain used the intercom again to give the order.

"Do you suppose they're going to come outside?" asked Clete.

Frank lifted his shoulders. "I don't know. They may be incapable of coming outside—even if they have space suits, the gravity may be too high for them to move around."

"Then why land on the *Kitty Hawk* at all?"

"Maybe they were just getting seasick being tossed on the ocean."

The helicopter was now leaving the Russian sub and heading back toward the *Kitty Hawk*.

Clete pointed at the gray-green markings on the ship's dark green hull. They were complex, consisting of a horizontal line with various spirals and curves descending from it. No way to tell if the whole thing was one character, or if it was meant to be a word, or just abstract art.

A sailor appeared next to the captain, holding a Geiger counter. The captain nodded for him to proceed. The man looked nervous, but headed out across the flight deck toward the lander.

"Captain," said Frank, "can you sail this ship to New York?"

"Want to take 'em to see *Cats?*" said Clete.

Frank frowned. "To the United Nations, of course."

The captain nodded. "Sure, we can go anywhere."

The helicopter landed. Two Russian men and a Russian woman disembarked, along with the copter pilot. They came over to the American captain.

"Sergei Korolov," said the Russian, a thickset man in his thirties. He saluted. "I'm—first officer, you'd call it, on the *Suvorov.*" He nodded to the woman. "Our doctor, Valentina Danilova, and our radio officer, Piotr Pushkin. Neither of them speaks English."

"Great," muttered Frank. "I'm Frank Nobilio, science advisor to the president of the United States. This is Cletus Calhoun, astronomer, and Captain Raintree."

"I point out," said Korolov, "that the lander only settled on your ship because it was not possible to settle on our submarine. But under international salvage laws, the lander is clearly ours—we got to it first."

Frank sighed. "It's not our intention to steal the lander, Mr. Korolov. In fact, I want to take it to the United Nations in New York."

"I will have to consult with my captain, and she will have to consult with Moscow," said Korolov. "It is not—"

The man with the Geiger counter returned. "It's clean, sir. Just normal background radiation."

"Very good," said Captain Raintree. "Do you want to go have a closer look, Dr. Nobilio?"

"By all means. Let's—*my God.*"

A portion of the curving wall of the lander was sliding up. The hatch had been completely invisible when closed, but the opening was obvious. Inside was a gray-walled chamber—an air lock, in all likelihood. And standing in the middle of the chamber was a figure.

A figure that was not human.

"Damn," said Captain Raintree, under his breath. "Sir, if that thing is carrying alien germs, we'll have to, er, *sterilize* this ship."

Frank spoke firmly. "I'll make that determination, Captain."

"But—"

"Captain, shut up." Frank stepped closer to the lander. His heart was pounding in his ears.

An alien.

An actual, honest-to-God alien.

It didn't have the big head, the large eyes, the tiny body, or any of the other characteristics associated with UFO sightings, of course. Frank had always taken such unimaginative descriptions of alien beings as proof that UFOs had nothing to do with extraterrestrial life, Packwood Smathers's ridiculous contentions notwithstanding. No, this was clearly something that had evolved somewhere else.

The creature was not humanoid.

It stood about five and a half feet tall and, at a wild guess, probably weighed a hundred and fifty pounds. It had four limbs, but all four of them seemed to be attached at the shoulders. The left and right ones were long, and reached down to the ground. The front and back ones were shorter, dangling freely. The head was a simple dome rising up from the shoulders, and on top of it there was a topknot or tuft of white tendrils that seemed to be waving independently of the gentle breeze. Positioned near the front of the dome were two mirrored convex circles that might have been eyes. Below them was an orifice that could have been a mouth. The being's hide was blue-gray. It wore a dun-colored vest-like affair, with many pockets.

Clete had moved to Frank's elbow. "No spacesuit," he said. "It's breathing our air, and it's standing in our gravity."

The alien began to walk forward. Its left and right limbs were joined at three places, and its stride length was close to six feet. Although it didn't seem to be hurrying, it managed to close half the distance between itself and Frank in a matter of seconds—then it stopped, dead, still about fifty feet away.

The meaning seemed plain enough: an invitation to come closer. The alien wasn't going to invade Frank's territory, and he clearly wasn't looking to grab Frank and steal him aboard the lander. Frank walked forward; Clete fell in next to him. The Russians began to move as well. Frank turned around. "Just one of you," he said. "We don't want it to think we're ganging up on it."

Korolov nodded and spoke briefly to Pushkin and Danilova. They both looked disappointed, but they obeyed the order and moved back to stand next to Captain Raintree.

The three humans closed the remaining distance. Clete held up a hand when they got within eight feet of the alien. "Better stop here, Frankie," he said. "We don't know what it considers to be its personal space."

Frank nodded. Up close, he could see that the creature's skin was crisscrossed with fine lines, dividing it into diamond-shaped scales or plates, and—Frank couldn't help smiling. There was a small adhesive strip, perhaps three inches long and three-quarters of an inch wide, attached to the side of the alien's domed head—apparently a bandage, as if the alien had bumped its head on something. Somehow, the small sign of fallibility made the alien seem much more accessible, much less formidable.

The alien was presumably studying the humans, but there were no visible pupils in the mirrored lenses—no way to tell where the alien was looking.

How to proceed? Frank thought for a moment about making the hand sign from *Close Encounters*—and that thought gave him a better idea. He held up one finger, then two—he was conscious that he was making a peace sign—then three, then five. He then brought up his second hand and added two fingers from it, for a total of seven.

The alien lifted its front arm and raised the hand attached to it, which ended in four flat-tipped fingers, equally spaced around the circular end of the arm. The fingers seemed undifferentiated—they were all the same length, with no obvious thumb. The first and third fingers opposed each other, and so did the second and fourth.

The alien raised one finger, then two, then three. It then reached its second hand around from behind its body, and raised two of its fingers—making a total of five—and then the remaining two, making a total of seven.

So far, so good. But then Frank thought perhaps he'd made a mistake. Maybe the alien would now assume humans communicated through a gesticular language, rather than a spoken one. He touched a hand to his own chest and said, "Frank."

"Frank." The alien was a gifted mimic—it sounded just like Frank's own voice.

No, no, that wasn't it—it had recorded his voice and immediately played it back to him. There must be some sort of recording equipment in the vest it was wearing.

Frank pointed at the alien. There was no reason to think the gesture would make sense to the creature—pointing might only be meaningful to beings who had been spear carriers in their past. But almost at once the alien's mouth moved. It was a complex structure, with an outer horizontal opening and an inner layer of tissue that had a vertical opening, letting it make a variety of rectangular holes. "Hask," said the alien. Its voice was smooth and deep—Frank had seen nothing on the being that might be genitalia, but it sounded male. The voice started softly, but the volume lifted by the end of the word.

But then Frank realized that he hadn't really established anything. Was Hask the being's personal name, or the name of its race? Or did the word mean something else? "Hello," maybe? Frank pointed at Cletus. "Clete," he said. The alien repeated the word back, and this time Frank was positive that the sound was coming not from the mouth, but the alien's chest. One of the pockets on its vest contained a small rectangular object; its outline was apparent by the way the fabric was distorted, and the top of the unit was peeking out of the pocket's flap. The sound had apparently come from it.

The alien pointed at Frank and said his name—this time it did come from the alien's mouth. He then pointed at Clete and said Clete's name. Both times the word started softly, but grew louder over the length of the syllable. The alien pointed at the Russian. Frank looked at him, but was damned if he could remember the man's name.

"Sergei," said the Russian.

"Sergei," repeated the device in the alien's pocket, and then, a moment later, the alien said "Sergei" on its own.

Frank then indicated himself, Clete, and Sergei. "Humans," he said.

"Wait," said Sergei. "I object to contact being made in English."

Frank looked at the man. "This isn't the time—"

"Certainly is time. You—"

Clete spoke up. "Don't be a pain. Dr. Nobilio is in charge here, and—"

"Nyet."

"For heaven's sake," said Frank. "We're getting this all on video. Let's not squabble."

Sergei looked angry but didn't say anything further. Frank turned back to the alien, repeated his pointing at each of the people in turn, then repeated the word, "Humans."

The alien touched its chest, just as Frank had touched his own moments before. "Tosok."

"Tosok," said Frank. "Hask."

"Humans," said Hask. "Frank. Clete. Sergei."

"Now we're cookin'," said Clete.

THREE

Captain Raintree and the remaining Russians came closer. Dozens of the *Kitty Hawk*'s crew members had found reasons to come up on the flight deck, and Hask was soon surrounded by an awestruck crowd. Frank and Clete spent hours teaching the alien English nouns and some simple verbs—such as "walk" and "run" and "lift."

Frank noted more details of Hask's appearance as time went by. The alien had four mirrored silver lenses—two on the front of his dome-shaped head above the forward arm, and two more in back above the rear arm, an arm that was somewhat less robust and a bit shorter than the one in front. There seemed to be some sort of rust-colored dental plates inside the mouth at the front of the head, but there was a second mouth that lacked such plates in the back of the head. There were also two small orifices at either side of the head, and it seemed that it was through these that the alien was breathing.

As they began building complex phrases it became clear that the Tosok manner of speech was to start each sentence at a low volume and raise it until the end of the sentence was reached. Hask seemed to have trouble following what Frank was saying because the human wasn't able to emulate this effectively; Hask was only able to parse Frank's speech if Frank paused for a full second between sentences.

After about an hour a seaman came to within ten feet of Frank, then motioned to catch his eye. Frank said, "Excuse me," to Hask—not that those were words Hask yet knew, but Frank hoped the alien would understand that they were meant to be polite. He walked over to the seaman. "What is it?"

"Sir, we just got a message from NORAD. They've located the alien mothership. It's in a polar orbit, about two hundred miles up. And, sir, it's huge."

The *Kitty Hawk* set course for New York. The alien came inside the aircraft carrier and allowed Frank and Clete to lead him to the wardroom. To Frank's astonishment, once they were inside, Hask reached up simultaneously with his front and back hands and let the four mirrored lenses fall into his square palms—he'd been wearing the Tosok equivalent of sunglasses, although Frank couldn't tell exactly how they'd been held in place. Hask stacked the mirrored lenses into a neat pile, and dropped them into one of the many pockets on his vest.

Hask's eyes were circular and moist. One of those in front was orange, the other green; one in back was also green, and the fourth was silver-gray. Each had a small vertically oval black pupil in it; each pair seemed to track together.

Hask couldn't use a chair with a back because of his rear arm. A yeoman got a stool from somewhere, but Hask didn't seem to have any desire to sit on it.

Clete and Frank continued teaching the alien English; so far, it had shown no interest in reciprocating by teaching the humans its language.

They showed Hask various objects, and spoke their

names aloud. The Tosok reached into one of his many pockets and pulled out the small rectangular device that had been helping him with translations. It was the first good look Frank and Clete had got at it. The object was made of something that looked more like ceramic than plastic or metal. There was a cross-shaped arrangement of buttons on it, with six green buttons in each arm of the cross and a blue one in the center, and on its side was a three-holed aperture for some sort of connector. The back of this handheld computer contained a viewscreen, and the computer apparently was also a scanner—Hask could display the interior structure of the objects Frank and Clete showed him, as well as magnify them enormously to study fine details.

The humans also drew pictures on a pad to represent a variety of mathematical and physical concepts. At one point Clete—who was a much better artist than Frank—produced an image of Earth, with an object in polar orbit around it.

"What is that?" asked Frank.

"Ship," said Hask.

"How many Tosoks?"

"Six."

"Six plus Hask?"

"Six plus Hask equals seven."

"Big ship," said Frank.

"Big ship for big walk," said Hask.

"Big *journey,*" corrected Frank.

"Big journey," repeated Hask.

They didn't yet have the vocabulary to ask from where the alien had come, but—

"How long journey?" asked Frank.

"Long. Big long."

Frank went to the porthole and motioned for Hask to follow. Hask placed mirrored lenses over his front eyes again and came over to stand beside Frank. Frank pointed at the sun, then made a circular motion with his arm, hopefully indicating the concept of a day.

"No," said Hask. It was frustrating. Sometimes Hask grasped what Frank was getting at quickly; other times it took repeated tries to get even a simple concept across. But Hask moved back to the table and took the marker from Clete's hand—the first direct physical contact between human and Tosok. He then took the drawing of the Earth that Clete had made, lifted it up in his front hand, and pointed at the porthole and the sun beyond with his back hand. Hask then moved the picture of the Earth in a circular motion.

"He's saying it's not a question of days, Frankie," said Clete. "It's a question of years."

"How many?" said Frank. "How many years?"

Hask used his front hand to manipulate the buttons on his pocket computer. The unit said something. Hask pushed another button, and this time the computer replied in English. "Two hundred eleven."

"You've been traveling for two hundred and eleven Earth years?" said Frank.

"Yes," said Hask.

Frank looked at Clete, whose mouth was hanging open in astonishment.

Hask picked up spoken English at a phenomenal rate. One of the things Frank had brought with him was the *Random House Unabridged Dictionary,* Second Edition, on CD-ROM, which had recorded pronunciations. There was no way to electronically interface Hask's pocket computer with Frank's multimedia notebook, but while Frank slept, Hask, who seemed to have no need for sleep, worked his way through the two thousand line drawings included with the CD, and for the ones that made sense to him, he listened to the pronunciations. By the time Frank woke up the next morning, Hask had substantially increased his vocabulary. How much of it was Hask's own native facility, and how much of it was the doing of his pocket computer, Frank couldn't say. Hask had explained that the computer could communicate directly to him, apparently by a receiver implanted in one of Hask's four evenly spaced ear slits (slits that were all but invisible against his gridwork of scales).

Concrete nouns were the easiest for him to learn—Frank had begun calling Hask *him,* rather than it, although they still hadn't worked out the being's gender. Synonyms confused Hask, though—the idea of having more than one word to express exactly the same concept was utterly foreign to him. Clete, who was trying to divine whatever he could about Hask's home world, suggested to Frank that this meant that Tosok culture had always been monolithic, with a single language—most English synonyms were adopted from other languages. Frank used this as another argument to keep on teaching Hask only English, despite the Russians' continued complaints.

The *Kitty Hawk* was still two days from New York. Hask could have flown there himself in his lander, or been taken there in one of the aircraft carrier's planes. But it seemed better to give humanity in general and the United Nations in particular a little time to prepare for the arrival of the alien.

"Is there a hierarchy among the seven Tosoks?" asked Frank. "Hierarchy" might be a big English word, but it was a simple concept that they'd already used repeatedly in discussions of scientific principles, such as the relationship between planets and stars and galaxies.

"Yes."

"Are you at the top?"

"No. Kelkad is at top."

"He's the captain of your ship?"

"Comparable."

Frank took a drink of water from a glass. He found himself coughing. Clete came over to thump him on the back, but Frank held up a hand and coughed some more. "Sorry," he said, his eyes red. "It went down the wrong way." Clete waited a moment to make sure Frank was okay, then went back to his chair.

"Who should speak to our United Nations?" asked Frank, once he'd regained control.

Hask's topknot was moving in strange patterns; it was apparent he had no idea what to make of the coughing fit. But at last he answered. "Kelkad."

"Will he come down from ship?"

"I will go get him and others."

"In your landing craft?"

"Yes."

Clete piped up from across the room. "Can I go with you?"

Hask didn't have to turn around; he had eyes in the back of his head. If the question struck him as impertinent, there was no way to tell. "Yes."

Frank shot an angry look at Clete. If anyone were going to go up, it should be Frank. But they'd agreed to minimize any signs of human conflict—Hask hadn't understood Sergei's exchange with Frank out on the flight deck at the time it had occurred, but the alien had doubtless recorded it and played it back now that he had an English vocabulary. They still didn't know why the Tosoks had come to Earth, but if it was what Frank was hoping—to invite Earth to join the community of intelligent races in this part of the galaxy— then the last thing they wanted to do was emphasize humanity's inability to get along. It was bad enough that the rendezvous with the alien lander had been performed by a military aircraft carrier and a nuclear sub.

Still . . .

"Can I go, too?" asked Frank.

"No room," said Hask. "Lander built for eight; only room for one more."

"If your ship has a crew of seven, why was the lander built for eight?" asked Frank.

"Was eight. One off."
"One dead?" asked Frank.
"One dead."
"Sorry."
Hask said nothing.

FOUR

The inside of Hask's lander was simple and elegant.
Frank and Clete had been hoping for a glimpse of some
fantastically advanced technology, but clearly almost all
aspects of the lander's operations were automated. There
was a single control console with a few cross-shaped key-
pads similar to the one on Hask's handheld computer. There
were also some recognizable mechanical devices, including
cylinders with nozzles that were most likely fire extin-
guishers.

The most intriguing thing were the Tosok chairs, which
were shaped something like tall, sideways saddles. Hask sat
on one. As he did so the raised sides rose up to—well, to
his "legpits" might be the appropriate term: the hollows
beneath where his long legs joined his shoulders. The sides
seemed to be spring-loaded. As Hask lowered his weight
into the chair, the sides compressed, then snapped into place
at just the right height to support him.

There were indeed eight chairs: two in the front row, then
two additional rows of three chairs apiece. Clete tried to sit
in one of the chairs, but found it excruciating. Hask went over

to the wall, which was pale green and waxy in appearance. He touched it, and a hatch popped open. Hask reached in and pulled out a device that looked a bit like a screwdriver, although no part of it seemed to be metallic. He then dropped down to the floor—it was a strange, fluid movement, his long legs folding in three places, and his front arm helping to support his weight. He ended up lying on his front, and his rear arm reached up with the tool held in his four-fingered hand. He did something with it, and the front part of the saddle seemed to come loose. Clete surged forward and grabbed that part of the chair before it toppled onto the Tosok.

Hask then rose to his feet. "Suitable?" he said.

Clete sat down sideways on it, leaning back against the remaining projection from the curving seat. He smiled at Frank. "Ain't no La-Z-Boy, but it'll do the trick."

"When are you going to leave?" Frank said to Hask.

"Whenever Clete is ready."

"Can I bring my video camera?" asked Clete, indicating an equipment bag sitting on the lander's floor.

"Yes."

"All right," said Clete. "Then let's go."

Frank left the spacecraft, and the air-lock door slid shut behind him.

It was three in the afternoon. The sky had been whipped by contrail lashes: dozens of media and government airplanes had flown over the area to get glimpses of the alien ship. The sea was reasonably calm; waves slapped softly against the *Kitty Hawk*'s hull.

All the arrangements had been made. Hask and Clete would fly up to the mothership, get the rest of the Tosoks, and then land in United Nations Plaza. There was going to be some delay aboard the mothership—Hask lacked the vocabulary to explain exactly why that was—so they would not be returning for about twenty hours.

Frank, meanwhile, would be flown by fighter jet direct from the *Kitty Hawk* to Washington, where he'd brief the president, who was already miffed that the meeting was taking place at the UN rather than on the White House lawn, as fifties SF films had predicted. They would both then fly to New York; other world leaders were making their way there as well. All in all, Frank was pleased: humanity was handling first contact much better than he'd expected.

The alien lander lifted off the flight deck, its deep green form stark against the pale blue sky. Frank waved as it rose higher and higher. Two F-14s provided an escort—as well as an opportunity to observe the alien ship in flight.

Inside the lander, Clete was getting it all on videotape. No live transmission was possible, unfortunately—the lander was shielded against radio waves, preventing Clete from broadcasting out, and there was no way of using the equipment on hand to interface his camera with the communications system employed by the Tosoks.

Although the four mirrored squares along the pointed bow of the shield-shaped craft did indeed turn out to be windows, Clete found he got a much better view through the wall display inside the ship. The lander rose up, higher and higher; the Atlantic Ocean receded beneath them, and the sky quickly changed from blue to purple to black. Soon Clete could see the east coast of Central America, and then the west coast of Africa as well. He was literally shaking with excitement—his whole life he'd wanted to go into space, and now it was happening! Adrenaline coursed through his system, and when he caught sight of his own reflection in the wall monitor, he saw that there was a huge grin spread across his face.

The lander continued to rise, and soon it passed over the terminator, into Earth's nightside. Above, the real stars were rock steady; below, the constellations of city lights twinkled with interference patterns.

Soon the ship was in orbit, and the invisible hand stopped

pressing against Clete's side—he was, after all, sitting side-saddle. He felt himself grow weightless, and his heart pounded even harder with excitement.

And then, there it was—floating majestically in front of them.

The mothership.

It was indeed gigantic. Almost all parts of it were flat black, making it hard to see against the backdrop of space. It seemed to be baton-shaped, with a bulbous habitat module at one end and what appeared to be an engine at the other. That the engine and the living quarters were so far apart suggested to Clete that the power source was nuclear. He'd have to get his colleagues to look over starplates they'd made in the last year or so; in all likelihood, the alien ship had come toward Earth tail first. Most ideas Clete had seen for starflight proposed a continuous acceleration to the halfway point, turning the ship around, then continuously decelerating until the destination was reached. Astronomers might well have inadvertently recorded the fusion exhaust of the braking starship—and from its spectra, something could be gleaned about Tosok technology.

Hask said the Tosok home world had a higher gravity than Earth, but the mothership, of course, was in microgravity now, although during its starflight its constant acceleration would have provided a sensation of normal weight.

Clete was still having trouble maintaining his composure. Flying through space was enough in and of itself to qualify as the greatest thrill of his life, but to have that coupled with actually being in the presence of an extraterrestrial lifeform was almost too much to bear. He'd been grinning so much that his cheeks hurt, and he felt positively giddy.

And weightlessness! My God, it was everything Armstrong and the other astronauts had told him it was! Once, for his PBS show, Clete had flown aboard the *Vomit Comet*—the KC-135 jet that NASA used to train astronauts. That had been fun, but this—this was spectacular!

Space travel.

Alien life.

Starships.

He'd come a long way from his poor upbringing in the hills of Tennessee. He was famous, a celebrity, rich, a frequent guest on *The Tonight Show*. But he'd always said he would trade all of that to go into space, to know for sure that life existed elsewhere.

Clete had guessed correctly: the lander was indeed fully automated; Hask never once touched the controls. But as the lander maneuvered along the baton's boom, something caught Clete's eye. Although it was hard to know what Tosok technology was supposed to look like, a portion of the ship seemed damaged. Clete pointed at it.

"Yes," said Hask. "An impact, as we entered your solar system. To our surprise, much junk at the edge."

"How far out?" said Clete.

"Perhaps fifty times Earth's orbital radius."

Clete nodded to himself. The Kuiper belt—the source of comets with orbital periods of twenty years or less. "Is the damage severe?"

"Must be repaired," said Hask. "Your help needed."

Clete felt his eyebrows rising. "Of course. I'm sure we'll be glad to."

The lander continued to approach the mothership, which Clete estimated was three hundred meters long. If its hull had been more reflective, it would have easily been visible from the ground.

Finally, the lander connected with the mothership's hull, clamping onto it just behind the bulbous habitat module; Clete could hear the clanging of docking clamps connecting with the ship. No clamshell-doored hangar deck like on the original starship *Enterprise*. Clete had always found that unbelievable anyway—it required pumping so much air in and out. Three other landers—two just like the one he was in now, plus one more that was much longer and narrower—were already clamped onto the hull. There was also one additional, unused docking port.

"Is the other empty port a spare, or is a ship missing?" asked Clete.

"Ship missing," said Hask. "One was knocked loose during the impact; we were unable to recover it."

Hask floated forward, and both the inner and outer doors of the air lock slid aside, revealing the interior of the mothership. The lighting was yellow-white, and rather dim. If the color matched that of sunlight on the Tosok world, then they must come from a G-class star. In the local stellar neighborhood, besides Earth's sun, only Alpha Centauri A and Tau Ceti were Gs.

It was cool inside the starship—perhaps fifty degrees Fahrenheit. The weightlessness was utterly intoxicating; Clete indulged himself with a few barrel rolls while Hask watched, his head tuft moving in a way that might indicate amusement. Soon, though, Hask floated down a corridor, and Clete followed, trying to maneuver while keeping an eye on his camcorder's small LCD screen. Since the Tosoks had apparently been traveling for two hundred and eleven years, Clete had expected the ship to be roomy on the inside, but there didn't seem to be much in the way of open spaces, and so far they had yet to see another Tosok.

"Where are the others?" asked Clete.

"This way," said Hask. Every few meters he gave a gentle push off the wall with his back hand to continue him on his way. It was clear which part of the corridor served as the floor and which as the ceiling when the engines were on: the ceiling had circular yellow-white light fixtures set into it at regular intervals. In between those were tiny, much dimmer, orange lamps, which Clete thought might be emergency lighting.

The floors were covered with—well, at first Clete thought it was deep-pile carpet, but as he pushed his own hand against it to propel him along, he realized it was some sort of plant material, with purple leaves. It wasn't grass; rather, it was more like a quilt of soft Brillo pads. Various possibilities ran through Clete's mind: that the plant carpeting was responsible for sucking up carbon dioxide, or some other waste gas, and replenishing it with oxygen; that it represented a food source for the Tosoks; or that they just liked the sensation of walking with their bare feet through it. Although he wouldn't presume to guess much yet about Tosok psychology, anything that helped them get through a multicentury voyage was doubtless to the good.

They finally arrived at the room Hask had been heading for. The door opened, and a puff of condensation billowed toward them, along with a blast of air so cold it gave Clete gooseflesh. He hoped it hadn't fogged his camera lens.

Inside the tiny room were six other Tosoks, strapped to special slabs, and mostly covered over with red plastic blankets. There were two empty slabs, with their blankets removed; one was presumably Hask's, and the other had belonged to the eighth crew member, who Hask had said had passed away. On these, Clete could see that there was a trough running down the slab's length to accommodate an arm. Clete couldn't tell if the other Tosoks were lying on their fronts or their backs; so far, the only difference between the two sides he'd noticed in Hask was in the interior of his mouth, the color of his eyes, and the robustness of the rear arm—and these Tosoks had their mouths and eyes closed, and the arm that was up was covered by the blanket.

"What are they doing?" asked Clete.

"Sleeping," said Hask.

All of them at once? Surely the crew would work in shifts, and—

And then it hit him—they hadn't just been sleeping for a few hours. Rather, they'd been sleeping for years—for centuries. This is how the Tosoks endured the long space-flight: in hibernation.

Clete tipped his camera to look around the room.

Illuminated panels were positioned on pedestals next to each slab. Each one had several animated bar charts and X-Y plots on it. Clete guessed they were medical readouts, monitoring the condition of the hibernating crew members. A careful study of the readouts might reveal a lot about Tosok physiology. Some of the panels had what looked like add-on pieces of equipment plugged into them; on others, three-holed connectors were exposed where no such equipment was in position. "I will turn up the heat," said Hask, "and they will wake. That one"—he pointed at a Tosok with a hide much bluer than Hask's own—"is Kelkad, the captain of this ship."

It wasn't cryonics—the kind of freezing for suspended animation humans had long dreamed off. Yes, this was cold—well below zero Celsius—but it was nowhere near absolute zero. The Tosoks seemed to have a natural ability to hibernate, just as many Earth animals did.

Clete was wearing blue jeans and a denim jacket; neither provided quite enough insulation against the cold. He looked around the room, still relishing the weightlessness. He found every detail of Tosok engineering fascinating. The only places he saw actual fasteners were where they were clearly meant to be undone for maintenance, like the bolts that secured the chair supports in the lander. Everything else seemed to have been molded in a single piece, mostly from ceramic, although there were a few places where metal was visible.

"They can hibernate for centuries without aid of equipment or drugs?" asked Clete.

"Yes."

Clete shook his head. "Y'know, before humans went into space we weren't even sure we could survive there. After all, we'd always lived under Earth's gravity—seemed reasonable that nature might've made some use of gravity feed, whether in our circulatory systems, our digestive systems, or somewheres else. But it didn't. We can live just fine in zero gravity.

The one part o' us that does rely on gravity—the sense of balance, which is controlled by fluids in our inner ears—simply shuts down under zero-g. Dreamers like me, we thought this meant that as a race we were *intended* to go into space."

Hask's translator had beeped a few times at unfamiliar words during Clete's comments, but the alien clearly got the gist of what the human had been saying. "Interesting thought," he replied.

"But you guys," said Clete, "being able to shut down for centuries, having that ability built right into y'all. You can fake gravity in space, 'course, through centrifugal force or constant acceleration. But there ain't nothing you can do about the time it takes for interstellar travel. With a natural suspended-animation ability, y'all sure got us beat. We might have been destined to go into planetary orbit, but your race seems to have been destined to sail between the stars."

"Many of our philosophers would agree with that statement," said Hask. He paused. "But not all, of course." There was silence between them for several moments. "I am hungry," said the Tosok. That didn't surprise Clete in the least; as far as he could tell, Hask hadn't eaten since his lander had splashed down. "It will take several hours for the others to revive. Do you require food?"

"I brought some with me," said Clete. "Navy rations. Hardly gourmet vittles, but they'll do."

"Come with me."

Clete and Hask killed time eating and talking. Clete found the Tosok approach to food utterly fascinating—not to mention disgusting—and he recorded it all on videotape. Eventually, the other Tosoks were revived enough to leave the hibernation chamber, and Clete heard the Tosok language for the first time as they spoke to each other. Although it contained many English-like sounds, it also included a snapping, a pinging, and something like two wooden sticks being clacked together. Clete doubted that a human could speak it without mechanical aids.

There was a lot of variation in skin color among the Tosoks. Hask's skin was blue-gray. One of the others had a taupe hide, another a neutral gray. Two had cyan skin. One was navy blue. Kelkad's was a bit lighter than that. Eye color seemed to vary widely; only one of the Tosoks had all four eyes the same color. They chattered endlessly, and one of the aliens took great interest in Clete, poking him in the ribs, feeling his skin and the hair on his head, and staring with two round eyes directly into Clete's face from only inches away.

Hask seemed to be briefing the others. As far as Clete could tell, hand gestures didn't play any significant role in Tosok communication—but the tufts on the tops of each one's head waved in complex patterns that seemed to add nuance to the spoken words. Hask's monologue contained several instances of a word that sounded like *kash-boom!* Clete wondered if it was onomatopoeic, referring to the explosion that must have accompanied the collision in the Kuiper belt; apparently only Hask and the now-deceased Tosok had been revived during that.

It was difficult to tell, but Captain Kelkad seemed displeased with Hask—his voice rose higher than was normal as his sentences progressed, and his tuft moved with great agitation. Perhaps, thought Clete, the alien captain felt Hask had exceeded his authority by making first contact before reviving the others, or maybe he was angry over the death of one of his crew.

At last, Kelkad turned to look at Clete. He spoke a few words, and Hask translated. "Kelkad says he will meet with your leaders now. We are ready to fly back down."

FIVE

The Tosok landing craft skimmed above the surface of New York's East River until it came to Turtle Bay, site of the United Nations. It zoomed over the low, concave-sided, dome-roofed General Assembly building, then did three loops around the thirty-nine-story slab of the Secretariat, before settling in the wide driveway in front of the General Assembly. No doubt about it—the Tosoks had a flare for the dramatic. Almost two billion people were watching the event live, and it seemed as though half of New York had been out on the streets, looking up.

The UN had been cordoned off. New York's finest on one side of the barrier and gray-uniformed United Nations guards on the other were carefully controlling who got access. Frank Nobilio hoped the precautions were sufficient. He'd spent hours poring over the photographs of the alien mothership taken by the Hubble Space Telescope (which had passed within line of sight of it repeatedly now). The guys at NASA Ames said the ship appeared to be fusion powered—and a fusion exhaust aimed at Earth could do enormous damage. Frank was terrified of the consequences if one of the Tosoks were assassinated.

Still, there was always something about being here at the UN that moved him deeply. Oh, sure, over its history, the United Nations had probably had more failures than successes, but it still represented the loftiest of human ideals, and that meant something to Frank, who in his early twenties had spent a year in the Peace Corps, and who, as a grad student at Berkeley, had been involved in protests against the Vietnam War.

"We, the People of the United States" were indeed great words, and even decades in Washington hadn't dulled Frank's faith in them. But "We the Peoples of the United Nations" were even greater words, he thought as he looked up at the giant plaque outside the General Assembly:

> WE THE PEOPLES OF THE UNITED NATIONS
> DETERMINED TO SAVE SUCCEEDING GENERATIONS
> FROM THE SCOURGE OF WAR, WHICH TWICE IN
> OUR LIFETIME HAS BROUGHT UNTOLD SORROW
> TO MANKIND, AND TO REAFFIRM FAITH IN FUN-
> DAMENTAL HUMAN RIGHTS, IN THE DIGNITY AND
> WORTH OF THE HUMAN PERSON, IN THE RIGHTS
> OF MEN AND WOMEN AND OF NATIONS LARGE
> AND SMALL . . .

Those were words the whole planet could be proud of. As everyone in the crowd waited for the air lock on the Tosok lander to open, Frank smiled to himself. Its critics notwithstanding, he was glad there was a place like this for the aliens to land.

The air lock did open—and out came Cletus Calhoun. The crowd, which normally would have been delighted to catch a glimpse of a celebrity, reacted with disappointment. A UN guard hurried over with a microphone stand, and Clete stepped up to it.

"Take me to your leader," he said, in harsh, mechanical tones.

The crowd laughed. Clete's face split in a toothy grin. "I suppose y'all are wondering why I called y'all here today."

More laughter.

"Ladies and gentlemen," he said, sobering. "It is my profound honor to present to y'all the first extraterrestrial visitors to Earth." He indicated the air lock, and the Tosok captain, Kelkad, strode out.

The entire audience gasped. Most of them had seen the pictures of Hask taken aboard the *Kitty Hawk,* but, still, to actually see an alien with one's own eyes . . .

It started at one side of the vast crescent of spectators: a single woman clapping. Within moments it swept like a wave over the entire crowd: a thunderous storm of applause.

Kelkad's long strides quickly brought him over to stand next to Clete. Frank could see Clete talking to the alien, probably explaining the significance of the clapping. Kelkad made a beckoning gesture with his back hand and the remaining six Tosoks filed out of the lander. They formed two rows of three behind Kelkad, who moved to stand in front of the microphone.

The applause died down at once, everyone anxious to hear what the alien leader had to say.

"Hello," said Kelkad—or rather, said his pocket translator. Frank assumed the vocabulary database from Hask's translator must have by now been copied over to those of the other Tosoks. "Nice planet you've got here."

The applause again, with hundreds of cheers mixed in. Frank recognized Clete's sense of humor in the comment; he'd obviously coached Kelkad on what to say.

Frank found himself clapping so hard his palms were stinging. And so were his eyes, at the beautiful sight of aliens standing in front of the rainbow row of one hundred and eighty-five flags outside of the United Nations of Earth.

"People of planet Earth," said Kelkad later that afternoon, standing at one of the two podiums inside the General Assembly hall, "we come to you as neighbors: our home world is a planet in the Alpha Centauri system."

Frank was sitting in the public gallery above the General Assembly, looking down on the concentric semicircular rows of delegate seating. His eyebrows went up. Although Alpha Centauri A was much like the sun, it was bound gravitationally to two other stars. Offhand, Frank wouldn't have thought that system capable of having an Earth-like world.

"We came here," continued Kelkad, "to bring you greetings from our people. But, unexpectedly, it seems we also need your help. Our starship has been damaged, and is in need of repair. We cannot build the required parts ourselves—the damage is beyond the limited resources of our mothership. But although many of the principles used in building the replacement parts we need will be unfamiliar to you, Dr. Calhoun assures me that you have the technology to manufacture complex items according to our plans. We therefore ask that some of you agree to build the parts we need. In exchange, those who do build the parts will be welcome to keep whatever knowledge and technology they can glean from the process."

Frank could see the rows of ambassadors salivating down below. Of course it would likely only be the technologically sophisticated countries, doubtless led by the U.S. and Japan, that would get contracts with the Tosoks.

Kelkad continued on for another half hour or so, with everyone listening intently. And then:

"And so," said Kelkad, "it is with great pleasure that we extend the front hand of friendship, and the back hand of trust, across the light-years to our closest neighbors, to a race of beings that we hope will also become our closest friends. Men and women of planet Earth, you are no longer alone!"

After the speech, every nation on Earth extended invita-tions to the Tosoks to visit. There was considerable pressure for them to head east from New York, across the Atlantic—it was felt that the United States had monopolized the alien visitors too much already, and a westward trip across the U.S. would be inappropriate.

And so it came to pass that the aliens toured London, Paris, Rome, Amsterdam, Moscow, Jerusalem, Giza, Calcutta, Beijing, Tokyo, Honolulu, and Vancouver. An entourage traveled with them, including Frank and Clete, and several other prominent scientists from various nations, along with a security detachment. The Canadian representative turned out to be Packwood Smathers, the same blowhard Clete had argued with on CNN.

One of the highlights of the trip—for Tosoks and humans alike—was observing one of the true wonders of nature. Clete tried to set the stage for it appropriately.

"Even now that I've actually been in space," he said to the Tosoks, "the most incredible astronomical sight I've ever seen I saw from the ground." He paused. "A total solar eclipse. There's nothing like it. And we're goin' to get to see one. I wish I could say we planned this for you guys, but we're jes' plain lucky. It's almost two years afore the next one. But this one—well, this one will be visible in lots of highly populated areas. I had to go to the Galápagos for the one in '98 and to Siberia for the one in '97—but it don't matter; wherever they are, I go. This one, though, will be visible from here in northern France all the way to Turkey—'prolly be seen by more people than any eclipse in human history." A pause. "Does your world have a moon, Kelkad?"

The alien captain's head tuft moved backward in what was now recognized as the Tosok sign of negation. "No. We were surprised to see how big yours is."

"Sure 'nuff," said Clete. "'Fact, Earth and its moon come purty near to bein' a double planet."

"It is remarkable," agreed Kelkad. "But even though we have no moon, I do know what an eclipse is—the partial or complete obscuring of one celestial body by another."

"That's true—but our eclipses are somethin' special," said Clete. "See, our sun is four hundred times wider than our moon—but it's also four hundred times farther away. That means when things line up jes' right, the moon *precisely* covers the sun, completely blockin' out the photosphere. When that happens you can see the corona—the sun's atmosphere—and sometimes even see prominences shootin' out into space."

"Incredible," said Kelkad.

Clete smiled. "That it is."

The eclipse occurred on a Wednesday at noon. The Tosoks and their entourage had just left Strasbourg, where they had toured the famous Gothic cathedral. To get an unobstructed view of the bowl of the sky, their specially modified tour bus had driven out into a vineyard in the French countryside.

The sun was fifty-five degrees above the horizon as the silhouette of the moon slowly bit into its blazing disk. The humans were wearing eclipse-viewing glasses with fluorescent green and pink cardboard frames and Mylar lenses; the Tosoks always wore pop-in sunglasses while outdoors during the day, but now were using extra-strength versions so that they, too, could stare up at the spectacle.

Slowly, ponderously, the black circular shadow of the moon covered more and more of the sun. As it did so the sky grew dim. A hush fell over the landscape; even the birds stopped singing to stare up in wonder. When the moon's disk had almost completely blocked the sun, a row of Bailey's beads was briefly visible at the disk's edge—bright spots caused by sunlight passing through irregularities on the moon's rim.

And then . . .

Totality.

The temperature dropped noticeably. The sky went dark. Those who were willing to take their eyes off the main attraction for a moment could clearly see bright Venus below and to the left of the sun, and dimmer Mercury above it and to the right, along with a smattering of stars; the sun was halfway between Leo and Cancer.

Around the black disk of the moon, a beautiful pink corona was visible, like wisps of hair, or a wild angel's halo.

It was absolutely incredible, absolutely breathtaking. Frank was deeply moved, and he saw Clete wipe tears from the corners of his eyes. The head tufts on the Tosoks were waving wildly in excitement.

All too soon it was over, the moon continuing on its way, and the sky brightening.

Kelkad strode over to Clete. "Thank you," he said, his tuft still moving with emotion. "Thank you for letting us see that."

Clete smiled. "Like you said, nice planet we've got here."

Finally, the aliens returned to the United States, touring California. They visited Rogers Dry Lake to watch the Shuttle *Discovery* land (it had been up taking photographs and radar scans of the alien mothership to aid in the repair effort). Next, they came to Los Angeles—which happened to be Clete's home now; he balanced his time between production of his TV series and teaching astronomy at UCLA. The aliens didn't know what to make of Disneyland. They understood that Mickey, Goofy, and Donald were supposed to be a mouse, a dog, and a duck, respectively—they'd seen all three types of animals during their tour of Earth. But they were absolutely flummoxed by the idea of portraying them as erect, sentient, articulate beings. They were also amazed by most of the rides—the idea that one could enjoy being frightened struck them as a contradiction in terms. They did rather seem to like the Teacups, though.

In the evening, a reception was held at Mann's Chinese Theatre, with a select guest list. Steven Spielberg was there, taking a possibly justifiable pride in having to some degree prepared the human race for the arrival of peaceful, friendly aliens. Captain Kelkad was invited to leave his footprints in cement. This was something that the aliens *did* understand: the idea of making one's mark, of being remembered after one was gone.

Three of the prime contracts for building the replacement parts for the alien mothership went to TRW, Rockwell International, and Hughes. The president of the University of Southern California sensed a golden opportunity, since all three were located within fifteen miles of its main University Park campus. He immediately offered long-term accommodation to the Tosoks in Paul Valcour Hall, a brand new six-story-tall residence facility. The residence had been completed behind schedule—too late for the current academic year, so it wouldn't be needed until next September. It was an ideal location—a hundred meters from any other campus building, meaning access to it was easy to control. The Tosoks accepted the offer, and they, and their scientific and security entourage, moved into the facility. Even Clete, whose home was in L.A., moved in, unable to give up a moment of time with the aliens.

"Thank you for helping arrange all the repairs," said Captain Kelkad one evening to Frank Nobilio, who had also taken up residence in Valcour Hall. "It is much appreciated."

"My pleasure," said Frank. Hask and Torbat—one of the other Tosoks—were sitting with him and the alien captain in the sixth-floor lounge. "Of course, you realize it will take a long time for the replacement parts to be built. They're saying perhaps as long as two years—"

"Two years!" said Kelkad, his tuft waving in shock. "Surely it can be done—"

Hask spoke a few words to Kelkad in the Tosok language.

"Oh—two of *your* years," said Kelkad. His tendrils came to rest. "That is not so bad."

Frank thought about telling the aliens that no human engineer's time estimate was ever to be trusted, but decided they'd do better to cross that bridge later. For now, he thought, sitting here, chatting amiably with pale-blue Hask, dark-blue Kelkad, and gray Torbat, first contact between the human race and aliens seemed to be going spectacularly well.

Until the murder.

SIX

Colin Elliot was an LAPD cop with ten years on the force. He was one of several officers doing rotating duty at Valcour Hall on the USC campus.

It was three in the morning. Valcour Hall was L-shaped, with the two wings meeting in a widened-out lounge area on each floor. Even this late, two of the Tosoks were sitting in the lounge on the fourth floor; dozens of special Tosok chairs had been built in the university's wood shop. Although the campus was pretty much deserted for Christmas break, most of the Tosoks, plus most of their entourage, had gone that evening to a public lecture being given by Stephen Jay Gould, held in the Davis Auditorium at the west end of the campus, just off McClintock Street. Still, they'd all gotten home several hours ago.

The two Tosoks raised their front hands in greeting at Elliot. He flashed a Vulcan salute back at them. The other Tosoks were presumably in their rooms. Since the residence was so large, each individual had taken quarters a goodly distance from everyone else's. As Elliot made his way down the corridors he passed a couple of rooms that had their doors open. Through one, he saw a Tosok working at an alien computer brought down from the mothership. Through another, he saw a Tosok watching TV—an old episode of *Barney Miller,* one of Elliot's own favorite shows. The Tosoks seemed to love sitcoms—maybe the laugh tracks helped point out for them what was funny to humans. He noted that the Tosok had the closed captioning turned on. They all could speak English with the aid of translating computers; perhaps the superimposed titles were helping this Tosok learn to read.

The long corridors were divided up into shorter sections by heavy glass doorways; they weren't fire doors, but they did provide some sound insulation. The Tosoks apparently had sensitive hearing, but weren't the least disturbed by background noise. On the three floors that housed Tosoks, these doors were generally kept open; only on the human floors were they usually closed at night.

Elliot came to the stairwell and made his way down to the third floor—one of the human floors. The humans, of course, were all asleep, and the main corridor lights were off. The only illumination came from lamps in a campus parking lot visible through floor-to-ceiling windows at the far end of the corridor, EXIT signs, and a few small safety lights. Elliot walked along, not expecting to see anything. He heard a sound as he passed one room, but, after pausing to listen for a moment, realized it was just snoring.

Elliot arrived at one of the closed glass doors that broke up the long corridors into sections. He opened it, passed through the doorway, and continued on along the hallway. At one point he heard a toilet flush. He wasn't surprised. Some of these eggheads were pretty old; they probably got up a couple of times a night to pee.

The carpeting was industrial-strength, of course, and dark gray—designed to survive years of student use. Although Elliot weighed over two hundred pounds, it did a nice job of cushioning his footfalls, so there was little chance he'd wake—

Squish.

Elliot looked down. The carpet was wet. A spilled beverage, probably—

No.

No. The liquid was thick, sticky.

And dark.

Elliot had a flashlight clipped to his belt. He brought it up, thumbed on the beam, played it over the puddle.

Red.

It was blood, seeping out from under a closed door. There was light spilling out, too—the lights inside the room were on. Elliot took a handkerchief from his pocket, and using the pressure of just two fingers so as to minimize disturbance of any fingerprints, he opened the door.

He'd expected it not to open all the way, but it swung freely back on its hinges, revealing the body.

It's one of those trivial facts that had stuck in Sergeant Elliot's mind for years: a human being has one quart of blood for every thirty pounds of body weight.

The dead man was skinny, but well over six feet tall. He'd probably weighed around one-seventy, which meant that he'd had something on the order of six quarts of blood—a gallon and a half.

And it looked like damn near all of it was spread around the body, in a vast dark pool.

It was surprising, in a way, that the first thing Elliot had noticed had been the quantity of spilled blood. Oh, certainly in any other murder that would have been the salient factor. But the corpse here had suffered far more than just a simple bleeding out.

The right leg was severed from the body halfway down the thigh. Whatever had cut it off had done a remarkably clean job, slicing through the man's jeans, leaving an edge on them as clean as if they'd been hemmed to that length. The leg had been severed just as neatly. Although the stump was now crusted over with a thick cap of dried blood, the cut looked as sharp as what a band saw would make through frozen meat. The actual leg, still wrapped in the tube of denim, its foot still socked and shod, was also present, bent gently at its knee, a short distance from the body.

But even that wasn't the worst of it.

The head had been severed from the body and—*God*—the lower jaw had been sliced free from the head. He couldn't see the jawbone anywhere, and—Christ—it looked like one of the eyeballs was missing, too.

The torso had been opened up, in one long line leading from the bottom of the neck down the center of the chest all the way to the groin. The decedent's shirt had been ripped open—not cut, but ripped, apparently before the cutting had begun. The individual buttons had been mostly torn free, and the shirt opened, its sides like wings, now stiff and dark and fused into the great pool of blood surrounding the body.

The breastbone had been split in two, and the ribs spread apart left and right, sticking up like the maw of a bear trap from—

—from the *empty* torso. The organs had been removed. Elliot knew enough anatomy to recognize the heart and lungs, lying a few feet from the body. The other lumps, all crusted over now, were doubtless spleen and liver and kidneys and more, but which was which, Elliot couldn't say.

At the bottom of the open chest cavity, there was all sorts of bluish-white connective tissue, and in places the vertebral column itself was exposed.

The last thing Sergeant Elliot looked at in any detail was the jawless face, now absolutely white, right down to the waxlike upper lip. This was only Elliot's second shift with the Tosok entourage; he didn't yet know most of the humans, but this one was familiar enough.

It was that guy from TV.

Cletus Calhoun.

———————

Frank Nobilio was having the dream again. He was at university, in the sixties, wearing bell-bottoms and a flowered shirt. He was walking down a corridor when another student passing by wished him luck.

"What for?" asked Frank.

"For the exam, of course," said the student.

"Exam?"

"In biochemistry."

Biochemistry. Oh, Christ. Frank remembered signing up for that course at the beginning of the academic year, but somehow he'd forgotten to go to every single one of the classes. And today was the final exam—an exam he'd not studied for at all. How in the hell did they expect him—?

Frank found himself stirring into consciousness. Decades since he'd left university, but he still had that same damned dream. Oh, the details changed—sometimes it was American history he'd forgotten to take, sometimes statistics—but the basic story kept coming up over and over again, and—

Insistent knocking at the door. An earlier barrage of it must have awoken him.

"What is it?" Frank called out. His voice was raw; he'd been sleeping with his mouth open.

"Dr. Nobilio? It's the police."

Frank disentangled himself from the sheet, got shakily to his feet, and made it over to the dorm room's door. He opened it, and his eyes squinted against the corridor light beyond. "Yes?"

Two men stood in the hallway. One was Sergeant Ellis, Elliot, something like that, wearing a police uniform. The other Frank didn't recognize: a compact man with an olive complexion, perhaps forty-five years old. He had wavy black hair, brown eyes, and a neat mustache. The small man flashed his ID. "Dr. Nobilio, I'm Detective Lieutenant Jesus

Perez, LAPD. I'm sorry to disturb you, sir, but there's been a murder."

Frank felt his jaw dropping. "Which one was it?"

"I beg your pardon, sir?"

"Which Tosok was killed?"

Perez shook his head. "It's not a Tosok, sir. It's a human."

Frank let out a sigh of relief. Perez looked at him in shock. "Sorry," said Frank. "I—I'm sorry. It's just that, well, Christ, I hate to think what would happen if one of the Tosoks were murdered."

"We want you to identify the body, sir."

Frank's heart skipped a beat. He was still waking up. "You mean it's someone I know?"

"Possibly, sir."

"Who?"

"We believe it's Cletus Calhoun, sir."

Frank felt like someone had driven a fist into his stomach.

The general commotion had awoken some of the other humans, too. By the time Perez got Frank over to Clete's room, Packwood Smathers and Tamara Slynova were already there, standing on the threshold just beyond the pool of blood. Smathers's white hair was wild, and Frank had never seen Slynova without makeup. Frank was in his pajamas; Smathers had a robe on over his; Slynova seemed to be wearing nothing but a robe.

Frank approached the doorway and looked in. Two LAPD criminalists were already working inside the room. Clete's body had been covered by a white sheet, which was now stained with blood. The sheet tented up over the spread rib cage. Frank looked down on his friend's face, missing its bottom part, the skin white as a marble statue's. He fought the urge to vomit.

"Well?" said Perez.

"That's him."

Perez nodded. "We thought so. Found his wallet on him. Do you know who his next of kin is?"

"He's not married. But he has a sister—Daisy, I think—in Tennessee."

"Any idea who would want to see him dead?"

Frank looked at Packwood Smathers, then back at the body. "No."

Frank made his way through the second, fourth, and sixth floors—each of which housed Tosoks—accompanied by the German scientist, Kohl. They went down the corridors, pausing at each occupied room to ask the Tosok within to join them. The aliens filed out, and they all made their way to the lounge in the middle of the sixth floor. It was now 4:30 a.m.

The Tosoks stood patiently. Frank did a quick head count—only six of them were present. Let's see: there's Captain Kelkad, and Rendo. Torbat. And—

"Sorry to keep you waiting," said a voice. "What's happening?"

Frank turned around and had a shock almost as great as the one that had overtaken him when he saw Clete's ruined body. Coming down the corridor with two-meter strides was a Tosok Frank had never seen before, with silvery skin.

"Who—who are you?" said Frank.

"Hask."

"But—but Hask has bluish skin."

"Had," said the Tosok. "I molted earlier today."

Frank looked at the being. He did indeed have an orange left-front eye and a green right-front eye. "Oh," said Frank. "Forgive me."

Hask moved in to take a seat. Frank looked at the seven aliens. They'd seen a lot of Earth. Although an effort had been made to present the best side of humanity, there had been no doubt that some of the worst had been displayed, too. The Tosoks had encountered poverty and pollution, and they knew that the security people were there to protect them from the possibility that a human being might want to do them harm.

Still, the violence humanity was capable of had all been abstract to this point. But now—now they had to be told.

"My friends," said Frank, into the sea of round, disk-like eyes, "I have sad news." He paused. Damn, he wished Tosoks made facial expressions; he still wasn't good at deciphering the waving of their cranial tufts. "Clete is dead."

There was silence for several moments.

"Do humans normally die without warning?" asked Kelkad. "He seemed healthy."

"He didn't die of natural causes," said Frank. "He was murdered."

Seven pocket computers beeped, slightly out of sync with each other.

"Murdered," repeated Frank. "It means killed by another human being."

Kelkad made a small sound. His computer translated it as "Oh."

SEVEN

"Sir," said Lieutenant Perez, stepping into the opulent office on the eighteenth floor of the Los Angeles County Criminal Courts Building, "we, ah, have a bit of a situation here."

District Attorney Montgomery Ajax looked up from his immaculate glass-topped desk. "What is it?"

"I'd like to go over the criminalist's report on the Calhoun murder with you."

Ajax was silver-haired with pale blue eyes and a long, deeply tanned face—a Bahamas tan, not a California one. "Something out of the ordinary?"

"You could say that, sir." He placed a photograph on the DA's desk. It showed a bloody U-shaped mark on a gray carpet.

"What's that? A horseshoe?"

"We didn't know what to make of it, sir. I thought maybe it was a heel mark, but the criminalist says no. But, well, have a look at this, sir." He placed a newspaper clipping next to the photograph. It contained a black-and-white photograph of Kelkad making his foot impressions at Mann's

Chinese Theatre. The imprint was almost identical in shape to the bloody mark.

"Christ almighty," said Ajax.

"My thoughts exactly, sir."

"Is there any way to tell which Tosok made the bloody footprint?"

"Possibly, although the print is not detailed."

"Is there any other evidence to implicate a Tosok?"

"Well, Calhoun's leg was severed with some sort of extremely sharp instrument. It went through the leg without compressing the muscle at all, and seemed to hardly catch on the bone. It cut through the femoral artery, and because it was a clean cut, Calhoun simply gushed blood out of it."

"And?"

"And the guys in the lab can't think of any human tool that could have done the trick. The slicing open of the abdomen seemed to be done mechanically as well. But the rib spreading—well, that seemed to be done manually. The cut edges of the ribs were razor sharp, and Feinstein found some chemicals on one of the rib tips that he couldn't identify. It might be Tosok blood."

The DA had already seen the crime-scene photographs. "Okay," said Ajax. "But whichever Tosok did it must have gotten soaked with human blood. Surely if it was one of the Tosoks, it would have had to have cleaned itself up somehow."

Perez nodded. "I thought of that, too."

"And?"

"And I interviewed all of the Tosoks today. But one of them looked different from any of the ones I'd seen on TV. You know they all had blue or gray hides, right?"

Ajax nodded.

"Well, this one had a silver-white hide."

"Like it had bleached itself clean?"

"More than that," said Perez. "I'm told it had shed its skin."

"Like a bloody snake, eh?"

"Yes, sir. Like a bloody snake."

The DA considered. "You know," he said slowly, "there is another possibility."

"What's that?"

"A frame-up." Ajax paused. "Not everybody liked Calhoun."

"If it *is* a frame-up, it would have to be someone who is part of the entourage traveling with the Tosoks. No one else could get into the USC dorm."

Ajax nodded. "True. Better check into their backgrounds." A pause. "Start with Smathers."

"Smathers?"

"I saw Calhoun show him up on national TV. That's got to sting."

"Will do."

"Be thorough, Perez. If I'm going to have to lay charges against an alien, I want to be dead certain we're right."

Frank was walking across the USC campus, passing by the Von KleinSmid Center. He looked up briefly at the one-hundred-and-seventy-six-foot tower visible through the portico; the tower was crowned by a five-thousand-pound gridwork globe, like a world picked clean.

Frank knew all about being picked clean; he had been divorced for five years, and his twelve-year-old daughter was with his ex-wife in Maryland.

It was the day before Christmas; the campus was almost deserted. Frank was used to it being cold at Christmas; he'd grown up in Canandaigua, New York, where winters were marked by bitter temperatures and hip-deep snow. But the path he was on was lined with palm trees, and Frank was more than warm enough in his black nylon windbreaker with the NASA logo on its back.

Christmases were the worst; Frank never got Maria at

Christmas. He'd actually been looking forward to this one—Clete had no family, either, and so they'd planned to mark the day together. They'd even been planning to exchange presents; Frank had bought Clete a trio of pewter starships from the Franklin Mint—a classic *Enterprise,* an original Klingon battle ship, and a Romulan Bird of Prey. Together, they'd cost six hundred dollars; far too much, really, but it had made Frank feel good to order them.

And now—

He made it a few more paces before he realized what was happening. If this had been upstate New York—if this had been proper Christmas weather—his breath might have escaped in great shuddering clouds, but here, in this warmth, palm trees obscenely decorated with Christmas lights, his sobs were escaping invisibly.

Clete and Frank had met in grad school; they'd been friends for twenty years.

God, how he'd miss him.

Frank found a bench beneath a palm, and lowered himself on to it, putting his face in his hands.

Merry Christmas, he thought.

And cried some more.

Three hours later Perez returned to DA Ajax's office. "Okay, I've got the scoop on Smathers."

"Go."

"When PBS was contemplating making a new astronomy series, they wanted someone who could fill Carl Sagan's shoes. Their first choices were Cletus Calhoun . . . and Packwood Smathers."

"Why'd they go with Calhoun?"

"It depends who you ask. One executive I spoke to there said it was his just-plain-folks image: PBS was under a lot of fire from Congress, you know. They were calling it an elitist service. The network was doing everything it could to appear more populist, in hopes of not getting its appropriation slashed further."

"Makes sense," said Ajax. "Heck, even I watched *Great Balls of Fire!*, and science always turned me off. But Calhoun was entertaining as hell."

"Right. But the other guy I talked to said they'd heard Smathers was difficult to work with, and that there were some improprieties in his research. He'd been a little too liberal, supposedly, with taking credit for work done not just by his grad students—which is par for the course, apparently—but also by other professors. They were afraid that might come out. *Great Balls of Fire!* was a coproduction with NHK—the Japanese television network. You know how the Japanese are about personal honor; they'd never be able to broadcast the show if there were a scandal about the host."

"Okay. So?"

"So the executive I spoke to at PBS said the source of the information about Smathers was Calhoun himself."

"Are the allegations true?"

"Apparently so. And if Smathers had learned that it was Calhoun who made PBS aware of them, costing him the host's job—"

"All right," said Ajax. "Let's bring Smathers in for questioning."

Parker Center was a large beige building two blocks from the Criminal Courts Building. Out front there was a black granite fountain dedicated to all the officers who had died in the line of duty. Part of the building was held up by a series of columns; behind these columns the main entrance was constantly guarded by armed cops.

The interrogation room was windowless, small, and dimly lit. Perez stood with one foot up on a chair. He took a sip of coffee. "I understand you had reason to dislike Cletus Calhoun," he said.

Packwood Smathers's white eyebrows went up. He considered for several seconds before responding. Finally, no longer looking at Perez, he said, "I object to all this, you know. I'm a Canadian citizen. If you'll just call the consulate—"

Perez moved into Smathers's field of view. "Professor, this won't take long if you cooperate. Simply tell me what you had against Calhoun."

"Nothing at all."

"There was some thinking that perhaps he had done an end run around you to get the PBS hosting job."

Smathers was quiet, sliding his lower teeth across his upper lip. Finally, he did meet Perez's gaze. "I think I'd like legal counsel."

"Why? You haven't been charged with anything."

Smathers rose to his feet. "Well, either *do* charge me and get me a lawyer, or I'm walking out that door."

Perez spread his arms. "Why the hostility, Professor?"

Smathers's tone was harsh. "You're implying I killed Cletus Calhoun. I suspect even the implication of that is actionable. Look—you're right, I didn't like that snot-nosed hick. He may be more personable than me, and he's got all that hillbilly charm, but he's not half the astronomer I am. He's just a *personality,* nothing but a popularizer. He dared to suggest that *my* work wasn't wholly original? Christ, he hadn't done dick on his own for years. But if you think I killed him, you're crazy. And if you want to question me about such an offensive suggestion, you'll do so with my lawyer present."

EIGHT

Jesus Perez returned to Monty Ajax's office. "I don't think Smathers did it."

Ajax looked up. "Does he have an alibi?"

"Not really. The ME says the murder took place around nine p.m., apparently. Most of the entourage and six of the Tosoks were attending an evening lecture at USC—Stephen Jay Gould was in L.A., promoting his newest essay collection. After Gould's talk, there was a big reception. They weren't home until after two. But Hask had begged off—to molt, he says now. And Calhoun and Smathers both stayed behind, too; Smathers didn't like Gould, apparently—he seems to have a thorn in his side about successful science popularizers. And Calhoun said he needed the time to work on his script for his next episode of *Great Balls of Fire!* But the criminalists have found no evidence at all that Smathers or any other human was involved. And a team at UCLA has confirmed that the substance on the rib is not of—what was the phrase?—'not of terrestrial origin.'"

"So it *is* likely Tosok blood—or, God help us, Tosok

semen or something like that," said Ajax. "Could it have been planted?"

"As far as we've been able to determine, the Tosoks have given up no tissue samples of any kind to human scientists. This apparently is a taboo with them: they consider the inner workings of the body extremely private. Apparently they were offered books on human anatomy early on, but reacted as if they'd been offered copies of *Hustler*. Given their approach to such things, it seems highly unlikely that Smathers had access to Tosok blood."

Ajax exhaled noisily. "So a Tosok did it?"

"Apparently."

"And you suspect Hask?"

"Yes. The shed skin makes it damned convenient, obviously. And we've had the bloody footprint blown up. It almost certainly wasn't made by Kelkad, and we've eliminated one of the other Tosoks—a female named Dodnaskak—because she has feet that are much too large.

"That still leaves five other possibilities, including Hask."

"But Hask had a bluish-gray hide."

"*Had* is right."

"And the criminalists found this inside Calhoun's room," said Perez, putting a tiny Ziploc pouch on Ajax's desk. Inside were three diamond-shaped flakes of blue-gray material. Perez was quiet for a moment while Ajax held the sample up to the light. "If Hask was about to molt," said Perez, "he could have been dropping scales all day."

Ajax put the pouch down and rubbed his temples.

Lieutenant Perez entered the sixth-floor lounge at Val- cour Hall, accompanied by four uniformed police officers, each at least a head taller than him. The Tosoks Kelkad and Ged, as well as Frank Nobilio, were there, talking. Frank rose. "What is it, Lieutenant?"

"Come with me, Doctor," said Perez. "Which one is Hask's room?"

"It's on the second floor."

"Take us there."

"What's this all about?"

"Just take us there, please," said Perez. "You're Kelkad, aren't you?" he said, looking now at the dark-blue Tosok. "You may want to come along, too."

Perez pressed the call button, and the elevator immediately reopened. He stepped in and held the door, waiting for Frank and Kelkad to join him and the four uniforms. Frank sighed, and they got in. The elevator dropped four floors, and Frank indicated with a hand gesture that they should head down the east wing. They passed through several open glass doorways, and finally came to Hask's room, at the end of the corridor.

Perez knocked on the door. "Hask, open up. This is the police."

There were sounds of movement inside the room, and a moment later the door opened. "Are you the Tosok known as Hask?" asked Perez.

"You know that," said Hask.

"Hask, I hereby arrest you for the murder of Cletus Calhoun."

Frank's eyes went wide. "Now, wait a minute—"

Perez reached into his jacket pocket and pulled out his well-worn Miranda card. He knew the rights by heart, but had to read them from the card, lest some lawyer later argue that part of them had been skipped. "You have the right to remain silent. If you give up—"

"Wait just a goddamn minute," said Frank, eyebrows climbing.

"—the right to remain silent, anything you say can and will be used against you in a court of law. You have the right—"

"You can't arrest an alien!" said Frank.

"—to have an attorney present during questioning. If you desire an attorney—"

"For Christ's sake, Lieutenant!"

"—but cannot afford one, one will be appointed for you without charge. Do you understand these rights as I've read them to you?"

Hask staggered backward. Even with eyes in the rear of his head, he still apparently didn't see where he was going. He bumped into his desk, and an object—a disk about thirty centimeters in diameter—fell from the desk. It hit the bottom shelf of a built-in bookcase on the way down, and cracked in two.

"Do you understand these rights as I've read them to you?" repeated Perez.

"Lieutenant, surely you can't think that Hask committed the murder," said Frank.

"Dr. Nobilio, we think there's sufficient evidence to bring charges, yes. Now, Hask, do you understand these rights as I have explained them to you?"

Hask's legs bowed out, allowing him to bring his two arms down to touch the floor. He picked up the two pieces and looked at them, one with his front set of eyes, the other with his rear set. The eyes Frank could see were blinking rapidly.

"Do you understand these rights?" said Perez for a third time.

"I—I believe so," said Hask. His tuft was waving back and forth in agitation.

Frank held out an impatient hand. "Show me the arrest warrant, Lieutenant."

"Hask?" said Perez.

"For Pete's sake, Lieutenant, he may *speak* English, but he can't read it. Give me the warrant."

Perez reached into his jacket and handed the papers to

Frank. Frank had never seen an arrest warrant before, but there was nothing obviously wrong with it. It said:

The undersigned is informed and believes that:

COUNT 1

On or about December 22 of this year, in the county of Los Angeles, the crime of murder, in violation of Penal Code Section 187 (a), a felony, was committed by Hask, a member of the Tosok species, who did willfully, unlawfully, and with malice aforethought murder Cletus Robert Calhoun, a human being.

Notice: The above offense is a serious felony within the meaning of Penal Code Section 1192.7 (c) (1).

It is further alleged that in the commission and attempted commission of the above offense, the said defendant, Hask, personally used a deadly and dangerous weapon, to wit, a knife or other extremely sharp instrument or tool, said use not being an element of above offense, within the meaning of Penal Code Section 12022 (b) and also causing the above offense to be a serious felony within the meaning of Penal Code Section 1192.7 (c) (23).

Jesus Perez
(LAPD Robbery-Homicide detective)
Declarant and Complainant

"Satisfied?" said Perez.

"Jesus," said Frank.

"It's *Hay-soos*."

"I wasn't talking to you. You can't possibly be serious about this."

"I am." The lieutenant turned to Hask. "Do you know what an attorney is?"

Hask was still holding the two broken halves of the disk; they seemed to be painted on one side—it was a decoration of some sort. "An advocate," said Hask slowly, "or someone who acts upon one's behalf."

"And do you know what I meant when I said you had the right to remain silent?"

"You meant you could not compel me to speak."

"Correct. Do you know what I meant when I said that if you do speak, the words may be used against you?"

"No."

"'Used against you.' Recorded, and presented as evidence."

"Oh. Yes, I understand that."

"If you make statements, they will be taken down in writing. If what you say can be used to prove your guilt, it will be so used."

"I understand."

"Do you have an attorney?"

Hask looked past Frank to Kelkad. "No."

"Of course he doesn't have an attorney!" said Frank. "He doesn't have an accountant, or a dentist, or a personal trainer, either."

Perez turned to the alien captain. "Are you or any of your colleagues qualified to serve as an attorney?"

"No," said Kelkad. "We do not have a system of laws comparable to yours. Oh, there are intercessors who will entreat God on one's behalf, and mediators for civil disputes. But we have nothing like your 'criminal-justice' system— indeed, I am not even sure I fully understand that term."

Perez turned back to Hask. "Hask, do you desire an attorney?"

"I am not—"

"Say yes, Hask," said Frank sharply. "Say yes."

Perez shot Frank a look, but Hask said, "Yes."

"All right, then. Come with me," said Perez.

"Suppose I choose not to?" asked Hask.

Perez indicated the four uniformed men. "These gentlemen are armed—do you understand that expression? They carry weapons capable of killing. If you don't come, they will be forced—"

"Oh, for Christ's sake, Lieutenant," said Frank. "You're not going to open fire!" He turned to Hask. "There's probably no way they can compel you to go with them." He swung on Perez. "Diplomatic immunity, Lieutenant."

Perez's gaze was unblinking. "What immunity, Doctor? There are no treaties between the United States and the Tosok government."

"But—"

"This is a completely righteous collar."

"How are you going to make him go?" asked Frank. "You can't shoot him."

Perez turned to Hask. "Hask, Dr. Nobilio is right. We won't use physical force to take you into custody. But I do have the power to prevent the materials needed to repair your mothership from being delivered. And I have the authority to order you to accompany me. Will you do so?"

Kelkad finally spoke. "My subordinate denies killing Clete."

Perez did a little half bow. "I mean no disrespect, sir, but that's not an unusual response in circumstances such as these."

Kelkad's natural voice rose as it always did, but his translated voice was absolutely even. "I vouch for my crew member."

"You will have an opportunity to do that in the appropriate venue at the appropriate time."

"But—"

"I will go," said Hask. "We need their help; cooperation is appropriate."

"You better know what the hell you're doing, Lieutenant," said Frank. "You better know exactly what you're doing."

"Thank you, Doctor. Now, unless you're aiding this being in resisting arrest—"

"Don't push it, Perez."

"And don't push me, Doctor. *A man is dead.* You're the one who is in over his depth." He turned again to Hask. "Come with me."

Hask began to move.

"Don't worry," said Perez. "We'll get you a lawyer."

"A *legal-aid* lawyer?" said Frank. "Jesus Christ, talk about being in over one's depth! Hask, don't say a word to anyone. Do you hear me? Not a word until we get a lawyer for you."

NINE

Frank immediately returned to his room and began making calls on his cellular, talking to a dozen different people in Washington. Two hours later the first phone call he'd made was returned. He put the phone to his now stubble-covered cheek. "Nobilio," he said.

"Dr. Nobilio, please hold for Olympus."

Frank waited through about a minute of static, then the familiar voice came on. "Frank?"

"Hello, Mr. President."

"Frank, we've got a problem here, don't we?"

"Yes, sir. I'm afraid we do."

"The phones here have been ringing off the hook, ever since CNN reported the arrest. There's not a single country on Earth that's happy about California wanting to try one of the aliens."

"I can imagine, sir," said Frank. "I'm not a lawyer, but does California even have jurisdiction?"

"Murder is only a federal issue if it's committed on federal lands, against federal officials, or if a fugitive crosses state lines," said the president, himself a lawyer. "None of those conditions pertain here." He sighed. "Several ambassadors have asked why we just didn't sweep this whole Calhoun mess under the rug, and—"

"No, sir."

"Pardon, Frank?"

"No—look, sir, Clete was my friend. He—" Frank paused, surprised to hear his own voice crack. "He was a good man, sir, and a good friend. I—I can understand the international feeling that maybe we're going too far in prosecuting an extraterrestrial, but we should *not* forget Calhoun. Not ever, sir."

"I know," said the president gently. "And, as my aides have tried to explain to the foreign ambassadors, we've got a strict separation between the executive and judicial branch. I can't be seen to be interfering with a court case, but . . ."

"Yes, sir?"

"Well, it's not that long until Super Tuesday. The vice-president had already agreed to appear on *Primetime Live* tonight before this broke; Sam Donaldson is sure to skewer him. Everybody seems to be asking why Washington didn't prevent this mess in the first place."

"I understand," said Frank. "Who are you sending out here to handle things?"

"Nobody, Frank. You're it. You're my man."

"Me, sir?"

"I'd love to fly half the attorney general's office out there, but it'd be suicide for me to be seen to be meddling directly. You're already there, and as part of the Tosok entourage, you've got a legitimate role apparently unrelated to the murder case. You're going to have to coordinate a defense for Hask, without being seen to be involved at all."

"What about money, sir? I'll need to hire a lawyer."

"That's a problem. We can't be seen to be underwriting the defense in any way."

Frank sighed, contemplating the magnitude of the task now facing him. "I'll do my best, sir."

"I know you will, Frank."

Olympus clicked off.

Frank went to Kelkad's room in Valcour Hall. "Captain," he said, "we will require money to hire a lawyer to defend Hask."

"Money?" said Kelkad. "That green paper stuff? I am sure Engineer Rendo can replicate whatever we need aboard the mothership."

Frank allowed himself his first faint smile since the murder. "No, you can't do that. Duplicating money is a crime."

"Oh. We have none of our own."

"I know," said Frank. "But I think I know a way . . ."

During his sixty-seven years of life, Dale Rice had heard the name for what he was change from Colored to Negro to Black to African-American. When he'd been born, there were still people alive who had been called slave.

Dale had white hair but black eyebrows, and large pouches of skin beneath his rheumy eyes. His nose was wide and misshapen. His three-hundred-pound body resembled an Aztec step pyramid; over it, he usually wore a charcoal-gray Armani suit, the pants held up by suspenders.

His wide, smooth face had seen a lot of history. Dale had been born in Montgomery, Alabama. He was a young man in 1955 when Rosa Parks was arrested there for refusing to give up her seat on a bus for a white man.

In 1961, Dale had become a Freedom Rider, testing the Supreme Court's order outlawing segregation in bus terminals. When the bus he was on pulled into Anniston, Alabama, a mob of white men with clubs, bricks, metal pipes, and knives was waiting. The bus was fire bombed, and as the black and white passengers escaped they were savagely beaten; it was during this fight that Dale's nose had been broken.

In 1963, he and two hundred and fifty thousand other people marched on Washington, D.C., and heard the Reverend Martin Luther King, Jr., give his "I Have a Dream" speech.

Dale Rice had known King, and he'd known Malcolm X. He knew Jesse Jackson and Louis Farrakhan. There were those who called him the top civil-rights lawyer in the United States. Dale himself thought that was probably true; he also thought it very sad that after all this time the United States still needed civil-rights lawyers.

The intercom on his desk buzzed. He pushed the talk button with a sausagelike finger. "Yes?" he said, his voice low and deep.

"Dale," said a woman, "there's a man here to see you. He doesn't have an appointment, but . . ."

"Yes, Karen?"

"He's shown me some ID. He works for the president of the United States."

The dark eyebrows rose toward the white cloud of hair. "Send him in."

A thin white man came into the room. He was wearing gold wire-frame glasses and a gray suit that looked much less expensive than Dale's. "Mr. Rice," he said, in a slightly nasal voice, "my name is Francis Nobilio. I'm the science advisor to the president."

Dale sat looking out at Frank over his own half glasses. Dale was a man of few movements, and he did not offer his hand. He indicated one of the empty chairs facing his desk not with a gesture, but simply with a glance of his old, tired eyes. "I've seen you on TV," he said. "You're part of the entourage living with those aliens."

"That's correct, sir. And that's why I'm here. One of the Tosoks has been arrested for murder."

Dale nodded. "I was at the county courthouse today. Everyone was talking about it. The victim was that gentleman from PBS, right?"

"Cletus Calhoun, yes."

"And you want me to defend the Tosok?"

"Yes."

"Why me?"

Frank shrugged, as if it were obvious. "Your track record."

"There are lots of good lawyers in this town."

"True. But, well . . ." He paused, apparently not sure what to say next. "Look, it's not exactly a civil-rights case, but . . ."

"But I'm black."

Frank looked away. "There's that."

"And many of my most prominent cases have involved black defendants."

"Yes."

"Including a number of blacks accused of murdering whites."

Frank shifted in his chair. "Well, yes."

"So you figured I'm an expert at defending individuals that the court might be inclined to view as second-class citizens."

"I, ah, I wouldn't put it that way."

"But that's the issue, isn't it? You're afraid the jury will consider the Tosok to be something less than human." Dale had a James Earl Jones voice; his every syllable was as a pronouncement from on high.

"The thought had crossed my mind, yes."

Dale's eyes were unflinching. "Would you have come to me if the deceased man had been black?"

"I—I don't know. I hadn't thought about that."

"Black stiff, alien killer—not quite the same issue, is it? A jury is less likely to be enraged over the death of a black man."

"I'd like to think that the color of the victim makes no difference."

Dale's eyes continued to bore into Frank's skull for a few moments. "But it does," he said simply.

"Look, I've got to find someone to represent Hask today. I called Janet Reno, and Janet says you're the best there is. But if you don't want the job—"

"I didn't say that. I just want to make sure that it's the right case for me—and that your expectations are realistic. I'm offered a hundred cases a day; I turn almost all of them down."

"I know. You were asked to be a part of the Dream Team for the O.J. Simpson criminal trial."

"True. And I passed."

"Why?"

Dale thought for a moment about whether he wanted to answer this. Finally, he said, "Too many chiefs. Too many egos. I don't work that way. You hire me, you get me—me, and one of my associates as second chair. Half the reason the Simpson trial lasted so long was that each of the gentlemen sitting at the defense table had to get his time in the spotlight."

"You would be lead counsel. The rest of the team would be up to you."

Dale considered. "You mentioned Simpson, Dr. Nobilio. Let me ask you a question. Why was he found not guilty in the criminal trial?"

Frank tucked his lower lip behind his teeth. He seemed to be trying to think of a politic answer. Finally, he shrugged. "Slick lawyering."

"You think he did it? Think he killed Nicole Brown and Ronald Goldman?"

"Well, yes."

"Was justice done in that trial?"

Frank shook his head.

"You need a different lawyer. My secretary will suggest some names to you." Dale heaved his massive bulk up from his leather chair, and this time he did extend a beefy hand.

Frank didn't get up. "Don't brush me off, Mr. Rice. I need you. If you think my opinion is incorrect, tell me why."

Dale knew his own natural expression was a frown; he now let Frank see what his real frown looked like. But then he lowered himself back down, the chair creaking as it took his weight again. "The Simpson criminal jury only deliberated for four hours," Dale said. "You know why? Because it was an open-and-shut case."

Frank raised his eyebrows. "Open-and-shut!"

"Certainly. The jury was asked a single question: was there a reasonable doubt about O.J. Simpson's guilt? And the answer was simple: of course there was. You and most of white America wanted the question to be: did Simpson do it? But no jury is ever asked to decide that. Instead, they're asked, is there a reasonable doubt? And there absolutely was, on a dozen different grounds. The clear proof that Mark Fuhrman had perjured himself on the witness stand, the suggestion that he might have planted evidence, the EDTA preservative in the Simpson blood specimens, the possibility of DNA contamination, the gloves that didn't fit, *et cetera, et cetera, et cetera.* That's reasonable doubt."

Frank said nothing.

"Since there was reasonable doubt, he was entitled to go free. Slick lawyering had nothing to do with it."

Frank sounded dubious. "Oh."

"Johnnie, Lee, and the others, they didn't pull off a miracle for Simpson. All they did was point out the reasonable doubt about his guilt. Any competent lawyer could have done the same thing—in that particular case. But you, Dr. Nobilio, are you shopping for a miracle worker?"

"Pardon?"

"Is there any reasonable doubt about whether your alien did it?"

Dale could see the surprise on Frank's face. "Of course there is. Hask wouldn't have committed murder."

"How do you know that?"

"I—well, I mean, he's an alien, and . . ."

"I saw you on *Nightline* a couple of weeks ago," said

Dale. "You said something about since the Tosoks are obviously technologically superior to us, they must also be morally superior. They'd faced all the demons of technological adolescence and come through it."

"I did say that, yes. And nothing has changed my opinion."

"Monty Ajax wouldn't have laid charges unless he thought he had an exceptional case," said Dale.

"I—I suppose," said Frank. It was clear from his expression that he hadn't considered the possibility that Hask might be guilty.

"If your alien is guilty, he will likely be found guilty," said Dale. "This isn't Perry Mason's Los Angeles. The DA in this town wins ninety percent of the time."

Surprise moved across Nobilio's face. "I—I thought it would be more like half the time."

"We elect our district attorneys, Doctor. You think the voters would keep voting in someone if he didn't usually win? If I take this case, you must have realistic expectations. If your alien did it, and if he premeditated the crime, then he will quite likely be found guilty of murder one."

"No. We need for him to go free."

"I can't guarantee that. And if he's guilty, and if the police did not violate his rights—hardly a given, I grant you—there is no reason he *should* go free."

"There's more at stake here than the simple issue of who killed Cletus Calhoun. This is our first contact with aliens, for God's sake. The repercussions of this going bad are beyond imagination. Look, you caught me off guard a moment ago: I did *not* come to you just because you're black. I came here because of the career you've had. You take cases in which larger issues are involved all the time—civil-rights cases, test cases against unjust laws. That's why I'm here. That's why I want you."

Dale considered. He kept his face impassive; the only sound in the room was the soft wheeze of his breathing.

"My race, of course, shouldn't be a factor—and I accept that it is not. But a reality that faces people of every race is the march of time. You're still a reasonably young man, Dr. Nobilio, but I'm just a few years shy of my allotted three-score and ten. I've got a cabin in Georgia that I've been planning to retire to. This could be an extremely complex and drawn-out case."

"I can't deny that," said Frank. "And I can't say that you need this case as a capstone; you will be remembered for a dozen major cases."

Dale's voice was dry. "Only a dozen?" He was quiet for a time, then: "I require a retainer of fifty thousand dollars. My fee is five hundred dollars an hour for my time, plus two hundred dollars an hour for my associate's time, plus expenses."

"Now, ah, that's a problem."

"You were expecting me to work *pro bono?*"

"No, no—you deserve to be paid; I understand that. But the Tosoks don't have any money, and of course my office can't be seen as getting involved."

"What do you propose?"

"Tosok technology will, of course, be introduced into Earth society; Captain Kelkad has agreed to patent the technology aboard his starship, and to pay you for your services a fee equal to one-quarter of one percent of all income generated from licensing that technology."

"In perpetuity?" said Rice. "And not contingent on the outcome of the case?"

"In perpetuity," agreed Frank. "And you get it whether you win or lose." He smiled. "Before you know it, you may be richer than Bill Gates."

"I don't crave money, Dr. Nobilio, but . . ."

"But think of all the good you could do with it."

Dale nodded. "Very well."

"You'll take the case?"

"I will."

"Thank you. Thank you. When can you see Hask?"

"Where is he? Parker Center?"

Frank nodded.

"I'll have Karen clear my afternoon." He rose again, slowly, ponderously. "Let's go."

Frank got up. "We'll want to go over his alibi, of course."

Dale had moved out from behind his wide oak desk. He placed a giant hand on Frank's forearm. "There is no 'we,' son."

Frank blinked. "Pardon?"

"You're not an attorney. You can't be with Hask when I speak to him."

Frank's eyes narrowed. "What? Why?"

"Because conversations between him and me are privileged—but only if they're in private. If they're not, then any of the participants—yourself, but also him or me—are subject to subpoena."

"But I want to be in on this. Hell, *the president* wants me to be in on this."

"I understand—but you cannot."

"Can't you—I don't know—deputize me? Something like that?"

"Make you an agent, you mean. No, I can't do that—after all, there's a reasonable likelihood that you'll be called as a witness by one side or the other." Dale began to move toward the mahogany doors to his office. "Sorry, son, but you've hired me, and now you've got to trust me."

TEN

Hask had been placed in a special cell at Parker Center, separate from the other prisoners. But that was the only concession to his unique status. The cell was filthy, with graffiti scrawled on its walls. There was a toilet and a sink, both in plain view. There was also a chair, but it wasn't suitable for a Tosok, so Hask had been standing for hours, his back hand grasping one of the bars for support.

Frank Nobilio and Dale Rice approached the cage, and the guard let them inside.

"Frank!" said Hask, his tuft moving excitedly. "Thank you for coming back."

"Hask, I apologize for all this," said Frank. "These people—the police—they've obviously made a terrible mistake. We'll get this all straightened out." A beat. "Let me introduce you to your lawyer. Dale Rice, meet Hask."

"The name again?" said Hask.

"Rice," said Frank. "R-I-C-E. Dale. D-A-L-E." He looked at the other human. "The Tosoks sometimes have trouble parsing human names."

"Greetings, Mr. Rice," said Hask. "You are the person who can get me out of here?"

"You may call me Dale. And I'll do everything I can."

"I will be grateful. Let me—"

"Wait. Frank, you have to leave now."

Frank frowned. "All right. Hask, I've got some other business to attend to, anyway, but I'll come back to talk to you when you and Dale are finished."

"I want you here," said Hask.

"Not possible," said Dale. "Hask, under our law, private conversations between an attorney and his client are *privileged*. That means they can never be introduced in court— but only if the conversations *are* private. You'll meet my associate, Ms. Katayama, soon; she's in court today, but I'll bring her by tomorrow. But only conversations you have while alone with either her or me are protected under law."

"It'll be okay," said Frank to Hask. "Dale is one of the most famous lawyers on this planet." Frank left, and Dale took the one chair; it protested loudly under his massive body.

"I tell you, Dale, I—"

"Shut up."

Hask took a half step backward. "Pardon?"

"Shut up. Shut up. You were about to tell me if you are guilty or innocent, right? Don't tell me *anything* unless I ask you. The Supreme Court has ruled that I can't put you on the stand to testify to your innocence if you've already told me you're guilty; it's tantamount to suborning."

"Suborning?"

"Inducing a witness to perjure himself."

"But—"

"Not a word, unless I ask for it. Understood?"

Hask's topknot waved in apparent bewilderment. But at last he said, "Yes."

"How are they treating you?"

"I have no chair that I can use."

"I'll send someone from my office to bring one for you from the USC dorm."

"I wish to leave this place," said Hask.

"I understand that—and we're working on that right now. There will be a bail hearing later today. If it's successful, you will be able to go."

"And this will be over?"

Dale shook his head. "No. No, it won't. But you'll be able to rejoin the other Tosoks, and have your liberty until the main trial."

"And when will that occur?"

"That's the first issue we have to address. You have a right to a speedy trial, but, well, I'm going to ask you to waive that right. We're going to need time to prepare your defense."

"If, as I am told, I am presumed to be innocent, then why must I mount a defense at all?"

Dale nodded. "Technically, you don't have to. But the prosecution will present the most compelling case it can. If we don't try to counter their arguments, they will likely win."

"I have already publicly declared my innocence. What other defense is possible?"

"Well, the simplest defense is just that—saying you didn't do it. But that means somebody else must have. The security at the USC residence was such that no one could get in or out without being seen. That means *somebody* inside killed Dr. Calhoun. It had to be either one of the seven Tosoks, or one of the eighteen humans who had access, including the members of the entourage and the LAPD officers. If it can be proved that none of the others did it, then your simple declaration won't be enough to find you innocent."

"Then we must find the killer."

Dale frowned. "It's not our responsibility to prove who did do it, and normally I'd not even try—but with so few possible suspects, it's certainly in our interest to consider the question. Without indicating one way or the other whether you yourself really did it, do you know anyone else who might have had reason to kill Calhoun?"

"No."

"A lot of the prosecution's case will probably hinge on proving that the crimes were committed by a Tosok rather than a human. Do you think it's possible that one of the other Tosoks did it?"

"We are not killers."

"Generally speaking, humans aren't, either. But a man is dead."

"Yes."

"One of my people will ask everyone in the residence this at some point, but did you ever see anyone fighting or arguing with Calhoun?"

"No."

Dale let out a hurricane of a sigh. "All right. We've certainly got our work cut out for us. Now, we better get prepared for the arraignment."

Frank Nobilio walked the two blocks to the Los Angeles County Criminal Courts Building, at the corner of Temple and Broadway. It was a great concrete cube, with wafflelike sides. Just inside the front door, Frank passed through a metal detector operated by two uniformed guards. Christmas decorations were hanging from the walls.

There was a shoeshine stand with four stations in the large, dim lobby. In front of it was a white foam-core board written on in brown Magic Marker:

A.J.'s Shoe Shine
Regular Shines (incl. Spit Shines)
Brief Cases / Police Belts + Accessories
Get your punch card, wherein every
6th shine is free!!!

Frank looked down at his own brown loafers. He was sweating a fair bit; the walk had been easy (although gently uphill), but L.A. was having a winter heat wave.

He made his way past the information desk—which seemed to specialize in giving bus maps to jurors—and found a building directory. The room he wanted was 18-709. He pushed the button to call an elevator that went to that floor.

He got into the elevator and heard the clacking of heels on the floor behind him. He held out a hand to keep the door from closing, and in came a severe-looking, thin white woman with short brown hair. Frank felt his eyes widen as he recognized her: Marcia Clark, the lead prosecutor in the Simpson criminal case. Clark must have just been dropping in for a visit, since she was now a TV host, rather than a member of the DA's office—Frank wondered if she got the same kind of flak about selling out from professional colleagues that Cletus Calhoun had. She punched a floor button; Frank pushed the one labeled 18 and tried not to stare at her. A sign in the elevator said "All Persons Will Be Searched on the 9th Floor." The warning was repeated in Spanish.

The elevator stopped. Marcia Clark got off. The cab resumed motion, and a moment later Frank exited. He found the door labeled "Montgomery Ajax, District Attorney," stopped to adjust his tie and smooth out his hair, then entered the outer office.

"I'm Frank Nobilio," he said. "I have an appointment with Mr. Ajax."

The secretary nodded, picked up her telephone handset, and spoke briefly into it. She then pushed a button on her desk, apparently unlocking the door to Ajax's private office. "You may go in," she said.

Frank walked into the large wood-paneled office with his hand extended. "Mr. Ajax," he said, "thank you for agreeing to see me."

Ajax's fox face was not smiling. "Frankly," he said, "I'm

not sure I should. In precisely what capacity are you here, Doctor?"

"A private citizen, that's all."

"Because if Washington is interfering—"

"No one is interfering, Mr. Ajax, believe me. But Cletus Calhoun was my friend—we'd known each other almost twenty years. Believe me, no one wants to see justice done more than I do."

"Well, then," said Ajax, sitting back down. The view of L.A. through his office windows was breathtaking.

Frank sat down, too. "But Hask is also my friend," he said. "I find it hard to believe that he killed Clete. Remember, I've spent more time with the Tosoks than anyone— anyone still alive, that is. I've seen no sign of malevolence in them."

"So?"

"So, I'm wondering—I'm just wondering, is all—I'm wondering, Mr. Ajax, if perhaps you've been a bit too hasty in going after one of the Tosoks."

Ajax stiffened noticeably. "Are you suggesting that my office should drop this case?"

"It might be prudent," said Frank gently. "After all, this is the first contact between humans and aliens. The Tosoks are much more advanced than we are. They could revolutionize our science and technology. We don't want to antagonize them."

"'We'?" said Ajax. "Who is 'we'?"

"Well—all of us. Humanity."

"One might say that it's the Tosoks who have antagonized us, not the other way around."

"But this case has an impact on the entire world."

"That may be so. But the fact is that one of your aliens committed murder. That crime has to be addressed."

Frank tried to keep his voice from rising. "No, sir. The fact is that a Tosok *may* have committed murder. But then again, he may be completely innocent. And if he is—"

Ajax spread his arms; Frank noticed he wore a Rolex watch. "If he is, he will be exonerated, and no harm done. But if he's guilty—"

"If he's guilty, you'll be seen as the great white knight in the fight against evil, the crusading DA who wouldn't back down."

Ajax's pale blue eyes flashed with anger, but he said nothing.

"I'm sorry," said Frank. "I shouldn't have said that."

"If there's nothing else, Doctor . . ." The DA gestured toward his office door.

Frank considered for a moment whether to go on. "Rumor has it that you're going to run for the governorship of California."

"I've made no public announcement."

"You could certainly use all sorts of support in that bid."

"Are you trying to bribe me into dropping this case, Doctor?"

"Not at all. I'm just pointing out that the ramifications run deep."

"Dr. Nobilio, *if* I run for governor, it'll be because I believe in law and order. I believe we shouldn't let criminals go free. And I think America can take a certain justifiable pride that one of its institutions is working the way it was intended to, as the great leveler and as the bastion of truth."

Frank nodded. "And therefore you can't be seen as being soft; I understand that. But surely you can see that you're letting political ambition blind you to the larger issues—"

Ajax held up a hand. "We're through here, Doctor. Good day."

Frank exhaled. "All I'm saying is think about what you're doing, Mr. Ajax."

"I *have* thought about it. And I intend to proceed against this alien killer with all speed."

ELEVEN

Judge Albert Dyck was almost seven feet tall. He entered the courtroom with a stride worthy of a Tosok and took his seat at the bench. Like most humans, he had trouble taking his eyes off Hask—he'd seen the aliens on TV before, but never one in the flesh.

"Mr. Rice," said Dyck, "on the primary charge of murder in the first degree, how does your client plead?"

Dale brought his massive bulk out of the swivel-mounted chair. "Not guilty, Your Honor."

"And on the secondary charge of using a deadly and dangerous weapon, how does your client plead?"

"Not guilty, Your Honor."

"Your client is entitled to a speedy trial, if he so desires."

"We waive that right, Your Honor."

"Very well. How long do you need to prepare?"

"Twelve weeks should be sufficient, Your Honor."

"How does March fifteenth sound, then?"

"Fine."

"The People?"

Deputy District Attorney Linda Ziegler rose; at forty-one,

she'd already had an illustrious career, and was one of the top lawyers in Monty Ajax's Special Trials Unit. She was thin, with jet-black hair cut in a short, punk style. Her nose was aquiline; her chin, strong. "Yes," she said, in a crisp, clipped voice, "that date's fine, Your Honor."

"Your Honor, I'd like to now raise the question of bail," said Dale.

Ziegler had sat down, but she immediately rose again. "Your Honor, the People oppose bail in this matter. The particularly brutal nature of the crime—"

"Your Honor, my client has a clean record."

"Your client has *no* record at all," said Ziegler, "which is hardly the same thing. For all we know, he's a notorious criminal on his home world. That starship could have been deporting dangerous offenders—sending them off into space to fend for themselves."

"Really, counselor," said Dale, his low voice filling the courtroom. "There's absolutely no basis for any of that. Presumption of innocence surely extends to the accused's background in the absence of direct evidence to the contrary, and—"

"Enough, Mr. Rice," said Judge Dyck. "We're satisfied that you've made your point."

"The People still oppose bail, Your Honor."

"On what grounds, Ms. Ziegler?"

"Flight risk."

"Oh, please!" said Dale. "A Tosok would be recognized anywhere."

"Granted," said Ziegler. "But there are many jurisdictions that might deny our extradition request."

Dale spread his giant arms. "My client has assured me of his intention to stand trial."

"Your Honor, the accused has access to a *spaceship*. That's a clear flight risk."

"The Court is cognizant of the larger issues in this case," said Dyck. "We're inclined to grant bail, in part to demonstrate to the Tosoks the reasonable nature of American justice."

"In that case, Your Honor, the People urge a high bail figure."

"Your Honor, my client has no money—absolutely none."

"Then how is he paying you?" asked Dyck.

"I've, ah, taken an interest in potential Tosok business dealings. My recompense shall be deferred until some time in the future. They really do have no money, and so bail of even a token amount will be a significant concern for Hask."

"We don't doubt that there are resources that can be made available to your client, Mr. Rice. Bail is set in the amount of two million dollars; ten-percent cash bond required." Dyck rapped his gavel.

Dale turned and looked at Frank Nobilio, who was seated in the gallery directly behind the defense table. Frank's eyes were wide; he clearly didn't know where the money would come from. But Dale simply reached into the jacket pocket of his Armani suit, pulled out his checkbook, and began to write.

After the arraignment, Dale and Frank took Hask back to Valcour Hall, where he was clearly delighted to be reunited with the other Tosoks. The two humans then returned to the offices of Rice and Associates, on the twenty-seventh floor of a Bauhaus high-rise in downtown L.A.

Dale sat behind his wide desk; Frank felt lost in a massive easy chair that faced the desk. Two of Dale's office walls were covered with oak bookshelves. The shelves were high quality—even in the middle, even supporting massive books of statutes and case law, they didn't sag. The third wall had the door in it. Mounted on it were Rice's law-school diploma (from Columbia), several award citations, and pictures of Dale with such notables as Colin Powell, Jimmy Carter, and

Walter Cronkite. There were also several pieces of framed art on that wall. Frank at first took some of the pictures to be very odd indeed—one was a giant, juicy cheeseburger; another seemed to be nothing more than a pile of pink satin ribbons. But as he'd moved close to examine one he discovered they were actually completed jigsaw puzzles, each made of thousands of pieces cut into almost identical shapes. On a large antique table across the room sat a partially finished puzzle, its border all filled in.

"We'll need to hire a jury consultant, of course," said Dale, looking over steepled fingers.

Frank frowned. "Oh."

"You don't sound enthusiastic."

"I—no, we've got to do whatever is necessary. It's just that tailoring a jury to favor our side . . . well, it seems to undermine the whole concept of a fair, impartial jury."

"That's right."

Frank's eyebrows went up. "You agree with me?"

"Certainly. You ever read *To Kill a Mockingbird?*"

"No. Saw the movie, though."

Dale nodded. "One of the few really good film adaptations of a novel. In both the book and the movie, Atticus Finch gives a speech to the jury about how the jury system isn't just an abstract ideal. 'I'm no idealist to believe firmly in the integrity of the courts and our jury system—that is no ideal to me, it is a living, working reality.' Well, you know what happened in *To Kill a Mockingbird:* the all-white, all-male jury convicted a black man of a crime he was physically incapable of committing. I've been checking up on you, Frank; you're an idealist, an Atticus Finch. But I'm afraid a lifetime in this nation's courts has taken the rose tint out of my eyeglasses; I don't believe in the integrity of the courts or the jury system. If you put an innocent person in front of the wrong jury, they'll find him guilty. Still, it's the system we're stuck with, and we owe it to Hask to try to sculpt a jury that will at least give him a chance."

"Still . . ." said Frank.

"You can be certain the prosecution is going to be trying to shape the jury to favor their side. Believe me, Frank, in a major case, it's tantamount to malpractice *not* to use a jury consultant." Dale paused for a moment. "In fact, there's an old joke lawyers tell. In England, the trial begins once jury selection is over. Here in the States, once jury selection is over, so's the trial."

"Okay, okay. So, what do we look for?"

"That, son, is indeed the question. There are many rules of thumb." Dale rose from his chair, which seemed to sigh in relief as he got off it, and moved over to one of the floor-to-ceiling bookcases. He searched for a moment, then plucked a book off the shelf. Frank could see its title: *The Art of Selecting a Jury.* Dale flipped it open, and read a passage, apparently at random. "'Women are often prejudiced against other women they envy, for example those who are more attractive.'"

Frank rolled his eyes. "Good grief! How old is that book?"

Dale turned to the copyright page. "Not very. It was published in 1988—and the author is a superior-court judge right here in L.A. County. But you're correct: It's all prejudice and stereotypes." He closed the book and looked at Frank. "For instance, prosecutors love northern Europeans—Germans, Brits, and especially Scandinavians. Real law-and-order types, see? The defense normally desires blacks, Hispanics, Natives, southern Europeans—cultures that are less likely to believe the authorities are always right. If you've got nothing else to go on, the prosecution will select jurors who are wearing gray—conservative, see? And the defense will select jurors who are wearing red—liberals."

"Okay, but—wait a minute! Wait a minute! Isn't Hask entitled to a jury of his *peers?* Obviously, his peers are Tosoks, and there are no disinterested Tosoks available—so maybe we can get this whole silliness set aside right now."

Dale smiled indulgently. "Although many Americans think they're entitled to a jury of peers, that's simply not true; that's a provision of British common law, not the U.S. Constitution. The Sixth Amendment simply provides for 'an impartial jury of the State and district wherein the crime shall have been committed.' It doesn't say a blessed thing about peers. In fact, consider the Simpson trial again: O.J.'s peers would be award-winning athletes, or perhaps mediocre actors, or commercial pitchmen, or millionaires, or those in interracial marriages—but every single person who fit any of those categories was excluded from sitting on the Simpson jury. No, Hask must face a human jury—a jury of beings as alien to him as he is to us. Still, as his defense counsel, I owe it to him to try to craft a jury that will be sympathetic to his case."

Frank sighed. "All right, all right. How much does a jury consultant cost?"

"The average fee is a hundred and fifty dollars per hour—although I tend to use people who charge at the high end of the scale. Total fees in a big case like this one can range from around ten grand to a quarter of a mil."

Frank frowned again. "I told you I don't have access to any funds."

"I'll take care of it," said Rice.

"Thank you." A pause. "But what you were saying before—I mean, isn't it illegal to discriminate in jury selection on the basis of race or gender?"

Dale nodded. "Of course; the Supreme Court has confirmed that. *Batson* v. *Kentucky,* among others. But all that means is if you don't want any blacks on the jury, you find some other reason to get rid of them. For instance, you see a black gentleman in the jury pool, and you want grounds to excuse him, ask him if he's ever had reason to distrust the police. Of course he's going to say yes, and—presto!—he's off the jury, without race ever being mentioned. The point is that with the right jury, it's possible to get someone off even if they committed the crime—"

"Like O.J."

"No, *not* like O.J.," said Dale. "We've been down that road before. But consider the case of Lorena Bobbitt—there was zero doubt that she'd cut off her husband's penis. Or *California* v. *Powell:* there was zero doubt that those officers had beat Rodney King within an inch of his life—the whole thing was caught on videotape. Still, in both cases, the undisputed perpetrators of the crimes were acquitted by juries."

Frank nodded slowly. "So in this case we want bright people, people who can follow a scientific argument?"

"I don't know about that. The standard advice is if you're defending a guilty party—which, my friend, despite your wide-eyed optimism, we might indeed be doing—then you want a dull-witted jury. Bunch of rubes who won't see through the tricks you're pulling. That means we're off to a good start right away. The jury pool is always skewed toward the poorly educated and the unemployed. A bright person can usually find a good reason to get out of jury duty." Dale paused. "You know why the DNA evidence failed in the Simpson criminal case? Because there were conflicting experts. You've got one side saying one thing, the other side saying something else, and the uneducated jury says, well, if these experts can't figure it out, then how can we? And so they simply *ignore* that whole line of evidence, and make their decision based on other considerations."

"Okay, so who do we want? Space buffs?"

"I wish. But you can bet the prosecution will get those eliminated."

"*Star Trek* fans? Science-fiction fans?"

"They'd probably be good, but, again, too obvious—the other side will strike them."

"People who think they've seen a UFO?"

"No—too unpredictable. Could be crazy, and the last thing you want on the jury is a crazy person. No way to guess what they'll do."

"Okay. So who *don't* we want on the jury?"

"The most important thing to watch out for is the ideologue—a person who wants to be on the jury to push for a particular verdict, no matter what. You find them a lot in abortion cases, civil-rights cases, and so on. Such people can be really crafty—they know exactly what to say and what not to say to get on the jury, then, once there, they hang the jury. We'll do our best to weed them out during *voir dire,* but in a case like this, we've got to be particularly careful not to get some aliens-are-devils nut impaneled . . ."

The intercom on District Attorney Ajax's desk buzzed. "Reverend Oren Brisbee is here to see you, sir."

Ajax rolled his eyes. "All right. Send him in."

The door to Ajax's office opened, and in came a thin black man of about sixty, with a fringe of white hair that, when he tipped his head down, looked like a halo.

"Mr. Ajax," said Reverend Brisbee. "How good of you to see me."

"I always have time for the pillars of the community, Reverend."

"Especially when about to announce a gubernatorial challenge," said Brisbee. His voice was a decibel or two too loud; Brisbee always spoke as if trying to reach the last pew, even when only one other person was present.

Ajax spread his arms. "My door has always been open to you."

"And let us hope, Mr. Ajax, that for a good long time to come you will always have a public door . . . either here in L.A., or up in Sacramento."

Ajax struggled not to sigh audibly. "What did you want to see me about, Reverend?"

"The murder of Cletus Calhoun."

"A tragedy," said Ajax. "But we will ensure that justice is done."

"Will you, now?" The words actually echoed slightly off of the office window.

Ajax felt the beginnings of heartburn. He reached into his desk drawer and took out a roll of Rolaids. "Of course. We've already had some pressure from Washington to drop the case—and I'm told Washington has been pressured by other nations." He forced a chuckle. "But if cases were dropped whenever Washington wanted them to be, Richard Nixon would have finished his term of office, Bob Packwood would still be in the Senate, and no one would ever have heard of Ollie North."

"I admire your stick-to-itiveness, Mr. Ajax. But tell me, sir, will you have the backbone to stick to it until the bitter end?"

Ajax narrowed his eyes. "What do you mean?"

"I mean, good sir, that this fine state of California recognizes the right of the people to do collectively that which individually we must not." Brisbee pointed a finger directly at Ajax. "We have capital punishment here, sir, and this is a capital crime. Will you have the moral courage to push for the death penalty in this case?"

The DA spread his arms. "Well, surely there are extenuating circumstances, Reverend. And although I won't bow to political pressure, I do accept that there are some gigantic issues at stake here."

"There are indeed. Would you like to know which issue is foremost in my mind, sir? Foremost in my mind is the fact that during your term as district attorney, you have called for the death penalty in sixty-four percent of the first-degree murder cases involving black defendants, whereas you've only asked for it in twenty-one percent of the cases involving white defendants."

"Those statistics don't tell the whole story, Reverend. You have to look at the severity of the individual crimes."

"And no crime is more severe than killing a white man, is it? In cases when a black person is accused of killing a white, you have sought execution *eighty-six* percent of the time. Well, good-ole-boy Cletus Calhoun was as white as they come, Mr. Ajax. If *I* had been the one to butcher him like a hog, sir, you'd be looking to fry my black ass."

"Reverend, I hardly think—"

"That, sir, is apparent. In your gubernatorial campaign, you can be sure the African-American constituency will be asking why you would execute a black man for killing a white man, but would demur from putting down an alien dog."

"It's more complex than that."

"Is it, sir? If you don't call for the death penalty in this case, what message are you sending? That this Tosok is more valuable than a black human being? That this alien traveler, with his advanced civilization and obvious education and great intelligence, is worthy of being spared, but a young Negro, victim of cruel poverty and racism, should be sent to the electric chair?"

"We are carefully weighing all the factors in deciding what penalty to seek, Reverend."

"See that you do, Mr. Ajax. See that you do. Because if you do not, sir, you will feel the wrath of a nation oppressed. We carry within each of us the divine spark of a soul, and we will not be treated as inferior, disposable products while you go easy on some soulless creature that has committed the most brutal killing and mutilation this city has ever seen."

Mary-Margaret Thompson was Dale Rice's usual jury consultant. She was a trim, birdlike brunette, who perched herself on the corner of Dale's wide desk. She looked at Frank, who was once again swimming in the giant easy chair. "There are several phases to the process, Dr. Nobilio.

First, there are the jury-selection surveys. For a normal case, they call in about fifty prospective jurors. For the Simpson criminal case, they called in twenty times that number—a thousand prospects. You can bet they're going to call in a similar amount this time. We'll get to consult with the prosecution on the survey that these people will have to fill out. That's step one—coming up with the right questions.

"Step two is *voir dire*—that's where the lawyers get to question the prospective jurors one-on-one. Now, we can end the consulting process there, but I suggest we go all the way. Once the jury is impaneled, we should set up a shadow jury—a group of people who are as closely matched as possible demographically to our real jury. We then monitor them throughout the trial; that way we can tell which arguments are working, which ones aren't, and how they're leaning day by day."

"A shadow jury," repeated Frank. "What does that cost?"

"We usually pay the shadow jurors seventy dollars apiece each day—which is ten times what the real jurors are making." A pause. "Now, the most important thing is to get someone on the panel who will serve as our virtual defendant—someone who will identify strongly with the defendant, taking on the role of Hask and presenting his viewpoint during deliberations. Of course, finding someone to do that is going to be rather tricky in this case . . ."

The squad room was bustling with activity—a blood-splattered black man being booked at one desk; two hookers, one white, one Asian, being booked at another; and three black gang members, maybe fourteen or fifteen, waiting to be processed. Dale looked at them, and shook his head. They looked back at him, at his three-thousand-dollar suit, at his gold cuff links and the chain for his gold pocket watch. "Oreo," said one to his homey as Dale walked by. Dale bristled, but didn't turn around. He continued along until he came to the door he was looking for. An engraved sign on the door said "J. Perez." Taped below it were a picture of a bale of hay, and a picture of an old white man holding a plush-toy Cat in the Hat. "Hay" "Seuss"—Perez's first name.

Oreo my ass, thought Dale. *Just call me Uncle Rebus.*

He knocked on the door. Perez barked out something, and Dale entered.

"Counselor," said Perez, not rising. "Haven't seen you for a while."

"Lieutenant." The stiff, formal word carried years of history behind it.

Perez jerked a thumb in the direction of the squad room. "I didn't think any of those lowlifes could afford you."

"My client is Hask."

Perez nodded. "So I'd heard. What's he paying you in? Gold-pressed latinum?"

"What?"

"Nothing." Perez paused. "You missed out on being part of Simpson's Dream Team, so now you've replaced the trial of the century with the trial of the Centauri." The detective chuckled at his own wit. "It's too bad, counselor. You had a pretty good winning streak going there."

"What makes you think I'm not going to win this time?"

"Are you kidding? Your buddy Mr. Spock offed one of TV's most popular personalities. This is Simpson in reverse: a celebrity stiff and a no-name defendant."

"Hask is famous as hell."

"Hask is *going* to hell."

Rice sighed. "Are you even looking for other suspects?"

"Certainly. But there are not many possibilities. There were only twenty-five people, including the seven Tosoks, who had access to the USC residence that night. But of the humans, the biggest question remains motive. Who would kill Calhoun? And who would kill him in that manner?"

"As you doubtless know, it could be someone wanting to frame the Tosoks—to incite ill-will toward them. And if that's the case, it could be a conspiracy involving two or more people—meaning the fact that someone has someone else as an alibi isn't worth anything."

"A conspiracy!"

"Why not? I should think you'd be glad that somebody is proposing a conspiracy *outside* of the LAPD."

Perez fixed Dale with a withering stare. "An eminent group of scientists hardly seems likely to frame an alien for murder."

Dale had gotten tired of waiting to be offered a seat. He took one—a metal-framed job, uncomfortably small for him; it groaned in protest under his weight. "Don't be so sure. Academic jealousy is the greenest of all. These gentlemen fight for ever-declining grant dollars and toil in obscurity, while some fellow from Pigeon Forge, Tennessee, makes millions and gets to hobnob with Jay Leno. They figure nobody's going to be crazy enough to arrest an alien—they didn't count on Monty Ajax's lust for power. It would be a perfect crime; they'd assume Washington would get it swept under the rug . . ."

"Which is precisely what they've been trying to do, apparently," said Perez. "No, counselor, we've got our— we've got our creature. It had to be a Tosok."

Dale's turn to fix a withering stare. "I would have thought, Lieutenant *Perez,* that you would have felt the sting of that kind of thinking enough in your own life not to apply it here. It has to be a Tosok. It must be a Latino. It was some black guy—and, hey, that guy over there is black, so it must be him."

"Don't accuse me of that, counselor. Don't you dare accuse me of that."

"Why not? 'It has to be a Tosok.' There are *seven* Tosoks on Earth. And unless you can prove that it's Hask in particular—Hask, and nobody else—my client is going to walk."

"Well, *of course* it's Hask."

"You can't prove that."

Perez smiled. "Just watch me."

TWELVE

Frank and Dale were meeting over breakfast in the restaurant at the University Hilton Hotel, just on the other side of Figueroa Street from the main USC campus. Frank was eating shredded wheat with skim milk, a half grapefruit, and black coffee. Dale was eating bacon, two fried eggs, and what seemed to be half a loaf's worth of toast with orange marmalade, all washed down with a pot of coffee with cream and sugar.

"Everybody on the planet is clamoring to interview your client," said Frank.

Dale nodded, and gulped more coffee. "I know."

"Do we let them?"

Dale stopped eating long enough to consider this. "I'm not sure. We don't care one whit about the public as a whole. The only people we're interested in are the twelve who will end up on the jury. The question is, do we do better if the potential jurors know Hask or not? We're probably not going to put Hask on the stand, after all, and—"

"We're not?"

"Frank, you *never* put your defendant on the stand, unless

you can't avoid it. So, yes, an interview could be our one chance to let the people who might end up on the jury get to know and like Hask. On the other hand, this is a bizarre crime, and if they decide he's just some weird alien, they may figure he probably did it."

"So, what do we do?"

Dale wiped his face with the napkin and signaled for the waitress to bring more coffee. "Let him do one interview—one of the biggies. Barbara Walters, maybe. Or Diane Sawyer. Somebody like that."

"What if it goes badly?" Frank asked. "Can you ask for a change of venue for the trial?"

"To where? The far side of the moon? There's no getting away from the media coverage *this* trial is going to get."

Barbara Walters was wearing her usual solicitous frown. "My guest today is Hask," she said, "one of the seven alien visitors to Earth. Hask, how are you?"

Dale, who was seated with the alien captain, Kelkad, just outside of camera view, had asked Hask not to wear his sunglasses, even though the camera lights were bothering him. Now, though, watching him squint at Walters, he thought perhaps he'd made a mistake.

"I have seen better days," said Hask.

Walters nodded sympathetically. "I'm sure you have. You're free on two-million-dollars bail. What is your assessment of the American legal system?"

"You have a huge number of people in jail."

Walters seemed taken aback. "Ah, yes. I guess we do."

"I am told your country has set a record. You have a greater percentage of your population in jail than any other country—even those countries that are referred to as police states."

"My question was intended more specifically," said Walters. "I was wondering how the Los Angeles Police Department treated you?"

"It was explained to me that I was to be presumed innocent until proven guilty—and yet I was put in a cage, something my race does not do to *anything,* and I had thought your race only did to animals."

"You're saying you were treated poorly?"

"I have been treated poorly, yes."

"You mean, as a guest on our world, you should be accorded more respect?"

"Not at all. There is nothing special about my status. I imagine if you were interviewing a human being who had been wrongly accused of a crime, he or she would also decry the treatment. Have you ever been imprisoned, Ms. Walters?"

"Me? No."

"Then you cannot understand."

"No," said Walters. "No, I guess not. What is the justice system like on your world?"

"On my world, there is no such thing as crime; allowing a crime to occur would imply that God had ceased to be vigilant over the affairs of her children. Besides, we do not prize material things the way they are prized here, so there is no theft of objects. And everybody has enough to eat, so there is no theft of food, or the means to acquire food." He paused, then: "It is not my place to say, but it seems that your legal system is designed backward. The root causes of human crime appear to my no-doubt ignorant eyes to be poverty and your ability to become addicted to chemicals. But instead of treating these, you devote your energies at the other end, to punishing."

"Perhaps you're right," said Walters. "But speaking of punishing, do you feel you can get a fair trial?"

Hask's topknot moved in agitation while he mulled this over. "That is a difficult question. A human is dead—and someone must pay for that. I am not a human. It is perhaps easier to make me pay, and yet . . ."

"Yes?"

"I am different. But . . . but your race continues to grow. My lawyer is Dale Rice, and his skin is black. He has told me how his kind were enslaved, were denied the right to vote, to use public facilities, and so on. And yet, in his lifetime, much of that has changed—although I saw in jail that much of it remains, too, just below the surface. Can twelve human beings look upon an alien and judge without prejudice?" He shifted slightly, looking directly at the camera with his orange and green front eyes. "I think yes. I think they can."

"There's been a lot of talk about what will happen if you are found guilty."

"I am given to understand that I may die," said Hask.

Barbara Walters pursed her thin lips, apparently disturbed by the baldness of the statement. "I mean, what will happen to Earth? What response will your government have?"

"It would be in my own interest to tell you that my people would descend on Earth and, because of the execution of one of their own, would wipe your planet clean of life." He paused. "Or I could simply tell you that the execution of me would result in the Tosoks leaving, never to return—a cutting off of all contact. But neither of these things is true, and so I will not claim them. As a people, the Tosoks believe in predestination. If it is my fate to be punished for a crime I did not commit, they will accept that. But I tell you, Ms. Walters, I did not kill Cletus Calhoun—why would I? He was my friend. If I am found guilty, it *will* be an error, for I did not commit this crime."

"You're saying we must find you innocent, then?"

"You will find me whatever God intends you to. But I *am* innocent."

Dale smiled broadly. Hask couldn't have done better.

———

"Kelkad!" shouted a man from the *Los Angeles Times* as Dale, Hask, and Kelkad left the ABC studios. "Kelkad! What did you think of tonight's broadcast?"

Captain Kelkad had his front hand up to shield his forward-looking pink and yellow eyes from the glare of the lights. "I thought my crew member presented himself well," he said.

The crush of reporters was overwhelming, but police were doing their best to keep them back.

"Kelkad," shouted a woman from CNN, "if Hask is found guilty, will your own people punish him as well?"

Kelkad continued to move forward through the crowd. "We would have to conduct our own investigation of the matter, of course."

"What have you done yourself about the murder?" shouted a woman from the CBC.

Kelkad paused, as if considering whether to answer. "I suppose there is no reason not to tell you. I have, of course, made a full report to my home world via radio. I told them earlier that we found intelligent life on Earth, and have now supplemented that report with news that one of our team has been apprehended, and is facing execution for a crime he denies having committed."

"How long will it take to get a reply?" asked a man from CBS.

Kelkad's tuft moved in an odd way, as if surprised that anyone covering this story could be unaware of the basic scientific truths involved. "Alpha Centauri is 4.3 of your light-years from here. It will take, therefore, 4.3 Earth years for my report to arrive, and another 4.3 Earth years for any reply to be received. Obviously."

A man with a European accent jostled to the front of the crowd. "It's been over two centuries since you left your home world. What response will they make?"

The alien captain considered this for quite some time. Finally, his tuft parted in the center, a gesture that the public had learned by now was the Tosok equivalent of a shrug. "I have no idea," he said.

THIRTEEN

During pretrial discovery, the prosecution and the defense each had to share the evidence it intended to present at trial so that an adequate study of it and response could be made. After the final discovery meeting, an exhausted Dale Rice returned to his office and sat down in his big leather chair. He rubbed the broken bridge of his nose between his thumb and forefinger, trying to fight off a headache. After a moment he picked up his desk phone, selected a line, and punched out the number for Frank's cellular.

The moment Frank Nobilio entered Dale Rice's private office, he felt his eyebrows drawing together. Frank had never seen the old attorney look so upset before. Dale's face was normally quite smooth—surprisingly so for a man his age—but deep worry lines creased his forehead. "What is it?" asked Frank, taking his usual seat.

"I don't think there's much question anymore," said Dale. "I think our boy did it. I think Hask killed Calhoun."

"I don't believe it."

"Politely, it doesn't matter what you believe. It doesn't even matter what *I* believe, for that matter. Only thing that matters is what a jury'll believe."

"So, if the jury is likely to find Hask guilty, what do we do?" asked Frank. He felt nauseous.

"Well, the DA is going to seek a murder-one conviction. That's murder in the first degree—premeditated murder. We could get our alien gentleman to confess to murder-two instead."

"Which is?"

"Second degree. Yes, he killed Dr. Calhoun, and, yes, he meant to, but it wasn't planned in advance. An argument that got out of hand, something like that. But even a second-degree conviction carries a mandatory sentence of fifteen years."

"No," said Frank, shaking his head. "No, that's not acceptable."

"Or we try to get the DA to come down to involuntary manslaughter. That means it was a criminal death, but Hask never intended to do it. Calhoun died because his leg was cleanly severed from his body. Say Hask did that without knowing it would be fatal—the fact that Calhoun died makes it a crime, but it isn't murder."

"But he'd still go to jail."

"Possibly."

"Any other options?"

"There are only two possible approaches that let Hask walk. First, there's self-defense. But you can only legally use deadly force in self-defense if deadly force is being used against you. Calhoun had to have been threatening Hask in such a way that Hask felt he was in immediate danger of being killed."

"I can't believe Cletus Calhoun was threatening an alien."

"Don't dismiss this so fast, Frank. There are possibilities here. Say Calhoun wanted to—I don't know—say he wanted to thump Hask on the back, all friendly-like, but being hit there, say that's fatal to a Tosok. Hask might have thought he was in imminent danger of being killed, and so responded with deadly force."

"It seems unlikely. Why wouldn't he have told us if that were the case?"

"I don't know."

"You said there's another possible defense."

Dale nodded. "Insanity."

"Insanity," repeated Frank, as though he'd never heard the word before.

"That's right. We prove that, by human standards, Hask is *non compos mentis.*"

"Can you do that?"

"I don't know. It may be that *all* Tosoks are bonkers by human standards. But if he did it, and it wasn't self-defense, pleading insanity is the only thing that will get him off."

"It's an interesting approach."

"That it is, but the insanity defense is used in less than one percent of all criminal cases. And of those, only fifteen percent are murder cases. In all cases, the insanity defense works—that is, results in an acquittal—only about twenty-five percent of the time."

"So it's not an easy out?" asked Frank.

"No—despite what the media claims. Eighty-nine percent of those who are acquitted under an insanity defense are done so because they've been diagnosed as being either mentally retarded, or having a severe mental illness, such as schizophrenia. Eighty-two percent of acquittees have already been hospitalized at least once for mental problems."

"Wait a minute—did you say mentally retarded?"

Dale moved his massive head in a slow nod.

"Is there a legal definition for that?"

"Doubtlessly. I can get my clerk to check."

"'Cause if it's a matter of IQ, you know, they often charge

that IQ tests are culturally biased. If Hask gets a really low score on a standard IQ test, he could qualify as retarded."

Dale shook his head. "We've got to sell this to a jury, remember? A jury isn't going to buy that he's retarded. Everybody on Earth saw him piloting that lander, and has seen how he picked up English. No, that's out. It's got to be insanity. But the problem is that normally a person acquitted under the insanity defense doesn't just go free. Rather, almost automatically, if they're found insane, they're committed to a mental institution. Remember the Jeffrey Dahmer trial? He tried the insanity defense. So did John Wayne Gacy and the Hillside Strangler. All of them failed on that defense, but if they had succeeded, I can guarantee they would have been committed for life. See, once you're found legally insane, the burden shifts dramatically. You're no longer innocent until the State can prove you guilty. Rather, once you're committed, you're insane until *you* can prove that you're not."

"What about temporary insanity?"

"That's a possibility, too," said Dale. "Some aspect of Earth's environment—whether it's pollution, pollen, or Twinkies, made him temporarily crazy. The problem with that, though, is that first Hask has to confess—and he still refuses to do that."

"Well," said Frank, "we certainly can't let them lock Hask up as a mental patient."

"No, of course not. And that means, if we can't prove temporary insanity, then we have to show that not only is Hask bonkers, but we also have to prove that human psychiatry is incompetent to treat him—that he's *so* bonkers that there's nothing we can do for him, and yet, at the same time, that he's not a menace to society and doesn't have to be locked up."

"And can we do that?"

"That's what we have to find out. The standard test for insanity is whether the person can distinguish right from wrong. The standard problem is that if the person has taken steps to avoid punishment—such as hiding the body—then he must know what he did was wrong, and therefore he's sane." Dale considered. "Of course, in this case, the body was as conspicuous as possible, so maybe we *are* onto something here . . ."

Dale and Frank went down to Hask's room in Valcour Hall, accompanied by Dr. Lloyd Penney, a psychiatrist Dale sometimes used as a consultant. Hask was sitting on the corner of his bed, propping his back up with his back hand. In his front hand, he was holding a piece of the disk that broke the night he'd been arrested.

"Hello, Hask," said Frank. "This is Dr. Penney. He'd like to ask you a few questions."

Penney was in his late thirties, with curly light-brown hair. He was wearing a Hawaiian shirt. "Hello, Hask," he said.

"Dr. Penney."

Dale sat down on the edge of the bed as well. The bed had been modified: a trough ran down its center to accommodate Hask's back arm when he was resting. Frank leaned against the wall, and Penney sat down on the one human chair in the room.

Hask was still holding the broken piece of disk. "What's that?" asked Penney.

Hask did not look up. "A *lostartd*—a form of art."

"Did you make it?" asked Penney.

Hask's tuft waved backward in negation. "No. No, it was made by Seltar—the Tosok who died during our flight to Earth. I kept it to remember her by; she had been my friend."

Penney held out a hand toward Hask. "May I see?"

Hask handed it to him. Penney looked at it. The painting on the disk was stylized, but apparently depicted an alien landscape. The other piece was sitting on Hask's desk. Penney motioned for Frank to hand it to him; Frank did so. Penney joined the two parts together. The picture showed a world with a large yellow sun and a small orange one in its sky. "A clean break," said Penney. "Surely it could be fixed."

Frank smiled to himself. Doubtless keeping a broken artifact around was pregnant with psychological meaning.

"Of course it can be fixed," said Hask. "But I would need to return to the mothership to get the adhesive I need, and the terms of my bail do not allow that."

"We have powerful adhesives, too," said Frank. "A couple of drops of Krazy Glue should do the trick."

"Krazy Glue?" repeated Hask. His untranslated voice seemed slow, sad.

"Cyanoacrylate," said Frank. "It'll bond almost anything. I'll go out and buy you a tube today."

"Thank you," said Hask.

Dr. Penney placed the two pieces of the *lostartd* disk on Hask's desk. "Dale and Frank have brought me here to ask you some questions, Hask."

"If you must," said the alien.

"Hask," said the psychiatrist, "do you know the difference between right and wrong?"

"They are opposites," said Hask.

"What is right?" asked Penney.

"That which is correct."

"So, for instance, two plus two equals four is right?" said Penney.

"In all counting systems except base three and base four, yes."

"And, in base ten now, two plus two equals five is wrong, correct?"

"Yes."

"Do the words right and wrong have any other meaning?"

"Right also refers to the direction that is to the south when one is facing east."

"Yes, yes. Right on its own has other meanings, but the

concept of 'right' and 'wrong,' do they apply to anything other than factual matters?"

"Not in my experience."

Penney looked briefly at Dale, then turned back to Hask. "What about the terms 'good' and 'bad'?"

"A food item that has an agreeable taste is said to be good; one that has putrefied is said to be bad."

"And what about the concepts of moral and immoral?"

"These apparently have to do with human religion."

"They have no bearing on Tosok religion?"

"Tosoks believe in predetermination—we do the will of God."

"You believe in a single God?"

"We believe in a single being that was foremother to our race."

"And this God—she is good?"

"Well, she has not begun to putrefy."

"You perform no actions that are not the will of your God?"

"*The* God."

"Pardon?" said Penney.

"It is not acceptable to speak of God possessively."

"Sorry. You perform no actions that are not the will of the God?"

"By definition, such a thing would be impossible."

"Is there a devil in your religion?"

Hask's translator beeped. "A—devil? The word is unfamiliar."

"In many Earth religions," said Frank, once again leaning against the wall, "there is a supremely good being, called God, and an adversary, who attempts to thwart God's will. This adversary is called the devil."

"God is omnipotent," said Hask, looking briefly at Frank, then turning back to Penney. "Nothing can thwart her."

"Then there is no continuum of behavior?" asked the psychiatrist.

"I have encountered this concept repeatedly in human thought," said Hask. "The idea that everything moves from one extreme on the left to another on the right, or that there are two equal 'sides' to every issue—using the word 'sides' in a way a Tosok never would." His topknot moved. "This is an alien way of thinking to me; I rather suspect it has something to do with the left-right symmetry of your bodies. You have a left hand and a right, and although each individual among you seems to favor one—Frank, I have noticed you favor your right, but Dale, you favor your left—in general, you seem to view the hands as equal. But we Tosoks have a front hand that is much stronger than our back hand; we have no concept—to use one of your words that does not translate fully—of what you call 'evenhandedness.' One perspective is *always* superior to the other; the front always takes precedence over the back. The aspect with the preponderance of power or weight is the side of God, and it always wins."

Frank smiled. Clete would have loved that kind of biology-based answer.

"Let me ask you some hypothetical questions," said Penney. "Is it all right to steal?"

"If I do it, God certainly must have observed it, and since she did not stop me, it must be acceptable."

"Is it all right to kill?"

"Obviously, God could prevent one from doing so if she wished; that she does not clearly means the killer must have been acting as her instrument."

Penney's eyebrows went up. "Are there any unacceptable actions?"

"Define unacceptable."

"Unacceptable: acts that cannot be countenanced. Acts that are not reasonable."

"No."

"If you killed someone because he was trying to kill you, would that be acceptable?"

"If it happened, it is acceptable."

"If you killed someone because he was trying to steal from you, would that be acceptable?"

"If it happened, it is acceptable."

"If you killed someone because the joke they told was one you had already heard, would that be acceptable?"

"If it happened, it is acceptable."

"In our culture," said Penney, "we define insanity as the inability to distinguish moral acts from immoral acts."

"There is no such thing as an immoral act."

"So, by the definition of the human race, are you insane?"

Hask considered this for a moment. "Unquestionably," he said at last.

Frank, Dale, and Dr. Penney walked out of the residence hall and ambled across the USC campus, passing by the statue of Tommy Trojan and then cutting diagonally across Alumni Park. It was an overcast January day. "We're not going to sell that insanity defense, are we?" said Frank.

A couple of students passed them going the other way. Penney waited until they were out of earshot. "I'm afraid not," he said. "Hask's thinking is radically different, but he doesn't seem out-and-out deranged. Most juries like to see illogic as part of insanity, but what Hask believes appears to be internally consistent." Penney lifted his shoulders. "I'm sorry, Dale."

"What about the self-defense approach?" asked Frank.

"Hask would have to admit to the crime before we could even begin to structure a defense based on that, and so far he's refused to do so," said Dale.

"So what are we going to do?" asked Frank.

Dale paused again, as more students, plus one old fellow who must have been a prof, passed them. "If he continues to plead innocent, then we've got to at the very least establish a reasonable doubt about his guilt. And that means attacking every aspect of the prosecution case."

"The Simpson criminal strategy?" asked Frank.

Dale shrugged. "Basically."

"But what if we get a Hiroshi Fujisaki instead of a Lance Ito?" asked Frank. "What if we don't get the latitude to do that?"

Dale looked first at Penney, then at Frank. "Then we're in deep trouble," he said. "The prosecution has an excellent case."

FOURTEEN

Linda Ziegler arrived at Valcour Hall late in the afternoon. She didn't want to see the murder site again, nor did she want to speak to any of the Tosoks. Rather, she went straight to Packwood Smathers's room. She knocked on his door, and he called out for whoever it was to come in.

"Hello, Dr. Smathers," she said, opening the door. "My name is Linda Ziegler, and I'm a deputy district attorney here in Los Angeles County."

Smathers was working at a desk mounted against one wall. He knit his bushy white eyebrows together. "I want legal counsel present."

Ziegler smiled her best, brightest smile. "Dr. Smathers, you're not a suspect for anything. I understand you were treated unpleasantly by the police earlier, and on behalf of—well, on behalf of Americans in general—I apologize for that. I know you're a visitor to our country, and I'm coming to you now for some help."

Smathers sounded dubious. "Help?"

"Yes, sir. We have a problem facing us in alien—well,

I guess 'alien physiology' would be the right term, and I'm told you're the top person in that field."

Like many an arrogant man, Smathers was apparently willing to be self-effacing so long as someone else was simultaneously singing his praises. "Well, as much as one can be—until recently, everything I've dealt with has been purely hypothetical, but, still, despite the way Calhoun twisted it on TV, so far I've seen nothing in the Tosoks that invalidates my basic work."

Ziegler moved fully into the room, taking the other chair. Smathers's bed was a mess, but otherwise the room was well kept. "And—do forgive me, Professor; I freely admit I'm in over my head here—but what exactly was your basic work in this area?"

Smathers seemed to be warming slightly. "Well, simply, that all lifeforms, no matter where they're from, must adhere to certain basic engineering principles in their fundamental body plan."

"Fundamental body plan?" said Ziegler.

Smathers nodded. "Our Tosok friends are vertebrates. Reduced to simplest terms, the Tosok body is a hollow tube, with an internal support structure, very much like our own." The Canadian paused. "I don't know if you're aware of this, but the Tosoks don't like talking about the insides of bodies—it's a taboo with them. It's like us and nudity: it's perfectly acceptable for a human to be seen nude by his doctor, but outside of that context, it takes on a completely different meaning. The Tosoks won't show us their medical texts, nor will they look at ours. Stant—he's the Tosok biologist—seems downright embarrassed by my curiosity about their inner workings."

Ziegler nodded.

"Anyway," said Smathers, "the Tosoks differ in several noticeable ways from the vertebrates of Earth. Our vertebrates have body parts that come either singly or in pairs: we have one heart, one liver, one spleen, one stomach, but two lungs, two kidneys, two eyes, two arms, two legs, and so on. Because of the pairing of our body parts, we have bilateral symmetry."

Ziegler nodded. "Right," she said.

Smathers smiled. "Right—exactly. And left. Just two sides. The Tosoks, on the other hand, have *quadrilateral* symmetry. Their body parts either come singly or in groups of four. Stant has at least admitted to that much."

"That's not true," said Ziegler. "They've got two arms and two legs, and their eyes come in pairs."

Smathers nodded. "Yes, yes. That's the way it appears superficially. It's hard when looking at the product of billions of years of evolution to see the underlying architecture. But let's consider a hypothetical primitive creature from Alpha Centauri. I suspect it had a body plan like so." He took a lined pad off his desk and drew a large central circle on it with four smaller circles clustered around it, like a café table and chairs as seen on a blueprint. "This is a view from above," he said. "The central circle is the animal's torso. Each of the four circles is the cross section of a limb, looking down from the shoulder. I suspect in early Centauri life-forms, the four limbs were undifferentiated, and were all used for locomotion—as flagella in aquatic forms, and as legs in land-dwelling ones. You can call these four limbs north, east, south, and west." He wrote the letters *N, E, S,* and *W* next to them.

"Well," said Smathers, "you've seen that the Tosoks have two arms—one in front, almost like a trunk; and another, more slender one, in back, where you'd expect a tail to be. And they have two legs, one on either side. Obviously, what happened through evolution is that the east and west limbs became the sole locomotor appendages, and the north and south ones shortened, so that they no longer touched the ground, freeing them up for manipulatory uses.

"A Tosok also has four orifices on the head. Two of the orifices seem to have specialized for breathing, and two more—the ones directly above the arms—have specialized for the intake of food."

"And the eyes?" said Ziegler.

"Right—the four eyes. I suspect they were originally evenly spaced around the head, but over time have migrated together forming two pairs, each of which is capable of stereoscopic vision."

Ziegler nodded, impressed. "All right," she said, "there's no doubt you've got a good handle on the basic physiology."

"As good as anyone can have without ever having seen the insides of a Tosok, yes."

"Then how do you kill one?"

Smathers visibly pulled back. "I—I beg your pardon?"

"If the jury finds Hask guilty, we're going to ask for the death penalty. We'll need a way to execute him."

"Oh."

"Well, how do you kill one?"

"I, ah—well, gee, that's a good question."

"They figured out how to kill our kind easily enough," said Ziegler bitterly.

"We, ah, don't have the death penalty in Canada," said Smathers. "I don't know if I'm really the right person for this job."

"My sources tell me you're damn near the *only* person for this job. The state of California will compensate you for your time, Professor, but we really do have to know how to kill a Tosok." She smiled at him. "Think of it as a puzzle in science."

Smathers scratched his chin through his white beard. "Well, you can kill just about anything by depriving it of oxygen."

Ziegler shook her head. "It has to be quick and painless; otherwise, it will be deemed unconstitutional cruel-and-unusual punishment. It also can't be gruesome; the public won't stand for that."

Smathers considered for a moment. "That makes it difficult. Hanging is out—Tosoks have no necks; having eyes in the back of their heads obviates the need for one. And using either lethal injection or a gas chamber depends on fine details of physiology; I can suggest all kinds of possible poisons, but can't guarantee any of them will work quickly or without causing pain."

"Electrocution?"

"Yeah, probably—but, again, I can't guarantee that it'll be painless or quick for a Tosok."

"Well, I need you to find a way."

Smathers shook his head. "Really, Ms. Ziegler, I—"

"And, of course," said Ziegler, "we would make the corpse available to you after execution." She paused. "It might be your only opportunity to ever study alien anatomy."

Smathers frowned for a very long time, obviously at war with himself. Then, at last, he spoke. "As you know, we don't have tissue samples or X rays of a Tosok; they've been quite shy about such matters. This really isn't an easy problem." He paused again, then: "Leave it with me, Ms. Ziegler. I'm sure I can work out a method." But then he shook his head and was quiet for a long moment. "I just hope," he said softly, "that I can live with myself after I do."

FIFTEEN

Dale and Frank were meeting in a restaurant over lunch. Dale was eating a clubhouse sandwich, French fries, and a Caesar salad; Frank was having a grilled chicken breast and tossed salad with fat-free Italian dressing. "Doesn't the fact that there are samples of Tosok blood at the crime scene create problems for us?" asked Frank, after swallowing a piece of radicchio.

"Why?" asked Dale.

"Well, if Tosok biochemistry is anything like human biochemistry, the prosecution should be able to get some sort of genetic fingerprint off it to prove it's Hask's blood."

"They could only do that if they had samples of the blood of the other Tosoks, to match it against."

"Well, surely they'll subpoena them."

Dale made a grim little smile. "If they try that, I'll be all over them like ugly on an ape." He took a bite of his sandwich.

"What? Why?"

The lawyer swallowed, and took a swig of Pepsi. "You know how DNA testing got started?"

Frank shook his head.

"It started in Leicester, England. In 1983, someone there raped and strangled a fifteen-year-old girl. The police couldn't come up with a single suspect. Three years later, in '86, the same damned thing happened again: another fifteen-year-old, raped and choked to death. This time, the police arrested a guy named—what was it now?—Buckley, Buckland, something like that. He confessed to the recent murder, but not the one three years before.

"Coincidentally, a British geneticist working right there at the University of Leicester had recently been in the news, because he'd invented a technique for finding genetic markers for disease. He called his technique restriction fragment-length polymorphism; that's the RFLP they kept talking about in the Simpson criminal trial. One of its incidental uses was that it could distinguish one person's DNA from another, so the cops called him up and said, look, we've got the guy who killed one of the girls, but we want to prove he killed both of them. If we send you semen samples collected from both bodies, can you prove that the DNA in them came from the same guy? The scientist—Jeffreys, his name was—said, sure thing, send them over."

Frank nodded, and took a sip of coffee.

"Well, guess what?" said Dale. "Jeffreys proved the semen samples both came from the same man—but that man was *not* the guy who had confessed. The police were furious, but they had to let Buckland go. Now, what to do? How to catch the real murderer? Well, the cops decided they'd ask all male residents of the area between seventeen and thirty-four to submit a blood specimen so that they could be 'eliminated from the inquiries.'" Dale shook his head. "Genteel Brits! Anyway, four thousand men came forward, but none of them matched the killer. Eventually, though, they found that a coworker of a man named Colin Pitchfork—the name should have tipped them off, don't you think?—had donated a sample in Pitchfork's place. The police took a sample from

Pitchfork, who, of course, was the murderer. That was the first case in which DNA fingerprinting was ever used."

"Terrific," said Frank.

"No," said Dale. "No, it stank to high heaven. Don't you see? A whole population of people were treated like suspects solely because they were males in a likely age group. They weren't forced to donate blood, but the idea caught on like wildfire in the community—and anyone who *didn't* make a donation was suspect. See? It was a gross violation of civil rights. Suddenly people were being compelled to prove themselves innocent, instead of being assumed to be so. If a cop came up to me and said, look, you're black and we think our criminal is black, so you prove to me you're not the criminal, I'd have that person busted off the force. Well, asking the Tosoks to give up blood specimens is the same thing: you belong to this group, therefore prove to us that you're innocent. No, we can prevent that from happening, I'm sure."

"But they're only seven of them!"

"It's still a civil-rights issue," said Dale. "Trust me."

"So the prosecution won't try to introduce the blood evidence?"

"On the contrary, I'm sure they will. It'll be a fight, but we'll win—at least on that point."

"You're sure?"

Rice took another bite of his sandwich. "Well—nothing's ever completely certain."

Frank frowned. "I was afraid of that."

Pretrial motions were supervised by the same judge who would preside over the actual trial: Drucilla Pringle. Pringle was forty-nine years old. She was the kind of woman usually referred to as "handsome" rather than "beautiful," with smooth, cold features. Her skin was white; her hair chestnut brown, cut short. She wore wire-frame glasses and little makeup.

The biggest fight at this stage was over whether the trial should be televised. Judge Pringle ultimately ruled that it would be, given the extraordinary interest the peoples of the entire world had in the outcome of the case. But there were dozens of other motions as well:

"Your Honor," said Dale, "we move that the jury be sequestered. The media interest in this trial will be huge, and there's no way to keep the jury from being exposed to possibly biased coverage."

"Your Honor," said Ziegler, "I think we've all been conscious ever since Simpson of the incredible hardship sequestration poses. Surely with a trial that may go on at great length, we can't make prisoners out of all the jurors and alternates."

"I've read your brief on this, Mr. Rice," said Drucilla Pringle, "but I agree with Ms. Ziegler. The jurors will be instructed to avoid media coverage, but they will get to go home and sleep in their own beds each night."

"Very well," said Dale. "We move that no photographic evidence of Dr. Calhoun's corpse be introduced. Such evidence could only serve to inflame the jury."

"Your Honor," said Linda Ziegler, rising, "the People vigorously oppose any limitation on photographic evidence. The jury questionnaire will enable us to screen out particularly squeamish individuals. Obviously, a significant portion of our case hinges on demonstrating that the method of killing is one no human would employ. There's no better evidence of the method than the crime-scene photos showing the mutilated corpse."

Judge Pringle frowned while she considered this. Finally: "You lose this one, Mr. Rice. But, Ms. Ziegler, I will shut you down so fast it'll make your head spin if your use of the photos ever goes beyond the merely probative."

"Very well," said Dale, "but we further move, Your Honor, out of deference to Dr. Calhoun's family, that *only* the jury be shown the photos of the corpse and removed organs."

"The public is entitled to something, Mr. Rice," said Pringle.

"We suggest stylized drawings be made, representing the injuries."

"You're setting me up for another battle with the media lawyers," said Pringle, "and I'm not convinced your concern is over the family's feelings. You're hoping for a hung jury, and don't want to inflame the potential jurors for any second trial."

Dale spread his arms. "You do me a disservice, Your Honor."

Pringle scowled, unconvinced. "Pending review of the arguments from the media attorneys, I'll agree to a ban on publication of the pictures while this trial is in progress; I'll reserve judgment on whether the ban should remain in place following the handing down of a verdict."

"Thank you, Your Honor," said Dale. "Next, the defense moves . . ."

The jury questionnaire, prepared jointly by the pros-ecution and the defense, contained three hundred and eleven questions. It started off predictably enough, asking for information about age, ethnicity, marital status, employment, level of education, spouse or partner's background, previous legal or courtroom experiences, political affiliation, organization memberships, and so on. It also asked if the potential juror knew the defendant, the decedent, any of the lawyers, the judge, or any of the courtroom staff.

In addition, it asked about the prospective juror's beliefs concerning the legal process:

> Do you believe that a defendant in a criminal case should testify or produce some evidence to prove that he or she is not guilty? If yes, please explain why.

To each of the following statements, indicate if you strongly agree, agree, disagree, disagree strongly, or have no opinion:

(A) "If the prosecution goes to the trouble of bringing someone to trial, the person is probably guilty."

(B) "Celebrities are treated better by our court system than other people."

The questionnaire also looked at possible bias from exposure to the extensive news coverage of the Calhoun murder:

Which of the following best describes how you would describe the media coverage overall? Biased in favor of the prosecution? Biased in favor of the defense? Basically fair to both sides?

It also asked about the Tosoks:

What was your first reaction to hearing that one of the Tosok explorers was a suspect in this case?

Have you ever seen a Tosok in person? If yes, please explain the circumstances.

Will you hold the prosecution to a higher standard than is legally required because the defendant is from another planet? Because of possible repercussions for the human race?

Does the fact the defendant comes from a civilization more technologically advanced than our own make it unlikely in your mind that he could commit murder?

And then came what Linda Ziegler had dubbed the "space-cadet questions":

Before the arrival of the Tosoks on Earth, did you read any nonfiction books, articles, or magazines concerning life on other worlds? If yes, please specify, and briefly describe what you recall having read.

Have you ever read any fiction (including science fiction) dealing with life on other worlds, or with aliens having come to Earth? If yes, please specify, and briefly describe what you recall having read.

Which of the following TV series have you watched regularly now or in the past? For those that you have seen, indicate whether you agreed with, disagreed with, or had no opinion about the portrayal of alien lifeforms:

> *ALF*
> *Babylon 5*
> *Lost in Space*
> *Mork & Mindy*
> Any *Star Trek* series
> *The X Files*

Members of LASFS, the Los Angeles Science Fantasy Society, helped in putting together a series of such questions. Apparently, anyone who agreed with the *ALF, Star Trek,* or *Mork & Mindy* portrayals of aliens would be biased in favor of the defense, whereas those who liked the *Babylon 5, Lost in Space,* or *X Files* portrayals would be biased toward the prosecution.

Regardless of which way they leaned, any out-and-out SF fans or space buffs had to be disqualified, hence these questions:

What's the name of Mr. Spock's father?
Do you know what the initials SETI stand for?
Have you ever attended a science-fiction convention?
Have you ever seen a UFO?

As with most Los Angeles trials likely to generate considerable media interest, *The People of California* v. *Hask* was scheduled into the main downtown Criminal Courts Building. That meant that jury pool had to be drawn from residents of central L.A. A thousand people were summoned. Of course, not all of them showed up. Men, in particular, often simply disregard jury-duty notices; since little follow-up is ever done, they usually get away with it.

Every one of those who did show up was asked to fill in the jury questionnaire. Over seven hundred prospective jurors were eliminated based on their responses.

Among the reasons potential jurors were excused: they were single parents, or had an elderly relative living with them, or were in a precarious financial situation. One man had the irritable bowel syndrome—and a doctor's note to prove it. Another was on a waiting list for a kidney transplant and could not guarantee he'd remain available until the end of the trial. A woman in her seventh month of pregnancy was let go as well.

Also struck from the list: all those who had difficulty seeing or hearing, or who couldn't read or write English effectively. Five people were dismissed because they knew one of the lawyers or court staff members—one had been to a lecture Dale had given once and had gotten him to autograph a book.

The remaining one hundred and eighty-five potential jurors—as always in central L.A., predominantly black, predominantly female, predominantly blue-collar or unemployed—were then examined by the lawyers during the process known as *voir dire*. And, at long last, a total of twelve jurors and six alternates were selected.

Kelkad, captain of the starship, had just returned to Valcour Hall from a meeting at Rockwell International. Frank was in the lounge on the fourth floor with Hask, and they greeted Kelkad as he came off the elevator. "How are the repairs going?" the human asked.

Kelkad's tuft waved in a way that signaled disappointment. "Slowly."

"I'm sorry to hear that," said Frank.

"I suppose it cannot be helped," said Kelkad. "But, although your race is backward technically, I am most impressed by the speed with which your engineers have grasped our concepts. They really are remarkable."

Frank grinned. "Darn clever, these humans, eh? Better watch it, Kelkad. Before you know it, we'll leapfrog right past you."

Kelkad didn't laugh. But there was nothing unusual about that.

SIXTEEN

Judge Pringle's courtroom was on the ninth floor of
the Los Angeles County Criminal Courts Building—the
floor the Simpson criminal trial had been held on, the floor
that required all persons to be searched before entering it.

The walls were paneled in California redwood. Pringle's
bench was mounted against the back wall, beneath a carved
wooden version of the California state seal. The California
flag, with its brown bear, was hanging from one pole to the
judge's right of the bench, and a U.S. flag hung from another.
On the bench the judge had a computer monitor, an open
laptop computer, and over a dozen law books held up by
black metal bookends.

Facing the bench was the defense table, on the judge's right,
and the prosecution table, on her left. Each of the tables had
a computer monitor and a video monitor mounted on it. In
between them was a lectern where the lawyer asking questions
could stand—the days when attorneys loomed right into the
witness's face, *à la* Perry Mason, were long gone.

The jury box was next to the prosecution table. It held a
double row of seven padded chairs; two of the alternates

would sit with the main jurors. The actual jurors—seven women and five men; six blacks, three Latinos, two whites, and an Asian—all wore bar-coded badges.

Next to the jury box, the camera for Court TV was set up; it was actually controlled by a technician at the back of the room, using two little joysticks.

At the side of the room, behind the bailiff's desk, six Tosok chairs had been installed so that Kelkad, Rendo, Torbat, Dodnaskak, Stant, and Ged could watch their shipmate stand trial; the Tosoks had spent the last several weeks screening videotapes of various previous murder trials so that they would understand procedures and proper conduct.

Frank Nobilio had a seat in the first row of the public gallery, directly behind where Dale Rice was sitting. Frank had been allowed this spot as a courtesy; he didn't have to line up overnight along with the other members of the public. On Rice's left sat Hask, in a special chair. As always, he was wearing a grayish-brown tunic covered with many pockets. On Rice's right sat Michiko Katayama, his associate, a slim thirty-five-year-old woman.

Judge Pringle, clad in black judicial robes, wrote something on a legal pad, then looked up. "Are counsel ready to proceed?"

"Ready, Your Honor," said Linda Ziegler.

"Ready, Your Honor," said Dale Rice. As was his tradition on the first day of trial, he was wearing an absolutely pristine white silk tie; he wouldn't get to speak, except for objections, until after the prosecution's opening statement, but he wanted to send a message of innocence to the jury in those crucial first moments.

"You may begin, Ms. Ziegler," said Pringle.

Ziegler got up from the prosecution table and came over to stand in front of the jury box. She was wearing a navy-blue jacket over a white blouse. "Ladies and gentlemen of the jury, as you know from *voir dire,* my name is Linda Ziegler, and I'm a senior deputy district attorney for Los Angeles County. My associate in this case is Trina Diamond; you'll hear from her later in the trial.

"You don't need me to tell you that this is an unusual case. The defendant in this trial is not a human being. Rather, he is an alien, an extraterrestrial, an entity from another world. We're all sophisticated people, ladies and gentlemen. We've all been around. But, still, I know from our discussions during *voir dire* that you are like me. You might have believed that life on other worlds was theoretically possible—we live in a big universe, after all, and it seemed unlikely, if we stopped to think about it, that this one tiny planet orbiting an unremarkable star, might be the only home of life in all of creation—but you never thought that the question would be anything more than the subject of documentaries on The Learning Channel, or shows like the decedent's *Great Balls of Fire!*

"But all that's changed in the last few months, hasn't it? Aliens have come to Earth! As a species, we rose remarkably well to this event. Perhaps remembering all of our own botched encounters between formerly isolated peoples on this world, we managed to deal with the arrival of the starship in a civilized manner.

"And, you know, it *was* wonderful to meet the Tosok aliens, wasn't it? We extended the hand of friendship to these new arrivals.

"But things did not stay wonderful for long, ladies and gentlemen, and that's why you're here today. Dr. Cletus Calhoun was—there's no other word for it, is there?—was *butchered,* his body carved up, his organs scattered about. I see some of you wincing, and I do regret, dear people, that we *will* have to dwell on the details of this grisly crime during the course of the trial.

"As you know, Hask, one of the seven Tosoks who have come to Earth, has been charged in the death of Dr. Calhoun. Ms. Diamond and I, on behalf of the People of California, will demonstrate to you, beyond any reasonable doubt, that Hask did, willfully, knowing full well what he was doing, murder Dr. Calhoun. We are seeking a conviction on the charge of first-degree murder. To substantiate such a charge, we have to demonstrate that the method was within the reach of the defendant—and it was, and we shall prove that to you, beyond all reasonable doubt. And, because we *are* seeking a first-degree conviction, we must also demonstrate that this crime was no spontaneous act of self-defense, nor a momentary lapse into unthinking rage, but rather was premeditated, was contemplated in advance, was planned by the defendant, and carried out—indeed, was *executed*— with purposeful deliberation—and this, too, we shall prove to you, beyond all reasonable doubt . . ."

Eventually, it was Dale's turn. He rose slowly and crossed in front of the prosecution's table as he made his way over to stand in front of the jury box. "Ladies and gentlemen," he said, "my name, as you may recall, is Dale Rice, and I'm representing the defendant, Hask. My co-counsel is Ms. Michiko Katayama.

"Now, I bet all of you have seen *Perry Mason,* but I don't want you to have any unrealistic ideas about what a defense attorney does. Good ol' Perry, he used to browbeat everyone on the witness stand until someone other than the defendant confessed. Well, that's unlikely to happen in this trial. The State has accused my client of murder, but as the judge will instruct you, the simple fact that he's been accused is not to be taken *at all* as evidence of guilt. My client has pleaded innocent. And you must understand that he has no obligation—absolutely none—to prove that innocence.

"Nor do we, as his defense lawyers, have any obligation to provide an alternative explanation of how Cletus Calhoun came to be dead. The most natural thing in the world for you to ask yourselves is, 'Well, if Hask didn't do it, who did?' But you *cannot* convict based on that question. You can only convict based on the actual evidence in this case. And if that evidence leaves a reasonable doubt in your mind about my client's guilt, then you must acquit him, even if that means the murder of Cletus Calhoun remains unsolved. Yes, the crime in question was horrible and brutal, and yes, we all want someone to pay for it. But you are in a tricky position: the only person you *can* make pay for it is my client. So, you must exercise great caution and great restraint: you must be sure that your natural desire to see someone pay, combined with the fact that the only person you have the ability to punish is Hask, does not sway you to find him guilty when there is still doubt in your mind about whether he really did commit the crime.

"There's another unusual circumstance in this case. It's conceivable that if Hask did not commit the murder, then perhaps one of the other Tosoks did. But you can no more allow the wrong Tosok to be punished than you could allow the wrong human to be punished. The mentality that 'one of them did it, so one of them should pay' can have no place in your deliberations. Each of the seven Tosoks is an individual. You must be convinced beyond reasonable doubt that *this* specific Tosok, my client Hask, committed the murder if you are to find him personally responsible for it . . ."

SEVENTEEN

Opening arguments consumed an entire day. At ten a.m. the next day, the prosecution's case-in-chief began.

"On the record now in *California* v. *Hask*," said Judge Pringle, taking her place at the bench. "The defendant is present, as are his attorneys, Mr. Rice and Ms. Katayama. The People are represented by Ms. Ziegler and Ms. Diamond. The jury is present. Are the People ready to proceed?"

"We are, Your Honor," said Ziegler.

"Very well. You may call your first witness."

"Thank you, Your Honor," said Ziegler, moving over to stand in front of the lectern. The Court TV camera panned to follow her. "The People call Dr. Anne Flemingdon."

Flemingdon was a tough-looking white woman in her forties, broad shouldered, round-headed, with short-cropped hair that she was content to let show its gray. She was wearing a dark-blue jacket over a pale green blouse, and matching blue pants.

Dr. Flemingdon moved through the little wooden gate that separated the spectators from the lawyers, and took a position next to the court reporter. She faced the clerk—a small Hispanic man—and raised her right hand before he had a chance to ask her to do so.

"You do solemnly swear or affirm," said the clerk in a slightly accented voice, "that the testimony you may give in the cause now pending before this Court shall be the truth, the whole truth, and nothing but the truth, so help you God?"

"Yes," said Flemingdon. Her voice was quite deep.

"Please have a seat in the witness box and state and spell your first and last names for the record," said the clerk.

Flemingdon sat down. "My name is Dr. Anne Flemingdon. Anne with an E: A-N-N-E; Flemingdon is spelled F-L-E-M-I-N-G, D as in David, O-N."

"Thank you," said the clerk.

"Dr. Flemingdon," said Ziegler, looking up from a sheaf of notes she'd placed on the lectern, "are you a medical doctor licensed to practice medicine in the state of California?"

"I am."

"By whom are you currently employed?"

"By the county of Los Angeles."

"In what capacity?"

"I'm the chief medical examiner and coroner for the county."

"In that capacity were you called upon to examine the body of Cletus Robert Calhoun?"

"I was."

"Where was this examination performed?"

"I did the initial examination at the crime scene at Paul Valcour Hall, a residence facility located on the University Park campus of the University of Southern California. I did further work on the remains once they were collected and moved to my lab."

"Your Honor, we would like to enter People's exhibits one through twenty-five: photos of the corpse taken at the USC crime scene."

"Mr. Rice?" said Pringle.

Dale exhaled. "Your Honor, we would like to preserve our objection."

"Understood," said Pringle. "Overruled."

Three easels were brought in. Each one held up a board with several large color photographs mounted on it. Flemingdon left the witness stand and went over to stand near them. The Court TV camera jockeyed to show her but not the photos.

Hask looked down at the cluttered surface of the defense table. Dale glanced back; the other Tosoks were averting their eyes from the photos as well, although one of them—Ged, it was—kept surreptitiously peeking at them.

"Dr. Flemingdon," said Ziegler, "could you please describe the cause of death?"

Flemingdon unclipped a slim black laser pointer from her inside jacket pocket. "Certainly," she said. "Death was caused by severe hemorrhagic shock. Dr. Calhoun suffered almost complete exsanguination—that is, his body was almost completely drained of blood. As you can see here in photo number four"—her laser pointer danced, a bright red dot amid all the dark-red blood—"Dr. Calhoun's right leg was severed from his body, by a diagonal cut that began just below his hip. The cut was incredibly clean, resulting in all the blood vessels in the leg, including the femoral artery, being sliced open. The femoral is the principal artery of the thigh, responsible for supplying blood to the leg, and because it was a diagonal cut, the opening was large. It was through this opening that most of Dr. Calhoun's blood drained out."

"Drained out?" said Ziegler, her eyebrows rising. "Surely it was more dramatic than that?"

"Well, yes. Until the loss of blood killed him, his heart would have been pumping, causing the blood to spurt out, actually."

Dale looked at Katayama and shook his head. But—then again—maybe the Sam Peckinpah quality of all this would numb the jury . . . and a numb jury wouldn't cry out for vengeance.

"How was this cut made?" asked Ziegler.

Flemingdon's laser dot danced again. "It started on the outside of the right hip, just below the groin line, and proceeded diagonally, at about a forty-degree angle, in toward the inner thigh."

"Actually, my question was meant to elicit what sort of implement was used to make the cut."

Dale rolled his eyes. Flemingdon knew damn well what Ziegler had meant; they'd doubtless rehearsed her testimony. But that little show was for the jury's benefit, to make it look as though they *hadn't* planned it all out.

"Oh," said Flemingdon. "Well, that's a tough one. I can make a clean cut through flesh with a scalpel, but Dr. Calhoun was wearing pants—Levi's blue jeans, to be precise." A couple of jurors smiled—who could picture Calhoun in anything else? "The cutting implement passed cleanly through the denim fabric, through the skin, through the muscles, through the femoral artery, and right on through the femur—the thighbone. I'd normally need a bone saw to go through the femur, and would never use a scalpel on denim—it would dull the blade. But this cut was made absolutely cleanly, without any snagging even on the bone."

"Are you sure it was a single cut?"

"Oh, yes. It aligns absolutely perfectly. One single slice was made through the pants and Dr. Calhoun's leg."

"What was the maximum diameter of Dr. Calhoun's upper thigh?"

"A little over eight inches."

"So if a knife was used, it had to have a blade at least eight inches long, correct?"

"Yes."

"The sharpest knives made are surgical scalpels, yes?"

"Yes," said Flemingdon.

"Do any scalpels have blades eight inches long?"

"No standard one does. Of course, medical-supply companies can custom-make surgical tools."

"But in all your experience, you've never seen a scalpel with an eight-inch blade?"

"Objection," said Dale. "Leading."

"Sustained," said Pringle. "Rephrase."

Ziegler nodded at the judge. "What's the largest scalpel you've ever seen?"

"I've seen one with a five-inch blade."

"Nothing bigger?"

"No."

"I'm sure the jury has noticed your fancy laser pointer, Doctor. Could the cut have been made by a laser beam?"

"No. A laser is a burning tool—it uses high temperatures to cut. It would have singed the denim, as well as Dr. Calhoun's skin, and the hairs on his thigh. And a laser—well, a laser *doesn't* leave arteries and veins open. Rather, it cauterizes them—sears them shut. That's why we use laser scalpels for delicate surgery: they sever and seal blood vessels simultaneously. No, this cut was not made with a burning implement."

"Thank you. Let's leave the leg cut for the moment. What about the rest of the injuries?"

Flemingdon turned to the photos, pointing with her laser. "The corpse had been severely—well, mutilated is probably the right word. The chest cavity had been carved open, and the ribs spread wide. Organs had been removed and scattered about, and the head was severed from the body."

"You said a moment ago that 'mutilated' is probably the right word. Why the hesitation in word choice?"

"Well, it *was* mutilation, by the dictionary definition: 'depriving of limbs or other essential parts, and/or irreparably disfiguring or damaging.' But, well, whether the *goal* was to mutilate or not, I can't be sure."

"What do you mean by the 'goal,' Dr. Flemingdon?"

"The purpose. This could have just as easily been a deliberate medical dissection, rather than an attempt to disfigure."

"Objection," said Dale. "Speculation. Move to strike."

"Dr. Flemingdon is certainly qualified to offer an expert opinion in this area," said Ziegler, looking up at the judge.

"Overruled," said Pringle.

"What makes you say it might have been a dissection, Doctor?"

"The thoroughness, for one. Disfigurement is often localized—the face will be scarred, or the genitals or breasts will be carved up. This process seemed to concentrate on no one part of the anatomy—or, more precisely, it seemed to involve *every* part of the anatomy."

"Would it be fair to say that whoever performed the procedures on this body had expert medical knowledge?"

"Yes and no."

"'Yes and no,'" repeated Ziegler. "What do you mean by that?"

"Yes, he or she clearly knew how to use surgical instruments. For instance, Ms. Ziegler, if I were to hand you or anyone else who had never used one before a scalpel and asked you to carve into a body, you'd likely make a tentative trial cut first—this would show as a hesitation mark, or shallow wound. Whoever dissected Dr. Calhoun showed no such inexperience. I would judge that the person doing it was quite familiar with dissecting technique."

"Then your answer is yes—the person *did* have expert medical knowledge."

"Expert knowledge of *equipment,* Ms. Ziegler. But the process by which the dissection was done was almost haphazard. No one who knew what they were doing would have spread the ribs in the way it had been done in this case; there are much easier methods. It was almost as if the person doing it, although familiar with general medical techniques, had no specific knowledge of human anatomy."

At the defense table, Dale sighed. Ziegler had doubtless

coached Flemingdon to volunteer this idea, neatly preventing Dale from objecting to a question that invited speculation from the witness.

"No specific knowledge of human anatomy?" repeated Ziegler.

"Yes."

"Can you give further examples that support this conclusion?"

"Well, whoever did the cutting opened the stomach up before removing it from the chest cavity—resulting in gastric acid spilling into the torso. If you'd known in advance that the stomach contained acid, you'd have removed it as a unit and dissected it separately."

"Thank you. Did you conduct an inventory of body parts?"

"Yes."

"Why did you do that?"

"In murder cases involving disfigurement or dismembering, it's not unusual for the killer to keep a souvenir of the crime."

"A souvenir?"

"Yes—a finger, perhaps, or, in some sex-related crimes, part of the genitals."

"So you inventoried Dr. Calhoun's body parts. What did you find?"

"Several pieces were missing."

"Which parts specifically, Doctor?"

"The right eye was gone."

Intake of breath from jurors four and six; Dale had identified both of them as queasy during *voir dire,* but had been unable to get them excused.

"The eye was removed?" repeated Ziegler, as if surprised by this piece of news.

"Yes."

"By the same cutting tool?"

"Well, sort of. The eyeball was prized from the socket,

possibly by fingers, but the muscles and optic nerve were indeed severed cleanly, quite probably by the same tool, yes."

"Was anything else missing?"

"The vermiform process."

"'The vermiform process,'" repeated Ziegler. She looked at the jury. "Is there another name by which we might be more familiar with that, Doctor?"

"It's commonly called the appendix."

"The same appendix that's down here?" She touched her lower right side. "The one that's prone to appendicitis?"

"That's right."

"How was it removed?"

"Well, not the normal way—that is, not like we do it in an appendectomy, going in from outside. Rather it was clipped out during the internal dissection."

"Are you sure about this?" said Ziegler. "Couldn't his appendix have been removed years before? Lots of people have no appendix—I don't myself."

"There was no appendectomy scar on Calhoun's body, and no signs of an old operation internally. Still, I did check with Calhoun's personal physician, and his health-insurance company. The doctor had no record of Calhoun ever having appendicitis, and the insurer has no claim on file for an appendectomy operation."

"Was anything else missing?"

"Yes. Dr. Calhoun's lower jaw and neck were gone."

More mock surprise. "His neck?"

"Yes, that's right. I said the head was severed from the body. In fact, the highest vertebra intact in the torso was the first thoracic one. And the head had no vertebrae left attached to it. All seven cervical vertebrae were gone, along with the throat and the Adam's apple. Also missing was the mandible—the lower jaw."

"Do you have any idea why the perpetrator would take these particular body parts, Doctor?"

"No."

"Are you sure that it wasn't the removal of these body parts that caused Dr. Calhoun's death?"

"I'm sure. He was dead by the time they were removed."

"How do you know that?"

"Well, you can tell by the pattern of blood splattering that the opening of the chest was done after the heart had stopped beating. Likewise the decapitation: in fact, there was very little blood left in the body by the time the head was severed. And the removal of the eye—well, it takes a lot of force to pull out an eye. If this had happened while Dr. Calhoun was still alive, there'd be bruising on his right cheek and the right side of his nose. As you can see here in photo fourteen, there's none of that."

"Thank you," said Ziegler. She turned to the jury. "And my apologies for the gruesome nature of the testimony—we should be on less gory ground from now on. I hope you all understand why it was necessary." She looked at Dale. "Your witness, counselor."

Dale rose. Damn, but Ziegler was good. She'd apologized for the graphic testimony, and promised the jury it was over—meaning Dale would look insensitive by going over it again in his cross. "Dr. Flemingdon," he said, "you spoke about 'hesitation marks.'"

"Yes?"

"The tentative initial cuts made by someone unfamiliar with using a knife?"

"That's right. They're best known as a feature of wrist-cutting suicides, but medical students make them all the time, too, until they're used to working with scalpels."

"Medical students," repeated Dale.

"Yes."

"Human medical students."

"Ah, well, yes. Yes, but—"

"No 'buts,' Doctor. Now, let's talk about the missing body parts. Dr. Flemingdon, wouldn't you say that Cletus Calhoun was a celebrity?"

"Well, this *is* Los Angeles, Mr. Rice. I'm sure Mr. Calhoun is a big fish wherever he's from . . ."

"Pigeon Forge, Tennessee."

"Right, well, by Pigeon Forge standards, I'm sure he's a big name, but out here? He was on *PBS,* for God's sake."

A few snickers from the spectators. Judge Pringle rapped her gavel to silence them.

"Actually," said Dale, "Dolly Parton is also from Pigeon Forge."

"You make my point, counselor. Even in Tennessee, he wasn't that big a name."

"I'm not sure everyone would agree," said Dale, turning to look at the jury. "I'm sure many of the people on the jury considered Dr. Calhoun to be quite a celebrity."

"Objection," said Ziegler, spreading her hands. "I fail to see the relevance."

"I'm frankly baffled, too," said Pringle. "Mr. Rice?"

"A couple more moments, if you please, Your Honor."

"Very well—but do get to the point."

"My pleasure. Dr. Flemingdon, didn't your lab handle the death last year of rock singer Billy Williger?"

Flemingdon stiffened. "Yes."

"And didn't parts of Mr. Williger's body go missing from your lab?"

"Yes."

"And were you reprimanded for that?"

Teeth clenched. "Yes."

"So body parts in your charge have disappeared before?"

"I've already said yes."

"And we have only your word for the fact that the parts you enumerated were taken by the perpetrator."

"The crime-scene photos show the missing jaw and the missing eye."

"Not exactly—none of the crime scene photos show those parts, but the photos hardly cover the entire room."

"You have my word that the parts were missing."

"Yes—your word. After all, it wouldn't do to have another case of overeager fans stealing body parts from your morgue, would it?"

"Billy Williger was a huge star, Mr. Rice. I'm not familiar with astronomers having obsessive groupies."

Laughter from the audience; Pringle was suppressing a chuckle herself.

"The defense would be glad to introduce Dr. Calhoun's fan mail into evidence," said Dale. "But so far, we have a murder mystery whose most mysterious elements rest on the testimony of someone who has lost body parts before."

"Objection," said Ziegler. "Mr. Rice is arguing his case."

"Sustained," said Pringle. "You've made your point, Mr. Rice. Move on."

"You mentioned that body parts are sometimes removed by *human* murderers," said Dale.

"Yes."

"For what purpose?"

"Well, as I said, a souvenir of the crime."

"Isn't it true that parts are sometimes removed for cannibalism?"

"Yes."

"Or as trophies from a sex slaying?"

"Yes."

"Define 'cannibalism' for us, Doctor."

"It's—well, it's the eating of human flesh."

"That's not quite right. It's actually the eating of the flesh of one's own kind, isn't it? When members of one species of fish eat other members of that same species, we say they're practicing cannibalism, don't we?"

"Umm, yes."

"So, the removal of parts for cannibalism would be possible only between members of the same species, no?"

"You're arguing semantics, Mr. Rice."

"And a sex slaying—again, sex is performed between members of the same species, isn't that right?"

"Usually."

"There's no reason to think that a Tosok would have either cannibalistic or sexual interest in human body parts, is there?"

"Well, no."

"But there are countless cases involving human murderers in which body parts are taken for those reasons?"

Reluctantly: "There are many such cases, yes."

"Thank you, Dr. Flemingdon," said Dale.

"Redirect?" asked Judge Pringle.

Ziegler shook her head.

EIGHTEEN

The trial took its noon recess at the end of Dr. Fleming- don's testimony. When court resumed, Ziegler picked up her case-in-chief.

"Please state and spell your name," said the clerk to the man now seated in the witness stand.

"Feinstein, Moshe." He spelled them both.

"Thank you."

Feinstein was forty-four, with a long, dour face and thick steel-gray hair. He wore horn-rim glasses and had a plastic pocket protector in the breast pocket of his short-sleeved blue shirt. Ziegler got up. "Mr. Feinstein, please tell the Court who you are."

"I'm a supervising criminalist for the Los Angeles Police Department."

"Your Honor, we have here Mr. Feinstein's curriculum vitae, which runs to six pages. We would like to enter it into evidence."

Judge Pringle looked at Dale, who nodded. "All right," said Pringle.

"Briefly, Mr. Feinstein, can you summarize your chief credentials?"

Feinstein smiled. It was not a pretty sight. "I've been with the LAPD for sixteen years. I have a master of science degree in criminology, and a second M.Sc. in chemistry. I'm on the board of directors of the California Association of Criminalists and am a Fellow of the American Academy of Forensic Sciences—and I hold certifications of professional competency from both those organizations."

"Thank you. Early on the morning of December twenty-third of last year, were you called to Valcour Hall, a residence on the campus of the University of Southern California?"

"I was."

"Why were you called there?"

"To be principal criminalist at the scene of the murder of Cletus Calhoun, and to supervise the other criminalists working there."

"Mr. Feinstein, did you find anything in Dr. Calhoun's dorm room that could have served as the murder weapon?"

"Objection," said Dale, rising to his feet. "Prejudicial. The term 'murder weapon' implies intent to kill. The People have not established that this was a first-degree crime."

"Sustained."

"Very well," said Ziegler. "Did you find anything in Dr. Calhoun's dorm room that could have been used to sever his right leg from his body?"

"I did not."

"Did you find any implement there that could have been used to spread Dr. Calhoun's ribs?"

"No, but I didn't expect to."

"Could you explain that?"

"Well, the incision down the center of Dr. Calhoun's chest was clearly made by a mechanical device—it's a perfectly straight line running from throat to groin. The cut split the breastbone, and dug into the heart and other soft tissues. But the actual spreading of the ribs was apparently done by brute force."

"What do you mean?"

"It was apparently done by hand—by someone grabbing either side of Dr. Calhoun's severed breastbone and pulling hard." Feinstein pantomimed the action against his own chest.

"What makes you think it was done by hand, Mr. Feinstein?"

"Well, whenever there's an open wound, we look at the edges of it, and—"

"Why do you do that?"

"Oh, you never know what you'll find. Say we're dealing with a naked corpse, killed by stabbing. We look to see if fabric fibers are embedded along the edges of the wound. If there are some, then the person was knifed while still clothed. If the knife is rusty, we'll find iron-oxide flakes along the periphery. Stuff like that."

"And did you find any iron-oxide flakes?"

"No."

"Did you find any embedded fabric?"

"No—meaning, as seemed likely at first glance, that Dr. Calhoun's shirt had been opened before the vertical cut was made."

"Did you find anything unusual at all?"

"Yes."

"What did you find?"

"Well, as I indicated, the breastbone had been split by an extraordinarily sharp cutting tool—and that meant the breastbone had sharp edges. On one of those edges we found pinkish crystals."

"Crystals, Mr. Feinstein?"

"Yes."

"Did you collect these for analysis?"

"Yes."

"And what did you find?"

"The crystals were quite complex chemically. I was unable to identify them, so I sent them to the department of chemistry at UCLA; we have a contract arrangement with them to do forensics work for us."

"Mr. Feinstein, let me pose a hypothetical: if a human being were to grab the sharp edges of a breastbone split as Dr. Calhoun's was, and that human yanked hard in order to open up the chest, what would happen to the hands of the human?"

"As I said, the breastbone had very sharp edges. Unless the person was wearing protective gloves, he'd probably cut his fingers in trying to do so."

"Presumably there was a lot of human blood on the edges of the breastbone."

"Oh, yes, indeed."

"Was all of it Dr. Calhoun's?"

"As far as I could tell, yes. It matched his blood in ABO grouping, Rh factor, and all other categorizations."

"Thank you. In addition to the pink crystals, what other evidence, if any, did you find at the crime scene?"

"I found certain objects."

Ziegler picked a small Ziploc bag off the prosecution's table. "Are these the objects?"

"Yes."

"Enter as People's twenty-seven," said Ziegler.

"No objection," said Dale.

"So entered," said Judge Pringle.

"Mr. Feinstein, please describe the contents of that pouch."

"Inside here are three flat diamond-shaped objects found in Dr. Calhoun's room at USC."

"Diamond-shaped objects? What do you think they are?"

"Objection," said Dale. "Calls for speculation."

"I'll rephrase. Mr. Feinstein, have you ever seen anything resembling these objects in shape?"

"Yes, they remind me of something I've seen before."

"What would that be?"

"To me they look like the scales covering the Tosoks' bodies."

"Your Honor, at this time, we would like to ask the defendant to stand so that we may directly compare the objects found at the crime scene to the scales on his body."

"Your Honor," said Dale, rising, "sidebar?"

"All right."

Dale and Ziegler moved to stand next to Judge Pringle's bench. "Your Honor," said Dale, "I object to the comparison between my client's skin and the scales found at the crime scene. There's been no foundation to establish that the scales came from Hask, as opposed to some other Tosok. That they generally match in shape and size Hask's scales will be prejudicial—they also generally match in shape and size the scales on all the Tosoks."

Pringle nodded. "I'm inclined to agree. Ms. Ziegler?"

Ziegler sighed. "I don't suppose you'd like to take judicial notice, Your Honor, of the fact that these *are* Tosok scales?"

"I'm in no position to do that," said Pringle. "You'll have to build the State's house one brick at a time."

"We have black-and-white blowups of photographs of Tosok skin that we could introduce for comparison purposes," said Ziegler.

"Would that be acceptable?" asked Pringle, looking at Dale.

Dale considered. "All right," he said at last, "as long as the photos are presented as generic Tosok skin, and not Hask's in particular."

"Stand back."

Dale moved back to the defense table, and Ziegler moved to the lectern to resume her direct. She made a gesture at one of her assistants, and he held up the black-and-white photo, measuring about two feet by a foot and a half. "This is an enlargement of a picture of Tosok hide," said Ziegler to Feinstein, who was still on the stand. She turned to Dale.

"I'll point out that this is a black-and-white photo so the gray color of the image is not to be taken as significant. Mr. Feinstein, you'll note that a ruler has been drawn in on the bottom of the photo, marked off in both inches and centimeters—this should give you some idea of the scale of the scales, so to speak." Feinstein made a toothy grin at the word play. "Can you tell the Court if there are any similarities in shape between those objects and the Tosok scales?"

"Yes indeed," said Feinstein. "They're very similar."

"And, again, noting the ruler, can you tell the Court if there is any comparison to the size of the Tosok scales?"

"They in fact seem to be very similar in size to the Tosok scales."

"Thank you, Mr. Feinstein. Now, in addition to the object resembling Tosok scales and the pink crystals on the sternum, what, if any, other evidence did you find at the crime scene?"

"We found what appears to be a mark made of blood."

"Can you be more specific?"

"Yes. If I can rise, Your Honor? Thank you. It's visible here in photo eleven, and again in photo fourteen. See? Here, and here?"

"Would you please describe what you're seeing?" asked Ziegler.

"It's a U-shaped or horseshoelike mark, measuring about five inches across."

"What could have made such a mark, Mr. Feinstein?"

"Well, I'd never seen anything like it myself, but Detective Schmitter—"

"Objection! Hearsay."

"Goes to effect on the listener," said Ziegler.

"Overruled," said Pringle.

"Detective Schmitter's comment's led directly to me checking this matter out for myself," said Feinstein, glaring at Dale and carefully measuring his words. "I have since with my own eyes seen a similar impression."

"Where?" asked Ziegler.

"At the suggestion of Detective Burt Schmitter, I went to 6925 Hollywood Boulevard."

"Which is what building?"

"Mann's Chinese Theatre."

"Go on."

"Outside the theater, I saw a pair of similar impressions. They were Tosok footprints made in the cement."

"Thank you. One final thing: the amount of blood spilled at the crime scene. Was it copious?"

"Objection. Leading."

"The jury has already seen the crime-scene photos, Mr. Rice," said Pringle. "No harm, no foul, in stating the obvious."

"Yes," said Feinstein. "'Copious' is a suitable word."

"In your estimation, what would have likely happened to the cleanliness of the person or persons who performed this dissection?"

"Objection. Speculation."

"Overruled."

"Given the rough nature of the work—the rib cage was spread by hand, remember, and the heart had a deep vertical gash in it made as part of the initial slicing of the torso—the person or persons doing this would have likely ended up covered in Dr. Calhoun's blood."

"Thank you. Your witness, Mr. Rice."

"Mr. Feinstein," said Dale, rising slowly to his feet and moving over to the lectern, "you say the perpetrator would likely have ended up covered in blood?"

"Yes."

"Do you know the previous witness, Dr. Anne Flemingdon?"

"Yes."

"She's chief medical examiner for the county, isn't she?"

"Yes."

"Have you ever had cause to visit her at work?"

"From time to time."

"When she greets you at the door to her lab, is she covered with blood?"

Feinstein snorted. "No."

"Not some monster-movie apparition, is she? Dripping crimson all over the carpet?"

"No."

"So, in point of fact, it's entirely possible to dissect a human body and not end up bloodstained from head to toe."

"Under controlled, laboratory condi—"

"Just answer the question, Mr. Feinstein. It is possible in your experience to perform a dissection even as extensive as the one apparently performed on Dr. Calhoun without getting covered in blood."

"It's possible, I suppose."

"Thank you. Turning now to the diamond-shaped objects—you think those might be Tosok scales?"

"Yes, sir, I do."

"What do you base that on?"

"The fact that they're the same shape and size as the Tosok scales in the photograph."

"But you've never seen loose Tosok scales before, have you?"

"Well, no."

"In fact, you don't know for sure that Tosok skin is composed of scales, do you? The diamond pattern might simply be made of crisscrossing lines, mightn't it?"

"I—I suppose."

Dale picked up an object from his desk. "This is a cardboard chessboard. It looks like it's made up of discrete red and black squares, doesn't it?" He flexed it. "But it's really all one piece, isn't it? The squares can't be separated, except by deliberate cutting with a saw, isn't that right?"

"I suppose so."

"And what was it you said? The putative scales are the same size as the objects shown in the photograph?"

"That's right."

"What do you mean by 'the same size'?"

"The same size—you know, the same dimensions."

"But the photograph only shows you the length and width of the diamond-shaped markings. This is real life, Mr. Feinstein, not a Saturday-morning cartoon. We live in a three-dimensional world. Yes, objects have length and width, but they also have thickness. How thick are the objects you recovered from the crime scene?"

"Approximately three one-hundredths of an inch."

"And how thick are the diamond-shaped objects that compose the Tosok hide, as seen in the photograph?"

"I—I have no idea."

"That's right, Mr. Feinstein. You have no idea at all. Further, I draw your attention to photo number eight. Isn't that one of the putative scales you recovered?"

"Yes," said Feinstein.

"And—speaking again in terms of our three-dimensional universe"—Dale's deep voice was rich with sarcasm—"the scale is covered with blood here, isn't it?"

"Yes."

"When you recovered the putative scale, was it blood-stained on both sides?"

"No."

"Which surface was free of blood?"

"The one that was on the bottom."

"In other words, fresh blood had flowed over the top of a scale that was already on the low-pile carpet, is that right?"

"That's the way it appears, yes."

"So the putative scale was *already* present before Dr. Calhoun started to bleed, correct?"

"That seems likely, yes."

"In fact, the putative scale could have been dropped well in advance of Dr. Calhoun's unfortunate demise, isn't that right?"

"No, sir."

"I beg your pardon?"

"The USC janitorial staff clean the rooms once a week. Dr. Calhoun's room was cleaned the morning of the day he died."

"Still the scale could have been lying there for a full day." Dale was flustered; he realized after a moment he'd forgotten to say "putative scale." He'd assumed, stupidly, that dorm rooms got no cleaning service—which was doubtless true when they were being used *as* dorm rooms.

"Actually, sir," said Feinstein, "Dr. Calhoun's room was cleaned just ten hours or so before he died, so, no, the scale could *not* have been lying there for a full day."

"I see. But it could have been there for one hour?"

"Possibly."

"Two hours?"

"Yes, possibly."

"Three hours? Four hours? Five hours?"

"Conceivably."

"Six hours? Eight hours? Ten hours?"

"Possibly—but it's a reasonably big object. Surely someone would have picked it up off the floor."

"Did you know Dr. Calhoun?"

"No, sir. Not at all."

"Would you like to be admitted as a character witness?"

"I—no, sir."

"Would you like to testify to his personal habits? His approach to cleanliness? His fastidiousness?"

"No, sir."

"Then please confine your testimony to areas you're competent in. You do not know whether or not Dr. Calhoun would have bent over to pick up a small piece of litter on his bedroom floor, and not knowing that, you can only say that the scale was definitely on the ground before Dr. Calhoun started bleeding, and might have been on the ground since—ten hours, you said—since perhaps eleven a.m. on December twenty-second, isn't that right?"

"I suppose."

"Thank you. Now, speaking of matters about which you *are* supposedly competent to testify, Mr. Feinstein, you told us your credentials at the outset—no doctorate, but a couple of master's degrees, correct?"

"Correct."

"And certifications from two different forensics organizations, correct?"

"Correct."

"You are obviously expert in chemistry—one of your master's degrees is in that subject."

"Yes."

"Any other areas of expertise?"

"I've had extensive training in fingerprinting, in fiber analysis, and in glass-shard analysis."

"What about footprints?"

"What about them?"

"Do you have expert qualifications in the area of footprint analysis?"

"Well, no."

"So, when you tell this jury that the U-shaped bloody mark is a Tosok footprint, you're not offering a considered, expert opinion. It's just a layman's observation—of no more value than my own, or anyone else's, casual comparison."

"I *am* a trained criminalist."

"But not expert in this specialized area. There *are* experts in footprinting, are there not? Jacob Howley in Boston is this country's top person in this field, isn't he?"

"Yes, I suppose so."

"And Karen Hunt-Podborski of the San Francisco PD, she's probably this state's top footprint expert, isn't she?"

"Yes. Her or Bill Chong."

"But you're not in the league of Doctor—*Doctor!*—Howley, are you, in the area of footprints?"

"No."

"Nor in the league of Ms. Hunt-Podborski, or Mr. Chong, are you?"

"No."

"So that U-shaped bloody mark *might* be a Tosok foot-print, but then it might be—well, we could have the court reporter read it back, but I believe you yourself likened it to a horseshoe?"

"Yes, I did, but—"

"Indeed, the mark is blurred and indistinct, isn't it? And the blood that made it was still wet enough to flow a bit, wasn't it? And so, really, you can't to a scientific degree of certainty say *what* made that mark, can you?"

Feinstein let his breath out.

"Can you?"

"No. No, I suppose I can't."

"Thank you," said Dale. "Thank you very much."

NINETEEN

It was pouring rain the next day. The courtroom was filled with the smell of moist clothing, and umbrellas were lined up against one of the wood-paneled walls.

"State and spell your name, please," said the clerk.

"My name is Jesus Perez, J-E-S-U-S, P-E-R-E-Z, and I will ask the court reporter to note with phonetic spelling that Jesus is pronounced 'Hay-soos,' not 'Jesus.'"

The Latino clerk winked at Perez.

Ziegler rose and moved over to the lectern, depositing a sheaf of notes on it. "Mr. Perez, what is your current job?"

"I'm a detective lieutenant with the homicide division of the Los Angeles Police Department."

"In that capacity, did you have cause to visit the University of Southern California on December twenty-second of last year?"

"I actually arrived after midnight, so it was early on the morning of December twenty-third."

"Why were you called there?"

"A police officer assigned to provide security for the Tosok delegation had found a badly mutilated body there."

"Did you ascertain whose body this was?"

"Yes."

"How did you do so?"

"Well, initially by the identification found on the body, and—"

"Excuse me, did you say identification?"

"Yes."

"Where was this identification?"

"In the man's wallet."

"This body still had a wallet on it?"

"Yes."

"Was there anything besides identification in the wallet?"

"Yes, there were four credit cards—Visa Gold, MasterCard, American Express, and Discover. There was also a phone card; an American Airlines frequent-flier card; a library card; a discount coupon for Bo-Jays, which is a pizzeria in Santa Monica; and the deceased man's driver's license."

"Did the wallet contain anything else?"

"Yes. It contained two hundred and fifty-three dollars in cash, plus one British twenty-pound note."

"Is it unusual to find cash on a murder victim?"

"Yes."

"Why?"

"Because many homicides occur during robberies. Clearly, that was not the motive in this case, and—"

"Objection!" said Dale. "Speculative. Move to strike."

"Sustained," said Pringle. "The jury will disregard the detective's comment as to motive."

"Lieutenant Perez, you said the wallet was only part of the identification."

"Yes, the body was also identified by two of Dr. Calhoun's associates, Dr. Packwood Smathers of the University of Toronto—who was part of the international entourage accompanying the Tosoks—and Dr. Frank Nobilio, science advisor to the president."

"And who did the dead man turn out to be?"

"One Cletus Robert Calhoun."

"Detective, were you the person who arrested Hask?"

"Yes."

"Was the arrest warrant sworn out in your name?"

"It was."

"Your Honor, we introduce that warrant now, as People's thirty-one."

"Mr. Rice?"

"No objection."

"Introduced and marked," said Pringle.

"Detective, is it therefore safe to say that it was you who made the determination that Hask was the most likely suspect in this crime?"

Rice nudged Michiko Katayama. "Objection!" she said. "Prejudicial."

"I'll rephrase: you made the decision to arrest Hask, correct?"

"In consultation with District Attorney Montgomery Ajax, yes."

"We've already heard compelling evidence that the crime was committed by a Tosok, and—"

Michiko was warming to this: "Objection! Counsel is arguing her case."

"Your Honor, is Ms. Katayama now—"

"No sale, Ms. Ziegler," said Pringle. "Sustained."

"There are seven Tosoks on Earth, Detective. Why did you bring charges against Hask in particular?"

"Three reasons. First, Hask and Calhoun spent considerable time alone together. They interacted in different ways than did Calhoun and the other Tosoks, who never saw him alone.

"Second, the marking I believe to be a bloody footprint at the crime scene is smaller and shaped differently than the one made by Captain Kelkad at the Chinese Theatre—that eliminates Kelkad from suspicion, and we were also able to eliminate Dodnaskak, who at a glance anyone can see has much larger feet."

"Objection. Facts not in evidence."

"Sustained," said Pringle. "The jury is advised that the bloody mark at the scene has not been proven to be a Tosok footprint."

"You were saying, Lieutenant . . . ?"

"Well, yes, then there's the fact that Hask shed his skin. The murderer—"

Michiko again: "Objection—there's no proof that a murder, as opposed to manslaughter, took place."

"Sustained."

Perez glowered at the Asian woman. "The *perpetrator*, then. The perp might very well have gotten covered in blood; shedding his entire outer skin would be a handy way to deal with that fact."

"Did you make an effort to recover Hask's shed skin?"

"I did, aided by my colleagues. Hask said he simply bagged it up and put it in the campus garbage."

"And have you managed to recover the skin?"

"No."

"Do you in fact believe Hask when he says he simply threw the skin out?"

"Objection!" shouted Michiko.

"Overruled."

"No, I don't. If it was blood-spattered, he'd have wanted to dispose of it more completely. It could have been chopped into small bits and flushed down a toilet; it could have been buried; it could have been eaten; it could have been burned—"

Dale's turn: "Objection. Pure speculation. There's no evidence that Tosok skin is flammable."

"Sustained," said Judge Pringle. "The jury will disregard Detective Perez's speculation; he is not qualified as an expert on—on Tosok dermatology."

"Besides the fact that they'd spent time alone together,

Detective," said Ziegler, "and beside the shed skin, did you have any other reason to suspect Hask over the other Tosoks?"

"Yes. He had no alibi. Most of the others were in broad public view attending a guest lecture by Stephen Jay Gould at USC during the time that Dr. Calhoun was killed."

"Thank you." Ziegler gathered up her notes. "Your witness, Mr. Rice."

Dale Rice squeezed out from behind the defense table and made his way to the lectern. "Detective Perez, is robbery the only human motive for committing murder?"

"No."

"Isn't it in fact true that robbery represents only a tiny fraction of the reasons why one human being might kill another?"

"It's a significant reason, but—"

"But it's a minority reason, isn't it?" said Dale. "There are all kinds of motives for one human being to kill another, yes?"

"Well, yes."

"You said Dr. Calhoun and Hask had spent considerable time alone together."

"Yes."

"Indeed, you testified that none of the other Tosoks were ever alone with Calhoun. Do you know that for a fact?"

"Well—"

"No, you don't, do you? You don't know that at all."

"Hask and Calhoun had a special bond; they had traveled together to the mothership from the *Kitty Hawk*."

"But you have no proof that over the last several months that Calhoun didn't spend a lot of time alone with other Tosoks, correct?"

"Well, yes. I suppose."

"You suppose. I see. Now, about this bloody mark, which you referred to as a footprint. You said it didn't match either of the ones Kelkad had left in cement outside Mann's Chinese Theatre, correct?"

"Yes."

"But those are the only known Tosok footprints you have to work with, and it's your testimony that the mark at the crime scene didn't match them in size or shape."

"Well, they didn't match exactly, but—"

"Not the same size, you said. Not the same shape."

"Not precisely."

"So, in fact, the bloody mark at the crime scene might not be a Tosok footprint at all."

"Oh, come on, counselor—"

"It doesn't match your one reference sample. The best you can say is that it's somewhat similar to a Tosok footprint."

"It's very similar."

"Just as, oh, say, Canada is very similar to the United States. Similar, sir, but not the same. Now, sir, still on the matter of the footprints at the Chinese Theatre: Harrison Ford's footprints are there—did you compare the impressions in the cement to Mr. Ford's actual footprints?"

"What? No."

"Eddie Murphy's are there, too. Did you track down Eddie Murphy and compare the shape and size of his actual feet to the footprints in the cement?"

"No."

"Dick Van Dyke? Tom Cruise? George Lucas? Paul Newman? Did you check to see how closely their real footprints match the cement impressions?"

"No."

"Cement expands in the heat and contracts in the cold, Mr. Perez; that's why sidewalks sometimes buckle on hot days. Even if the mark at the crime scene is a footprint—which I doubt—the fact that it's smaller than the marks you measured in the cement outside Mann's Chinese Theatre doesn't prove anything, does it?"

Ziegler's second chair, Trina Diamond, decided that she, too, should get into the act: "Objection! Argumentative!"

"Withdrawn," said Dale, with a courtly bow at Ms. Diamond. "Now, to the question of what happened to Hask's shed skin. You testified he told you he threw it out."

"That's right."

"In a garbage bag, put out with the campus trash."

"That's what he claimed."

"Did you determine which dump the University of Southern California's trash is taken to?"

"I did."

"Did you visit that dump and try to find the bag containing the skin?"

"Yes."

"But you say you did not find it."

"I did not find it."

"Let's reflect on that a moment, Lieutenant. If you found the shed skin, and it was clean and free of bloodstains, your case pretty much evaporates, doesn't it?"

"Not at all."

"Indeed, the fact that Hask's old skin is missing is the best thing that could have happened to you, isn't it? You don't have to see if the diamond-shaped objects found at the crime scene match any possible holes left by any missing scales in that old skin. And you don't have to explain why it might be clean and free of bloodstains."

"Objection," said Ziegler. "Counsel is arguing his case."

"Overruled," said Pringle, "but tread softly, Mr. Rice."

"On what day did you go to the dump, Detective?"

"I'd have to consult my notes."

"During pretrial deposition, you said it was December twenty-fourth."

"That sounds about right."

"Do you remember what the weather was like that day?"

"Not offhand."

"Your Honor, I would like to now enter into evidence this report from the LAX meteorological office, showing that last December twenty-fourth was exceptionally hot—seventy-five in the shade."

"Ms. Ziegler?" asked Pringle.

"No objection."

"So entered."

"Seventy-five in the shade," repeated Dale. "One can well imagine that you didn't really feel like poking through garbage in that heat."

"I do my job."

"And the smell—let's not forget about the smell. Even on a normal winter day, a garbage dump reeks, Detective. On that exceptionally hot day, the smell must have been overpowering."

"Not as I recall."

"Surely no one could blame you for not spending too much time rooting around, opening green garbage bag after green garbage bag, while the sun beat down upon you—especially since it was, after all, Christmas Eve. No doubt you were in a hurry to get home to your family."

"I did a thorough search."

"You pretty much have to say that, don't you?"

"Object—"

"Of course I have to say it. I'm under oath, and it's the truth."

Dale smiled. "Smooth, detective. Very smooth. No further questions."

TWENTY

"The People call the Tosok named Stant."

Stant rose from one of the six Tosok chairs in the seating gallery and strode through the gate into the well in front of Judge Pringle's bench.

"You do solemnly swear or affirm," said the clerk, "that the testimony you may give in the cause now pending before this Court shall be the truth, the whole truth, and nothing but the truth, so help you God?"

"I do."

"State your name, please."

"Stant. Phonetically: S-T-A-N-T."

"Be seated." While Stant was being sworn in, a bailiff had removed the standard chair from the witness stand and replaced it with another Tosok one. Stant made himself comfortable, the high sides of the chair nestling in the hollows beneath where his legs joined his torso.

Linda Ziegler rose. "Stant, before we begin, I think it's necessary to talk a bit about that oath you just swore. Do you know the difference between lying and telling the truth?"

"Of course."

"You said 'I do' when the clerk said, 'So help you God?'"

"Yes."

"Do Tosoks in general believe in a higher being?"

"Yes."

"This being—he or she is held to be the creator?"

"She is the creator of the universe, yes. And of certain lifeforms."

"And do you personally subscribe to a belief in this being?"

"Yes."

"So when you invoke God's aid in helping you tell the truth, you are in fact calling on a power in which you personally believe?"

"I am."

"You understand the weight we place on telling the truth during a trial, don't you?"

"It has been explained to me at length. I will tell the truth."

"Thank you—and forgive me for asking those questions. Now, please, Stant, tell us what your relationship is to the defendant, Hask?"

"I am his half brother."

Ziegler was visibly flustered. "I—I beg your pardon?"

"I believe I have used the term correctly. We have the same mother, but different fathers."

Ziegler glanced over at Dale. Dale was as shocked by this revelation as Ziegler was, but he kept a poker face. She then looked behind Dale to where Nobilio was sitting; he, too, had an expression of complete surprise on his face: eyebrows high, open mouth rounded into a circle. It had been a simple, *pro forma* opening question, and she'd doubtless anticipated the answer to be, "I'm his shipmate" or "he's my coworker" or something equally obvious. She visibly tried to regain her own composure. "Your half brother," she repeated.

Stant's tuft waved front to back; the Tosok equivalent of a nod. "Yes."

"Your Honor," said Ziegler, "permission to treat the witness as hostile."

"I am not hostile," said Stant.

Judge Pringle looked at Stant. "By hostile, she means vehemently opposed to the prosecution's case. Now please don't speak again until I've ruled in this matter."

"Your Honor," said Dale, rising to his feet and spreading his giant arms, "the defense objects. Stant has exhibited no hostility."

"Your Honor," said Ziegler, "some latitude would be appropriate."

Pringle frowned. "Being someone's brother doesn't necessarily confer hostile status. Besides, we don't know anything about Tosok family relationships. I'm going to reserve judgment until we do."

"Very well," said Ziegler. She turned to Stant. "Let's find out a bit about them, then. Stant, how is that you come to be Hask's half brother?"

"I have male genitalia. Otherwise, I would be his half sister."

The jury laughed. Ziegler looked annoyed. Dale sympathized with her. She had no idea what was going to come out here, and that was a position no lawyer liked to be in. "Are you the product of a broken home?"

"Our domicile was intact."

"No, no. What I mean is, did your parents divorce? Why is it that the same female had children by two males?"

"My mother had children by *four* males, of course," said Stant.

"Four males," said Ziegler, blinking.

"That is correct."

Ziegler paused, apparently trying to formulate a proper question. Finally, she looked again at Dale, as if entreating him not to object simply for the sake of objecting, and said to Stant, "Perhaps you could explain Tosok reproduction to us . . . if that's not a private matter, that is."

"It is not private, although our custom is not to speak of the inner workings of the body, except when consulting with a priest-physician. The outer self is one's own responsibility, but the inner self is the province of God."

Everyone waited for Stant to go on. After a few moments Judge Pringle said, gently, "Stant, you are required to answer the question."

The Tosok was silent for a moment longer, then his top-knot parted in a shrug. "For one short period during her lifetime a Tosok female is able to reproduce." He averted his eyes from the other Tosoks in the room. "During that period each of her four wombs will be inseminated on the same day—usually by four different males, but in some deviant cases, individual males will be responsible for multiple wombs. In the usual case, though, all offspring will have the same mother, but each will have a different father."

"I see," said Ziegler. "Well, then—"

"Ms. Ziegler," said Judge Pringle, interrupting from her position high up on the bench, "there's only one relevant point here, so let's get to it." The judge herself turned to face Stant. "Stant, on Earth it's common for people to feel extraordinary loyalty to their close relatives—so much so that they might be inclined to shelter them, even if they've committed an illegal act. Is this in fact the case on your world?"

Stant considered for a moment, then: "In addition to Hask, I have two other half siblings on my mother's side. Beyond that, my father impregnated three other females, of course, and so the products of those unions are also my half siblings. Being one's half sibling is a common enough occurrence, and most everyone I know is related to me to some degree. For instance, Rendo"—he pointed to a Tosok with cyan-colored skin—"and I are related maternally as well, although not as directly as Hask and I. These are points of mild interest to us; they do not circumscribe our interpersonal relationships."

"Thank you," said Judge Pringle. "Motion to confer

hostile status denied. Please proceed with normal questioning, Ms. Ziegler."

Ziegler nodded. "Stant, tell us what your profession is."

"I am a biochemist."

Ziegler looked relieved to have this time gotten the
answer she'd expected. "And where did you receive your
training in this discipline?"

Dale rose. "Objection, Your Honor. The Court has no
way to verify any of this."

"Overruled."

"You may answer the question, Stant."

"I trained under Kest<*click*> in Deta<*pop*>darl."

Dale rose again. "Your Honor, this is gibberish. We
object strenuously."

"Overruled. Sit down, Mr. Rice."

Ziegler nodded thanks at the judge. "Let's try it this way,
Stant. How long have the Tosoks been on Earth?"

"Approximately 1.2 Earth years."

"And did your training in biochemistry last longer than
1.2 Earth years?"

"Much longer."

"So, it is a chronological impossibility for any human
being to have more experience in Tosok biochemistry than
you do?"

"That would follow, yes."

"There are seven Tosok on Earth, correct?"

"Correct."

"Are you more expert in Tosok biochemistry than is
Hask?"

"Yes."

"More expert in Tosok biochemistry than is Kelkad?"

"I am, yes."

"More expert than Rendo?"

"Yes."

"More than Torbat? Than Dodnaskak?"

"Yes. Yes."

"More than Ged?"

"Yes."

"So, Stant, is it fair to say that you are the greatest expert on Tosok biochemistry among the seven of you?"

"Yes."

"And we've already established that you are more expert in Tosok biochemistry than any human could possibly be, isn't that so?"

"It is so."

"So that means that you are, in fact, the greatest expert on Tosok biochemistry on this entire planet."

"Yes."

"Objection," said Dale, again. "Improper foundation."

"Overruled. The Court is satisfied with Mr. Stant's credentials, and is pleased to have the world's foremost expert in *anything* appearing before us."

"Now, Stant," said Ziegler, "I want to ask you about Tosok skin."

"Go ahead."

"We are given to understand that Tosoks can shed their skin."

"That is correct."

"How often do they do this?"

"The cycling is very precise. It occurs once every . . ." He paused, pulled his pocket computer out, and tapped on the cross-shaped keypad. "Once every eleven hundred and forty Earth days."

"And why is the skin shed? Is it to accommodate increased size?"

"Objection! Leading."

"I'll allow some latitude here," said Pringle. "We're trying to cover new territory without unduly tying up the Court's time. Overruled."

"Yes, that is correct," said Stant. "Tosoks continue to grow in size throughout their lives—not by much, but enough that the tegument eventually splits and is shed."

"Is this a voluntary or involuntary action?"

"It is normally involuntary."

"What do you mean by 'normally'?"

"Normally, the shedding occurs without intervention. But there is a chemical agent that can induce shedding."

"This chemical," said Ziegler. "How is it applied?"

"As a topical solution."

"In other words, you mean it's spread on the skin, right?"

"Yes. And once applied to the skin, it causes a slight shrinking of the hide—which has the same effect as the body beneath the hide having grown slightly: it causes the hide to split."

"Is the Tosok hide in fact composed of scales?"

"Yes, although our scales simply abut one another; they do not overlap as do the scales of your fish or reptiles."

"Do scales sometimes come loose during this process?"

"Yes, but they also come loose in advance of normal shedding."

"This chemical substance you've referred to—is it common?"

"On Earth? I doubt it exists at all."

"But would it be among your ship's store of chemicals?"

"Yes."

"Why?"

"In case of severe burns, for instance, the appropriate treatment is to force the damaged skin to shed prematurely."

"What is normally done with a shed skin?"

"It is disposed of."

"In any special way?"

"No. It is just thrown out."

"Thank you, Stant. Now, on another topic, do Tosoks have a circulatory system?"

"Yes."

"Would you describe it, please?"

Stant swiveled his front eyes to look at Judge Pringle. "Talking about the outer covering of the body is one thing, but interior workings really are something we do not discuss in public, Your Honor."

"I appreciate that," said the judge. "But we do need this information."

Stant was quiet for a moment. "I—perhaps my embarrassment would be lessened if no other Tosoks were present."

"Our laws require the defendant to be present throughout these proceedings," said Pringle, "but if you like, I will ask the other Tosoks to leave."

Dale swung around to look at the six aliens sitting near the bailiff's desk.

"We would be more comfortable to leave as well," said Kelkad.

"Very well," said Pringle.

The Tosoks rose from their special chairs. Their long strides carried them quickly across the room. Dale could see that four of their tufts were moving in ways he associated with relief. Ged's wasn't moving at all, though—but then, Ged might just be the Tosok equivalent of a dirty old man.

Once the courtroom door had closed behind the last Tosok, Dale and everyone else turned their attention back to Stant.

"Thank you, Your Honor," said the witness.

"Now," said Ziegler, "I'd asked you about the Tosok circulatory system."

"Yes," said Stant. He paused for a moment, as if working up the nerve to discuss the matter, then: "We have four hearts, located here, here, here, and here." He pointed to four points spaced evenly around the bottom of his torso. "We also have four lungs, each of which is semicircular in cross section, located directly above each heart. The hearts pump blood oxygenated by the lungs throughout the body."

"Except for the number and placement of organs involved, this is substantially the same as what happens within a human body, correct?"

"So I would assume."

"You mentioned blood. What are the constituents of Tosok blood?"

"It consists of a plasma the chemical composition of which resembles the seawater of our world. In this plasma float various specialized structures, including oxygen conveyors, tools for repairing damage and fighting infection, and free-floating nerve components."

Dale could hear Frank Nobilio mutter "Fascinating" behind him.

"Free-floating nerve components?" repeated Ziegler.

"Yes. We each have a *kivart*—an organ that produces these. The floaters are crucial to our muscular control."

"What happens to your blood when exposed to air?" asked Ziegler.

"It crystallizes, forming a protective covering over the wound."

"And what color are these crystals?"

"Pink."

"I show you People's exhibit forty-two, which is the sample of pink crystals taken from Dr. Calhoun's breastbone. And, Your Honor, I'd like to enter People's sixty-three—the UCLA Department of Chemistry analysis on these crystals."

"Mr. Rice?"

"All right."

"So entered."

"Now, Stant, looking at these crystals, and the analysis of their chemical make-up, do you have an opinion about what substance they are?"

"It is blood—Tosok blood."

"Blood from one of you seven?"

"I cannot say that from the evidence presented here. It

could be blood from a Tosok, or conceivably from an animal from our world."

"But it is blood from a Tosok, or a related lifeform?"

"Certainly."

"You mentioned the specialized structures in Tosok blood, Stant. Are they cells?"

"Many are, yes."

"And do Tosok cells contain within them the genetic blueprint of the individual?"

"They do."

"Is this blueprint encoded by deoxyribonucleic acid?"

"No."

"Is the encoding chemical similar to DNA?"

"I really do not know anything about DNA, although early on, before they understood our discomfort in discussing interior workings, Dr. Smathers and Dr. Nobilio did mention it to me. Our genetic molecule encodes in binary, indicated by the presence or absence of methyl groups."

"Without delving further at this stage into the precise details of the coding method, is it fair to say there is a wide range of information that can be encoded?"

"Yes."

"So, since Tosok blood contains cells, and these cells contain widely varying genetic information, is it possible to identify the individual from whom a sample of Tosok blood was taken?"

Stant looked at the judge, looked at Dale, then looked back at Ziegler. There was a large analog clock on the back wall of the courtroom; it whirred loudly as its minute hand advanced one position. "I wish to assert my Fifth Amendment privilege," Stant said at last.

There were gasps from the audience. "I—I beg your pardon?" said Ziegler.

"I believe I have phrased the statement correctly. I assert my Fifth Amendment privilege."

Dale Rice and Michiko Katayama were consulting at the

defense table. Frank leaned in from the row behind them. Journalists were furiously making notes.

"Which part of the Fifth Amendment are you referring to?" asked Ziegler.

"'No person shall be compelled in any criminal case to be a witness against himself.'"

"How does that possibly apply here?" asked Ziegler.

Dale rose. "Objection, Your Honor! The witness *has* asserted the privilege."

"Counsel, approach," said Pringle.

Dale, Ziegler, and their second chairs came to sidebar. "What's going on, Ms. Ziegler?" asked Pringle impatiently.

"I have no idea, Your Honor."

"Does Stant have legal counsel?"

"I'm willing to serve," said Dale.

"I hardly think that's appropriate," said Pringle. "Is there any reason to think he doesn't understand the Fifth Amendment?"

"Of course he understands it," said Dale. "It's obvious. Ms. Ziegler wants to introduce the concept that Tosok blood can be genetically fingerprinted. By taking the Fifth, Stant is clearly saying no, it cannot—and therefore what you've taken as evidence against Hask could also be evidence against him."

"Or else," said Michiko, "there's another possibility. He's saying that because Hask is his half brother, they have the same Tosok blood type, and that the evidence would incriminate Stant as well as Hask."

Judge Pringle pursed her lips. "I wish this hadn't come up before the jury. All right, stand back."

The lawyers moved away from the bench.

"Ms. Ziegler," said Judge Pringle. "You may proceed if you have questions in areas other than the one in which Mr. Stant has asserted his constitutional right not to answer."

Ziegler looked at Stant, then shrugged. "No further questions."

"Mr. Rice?"

Dale hadn't yet made it back to his seat. He turned around. "Mr. Stant, are there circumstances under which a Tosok can lose scales that are unrelated to the shedding of skin?"

"Certainly."

"Such as?"

"Abrasions."

"You mean if you bumped into something, some scales might flake off."

"It would take a big bump, but, yes, that can happen."

"Could one deliberately pry off one's own scales?"

"It would hurt, but it could be done."

"You mentioned a chemical that can induce shedding."

"Yes. It's called *despodalk.*"

"This *despodalk*—you said it's something normally kept in your ship's stores?"

"Correct."

"For medicinal purposes?"

"That is right."

"Presumably you have an inventory of what supplies are aboard your ship."

"Yes."

"And did you check that inventory to see if any *despodalk* was missing?"

"At the request of Detective Perez, yes, I did that."

"And was any?"

"Not according to the inventory, but—"

"Thank you. Now—"

"No, wait—"

"I control the asking of questions at this phase, Mr. Stant. You can't interrupt me."

"But you made me swear—invoking God as I did so—to tell the truth, the whole truth, and nothing but the truth, and—"

"I'd like to move on," said Dale.

Stant turned to the judge. "My answer is not complete."

Pringle nodded. "I will allow Mr. Stant to complete his answer."

"Thank you," said Stant. "The quantity of *despodalk* aboard our ship matched the quantity specified in the inventory. But the inventory is kept in what you would call an open computer file; if anyone wished to modify it, they could. It would be an easy matter to take a container of the chemical and to alter the inventory to make it appear that none had been removed. I have no personal knowledge of the quantity of *despodalk* we had when we left our world, and so no way of knowing whether the current inventory is depleted from its original amount."

"Your Honor," said Dale, "I move that the last be stricken from the record."

"Your Honor," said Ziegler, "I'll simply reintroduce the same material on redirect."

"The comment will stand," said Judge Pringle. "Let's move along."

"Once bitten, Your Honor," said Dale. "No further questions."

"Redirect?" said Pringle.

Ziegler rose. "Just a few points, Your Honor. Mr. Stant, this chemical agent that can induce shedding—"

"*Despodalk.*"

"I assume each of your landing craft contains a first-aid kit, no?"

"Yes."

"And would such kits contain *despodalk?*"

"No."

"So the only way some of it would be available here on Earth is if someone had thought *in advance* to bring some down from your mothership, correct?" Ziegler was clearly making the case for premeditation.

"That is right."

"Thank you. Now, Mr. Stant, you said you were the defendant's half brother—"

It hit Dale in a flash—just as it had doubtless occurred to Ziegler just after she'd completed her direct examination. If Stant and Hask were half brothers, and if they'd been born nearly simultaneously, and if sheddings occurred on a regular schedule, then their natural shedding of skin should have been synchronized. But Stant hadn't shed his skin since arriving on Earth, whereas Hask's had been shed almost four months ago—strongly suggesting that Hask's shedding must have been deliberately induced, presumably to enable him to dispose of his blood-covered hide. Dale was immediately on his feet. "Objection! Improper redirect! The question of Stant's relationship to Hask came up during direct, and should have been dealt with then."

"Your Honor, I simply want to clear up some points about Tosok family relationships."

"No way, Linda," said Dale.

"Mr. Rice—" said Pringle.

"Sorry, Your Honor," said Dale, turning now to face the judge. "But family relationships were covered in Ms. Ziegler's direct; her redirect can only cover material I touched on in my cross."

"Sustained," said Pringle. "You know the rules, Ms. Ziegler."

"Very well. Stant, you'll recall that Mr. Rice *did* talk to you about the shedding of skin during his cross-examination. Now, you said that this event naturally occurs on a fixed, predictable schedule, correct?"

"Correct."

"And would that schedule be synchronized with—"

"*Objection!*"

"Freeze right there, Ms. Ziegler."

"But, Your Honor—"

"*Freeze.*"

"Yes, Your Honor."

"If you have proper redirect, you may continue. Otherwise, take your seat now."

Ziegler considered for several seconds. Finally, she shrugged and sat back down. "No further questions, Your Honor."

Dale looked over at the jury. Some of the faces were perplexed, but several others were nodding slowly. They'd come to the same realization as Ziegler and Dale had, and would doubtless share it with the others after today's session, the admonition not to discuss the case notwithstanding.

The damage had been done.

TWENTY-ONE

"The People call Kelkad," said Linda Ziegler.

The alien captain was sworn in.

Ziegler stepped up to the lectern. This time, she chose her words carefully. "Kelkad, what is your working relationship to the defendant?"

"I am captain of a starship on which he serves."

"So you are his boss?"

"Yes."

"Are you also his friend?"

"We are not close emotionally."

"Kelkad, how long have you known Hask?"

"Two hundred and nineteen of your years."

"But you spent most of that time in hibernation, no?"

"That is correct."

"How long were you in hibernation?"

"Two hundred and eleven Earth years."

"So, setting aside that time, you've still known Hask for eight years."

"Correct."

"Have you ever had to discipline him?"

"Of course. I am his commanding officer."

"In other words, Hask in the past has failed to observe regulations?"

"From time to time."

"Would you please give an example of Hask's disobedience?"

"Certainly. Regulations require venting the reclamation facilities aboard our ship after each use; Hask has occasionally failed to observe this protocol."

A couple of jurors laughed.

"I beg your pardon?" said Ziegler.

"It is comparable to forgetting to flush the toilet," said Kelkad.

The rest of the jurors laughed, and so did Judge Pringle. Ziegler turned slightly red. "Can you give a more significant example of his disobedience?"

"I have no way of knowing what you would consider significant," said Kelkad.

"Isn't it true that your crew originally consisted of eight members?"

"Objection," said Dale. "Irrelevant."

"Overruled."

"Yes," said Kelkad.

"And isn't it true that one of those crew members died *en route* to Earth?"

"Objection," said Dale. "Irrelevant."

"Overruled."

"Yes," said Kelkad.

"What was the name of this dead crew member?"

"Seltar."

"Did you have to discipline Hask over Seltar's death?"

"I was not pleased about it, but it seemed unavoidable. However, I did discipline him for making contact with you humans before I was revived; I felt that Hask had been presumptuous in exceeding his authority."

"Do you personally know for a fact what killed Seltar?"

"Hask told me that—"

"Hearsay is inadmissible," said Ziegler. "Do you personally know for a fact what killed Seltar?"

"Yes."

"How?"

"I was informed by Hask that—"

"Again, that is hearsay."

"I trust Hask," said Kelkad.

"Non-responsive," said Ziegler. "Move to strike."

"The jury will disregard the witness's last comment," said Pringle.

"Did you yourself examine Seltar's body?"

"No."

"Why not?"

"I was still in hibernation when the accident occurred."

"But Seltar was not?"

"That is correct."

"Who else was not in hibernation?"

"Hask had also been revived."

"Hask and Seltar were the only ones conscious aboard your ship at that time?"

"Correct."

"And Hask was the only possible witness to Seltar's death?"

"Correct. However, I do not know if he actually did witness the death. She died while performing repairs to our ship."

"I didn't ask you that. What became of Seltar's body?"

"It was expelled into space."

"The whole thing?"

Kelkad's tuft waved in confusion. "I beg your pardon?"

"Was the whole, intact body expelled into space?"

"No."

"In what way was it not intact?"

"Its significant component parts were harvested prior to ejection."

"'Harvested.' What do you mean by that?"

Kelkad paused. He glanced uncomfortably at the other Tosoks. "Her organs were removed and stored in case they might be required for transplant at some future time. Of course, if a single organ is damaged, it can usually be regenerated internally, but if two or more are damaged simultaneously, a transplant may be required."

"Who performed the organ harvesting?"

"Why, Hask, of course."

"Let me get this straight," said Ziegler, now facing the jury. "Prior to your arrival at Earth, Hask had been awoken early, and one of the principal tasks he performed at this time was carving the organs out of a Tosok body."

"It was not a principal task."

"But he did do it."

"Yes. I have seen Seltar's organs in cold storage aboard the mothership."

"So Hask opened up her body, removed the hearts, the lungs, and so on."

"Yes."

"Blood spilling everywhere."

A sucking in of breath from juror four.

"Your Honor!" said Dale. "Objection."

Judge Pringle frowned at the prosecutor. "Sustained. Ask a question, Ms. Ziegler."

"Hask is not a doctor, correct?"

"That is correct. But he was consecrated by a priest-physician to perform certain medical procedures; we all had such training."

"Despite the Tosok taboo about such matters?"

"We view the internal workings of the body the way you view sexual intercourse. They are private matters, but at appropriate times they can be appropriately explored. Given that five individuals are involved in Tosok mating, we have no privacy taboos associated with that act, and I assure you, Ms. Ziegler, that human embarrassment over sexual matters seems as strange to us as our reticence about interior biology is to you."

"Understood," said Ziegler. "When Hask was confronted with the task of harvesting Seltar's organs, this would have been his first time performing such a procedure on an actual corpse, no? His training would have been done on simulations or dummies, correct?"

"Objection, Your Honor," said Dale. "Compound question."

"Sustained."

"To your knowledge," said Ziegler, "Hask would never have dissected an actual corpse before?"

"Object to the term 'dissected.' Inflammatory."

"Sustained."

"To your knowledge, Hask would never have removed organs from a real body before, correct?"

The clock whirred again. Someone coughed in the back of the courtroom. "Correct."

Ziegler locked her gaze on the alien captain. "Is it conceivable that Hask took pleasure in this act?"

"Objection! Calls for speculation."

"Sustained."

"Very well. As leader of your expedition, you no doubt received training in psychology, correct?"

"Correct."

"Tosok psychology, right?"

"Yes."

"So you are qualified as an expert in this area—more so than any human psychologist?"

"Yes."

"And of all your crew, you've had the most psychological training?"

"Your Honor," said Dale, spreading his arms. "Objection. Ms. Ziegler has tried this same stunt before. We've got no way to verify any of this. Surely the Court can't rely on such opinions."

"The People are not asking you to accept Kelkad's opinions, Your Honor," said Ziegler, "but the Tosoks are the only witnesses who can offer any sort of testimony in these areas. To that extent, these are factual matters, not matters of opinion, and they are clearly probative."

"Normally I wouldn't allow it," said Pringle, "but, Mr. Rice, I'll give you similar latitude should you wish to pursue similar lines of questioning during your case-in-chief."

"Thank you," said Ziegler. "Kelkad, as an expert in Tosok psychology, let me ask you a hypothetical question. Given the taboos surrounding internal bodily processes in your culture, is it conceivable that a Tosok could find pleasure in performing organ extraction?"

"Not a normal Tosok."

"No, not a normal Tosok," said Ziegler. "But in the annals of Tosok psychology, have there been cases of aberrant individuals taking pleasure in carving into other people's bodies?"

Kelkad said nothing.

"Come now, Kelkad. I realize you're trying to put the best foot forward for your people, just as our race has been trying to portray itself positively in your eyes. There *are* human beings who take pleasure in such matters. We consider it sick and deviant, and it is mercifully rare, but such human beings *do* exist. Are you telling me that no such Tosoks exist?"

"They exist," said Kelkad slowly.

"In Tosok psychology, are there predictive tests for such a predilection?"

"I do not understand the question."

"I mean, how is it that you discover that a Tosok has this particular aberration? Can you determine it just by looking at the Tosok?"

"No."

"Would a normal Tosok psychological test—say, the kind your crew might have undergone before being assigned to this mission—reveal this predilection?"

"I doubt it."

"In fact, in most such cases, a Tosok would not know that he found this pleasurable until circumstance forced him to actually expose the internal organs, isn't that correct?"

"Yes, I suspect that is probably true."

"And if a Tosok did find itself stimulated by this action, he or she might be as surprised as anyone, no?"

"It would certainly shock me to discover it about myself," said Kelkad.

"I'm sure it would," said Ziegler. "Psychologically speaking, do individual Tosoks desire to repeat experiences they have found stimulating?"

"Possibly."

"You're hedging, Kelkad. The answer is surely more direct."

"Objection," said Dale. "Badgering."

"Overruled."

"Yes, they may well desire to repeat pleasurable experiences."

"So," said Ziegler, "if Hask had found himself enjoying the act of removing the organs from—"

"Objection! Your Honor, counsel is arguing her case."

"Sustained."

"Very well," said Ziegler. She looked at the jury. "Very well. Your witness, Mr. Rice."

Dale rose. "Mr. Kelkad, in your experience, has Hask ever exhibited signs of sadism?"

Kelkad's translator beeped. "Sadism?"

"Deriving satisfaction from inflicting pain on others."

"No, Hask never exhibited any such thing."

"Did he demonstrate an unnatural fondness for the gory?"

"No."

"Any bloodthirstiness?"

"No."

"Have you ever seen him cause deliberate injury to other Tosoks?"

"No."

"What about animals on your world?"

"Hask in fact had a pet *kogloo* he was quite fond of; he treated it extremely well."

"Thank you," said Dale, returning to his seat. "No further questions."

TWENTY-TWO

A number of lesser witnesses occupied the next two weeks—other Tosoks, experts on deviant human psychology, and a variety of individuals who tried to shore up the State's shaky case for premeditation, which seemed to hinge on two facts: first, that Hask had arranged to stay back at the dorm while the others went to the Stephen Jay Gould lecture, knowing Calhoun was also staying back, and, second, that to induce his skin shedding, he must have thought in advance to bring the chemical agent down from the mothership.

Finally, though, it was time for the People's most compelling bit of evidence. Linda Ziegler rose from her place at the prosecution table. "If it pleases the Court," she said, "the People would now like to introduce a segment of the videotape made by the decedent while he was aboard the Tosok mothership."

"Mr. Rice?"

Dale had fought long and hard before the trial began to get this suppressed, but Judge Pringle had ruled it admissible, and the appeals court had agreed with her. "No objection."

"Please proceed."

Two large color television monitors were mounted on the walls of the courtroom, one facing the jury box, the other facing the spectators. In addition, Judge Pringle had a smaller TV on her bench, as did the prosecution and the defense. The bailiff dimmed the lights in the room . . .

All the still pictures of the *Apollo 11* crew walking on the moon have one thing in common: they all show Buzz Aldrin, for the simple reason that it was Neil Armstrong who was holding the camera. Although Armstrong was the first man on the moon, there are, in fact almost no pictures of him there.

The videos shot in microgravity aboard the Tosok mothership were taken by Cletus Calhoun, and except for the occasional glimpse of one of his gangly limbs, he himself was therefore completely absent from the footage. Dale Rice was pleased by this. The more the jury forgot about Calhoun—the amiable hillbilly who could trade jokes with Jay Leno—the better.

Still, Clete's drawling voice was heard loud and clear throughout the videotape. The tape began with him chatting with a floating Hask, who was plainly visible; Dale had forgotten just how blue Hask's old hide had been.

"But you guys," Clete was saying in that rich Tennessee accent, "being able to shut down for centuries, having that ability built right into y'all. You can fake gravity in space, 'course, through centrifugal force or constant acceleration. But there ain't nothing you can do about the time it takes for interstellar travel. With a natural suspended-animation ability, y'all sure got us beat. We might have been destined to go into planetary orbit, but your race seems to have been destined to sail between the stars."

"Many of our philosophers would agree with that statement," remarked Hask. Then, after a second: "But not all, of course." They were both quiet for a time. "I am hungry," said Hask. "It will take several hours for the others to revive. Do you require food?"

"I brought some with me," said Clete. "Navy rations. Hardly gourmet vittles, but they'll do."

"Come with me," said Hask. The alien folded his three-part legs against a bulkhead and kicked off. Clete started off with a hand push—his long arm darted into the shot for a moment—but then apparently kicked off the wall as well. They floated down another corridor, large yellow lights overhead alternating with small orange ones.

Soon they came to a door, which slid aside for Hask. They floated into the room. As they did so more lights came on overhead.

There was a sound of Clete sucking in his breath. No way to know what he'd been thinking, but Dale Rice always felt like vomiting when he saw this part of the tape. In the dimmed light of the courtroom, he could see several jurors wincing.

There was a great bloody mass in the middle of the picture. It took several seconds for the shape of the thing to register as Clete panned the camera. It seemed to be an enormously long tube of raw meat, its surface glistening with pinkish-red blood. The tube wound around itself like a pile of spilled intestines. Its diameter was about five inches, and its length—well, if it were all stretched out, instead of coiled up, it might have run to fifty feet, a great, gory anaconda stripped of its hide. One end was plugged into one of the room's walls; the other end, which terminated in a flat circular cross section, was propped up by a Y-shaped ceramic support.

"God a'mighty!" said Clete voice. "What is it?"

"It is food," said Hask.

"It's meat?"

"Yes. Would you like some?"

"Ah—no. No, thanks."

Hask floated over to the tube's free end. He reached into

one of the pouches on his dun-colored vest and removed a small blue cylinder about ten inches long and two inches in diameter. He took one end of it in the fingers of his front arm and the other in his back arm, then bent it. It split down the middle into two five-inch cylinders. He then moved his hands as if he were drawing an invisible loop of string stretched between the two cylinders around the great tube of meat, about four inches from its end. He pulled the two blue handles away from each other, and to the jury's amazement, the last four inches of the great meat sausage separated from the rest. It just floated there, but the picture clearly showed a receptacle attached to the Y-shaped support that obviously would have caught it had the ship been undergoing acceleration.

"How did you do that?" said Clete, off camera.

Hask looked at him, puzzled. Then he seemed to realize. "You mean my carving tool? There is a single, long, flexible molecular chain connecting the two handles. The chain cannot be broken, but because of its thinness, it cuts easily through almost anything."

Clete's voice could be heard to say, "It slices! It dices!"

"Pardon?" said Hask.

"A line from an old TV commercial—for the Ronco Veg-O-Matic. 'It slices! It dices!'" Clete sounded impressed. "Purty neat device. But if you can't see the thread, isn't it dangerous?"

Hask grabbed the two parts of the handle and pulled them as far apart as he could. Every fifteen inches or so, a large blue bead appeared along the otherwise invisible filament. "The beads enable you to see the filament," said Hask, "as well as letting you handle it safely. They are lined on the inside with a monomolecular weave that the filament cannot cut through, so you can slide the beads along the filament if they get in the way." Hask's tuft moved in a shrug. "It is a general-purpose tool, not just for carving meat; nothing sticks to the monofilament, so you do not have to worry about keeping it clean."

Dale had his eyes glued to the jurors. First one got it, and then another, and soon they all had reacted with either widened eyes or noddings of their heads: they had just seen what could very likely have been the murder weapon.

Hask brought the two handles together—the molecular chain and its beads were reeled in as he did so—and he placed the unit back in a pocket. He then reached out with his front hand and plucked the floating disk of meat out of the air. Very little blood had been shed—a few circular drops had come free as the molecular chain went through the meat, but something—a vacuum cleaner, perhaps—had sucked them down into the Y-shaped support.

"What kind of critter *is* that?" said Clete. His arm was visible again, pointing at the skinless snake.

"It is not an animal," said Hask. "It is meat." The image bounced as Clete pushed off the wall to have a closer look at what Hask was holding. Clete apparently wasn't good at maneuvering while weightless; Hask had to reach out with a leg—which bent in a way that would have snapped the joint had Hask been human—to stop Clete's movement. Clete thanked Hask, then took a close-up shot of the piece of meat. It was clear now that it *did* have a skin, made up of diamond-shaped plates just like Hask's own hide. But the skin on the meat was thin and crystal clear.

"Meat, but not an animal?" said Clete's voice. He sounded perplexed.

"It is *just* meat," Hask said. "It is not an animal. Rather, it is a product of genetic engineering. It has only what nervous system is required to support its circulatory system, and its circulatory system is simplicity itself. It is not alive; it feels no pain. It is simply a chemical factory, converting raw materials fed to it through the wall receptacle into edible flesh, balanced perfectly for our nutritional needs. Of course, it is not all we eat—we are omnivores, as you are."

"Ah," said Clete. "Y'all couldn't bring animals on your long space voyage, but this lets y'all enjoy the taste."

Hask's front eyes blinked repeatedly. "We do not eat animals on our world," he said. "At least, not anymore."

"Oh," said Clete. "Well, we don't have the ability to create meat. We kill animals for their flesh."

Hask's tuft waggled as he considered this. "Since we do not *have* to kill for food, we no longer do so. Some say we have sacrificed too much—that killing one's own food is a release, the outlet nature intended for violent urges."

"Well, I'm an old country boy," said Clete. "I've done my share o' huntin'. But most people today, they get their meat prepackaged at a store. They don't ever see the animal, and have no hand in the kill."

"But you say you have killed?" said Hask.

"Well, yes."

"What is it like—to kill for food?"

The camera bounced; Clete was apparently shrugging as he held it. "It can be very satisfying. Nothing quite so delicious as a meal you tracked and bagged yourself."

"Intriguing," said Hask. He looked at his disk of meat, as though it were somehow no longer all that appetizing. Still, he brought it to his front mouth, the outer horizontal and inner vertical openings forming a square hole. His rust-colored dental plates sliced a piece off the edge of the meat disk, and to the jury's evident surprise, two long flat tongues popped out of the mouth after each bite, wiping what little blood there was from Hask's face.

"You eat the meat raw?" said Clete.

Hask nodded. "In ancient times we cooked animal flesh, but the reasons for cooking—to soften the meat, and to kill germs—do not apply to this product. Raw meat *is* much more flavorful . . ."

"That's fine," said Linda Ziegler, rising in the darkness. The bailiff pushed the pause button, and a still image of the floating Tosok, holding the now half-eaten piece of raw flesh in his hand, jerked and flickered on the monitors. The lights in the courtroom were brought back to full illumination; jurors and audience members rubbed their eyes.

Linda Ziegler then introduced into evidence one of the Tosok monofilament tools—the one that had belonged to Hask. There was no way to demonstrate that it was the specific one that had been used in the murder; forensics had been unable to find any evidence of that, and so she didn't bother pursuing this line of questioning.

Of course, Hask possessed a new monofilament tool now; the mothership had dozens in its stores. A smaller version of the Tosok meat factory had been installed at Paul Valcour Hall; Hask needed one of the tools in order to feed himself, and Dale had successfully argued that one accused of killing with a knife is normally not denied access to cutlery.

Still, there was no doubt that the shipboard videotape, and the presentation of Hask's cutting tool in court, had a huge impact on the jury. And so, with smug satisfaction, Linda Ziegler returned to her seat and said, "Your Honor, the People rest."

TWENTY-THREE

Hask and Frank had returned with Dale to Dale's twenty-seventh-floor office. As soon as they arrived, though, Hask excused himself to use the bathroom. Like humans, Tosoks eliminated both solid and liquid waste, and with some difficulty they could make use of human toilets.

Once Hask had left the room, Frank leaned forward in his usual easy chair. "Ziegler's case was quite devastating," he said. "What does our shadow jury say?"

Dale heaved his massive bulk into his leather chair and consulted a report Mary-Margaret had left on his desk. "As of this moment they're voting unanimously to convict Hask," he said with a sigh.

Frank frowned. "Look, I know you said we shouldn't put Hask on the stand, but at this stage surely the real jury will be expecting to hear from him."

"Possibly," said Dale. "But Pringle will tell them that the defendant is under no obligation to testify; the entire burden is on prosecution. That's part of CALJIC. Still . . ."

"Yes?"

"Well, this is hardly a normal case. You know what it

says in the charge—'did willfully, unlawfully, and with malice aforethought murder Cletus Robert Calhoun, a human being.' In previous cases, it always seemed funny to me that they specify 'a human being,' but that *is* the key point in this case. The deceased *is* human, and the defendant is not—and the jury might well feel the prosecution has less of a burden in this case." He waved the report at Frank. "That seems to be what our shadow jury is saying, anyway: if they make the wrong verdict, well, it's not as though a human being would end up rotting in jail. If we can put Hask on the stand, and convince the jury that he's every bit as much a person, every bit as real and sensitive as anyone else, then they may decide the way we want them to. The key, though, is to get them to like Hask."

"That's not going to be easy," said Frank, shaking his head. Late-afternoon sunlight was painting the room in sepia tones. "I mean, we can't win the jurors over with Hask's smile, or anything like that—he physically can't smile, and frankly, those rusty dental plates give me the willies. And shouldn't a good defendant show more horror when crime-scene photos are displayed? I was hoping the Tosok taboo about internal matters would have worked in our favor there, but all Hask did was wave that topknot around in various patterns. The jury will never understand what those mean."

"Don't underestimate juries," said Dale. "They're a lot smarter than you might think. I'll give you an example: I once handled a personal-injury case; not my normal thing, but it was for a friend. Our position was that the reason the person had been injured was because the car's seat belt was faulty. Well, during our case, every time I mentioned that, I took off my glasses." He demonstrated. "See? After I'd done that a few dozen times, the jury was conditioned. Then, whenever the automaker's lawyer tried to point out alternative possible causes for the accident, I'd just take off my glasses. Never said a word, see, and there's nothing in the transcript. But I'd take off my glasses, and the jury would be reminded of the faulty seat belt. We won 2.8 million in that case."

"Wow."

"If the jury can learn that 'glasses coming off' means 'defective seat belt,' it can also learn that 'topknot waving side to side' means Tosok laughter, or that 'topknot lying flat' means Tosok revulsion. Don't worry, son. I think our jury knows Hask and the other Tosoks a lot better than you think they do."

"So then we *should* put Hask on the stand."

"Maybe . . . but it still worries me. Nine times out of ten, it's a disaster, and—"

The door to Dale's office opened, and Hask strode in. "I wish to testify," he said at once, lowering his weight onto the single Tosok chair.

Dale and Frank exchanged glances. "I advise against it," said Dale.

Hask was silent for a moment. "It *is* my decision to make."

"Of course, of course," said Dale. "But you've never seen a criminal case before; I've seen hundreds. It's almost always a mistake for the defendant to take the stand."

"Why? What chance is there that they will find me innocent if I do not testify?"

"No one ever knows what a jury is thinking."

"That is not true. Your shadow jury has already voted to convict me, has it not?"

"No, it hasn't."

"You are lying."

Dale nodded. "All right, all right. But even if it has, taking the stand is almost always the wrong move. You only do that when you have no other choice."

"Such as now," said Hask. As always, his natural voice rose as the words were spoken, making it impossible to tell if it was a question or a statement.

Dale sighed again. "I suppose. But you know that Linda Ziegler will get to cross-examine you?"

"I understand that."

"And you still want to do it?"

"Yes."

"All right," said Dale, resigning himself to it. "But we'll put you on the stand first."

"Why first?" asked Hask.

"Because if Linda eviscerates you—forgive the metaphor—we'll have the rest of our case-in-chief to try to recover." Dale scratched his chin. "We should talk about your testimony—figure out what you're going to say."

"I am going to tell the truth, of course. The truth, the whole truth, and nothing but the truth."

Dale raised his eyebrows. "Really?"

"You cannot tell, can you?" said Hask.

"Tell that you're innocent? Of course I believe that, Hask, but—"

"No, tell if I am telling the truth."

"What? No. Aren't you?"

Hask fell silent.

There was an even bigger than normal crowd of report- ers outside the Criminal Courts Building the next morning. Many dozens of reporters shouted questions at Dale and Frank as they entered, but Dale said nothing. Inside the courtroom, the excitement was palpable.

Judge Pringle came in, said her usual good morning to the jurors and lawyers, and then looked at Dale. "The defense may now begin its case-in-chief," she said.

Dale rose and moved to the lectern. He paused for a moment, letting the drama build, then, in that Darth Vader voice of his, he boomed out, "The defense calls Hask."

The courtroom buzzed with excitement. Reporters leaned forward in their chairs.

"Just a second," said Judge Pringle. "Hask, you are aware that you have an absolute constitutional right not to testify? No one can compel you to do so, if it is not your wish?"

Hask had already arisen from his special chair at the defense table. "I understand, Your Honor."

"And no one has coerced you into testifying?"

"No one. In fact—" He fell silent.

Dale kept an expressionless face, but was relieved. At least he'd taught Hask *something*. He'd closed his mouth before he'd said "In fact, my lawyer advised me against testifying," thank God.

"All right," said Pringle. "Mr. Ortiz, please swear the witness in." Hask made his way to the witness stand. As he did so, a court worker removed the human chair and replaced it with a Tosok one.

"Place your front hand on the Bible, please." Hask did so. "You do solemnly swear or affirm," said the clerk, "that the testimony you may give in the cause now pending before this Court shall be the truth, the whole truth, and nothing but the truth, so help you God?"

"I do so affirm," said Hask.

"Thank you. Be seated, and please state and spell your name for the record."

"Hask, which I guess is H-A-S-K."

"Mr. Rice," said Judge Pringle, "you may proceed."

"Thank you, Your Honor," said Dale, slowly getting to his feet and making his way to the lectern. "Mr. Hask, what is your position aboard the Tosok starship?"

"My title was First."

"'First'—is that like 'first officer'?"

"No. The First is the person who comes out of hibernation first. It was my job to deal with any in-flight emergencies, and also to be the first revived upon arrival at our destination, in order to determine if it was safe to revive the others."

"So you are a very important member of the crew?"

"On the contrary, I am the most expendable."

"The prosecution has suggested you had the opportunity to kill Dr. Calhoun. Did you have that opportunity?"

"I was not alone with him at the time he died."

"But you can't account for your presence during the entire window of opportunity for this crime."

"I can account for it. I simply cannot prove the truth of the account. And there are others who had equal opportunity."

"The prosecution has also suggested that you had the means to kill Dr. Calhoun. Specifically, that you used a monofilament carving tool to sever his leg. Would such a tool work for that purpose?"

"I suspect so, yes."

"But a murder conviction requires more than just opportunity and means. It—"

"Objection. Mr. Rice is arguing his case."

"Sustained."

"What about motive, Hask? Did you have any reason to want to see Dr. Calhoun dead?"

Ziegler was on her feet. "Objection, Your Honor. CALJIC 2.51: 'Motive is not an element of the crime charged and need not be shown.'"

"Overruled. *I'll* present the jury instructions, counselor."

"Hask, did you have any motive for wanting to see Dr. Calhoun dead?"

"None."

"Is there any Tosok religious ritual that involves dissection or dismemberment?"

"No."

"We humans have some rather bloody sports. Some humans like to hunt animals. Do your people hunt for sport?"

"Define 'for sport,' please."

"For fun. For recreation. As a way of passing the time."

"No."

"But you are carnivores."

"We are omnivores."

"Sorry. But you do eat meat."

"Yes. But we do not hunt. Our ancestors did, certainly, but that was centuries ago. As the Court has seen, we now grow meat that has no central nervous system."

"So you've never had the urge to kill something with your own hands?"

"Certainly not."

"The tape we saw of you and Dr. Calhoun talking aboard the mothership implies differently."

"I was engaging in idle speculation. I said something to the effect that perhaps we had given up too much in no longer hunting our own food, but I have no more desire to slaughter something to eat than you do, Mr. Rice."

"In general, is there any reason at all you'd want to kill something?"

"No."

"In particular, is there any reason you'd want to kill Dr. Calhoun?"

"None whatsoever."

"What did you think of Dr. Calhoun?"

"I liked him. He was my friend."

"How did you feel when you learned he was dead?"

"I was sad."

"Reports say you didn't look sad."

"I am physically incapable of shedding tears, Mr. Rice. But I expressed it in my own way. Clete was my friend, and I wish more than anything that he was not dead."

"Thank you, Mr. Hask." Dale sat down. "Your witness, counselor."

"Hask," said Ziegler, rising to her feet.

"Your Honor," said Dale, "objection! Mr. Hask is entitled to common courtesy. Ms. Ziegler should surely precede his name with an honorific."

Ziegler looked miffed, but apparently realized that any argument would just make her look even more rude.

"Sustained," said Pringle. "Ms. Ziegler, you will address the defendant as 'Mr. Hask' or 'sir.'"

"Of course, Your Honor," said Ziegler. "My apologies. Mr. Hask, you said you weren't alone with Dr. Calhoun at the time of his murder."

"Correct."

"But you had been alone with him on other occasions?"

"Certainly. We took the trip up to the mothership together."

"Yes, yes. But, beyond that, hadn't you and he spent time alone at the USC residence?"

"From time to time he and I happened to be the only people present in a given room."

"It was more than that, wasn't it? Is it not true that you often spent time alone with Dr. Calhoun—sometimes in his room at Valcour Hall, sometimes in your own?"

"We talked often, yes. Friends do that."

"So it would not be at all unusual for him to admit you to his room?"

"Clete had singular tastes in music. No one else would join him there when he was using his CD player."

"Singular tastes?"

Hask made a sound very much like human throat-clearing, then sang, "'Swing your partner, do-si-do—'"

The jury erupted into laughter.

"Thank you for that recital," said Ziegler coldly. "Mr. Hask, if you were often a guest of the deceased in his room, then why should we believe that you were not in his room when he was killed?"

"You should believe it because of the presumption of innocence, which is supposed to be the underpinning of your system of jurisprudence."

"Move to strike as nonresponsive," snapped Ziegler.

But Judge Pringle was smiling. "It seemed an excellent response to me, Ms. Ziegler. Overruled."

Ziegler turned back to Hask. "You admit, though, that you were frequently alone with Dr. Calhoun."

"'Occasionally' would be a more correct word."

"Fine. You were occasionally alone with him. And on the night that he died, you chose not to go see Stephen Jay Gould."

"That is correct."

"Why is that?"

"I knew that I would likely shed my skin that evening."

"And you wanted privacy for that?"

"Not at all. But I have observed the incredible attention you humans give to us Tosoks, even under the most banal circumstances. I felt it would be rude to create a distraction during Professor Gould's lecture by shedding my skin in public."

"Very considerate," said Ziegler sarcastically. "Yet you were not due to shed that day. How could you possibly know it was going to happen?"

"I had begun dropping scales earlier that day, and I was experiencing the itchy feeling that is normally associated with the shedding of skin. I grant that my shedding was unscheduled, but I *was* aware in advance that it was going to happen."

"And how do you explain the presence of objects resembling Tosok scales being found in Dr. Calhoun's room?"

"Objection," said Dale. "Calls for speculation."

"I'll allow it," said Pringle.

Hask's topknot waved slightly. "I visited him earlier in the day; perhaps I dropped some scales then. Or perhaps I had dropped scales elsewhere in the dormitory, and Dr. Calhoun, intrigued by them, picked them up and took them to his room for study; they could have then been knocked to the floor from his desk during whatever melee might have accompanied his murder."

"What were you doing while Dr. Calhoun was murdered?"

"I believe the People have been unable to establish precisely when that occurred," said Hask.

"Very well. What were you doing between eight p.m. and midnight last December twenty-second?"

"From eight p.m. to eight-thirty p.m., I watched TV."

"What program?"

"I believe I was 'channel surfing,' if I understand the term. I watched a variety of programs." His tuft parted in a Tosok shrug. "I *am* a male, after all."

The jury laughed. Ziegler's cheeks turned slightly red. "And after your channel surfing?"

"Meditation, mostly. And, of course, the shedding of my skin."

"Of course," said Ziegler. "The very convenient shedding of your skin."

"It is never convenient, Ms. Ziegler. I do not know if you are prone to any periodic biological function, but, trust me, such things are just plain irritating."

Judge Pringle was struggling to suppress a grin.

"The tool used to kill Dr. Calhoun," said Ziegler. "Was it yours?"

"It certainly looks as though he was killed with a Tosok monofilament, yes. It could have been mine or that of any of the others; it is a common tool—we have dozens of them aboard our starship. But even if it was mine, it was hardly an item I kept under lock and key."

Dale allowed himself a small smile. Hask was being a wonderful witness—funny, warm, reasonable. It was clear that he was winning the jury over.

Linda Ziegler must have been thinking the same thing. Dale could almost see her changing mental gears. Her manner became much more aggressive, her voice much harsher. "Mr. Hask, isn't it true that you were awoken prematurely from hibernation to deal with a shipboard emergency?"

"Yes."

"You were awoken because you were the crew member designated as 'First,' correct?"

"Yes."

"What about Seltar? What was her title?"

"She was Second—if a situation arose that I could not deal with alone, she, too, would be revived. I was more expendable than she, but she was more expendable than all the others."

"And the two of you were revived to deal with an accident affecting your ship?"

"Yes."

"Simultaneously? Or did you revive first?"

"Simultaneously. The on-board computer recognized that both of us would be required, and so began heating our hibernation pallets and blankets to awaken us."

"But Seltar died during repairs?"

"Yes."

"How?"

"She was working in the engineering compartment. A containment plate ruptured and blew out toward her. The impact killed her instantly."

"Was her body severely damaged?"

"No. The injury was to her head."

"And so what did you do with the body?"

"As per the standard procedures of my ship, I dissected it to harvest her organs, in case they might be needed for transplant."

"And didn't you find yourself aroused by the process of doing so?"

"No."

"Didn't you find the cutting of flesh pleasurable?"

"No."

"You didn't feel compelled to experience the same sensation again?"

"No."

"And once you arrived at Earth, weren't you curious about human anatomy?"

"No. Such curiosity would be prurient."

"Come now, Hask! You're an explorer, and you're on what is, to you, an alien world. Weren't you curious about the lifeforms you found here?"

"When you put it that way . . ."

"So you lied a moment ago when you said no."

"I misspoke."

"How many other times have you misspoken?"

"Objection!" said Dale. "Argumentative."

"Sustained," said Pringle.

"So you admit that you had recently experienced the opening up of a body, and that you were fascinated by human anatomy—even if such fascination was not polite by the standards of your race."

"You are overstating my curiosity."

"On December twenty-second, you found yourself with Dr. Calhoun while almost everyone else was away. Did your urge to see human innards get the best of you?"

"No."

"Did you pull out your cutting device and sever his leg?"

"No."

"And did you then slit open his belly and carve out his organs—just as you had carved out Seltar's organs?"

"No. No. None of what you say is true."

"You're a monster, aren't you, *Mister* Hask? A killer, and, even by the standards of your own people, a deviant."

"Objection!" said Dale.

"That is not true," said Hask. His topknot was flailing wildly.

"The one inescapable truth, though," said Ziegler, "is that Cletus Calhoun *is* dead."

Hask was quiet for several seconds. His topknot slowly calmed down. "That," agreed Hask, at last, "is the one inescapable truth."

TWENTY-FOUR

The media excitement was slightly—but only slightly—
less the next day, when the defense's case-in-chief continued.

"The defense calls the Tosok named Rendo," said Dale
Rice.

Rendo strode to the witness stand and was sworn in.

Dale rose. "Mr. Rendo, what is your job title aboard the
Tosok starship?"

"I am Sixth."

"And what specialty did you perform?"

"I am chief engineer."

"Prior to embarking on your starflight, where did you
live?"

"In the city known as Destalb<*pop*> on the planet my
people call home."

"And that planet," said Dale, "where is it located?"

"In the scheme of naming used by your species, it is part
of the Alpha Centauri system."

"Why did your people come to Earth?"

Rendo looked at the jurors. "In our skies, your sun

appears in the constellation you call Cassiopeia. From Earth, Cassiopeia looks like your capital letter W. From our world, your sun forms an extra jag off the W. We call that constellation the serpent. Your sun is the bright eye of the serpent; the rest of what you call Cassiopeia makes up the fainter tail." Rendo's tuft parted in the center. "Every young Tosok has looked up at the eye of the serpent, knowing that, save for Orange and Red, it is the nearest star. It is only natural that we should wish to visit here."

"Orange and Red?"

"Our names for Alpha Centauri B and C. We call Alpha Centauri A 'Yellow,' B 'Orange,' and C 'Red.'"

"What is the purpose of your mission?"

"We are explorers. We came in peace, and in friendship."

"Your mission is, to quote an Earth TV show, to seek out new life and new civilizations?"

"Yes."

"Something is wrong with your starship, the *Ka*<click>*tarsk,* isn't there?" Dale did a credible job of imitating the Tosok name.

"Yes."

"What, exactly?"

"The ship has two engines. The main one is a large fusion engine, used for interstellar travel. The other, smaller one, is a standard rocket engine, used for maneuvering within a star system. Although this secondary one still operates, the main one was damaged and requires repair."

"How was it damaged?"

"As we approached the orbit of your planet Neptune, a chunk of ice impacted the fusion engine."

"Is the damage irreparable?"

"No. With the proper parts, it can be fixed."

"Are you capable of manufacturing the proper parts aboard your mothership?"

"No."

"Could humans manufacture the proper parts here on Earth?" asked Dale.

"With guidance from us, yes. In fact, they are doing that even as we speak."

"Let me get this straight, Mr. Rendo. Without human goodwill, you and your crew are stranded here, unable to ever return home, is that right?"

"That is correct."

"So the last thing you Tosoks would want to do is to make us humans angry, lest we be unwilling to help you?"

"Objection," said Ziegler. "The witness can only speak on his own behalf."

"Sustained."

"Chief Engineer," said Dale, "speaking personally, since you require our help to get home, is it not in your best interest to treat us well?"

"Absolutely."

"Just so there's no misunderstanding, killing someone would not be considered treating them well in Tosok society, would it?"

"Like Captain Kelkad, I wish for you humans to think well of Tosok society. I would like to be able to tell you that murder is unknown on my world, but it is not. But committing murder most certainly would not be the appropriate thing to do to one from whom we wanted help."

"Thank you, Rendo. I'm sure the jury appreciates your candor and honesty. Your witness, Ms. Ziegler."

Linda Ziegler stood up and moved to the lectern. "Hello, Mr. Rendo."

"Hello, Ms. Ziegler."

"I'm curious about the accident that befell your ship."

"What would you like to know?"

"I wonder how it is that such advanced beings as yourselves would not have prepared for the possibility of collisions in space?"

"We were prepared for the possibility of micrometeoroid

collisions in the inner solar system, by which point our crew would be revived from its long sleep and therefore able to deal with them. We had expected the outer solar system to be virtually empty, and so our ship was undertaking only the most cursory of automated monitoring. We knew about your Oort cloud, of course—the halo of cometary material that surrounds your sun at a distance of up to one hundred thousand times your planet's orbital radius, but we had not known about the disk of cometary nuclei, ice, and other junk approximately forty times your orbital radius from the sun."

Ziegler consulted her notes, refreshing herself on the briefing she'd had on this topic. "We call that region 'the Kuiper belt.'" She looked at the jurors. "The jury may have heard of the asteroid belt between Mars and Jupiter, but that is a different phenomenon; the Kuiper belt is much farther out, past the orbit of Neptune." She turned back to Rendo. "Our theories of planetary formation suggest that any star with planets is likely to have such a region surrounding it."

"And we have learned from that insight," said Rendo. "Dr. Calhoun explained short-period comets to me, which, I understand are debris from the Kuiper belt that has fallen in toward the inner solar system. I suspect such comets are spectacular to behold, but my world has never seen one, at least not in all of Tosok recorded history." Rendo paused, as if considering how best to make his point. "Alpha Centauri is a triple star system, Ms. Ziegler. Each of these three stars has a gravitational effect on matter orbiting beyond a certain distance from the others. From what I learned from Dr. Calhoun, I would say it was likely that Alpha Centauri A, B, and C did indeed have Kuiper belts left over after they coalesced out of primordial dust and gas, just as such a belt was left over after your sun did the same. But the gravitational dance of A and B long ago cleared out each other's Kuiper belts. Without the clue of having seen short-period comets in our own sky, it never occurred to us that a disk of debris would ever have existed close in to our own sun, let alone around other suns. The accident did indeed occur as I described, we do indeed need human assistance, and as I told Mr. Rice, none of my people would have jeopardized that assistance by committing murder."

Ziegler realized she wasn't helping her cause. "No further questions," she said.

TWENTY-FIVE

Something about the courtroom discussion of the orbital dynamics of the Alpha Centauri system was bothering Frank Nobilio, but he wasn't exactly sure what. Of course, Frank wasn't an astronomer himself (his doctorate was in the history of science), but he'd taken one undergrad astronomy course. Still, there was something that didn't quite add up. In the past, when he'd had an astronomical question, Frank had simply put it to Cletus Calhoun, but now that wasn't possible.

Or was it?

Frank drove out to KCET, the Los Angeles PBS affiliate. The people there were only too happy to give him access to a viewing room, with a thirty-one-inch TV and a stereo VCR. Frank's memory was right: there *had* been an episode on this very topic. He sat in the dark, sipping Diet Pepsi from a can.

The screen filled with a corporate logo. "This program," said a female voice, "is made possible by a grant from the Johnson & Johnson Family of Companies, and by annual financial support from viewers like you."

The camera started tight on a campfire, then pulled back to show that it was surrounded by primitive, beetle-browed humans. Sparks rose from the fire, and the camera tilted up, following them as they continued up toward the moonless night sky. The sparks soon disappeared, but the sky was filled with stars, the Milky Way arching overhead. The camera kept tilting up, and the pounding rhythm of Jerry Lee Lewis's piano started in the background. Soon the camera was zooming into space, then the image flipped around to show Earth's nightside and, rising over its curving edge, the sun. The camera moved in toward the sun, its spotted face filling the screen, a prominence arcing up from the surface. Lewis's voice belted out the words "Goodness gracious! Great balls of fire!" The prominence fell back toward the surface of the sun, but the series title was left in flaming letters glowing in space: *Great Balls of Fire!*

The camera moved through space as the song continued, past a bloated red giant star adjacent to a black hole, which was pulling material from it; past a binary star system; past a pulsar flashing on and off; through the Pleiades, their blue light diffused by the nebulosity surrounding them . . .

A second title appeared: "With Cletus Calhoun." Jerry Lee Lewis sang the words "Great Balls of Fire!" once more, and the credit sequence ended. After a brief fade to black, the image of Clete himself came up, all gangly limbs and goofy smile. It was twilight, and he was standing on a boardwalk at the edge of a subtropical swamp.

A third title appeared: "Program 3: Just Over Yonder."

"Evening, y'all," said Clete, smiling. Frank felt his eyes stinging. God, how he missed that man. In the darkened room, it was almost like he was really there with him.

"Y'all know I come from the South," continued Clete, looking straight into the camera—straight at Frank. "From Tennessee, t'be 'zact. But tonight we've up and gone even farther south than that—just 'bout as far south as a body can go and still be in the good ol' U.S. of A. We're here in

Everglades National Park, right down near the tip o' Florida." In the background, an egret flew against the pink sky, its long legs and neck not unlike those of Calhoun himself. "We've come on down here to see something y'all can't see farther north." He pointed with a skinny arm and the camera followed until it had centered its view on a bright star, just above the horizon, framed between two bulrushes.

"That there's Alpha Centauri," said Clete. "Don't look like nothin' special, but it's the closest star to the Earth, 'cepting the Sun. It's 'round 'bout twenty-five trillion miles away—just over yonder. Our nearest neighbor in space."

Frank hit the fast-forward button. Clete zipped around silently, like a Keystone Kop. He was intercut with graphics showing the constellation of the Centaur. After a time Frank released the button.

"—but Alpha Centauri ain't just one star," said Clete. "It's actually three of 'em, all very close together. We call 'em— Alpha Centauri A, Alpha Centauri B, and—wait for it— Alpha Centauri C. Us astronomers—we got the souls of poets." His broad face split in a grin. "Actually, Alpha Centauri C is the closest of the bunch to us, so sometimes we *do* call it by a fancier name: Proxima Centauri—Proxima like in 'proximity.' Nuther thing y'all should know about astronomers: we like fifty-dollar words, 'cuz that's as close as most of us ever gets to a fifty-dollar bill." He grinned again.

The image changed to Mardi Gras in New Orleans, with Clete walking down a street at night. He paused to watch a man in gaudy dress juggling three flaming torches. "Course," said Clete, "when you got three stars close together, things get very interesting indeed." The camera zoomed in on the dancing torches, then pulled out of the fireplace inside Clete's mountain cabin—a common sight in the series. He was sitting behind an old wooden desk. A potbelly stove was in the background, and a hunting rifle hung on the wooden wall behind him. A bowl of fruit sat on the desktop.

"A and B are big stars," Clete said. He picked a grapefruit

out of the fruit bowl. "This here could be A—a big yellow star, very much like our own sun. 'Fact, A's a tetch bigger than our sun, and about fifty percent brighter."

He reached into the fruit bowl and pulled out an orange. "Now this here, this could be B—a smaller, dimmer, orange star. B's about ten percent smaller than our sun, and not even half as bright—kinda like my cousin Beau." Clete winked at the camera. He rummaged around in the fruit bowl, and found a cherry. "And C—well, shoot, C's just a l'il peckerwood of a star, a cold, dim red dwarf. Dang thing's so small and dim, nobody even noticed it was there till 1911."

"Now, A and B—they orbit 'round each other like this." He moved the grapefruit and the orange to demonstrate. "But the distance between 'em ain't constant." The sound of a buzz saw had started in the background. "Y'all know how I hate jargon, but here's one little bit that'll help us out." He turned and shouted into the distance, "Hey, you! Y'all stop that, hear?" The buzz saw died down. Clete then looked back at the lens and grinned again. "For things that are purty close together—close enough for shoutin'—we astronomers use the 'Hey, you!' as our yardstick. Okay, truth be told, it's really an 'AU' not a 'Hey, you!' AU stands for 'astronomical unit,' and it's equal to the distance 'tween the Earth and the sun." A diagram appeared, illustrating this.

"Well, when they's as far apart as they ever get, Centauri A" (he held up the grapefruit with one fully extended arm) "and Centauri B" (he held up the orange in his other fully extended arm) "are thirty-five AUs apart. That's 'round 'bout the distance 'tween here and Uranus."

He paused and grinned, as if contemplating making a joke about the planet's name, but then shook his head in a "let's not go there" expression.

"But when A and B are as close as they ever get" (he drew his arms together) "they is just eleven AUs apart—practically spittin' distance. It takes 'em about eighty years to orbit round each other."

He placed the grapefruit and the orange on the desktop and then picked up the cherry. "Now, Centauri C is a bunch farther away from A and B." He used his thumb to flick the cherry clear across the room and right out an open window. "It's a wallopin' thirteen *thousand* AUs from the other two. The little guy might not even be really bound by gravity to the others, but if it is, it more'n likely takes a million years or so to revolve around them in what's probably a highly elliptical orbit—"

Frank hit the pause button, and sat in the dark, thinking.

TWENTY-SIX

"Our next order of business," said Dale Rice, leaning back in his leather chair, "is the missing body parts."

Something was different about Dale's office. It took Frank a minute to realize what it was. His normal chair was now on the left, and the Tosok chair was on the right; the cleaning staff must have moved them in order to vacuum the rich brown carpet. Indeed, in the late-afternoon sunlight, the paths made by the vacuum were clearly visible.

On the table across the room, Dale's latest jigsaw puzzle had gaping holes in it.

"I wish we had some idea why those parts were taken," said Frank.

Dale nodded. He'd put some witnesses related to them on his witness list, but hadn't made up his mind whether he'd actually call them all. "The question we've put to our shadow jury is this," he said. "'Given the unusual choice of missing body parts—an eye, the throat, the appendix—are you more or less likely to think an alien was involved in the crime?' The answer, of course, is more likely."

"Then do we do any good by examining the question of the missing parts at all?" asked Frank.

"Well, you can be sure Linda is going to harp on them during her closing argument, so . . ."

Frank was quiet for a moment, thinking. Suddenly he sat up straight. "What about the Simpson case?" he said. "The DNA in the Simpson case."

"What about it?" said Dale.

"Well, you said the Simpson criminal jury simply ignored that entire portion of the evidence. On the one hand, you had Robin Cotton from CellMark presenting the prosecution's view of the DNA evidence, and on the other, you had all the defense experts presenting their view of it. You said the jury essentially just threw up its hands and said, hell, if these experts can't find the truth in it, how can we? And so they ended up simply ignoring that entire line of evidence."

Dale spread his arms, humoring the layman. "But Linda didn't present anything for us to counter about those body parts during the prosecution's case-in-chief."

"That's true," said Frank, "but what if *we* present conflicting testimony about those parts? If we put people on the stand giving two mutually contradictory interpretations, the jury might still throw the whole line of evidence out. A human could have used the Tosok cutting tool, after all; the missing body parts are the thing that points most directly to an alien perpetrator—and getting the jury to ignore them is the best thing we can do."

Dale opened his mouth to say something, closed it, then just sat there, frowning thoughtfully.

The next day, Dale Rice stepped up to the lectern in Judge Pringle's ninth-floor courtroom. "The defense calls Dr. James Wills."

Wills, a brown-haired white man in his late forties, was

sitting in the third row, doing *The New York Times* cross-word puzzle in ink with an antique silver fountain pen. He put the cap back on the pen, rose, and was sworn in: "James MacDonald Wills," he said. "That's James the usual way, although I'm commonly called Jamie, M-A-C-capital-D-Donald, and Wills, W-I-L-L-S."

Dale went through the business of establishing Wills' credentials—he was an anatomy professor at UC Irvine. Wills stood five-eight and weighed maybe a hundred and fifty-five pounds. Frank noticed he wore no watch, but was remarkably well dressed for a professor.

"Dr. Wills," said Dale, "the prosecution has spent a lot of time on the missing parts—the items apparently removed form Dr. Calhoun's body by whatever person killed him. Would you start by telling the jury what the significant characteristics are of the human throat and lower jaw?"

"Certainly," said Wills, who had a pleasant, deep voice. "The shape of the cavity made by the throat and the lower jaw is what allows us to produce the complex range of sounds we're capable of. In other words, it makes human speech possible."

"Is the throat shape significant in any other way?"

"Well, the Adam's apple serves as a secondary sexual characteristic in humans; it's much more prominent in adult males."

"Anything else?"

"I'm not sure I know what you mean."

Dale was pleased with Wills's performance; the defense could play the "see, we don't rehearse expert testimony" game every bit as well as the People could. "Well," said Dale, "consider a chimpanzee's throat and a human throat. What differences are there?"

Wills adjusted his wire-frame glasses. "The angle made by the path between the lips and the voice box is quite different. In a human, it's a right angle; in a chimp, it's a gentle curve."

"Does that cause any problems?"

"Not for the chimp," said Wills, grinning widely, inviting everyone in the court to share in his joke.

"How do you mean?"

"In humans, there's a space above the larynx in which food can get caught. We can choke to death while eating; a chimp can't."

"Thank you, Dr. Wills. Now, what about the appendix? We've all heard of it, of course, but can you tell us a bit about it?"

"Certainly. The appendix is a hollow tube of lymphoid tissue between two and twenty centimeters long, and about as thick as a pencil. In other words, it looks like a worm— which is why we call it the vermiform process; *vermiform* is Latin for 'wormlike.' One end of this worm is attached to the cecum, which is the pouch that forms the beginning of the large intestine. The other end is closed."

"And what does the appendix do?"

Wills blinked his blue eyes. "The common wisdom is that it does nothing at all; it's just a vestigial organ. Our primate ancestors were herbivores, and in its original form, the appendix was probably of some use in aiding digestion— modern herbivores have an extended cecum that resembles a longer version of our appendix. But for us, the appendix does little, if anything."

"And are there any dangers associated with the appendix?"

"Oh, yes. It's prone to infection and inflammation. About one out of every fifteen people will come down with appendicitis during their lifetimes."

"This is a minor condition, no?"

"No. It's a major, excruciating, and potentially fatal problem. Usually, the appendix has to be surgically removed."

"Thank you, Professor. Your witness, Ms. Ziegler."

Ziegler consulted briefly with her second chair, Trina Diamond, then shrugged. "No questions."

"All right," said Judge Pringle. "In view of the lateness of the hour, we'll recess until ten a.m. tomorrow morning." She looked at the jury box. "Please remember my admonitions to you. Don't discuss the case among yourselves, don't form any opinions about the case, don't conduct any deliberations, and don't allow anyone to communicate with you regarding the case." She rapped her gavel. "Court is in recess."

Hask still spent his nights in his room at Valcour Hall. As usual, Frank escorted him back home, along with a total of four LAPD officers—two in the same car as Frank and Hask, and two others in a second cruiser. The one problem with Valcour Hall was that although the building had been finished, the parking lot adjacent to it hadn't been surfaced yet, and so the police cruiser had to let Hask out about two hundred yards from the residence. Wooden stakes had been driven into the grass all around the dorm, with yellow "Police Line—Do Not Cross" tape stretched between them. Still, every day after the trial, hundreds of students, faculty members, and other Angelenos could be seen waiting behind the line for a glimpse of Hask. Frank and Hask left the police cruiser together. As usual, Frank was having trouble keeping up with the Tosok, whose stride was much longer than his. It was only four-forty in the afternoon. The sun was still well up the bowl of the cloudless sky.

To Frank's ears, the two sounds seemed to begin simultaneously, but, of course, one of them had to have come first. The first sound was a cracking so loud it hurt the ears, like thunder or bone breaking or a frozen lake shattering beneath the weight of a stranded man. It echoed off walls of glass and stone, reverberating for several seconds.

The second sound was high-pitched and warbling, unlike anything Frank had ever heard before. It was partly the sound of shattering glass, and partly the sound of train wheels screeching to a halt on metal tracks, and partly the wail of a hundred phones left too long off the hook.

Frank had thought—*hoped*—the first sound had been a car backfiring, but it wasn't. In a blur of motion, two of the four police officers surged forward, running toward the crowd of people behind the police line. They had a man to the ground almost at once. Frank looked down at his own chest, and saw a spiderweb splash of pink across his jacket, shirt, and tie.

And then he realized what the second sound had been.

Hask was still standing, but as Frank watched he crumpled as if in slow motion to the ground, each of his legs folding first at its lower joint then its upper one. His torso tumbled backward, and the alien's scream died as the square of his mouth diminished in size until nothing was left but the horizontal slit that marked the outer opening. He continued to fall, his rear arm splaying out behind him. Frank moved forward, trying to catch him, but the Tosok's collapse was completed before the human reached him.

The assailant—a white man in his late twenties—was pinned to the ground. He was yelling, "Is the devil dead? Is the devil dead?"

The bullet hole in Hask's tunic was obvious, surrounded by a pink carnation of Tosok blood. What to do was less obvious, though. Frank was certified in CPR—anyone who got to spend time alone with the president was required to be. Spectators were ignoring the police tape now, and had rushed to reach the downed alien, clustering around him in a circle. Frank leaned in and placed his ear next to one of Hask's breathing orifices. Air *was* being expelled; he could feel it on his cheek. But he had no idea where to check for a pulse. Not much blood had spilled out of the wound—possibly a sign that the being's four hearts had stopped pumping.

Frank looked up, about to tell someone to call for an ambulance, but one of the cops was already on his cruiser's radio, doing that. Frank reached into his own jacket pocket and pulled out his cellular flip phone. He hit the speed-dial key for the cellular that had been given to Captain Kelkad, and then handed the phone to the other officer, not waiting for Kelkad to answer. Frank bent down over Hask again. "Hask," he said. "Hask, can you hear me?"

There was no response from Hask. Frank loosened his tie and pulled it up over his head, then wadded it up into a ball and used it as a pressure bandage on the entrance wound. He had no idea if that was the right thing to do, given how little he knew about Tosok physiology, but—

"Frank," said the cop. "I've got Kelkad on the phone." She handed the cellular to him. He took it in his left hand while continuing to lean on the wadded-up tie with his right.

"Kelkad, what should I do?" said Frank. "Hask has been shot."

Kelkad and the other Tosoks were in separate cars, on their way back from the Criminal Courts Building. The connection was staticky. There was a long pause, then a spate of faint Tosok language—but not in Kelkad's voice— then some more of the alien tongue; this time it *was* Kelkad. And then the voice of the translator. "Describe the injury, and the way in which it was made." Frank realized Kelkad had to be moving the cellular back and forth between his translator and his ear slit.

Frank lifted his hand up off his pressure bandage. Although the tie was covered with Tosok blood—which was crystallizing, like a thin layer of ice, rather than clotting the way human blood did—the total volume of bleeding seemed to be tiny. "He's been shot by a metal projectile—presumably lead. He's lying on his back, is still breathing, but appears to be unconscious. The bullet entered between the front arm and the left leg, about eight inches below the breathing orifice. I can't tell what angle it moved through the body. I was applying pressure to the wound, but it seems to have stopped bleeding, and the blood is crystallizing."

There was a sound from Kelkad, and noises from the

translator—plus traffic sounds, and a siren. The car Kelkad was in was now rushing to the scene.

"You will probably not harm him by rolling him over onto his front," said Kelkad. "Did the bullet go all the way through the body?"

Frank handed the phone to the cop and grabbed the upper part of Hask's left leg with both hands, feeling the odd alien skeleton beneath the skin, then rolling him ninety degrees. He examined the back of Hask's dun-colored tunic, but could find no exit hole. He looked at the cop. "Tell him there's no sign that the bullet came out."

She did so, then she listened for a moment. "Kelkad asks you to confirm that lead is atomic number eighty-two."

"What?" said Frank. "Christ, I have no idea."

"He says lead is highly toxic to Tosoks. He says the bullet will have to be removed within the hour."

"Where's that damn ambulance?" said Frank.

"It's coming," said the other cop, who had rejoined them. He pointed in the distance. A white van with flashing lights on its roof was approaching.

Frank rose to his feet. One of the other police officers came over to him. "The assailant's name is Donald Jensen, according to his ID. I called it in; he's got a small record—disturbing the peace, mostly."

Frank looked over at the man, who was now on his feet with his hands cuffed behind his back. He was clean-cut, with short blond hair, and he was wearing a sports jacket with patches on the elbows. The left side of his face was badly scraped from where the officers had forced him down onto a paved walkway. His blue eyes were wide. "Death to all the devils!" he shouted.

The ambulance pulled up at the curb, and two burly men got out. They immediately opened the vehicle's rear doors and brought a stretcher over to Hask.

Just behind the ambulance, the cars carrying the other Tosoks pulled up on the access road. Their doors flew open, and the six Tosoks came running across the field with giant strides. Lagging far behind them were the police officers who were supposed to be their escorts.

Frank looked like he expected a lynching. "Get him out of here," he ordered the cops, pointing at the blond man. "Get him out of here right now."

The cops nodded, and hustled the assailant into a car. Meanwhile the two ambulance attendants had transferred the alien to their stretcher and were now lifting him off the ground.

The Tosoks arrived. Their breathing orifices seemed to be spasming, and they each lifted their arms away from their bodies, possibly to help dissipate heat. Kelkad and Stant came immediately over to Hask and began peering at the wound. They chatted among themselves, then Stant's translator spoke: "There is insufficient time to get him up to the mothership. Your germs are no problem for us, so we do not need a particularly sterile place to work. But we will need surgical implements."

"We're taking him to the Los Angeles County-USC Medical Center," said one of the attendants. "It's a huge hospital; they'll have everything you'll need there."

"I'm coming with you," said Frank.

They got the alien body into the back of the ambulance, and then Kelkad and one of the attendants climbed in the rear door. The other attendant got into the driver's seat and Frank hopped into the passenger's seat. The ambulance took off, a police car carrying Stant providing an escort.

"Frank," said Kelkad's voice, from the back of the ambulance. Frank turned around and looked into the rear compartment. "Who is responsible for this act, Frank?"

"We have the man," said Frank. "He sounded like a religious fanatic to me. Don't worry, Kelkad. He will pay for his crimes."

"Shooting one of our people could be construed as an act of war," said Kelkad.

"I know, I know. Believe me, you will have every apology possible, and I promise you the man will be punished."

"A fanatic, you said?"

"He called Hask a devil—a demon, a supernatural creature."

"His lawyer will try the insanity defense, then."

The ambulance's tires squealed as the driver took it through a tight turn. Frank shrugged. "It's possible."

"See to it that my faith in this thing you call justice is not betrayed," said Kelkad.

They continued on to the hospital, siren wailing.

TWENTY-SEVEN

Frank and Kelkad got out of the ambulance at emer-gency admitting. "Of all our crew, the best choice for performing the surgery now is Stant, our biochemist."

Stant had arrived in one of the police cruisers at the medical center moments after the ambulance did. He was still rubbing his back arm, which had been crushed behind him in the car's unmodified seat, but his tuft moved forward in agreement. "I can do the operation," he said, "but I will need a human to assist me—not so much in procedures, but in equipment." He looked out at the large crowd of doctors and nurses who had gathered in the ER lobby, as well as the many often-bloodied, mostly Latino, mostly indigent patients waiting for treatment. "Is there someone who will help?"

"Yes, certainly," said a black man of about fifty.

"I'd be glad to," said a white man in his forties.

A third person simply cleared her throat. "Sorry, boys—rank hath its privileges. I'm Carla Hernandez, chief of surgery here." She looked at Stant. "I'd be honored to assist you." Hernandez was in her mid-forties, with short-cropped salt-and-pepper hair.

"Very well. Let us get to work. Do you have devices for seeing into the body?"

"X rays. Ultrasound."

"X rays are acceptable. We will need pictures to determine the depth of the bullet."

Hernandez nodded. "I'll take Hask down to radiology, then prep him for surgery." She pointed to the black man who had volunteered a few moments before. "Paul, take Stant to surgical supplies and let him select whatever tools he'll need . . ."

The operation went quickly. Stant was obviously a practiced surgeon—so practiced that it occurred to Frank, watching from the packed observation gallery above, that he would have been quite capable of doing the dissection of Calhoun.

There was very little blood, despite the deep incision Stant made. The other doctors watching with Frank seemed amused by the way Stant operated: he held the x ray up to his rear pair of eyes with his back hand, and watched the operation with his front eyes, wielding the scalpel with his front hand. It took about eight minutes to complete the extraction of the bullet, which Stant pulled out with tongs and dropped into a stainless-steel pan Hernandez was holding.

"How do you close wounds?" asked Stant. His translated voice was difficult for Frank to make out over the staticky speakers in the observation gallery.

"With suture," said Hernandez. "We sew the wound shut."

Stant was quiet for a moment, perhaps appalled by the barbarism of it all. "Oh," he said at last. "You can do it, then." He stepped aside, and Hernandez moved in over the wound, and, in a matter of about two minutes, had it neatly closed.

"When will he regain consciousness?" said Hernandez.

"Do you have acetic acid?"

"Acet—do you mean vinegar? Umm, maybe in the cafeteria."

"Get some. A small amount given orally should wake him up." Stant looked at Hernandez. "Thank you for your help."

"It was an honor," said Hernandez.

Hask was still recuperating the next day, and so court could not sit; the defendant had to be present for all testimony. But Dale and Linda Ziegler started the day in Judge Pringle's chambers. "Your Honor," said Ziegler, "the People would like to move for a mistrial."

Judge Pringle was obviously expecting this. She nodded, and began writing on a legal pad. "On what grounds?"

"On the grounds that, given that our jury is not sequestered, its members have doubtless become aware of the fact that an attempt has been made on the defendant's life."

Dale spoke firmly. "Your Honor, the defense is quite content with the current jury. We vigorously oppose the motion to throw so many months of work—not to mention so many thousands of taxpayer dollars—out the window."

Ziegler's voice had taken on an earnest note. "Your Honor, surely seeing the defendant staggering into the courtroom all bandaged up will cause the jury to feel undue sympathy toward him, sympathy that could color their verdict in this case."

Judge Pringle raised her eyebrows. "You're not going to find another twelve people anywhere who haven't heard about the shooting of Hask, Ms. Ziegler."

"And," said Dale, "surely knowing that at least one person felt so strongly that Hask was evil would have a prejudicial effect *against* my client."

"Your Honor, if counsel thinks it's prejudicial, then he should be arguing for a mistrial, too," said Ziegler sharply. "The reason he isn't is obvious: this fanatic, this Jensen, clearly felt Hask was going to go free, or he wouldn't have bothered trying to kill him. His act is a clear signal to the jury of how they are being read."

"Being read by *one* person," said Dale, also facing Pringle. "Anyway, I'm sure there's no need to remind my colleague of this, but Hask was supposedly under the protection of the LAPD when the attempt was made on his life. The State is at fault here; let's not compound the State's damage to my client by asking him to go through another trial."

"But the prejudicial effect—"

"As Ms. Ziegler surely knows, Your Honor, I've built my whole career on believing that juries can rise above their prejudices. Ms. Katayama and I have faith in this one."

"What's the case law?" asked Judge Pringle. "I can think of cases where the defendant was killed during the trial, but I can't think of any offhand where he was shot but survived."

"We haven't found anything yet," said Ziegler.

"Well, unless you get me something compelling, I'm inclined to agree with Mr. Rice. Mistrials are expensive."

"In that case, Your Honor," said Ziegler, "may I request a special jury instruction?"

Drucilla Pringle frowned, but then nodded. "Agreed. I'll advise them that they are to avoid any feelings of sympathy because the defendant is injured." She turned to Dale. "And I'll also instruct them that they are in no way to take the fact that Hask was considered a devil by one man to be any indication of his guilt."

TWENTY-EIGHT

Carla Hernandez was never home during the day to watch the live coverage of the Hask trial. CNN did an hour-long recap at nine p.m. Pacific, but that was more than she had time for; her job as chief of surgery required at least an eighty-hour week. Besides, she'd gotten sick enough of Greta Van Susteren and Roger Cossack during the two Simpson trials. Fortunately, every L.A. station had its own nightly special on the trial; she was partial to Bob Pugsley's 10:30 p.m. commentary on Channel 13.

She'd thought that after she'd assisted Stant in operating on Hask, her involvement with the Tosoks would cease. But she'd seen something when prepping Hask for surgery, something that bothered her. Something she couldn't explain.

There, on the TV, was Dale Rice, surrounded by a hundred reporters outside the courthouse. They were shouting questions at him about his client's chances and the effect the shooting would have on the case.

Of course, Rice would have an unlisted home number—that was something most doctors and lawyers had in common. But he must have a business listing—although

Hernandez had no idea what Rice's firm's name was. Still, it was worth a try. She got up and found her phone book.

A firm called Rice and Associates did indeed have offices on West Second Street.

She'd call them tomorrow.

Frank came by Rice and Associates each morning at eight-thirty for a quick update on the day's strategy. When he entered Dale's office this morning, Dale leaned back in his chair and interlocked his thick fingers behind his head. "I think Stant did it."

Frank's eyebrows went up. "Why?"

"Well, he took the Fifth on testifying about blood—so he's got something to hide. And, more than that, he's trained as a surgeon—he performed the bullet extraction from Hask, after all. The murderer was somebody who clearly had medical skill."

"But what about his alibi?"

Dale shrugged. "His alibi is entirely other Tosoks. They were all seated alone at the back of the lecture hall—they'd put in Tosok chairs for them behind the last row of normal chairs. Stephen Jay Gould's lecture was illustrated with slides, and it lasted seventy-five minutes, before the house-lights were brought up for a question-and-answer session. The theater is only five minutes from the dorm. Stant could have easily slipped out—excusing himself to use the bath-room, maybe—done the deed, and returned. He's got his own key for the dorm; he could have entered through the back door."

"Unseen?" said Frank. "Going clear across the campus?"

"It was a dark night, and it was during Christmas holidays—the university was mostly deserted."

Frank scratched his chin. "I suppose. So you want to demonstrate that there's enough slack in the prosecution's time line for this to be possible?"

Dale nodded. "It's a little late for a new strategy, but the shadow jury is still saying Hask is almost certainly going to be convicted if we don't come up with something new; I'd hoped the shooting of Hask would have swayed them toward leniency, but apparently it didn't."

"You won't get any help from the Tosoks if they're shielding Stant—and I'm not sure why they'd want to protect him at the expense of Hask."

"Hask said it himself," said Dale. "He is 'First'—the most expendable member of the crew. Kelkad may have decided that if someone has to take the fall for this, it should be Hask."

Frank considered this, then nodded. "And Hask seems to be a loyal enough officer that he's willing to abide by that."

"Exactly." Dale looked at his antique brass desk clock. "We better get going."

"Rice and Associates."

"Hello. Dale Rice, please."

"Mr. Rice has already left for the courthouse. Would you like to leave a message?"

"Umm, yes. Sure. Could you tell him that Dr. Carla Hernandez called. I'm the chief of surgery at Los Angeles County-USC Medical Center, and I assisted in the operation on his client Hask."

"I'll give him the message."

"Good morning, everyone," said Judge Pringle. **"On the** record now in *California* v. *Hask*. The jury is present, as is the defendant and his counsel, Mr. Rice and Ms. Katayama. The People are represented by Ms. Ziegler and Ms. Diamond."

Judge Pringle looked up—and something caught her eye. A small commotion in the bank of chairs set aside for the

Tosoks. Stant had folded his front arm at its upper and lower elbows so that his hand could reach to the area between that arm and his left leg. He used one of the four fingers on that hand to pry free a diamond-shaped scale from there; it had apparently already begun to pop loose on its own. The scale fell to the floor. Stant picked some more at the spot where the scale had come from, and an adjacent patch of six or seven scales came free. He used the stubby, flat ends of his fingers to scratch the white skin underneath, and his tuft rippled back and forth, conveying some emotion, although Judge Pringle couldn't say what it was.

"You there," she said. "The Tosok in the middle of the first row."

Stant looked up. "My name is Stant."

"Are you all right?"

"I am fine, but—"

"What's happening to your skin?"

A rift had begun to appear in Stant's hide, continuing down from the exposed patch where the scales had come free. The split had a zigzag edge, neatly following the edges of the diamond scales.

"I am shedding. Apologies; I should leave the courtroom." He rose to his feet.

"This isn't an intensely personal or private experience, is it?" said Pringle.

"Of course not—it relates to the *outer* body, after all. Still—"

"Then do not feel pressure to leave."

Stant hesitated for a moment, then sat back down. But as he went down, Dale Rice got up, almost like a counterbalance. "Your Honor, surely this shouldn't be displayed in front of the jury."

Linda Ziegler apparently hadn't been sure what to make of it, either, so she simply fell into the comfortable old role of disputing whatever her opponent said. "On the contrary, Your Honor, had such a demonstration been possible at the

Court's convenience, I would have arranged for it as part of the People's case-in-chief."

"But your case-in-chief is over," said Dale, "and it's time—"

"Enough," said Pringle. "Mr. Stant is hardly being deliberately disruptive. He will remain in the courtroom. If need be, *I'll* call him as a witness."

Dale was fuming. Across the room, Stant had brought his back hand around to the front side of his body, and was now using both arms to help widen the gap. The old skin peeled away without difficulty, although it did make a sound like Scotch tape being pulled off a hard surface. Stant worked the joints where his legs and arms met his torso back and forth, and soon a second split and then a third appeared in his old hide. Meanwhile, he was now using his fingers to scratch itches in a variety of newly exposed places.

It took a total of about fifteen minutes for Stant's entire old hide to be shed, and everyone in the courtroom watched. Most were fascinated, although one man with a severe sunburn was wincing throughout. The hide came off in four separate pieces. Stant wadded them up and stuffed them into a canvas carrying bag that he'd had stored under his chair. His new skin was white with just a tinge of yellow, and it glistened brightly under the harsh fluorescent lights.

Judge Pringle appeared satisfied. "Fascinating," she said. "Now, on to today's testimony. Mr. Rice, you may call a witness . . ."

TWENTY-NINE

Dale pushed open the door to his office and held it open for Frank, who walked in and took his now familiar seat. Dale looked at his watch—5:40 p.m—then picked up a bottle of brandy from the bar along the back wall of the room. He held it up so that Frank could see it. Frank nodded, and Dale poured some into two snifters. He walked back toward his desk, paused to hand one snifter to Frank, then took his seat in the high-backed leather chair.

Dale's receptionist had left a small stack of yellow telephone-message slips on his desk, neatly squared off in a pile. After taking a sip of brandy, he picked up the pile and glanced at each one. His broker. Larry King's people. Someone from the NAACP asking him to give a guest lecture. And then—

"Frank, forgive me, but I should return this one. It's Carla Hernandez."

Frank's mouth had already formed the word "who?" but he yanked it back before giving it voice, recognizing the name.

Dale punched out seven digits on his phone. "Hello," he

said. "Dale Rice calling for Dr. Hernandez. No, I'll hold. Thanks." He covered the mouthpiece. "She's on another call," he said to Frank, then: "Hello? Dr. Hernandez? It's Dale Rice, returning your call. Sorry to be so late getting back to you—I've been in court all day. No, no, that's okay. What? No, I suspect it would be all right to tell me. What's that? *Three* of them? Are you sure?" Frank was now leaning forward on his chair, openly intrigued. "They couldn't have been anything else? Did you take pictures? No, no I suppose not. They don't show up in the x rays, do they? But you're sure that's what they are? Okay. No, you were right to tell me. Thank you. I'll be in touch. Thanks. Bye." He put down the handset.

"What is it?" said Frank.

"I'm not sure. Maybe the break we've been looking for."

Dale had used the Reverend Oren Brisbee as an expert witness in other cases—no one could captivate a jury like a Baptist preacher. Brisbee was perhaps an odd choice, given his public clamoring for the death penalty for Hask. Still, it wasn't out of any presumption that Hask was guilty. And so:

"Reverend Brisbee," said Dale, "one of Dr. Calhoun's eyes was missing. Will you tell the Court what's significant, in your view, about the human eye, please?"

Brisbee smiled broadly, as if warming to a favorite topic. "Ah, my brother, the human eye! Testament to God's genius! Proof of divine creation! Of all the marvels of the universe, perhaps none bears stronger testament than the human eye to the lie of evolution."

"Why is that, Reverend?"

"Why, Brother Dale, it's simply because nothing so complex as the human eye could possibly have evolved by chance. The evolutionists would have us believe that life progresses in tiny incremental stages, a little at a time, instead of having been created full-blown by God. But the eye—well, the eye is a perfect counterexample. It could not have evolved step-by-step."

Someone in the courtroom snickered, presumably at the mental picture of eyes marching along. Brisbee ignored the sound. "The evolutionists," he went on, his voice filling the courtroom as it had so many churches, "say complex structures, such as feathers, must have evolved by steps: first as scales for insulation, which then perhaps elongated into a frayed coat to aid running animals in catching small insects inside this fringe, and only then, fortuitously, would the proto-bird discover, lo and behold, that they were also useful for flight. I don't believe that for one moment, but it's the kind of stuff they spout. But that argument falls down completely when we contemplate God's masterwork, the human eye! What good is half an eye? What good is a quarter of an eye? An eye either *is* an eye, or it isn't; it can't evolve in steps."

Brisbee beamed out at the courtroom. They were all his flock. "Consider the finest camera you can buy today. It's still not nearly as effective as our eyes. Our eyes adjust automatically to wide variations in lighting—we can see by the light of a crescent moon, or we can see by the brightest summer's sun. Our eyes can adjust easily between natural light, incandescent light, and fluorescent light, whereas a photographer would have to change filters and film to accommodate each of those. And our eyes are capable of perceiving depth better than any pair of cameras can, even when aided by a computer. A basketball player can routinely determine the precise distance to the hoop, throwing perfect shot after perfect shot. Yes, I can see why the Tosok took the human's eye as a souvenir—"

"Now, now, Reverend," said Dale. "You don't know that that's what happened."

"I can see," continued Reverend Brisbee, somewhat miffed, "why anyone from anywhere would admire the human eye, as a sterling example of God's craftsmanship."

At nine a.m. the next morning, Dale and Frank entered Judge Pringle's chambers. Linda Ziegler was already there, as were juror number 209—a pudgy white woman of forty-one—and a man Dale had seen around the courthouse over the years but didn't know. A moment later, Judge Pringle entered, accompanied by a stenographer. Pringle waited for the stenographer to get set up, then said, "Mr. Wong, will you please introduce yourself to the others?"

"Ernest Wong, representing Juror 209."

"Thank you," said the judge. "Let the record show that also present are Ms. Ziegler for the People, and Mr. Rice for Mr. Hask, who is not here. Also present with my permission is Dr. Frank Nobilio, American delegate to the Tosok entourage. Now, Juror 209, good morning to you."

"Good morning, Judge," said Juror 209, her voice nervous.

"Okay," said Judge Pringle, "Juror 209, your attorney is here. Feel free to stop me anytime you want to consult with Mr. Wong, and Mr. Wong, of course anytime you wish to interpose an objection or make an inquiry, you are entitled to do so."

"Thank you," said Wong.

"Now, Juror 209, some questions have been raised." Pringle held up a hand, palm out. "I'm not saying you've done anything wrong, but when questions are raised relating to juror conduct or juror impaneling, the appellate law here in California requires me to make an investigation, so that's what we're doing. Okay? Okay. You were asked to fill out a questionnaire prior to serving on this jury, correct?"

"That's right."

"Did you fill out the questionnaire truthfully?"

"Objection!" said Wong. "Calls for self-incrimination."

Judge Pringle frowned. "Very well. Juror 209, we have a problem here. Question 192 on the jury questionnaire asked if you had ever seen a flying saucer. Do you recall that question?"

"I don't recall a question using that term, no, Your Honor."

Judge Pringle looked even more irritated. "Well, let me read the question to you." She rummaged on her desk, looking for the questionnaire. Linda Ziegler rose to her feet, her copy in hand. Pringle motioned for her to bring it forward. The judge took the sheaf of papers, flipped through it until she found the appropriate page, and read, "'Have you ever seen a UFO?' Do you recall that question?"

"Yes."

"You recall it now," said Pringle.

"I've always recalled it—but you asked me about flying saucers, not UFOs."

Pringle was getting more annoyed by the minute. "What's the difference?"

"A UFO is an *unidentified* flying object. By definition, it's something the nature of which you don't know."

"And you put on your survey that you'd never seen a UFO."

"That's right."

"The Court has received a letter from a member of the Bay Area chapter of MUFON. That's the . . . the—"

"The Mutual UFO Network," said Juror 209.

"Yes," said Pringle. "A member of the Bay Area chapter of the Mutual UFO Network, saying that you were a speaker at one of their meetings about eight years ago. Is that true?"

"Yes. I lived in San Rafael back then."

"What was the subject of your talk?"

"My abduction experience."

"You were kidnapped?" said Pringle.

"Not that kind of abduction. I was taken aboard an alien spacecraft."

Judge Pringle visibly moved away from the woman, shifting her weight on her chair. "Taken aboard an alien spacecraft," she repeated, as if the words had been unclear the first time.

"That's correct, Your Honor."

"But you specified on your questionnaire that you had never seen a UFO."

"And I never have. What I saw was wholly identified. It was an alien spaceship."

"Alien—as in from another world?"

"Well, actually, I believe the aliens come from another dimension—a parallel time track, if you will. There's a lot of good evidence for that interpretation."

"So you're making a distinction between a UFO— something unknown—and an alien spaceship?"

"Yes."

"Surely you're splitting hairs, Juror 209."

"I do not believe so, ma'am."

"You felt completely comfortable denying having ever seen a UFO on your jury questionnaire?"

"Yes."

"But surely the spirit of the question—"

"I can't comment on the spirit of the question. I simply answered the question that was asked of me."

"But you knew what information we were looking for."

"With all due respect, Your Honor, it says right on the questionnaire, it says—may I see that? May I see the questionnaire?" Pringle handed it to her. "It says right here, right at the top, it says, 'There are no right or wrong answers. Do not try to anticipate the answers likely to get you placed on or removed from the jury panel. Simply answer the questions as asked truthfully and to the best of your knowledge.'"

Pringle sighed. "And you felt what you gave was a truthful answer?"

"Objection!" said Wong. "Self-incrimination."

"All right," said Pringle. "Did you—"

"No, I don't mind answering," said Juror 209. "Yes, I felt my answer was truthful."

"But you know in court we want the truth, the whole truth, and nothing but the truth."

"Forgive me, Your Honor, but it's been quite clear throughout this case that you want nothing of the kind. I've seen Mr. Rice, there, and Mrs. Ziegler, cut off all sorts of answers because they were more than either of them wanted the jury to hear. By every example I've ever seen, the Court wants specific answers to the narrow, specific questions posed—and I provided just that."

"Did you have a special reason to want to be on this jury?"

"Objection!" said Wong. "Self-incrimination again."

"All right, all right," said Pringle. "Juror 209, I don't mind telling you I'm extremely disappointed in you. As of this moment, you're dismissed from the jury panel."

"Please don't do that," said Juror 209.

"You've given me no choice," said Pringle. "Just be happy that I'm not finding you in contempt. Deputy Harrison will take you home. We'll try to get you there before the press gets wind of this, but I suspect they'll be all over you by this evening. I cannot order you to be silent, but I do ask you to please consider the impact any statements you might make to the media will have. All right? You're dismissed." Pringle sighed, then turned to the lawyers. "We'll move up the appropriate alternate juror. I'll see you in the courtroom in"—she looked at her watch—"twenty minutes."

The lawyers rose and filed out of the judge's chambers. Frank sidled over to stand next to Dale. "Does this happen often?"

"People with a particular ax to grind trying to get on juries?" Dale shrugged. "It's most common in cases like this one, with big potential jury pools. Obviously, you can't volunteer for jury duty, but if you ask a big enough group of people to come on down, there's bound to be someone who wants on."

Frank waited for Ziegler to drift far enough down the

corridor. "This woman—actually, she would have been on our side, wouldn't she?"

Dale nodded. "Probably. A real alien-lover. Anyway, one of the alternates will replace her."

"Let's hope that it's somebody who isn't crazy but will still support us."

Dale grunted.

"What?" said Frank.

Dale lowered his voice. "I still haven't figured out what to do with the information from Dr. Hernandez, but, well, it may only be crazy people who *will* support us."

Frank looked like he was going to protest this, but after a moment he nodded. "Yeah."

THIRTY

Dale Rice came into the courtroom. He looked at the
new juror. Of course, he'd been in the room since the beginning, but this was his first day as an actual voting member
of the panel. He was an Asian man, perhaps twenty-five or
thirty. There was nothing in his face to convey which way
he would vote. Dale smiled at him—a warm smile, a "trust
me" smile, a "we're all in this together" smile.

It couldn't hurt.

The day had been devoted to minor witnesses and ar-
guing points of law. Dale got home after nine p.m.,
exhausted—as he was more and more these days; he couldn't
deny his age.

Years ago, after having received a Los Angeles County
"Lawyer of the Year" award, Dale Rice was asked by a
reporter "whether he was proud today to be a Black American."

Dale gave the reporter the kind of deadly cross-
examinational stare normally reserved for lying police

officers. "I'm proud *every* day to be a Black American," he said.

Still, there weren't many times when it was an actual advantage to be African-American. He was used to the screwups in restaurants. Waitresses bringing him the wrong meal—mixing up his order with that of the only other black person in the entire place. White people constantly confused him with other black men, men who, except for their skin color, looked nothing like him, and were often decades younger.

But the one time it perhaps was to his advantage to be big and black was when he wanted to go for late-night walks. Even here in Brentwood, most people were afraid to be out on the streets after midnight, but Dale knew that no one would try to mug him, and since he rarely got home from the office before nine p.m., he was grateful that at least the streets weren't denied to him after dark, as they were to so many others. Of course, there was always the problem of police cars pulling up to him and asking to see his ID—for no good reason other than it was night, and he was black, and this was a rich white neighborhood.

Tonight, as he walked along, he thought about the case. The evidence against Hask seemed compelling. His lack of an alibi; his having shed his skin the night of the murder; the fact that he was experienced at dissection, having recently carved up the body of the dead Tosok, Seltar; the video showing him wielding precisely the sort of cutting device used to commit the crime—and his musings on that video about his people having given up too much by no longer hunting their own food.

Dale continued along the sidewalk. Up ahead, coming toward him, a white man was walking a small dog. The man caught sight of Dale, and crossed over to the other side of the road. Dale shook his head. It never ended—and it never ceased to hurt.

Judge Pringle should never have allowed the jury to watch Stant shed his skin. Perhaps that alone would be grounds for an appeal, should the likely happen and the jury find Hask guilty. And even if Ziegler hadn't been able to raise the point in the courtroom at that moment, she'd doubtless make it in her closing argument: Hask and Stant were half brothers, and their regular shedding should have been closely synchronized. That it wasn't was apparent proof that Hask's shedding had been induced—and why else induce it on the day of the murder, except that he himself had committed the crime?

Dale's footsteps echoed in the night. A few dogs, behind high stone fences, barked at him, but he didn't mind that; dogs barked equally at everyone. If Dale's life hadn't been so busy, he'd have liked to have had a dog of his own.

Or a wife, for that matter.

He'd been engaged during law school, but he and Kelly had broken up before he'd graduated. She'd seen then what the work was like, the commitment, the fact that there really was room for nothing else in his life beside his career. Dale thought of her often. He had no idea what had become of her, but he hoped, wherever she was, that she was happy.

He was approaching a corner, a pool of light shining on the concrete sidewalk from the street lamp overhead. He stepped into the light and began walking now down the perpendicular street.

And then it hit him—how all the pieces of the jigsaw puzzle fit together.

Christ, if he was right—

If he was right, then Hask *was* innocent.

And he could prove it.

Of course, Hask would not cooperate. But it wouldn't be the first time Dale had saved a client despite the client's wishes. As he headed down that dark street Dale felt sure he knew who Hask was protecting.

He'd already arranged to examine Smathers tomorrow, but after that he would call Dr. Hernandez. And then—

Dale turned around and headed back home, moving as fast as his ancient form would allow.

THIRTY-ONE

"State and spell your name, please," said the clerk.

The square-headed man with white hair and a white beard leaned into the microphone on the witness stand. "Smathers, Packwood. S-M-A-T-H-E-R-S."

Dale could have called someone else at this point, but by using Smathers as an expert witness for the defense, he hoped to communicate to any jurors who had gotten wind of Smathers's attempts to devise a method to execute a Tosok that Smathers did not, in fact, necessarily believe Hask was guilty; it would, after all, be particularly damning if the jury believed that a member of the Tosok entourage thought Hask had indeed killed Calhoun.

Dale moved over to the lectern. "What is your profession, sir?"

"I'm a professor of exobiology and evolutionary biology at the University of Toronto."

Dale introduced Smathers's massive CV into evidence, then: "Dr. Smathers, you heard Reverend Brisbee's discourse on the human eye. Do you agree with it?"

"No, sir, I don't."

"You don't believe that the complexity of the human eye represents clear proof of divine creation?"

"No, sir."

"Your Honor," said Ziegler, rising. "We object to this. What has the nature of the eye got to do with this case?"

"Your Honor," said Dale, "Ms. Ziegler has put much emphasis on the missing parts of Dr. Calhoun's body. Surely we're entitled to explore whatever reasons there might be for those particular parts to be taken."

"I'm inclined to grant some latitude," said Pringle, "but don't let this go on too long, Mr. Rice."

"I shall be the very soul of brevity, Your Honor," said Dale, with a small bow. "Now, Dr. Smathers, you heard the reverend's contention that the eye could not possibly have evolved in stages. I can have the court reporter read back the exact quote, if you like, but I believe the gist of it was, 'What good is half an eye? What good is a quarter of an eye?' Do you agree with that?"

Smathers smiled and spread his hands. "Today, we consider a one-eyed man to be at least partially disabled: he has a drastically reduced field of view including no peripheral vision on one side of his body, and, of course, he has no depth perception, since depth perception is a function of stereoscopic vision—which requires two simultaneous views of the same scene from slightly different angles."

Smathers paused, and took a drink of water from the glass on the witness stand. "Well, there's an old saying, sir. In the country of the blind, the one-eyed man is king. If *nobody else* had two eyes, one eye would be a spectacular improvement over no eyes. You wouldn't be considered disabled; rather, you'd be considered incredibly advantaged."

"But, still," said Dale, "that one eye is a miraculous creation, no?"

"Not really. A human eye consists of a lens for focusing light; a retina, which is a delicate, light-sensitive membrane at the back of the eye—sort of like the eye's 'film'; and the optic nerve for transferring information to the brain. The reverend is right, of course, that three such complex structures couldn't simultaneously appear as the result of a single mutation. The eye, evolutionarily, started out as light-sensitive tissue—which had the ability to distinguish light from shadow. Now, that's not half an eye. That's not a quarter of an eye. It's the tiniest, least significant fraction of an eye. There's nothing miraculous about light-sensitive cells. Our skin is full of their precursors; you tan because of exposure to ultraviolet light, after all. Well, not *you,* sir, but—"

"Go on, Doctor."

"Well, this tiny, barest fraction of an eye is enough to make you king if everyone else is totally blind. What good is a partial eye? If it lets you detect that some creature is coming toward you—a creature that might eat you—if it lets you sense that, even as an indistinct shadow, so that you can get away before it's upon you, well, yes, that's an advantage, and yes, evolution would select for it.

"And as time goes by, if a transparent membrane developed over those light-sensitive cells, to protect them from damage, well, if that membrane lets you keep your light-sensitive cells when others are losing theirs, then, yes, that's an advantage, and evolution would select for it.

"And if that transparent membrane became thicker in the middle by random chance, and that thickness had the effect of focusing the light somewhat, giving you a slightly sharper view of whatever was approaching, then, yes, that's an advantage, and evolution would select for it, too.

"Bit by bit, tiny change by tiny change, you do go from no vision at all to a highly sophisticated eye, like the one we possess. In fact, in Earth's fossil record, it seems that vision didn't evolve once—it appears that it evolved as many as *sixty* different times. It takes all sorts of forms: our single-lens eyes, the compound eyes of insects, the lensless pinhole-camera eyes of nautiluses. Yes, the eye evolved, on its own, unguided, unplanned, through natural selection."

"But the eye is so refined, Doctor, so sophisticated. Do you really believe it isn't the handiwork of God?"

Smathers looked out at the courtroom. "About half the people I see here today are wearing glasses; I'll bet of the remaining half, a goodly number are wearing contact lenses. Now, it may be a miracle that LensCrafters can make glasses in about an hour, but I'd have actually expected an omnipotent God to have designed eyes that focused properly *on their own,* without mechanical aids.

"Of course, one could argue that God never intended us to watch TV all night long, or to read so much, or to sit in front of computers, or to do delicate work with our hands. But poor eyesight is not just a modern ailment. The ancient Indians of North America used to have their own eye tests. The second-last star in the handle of the Big Dipper is actually a double star. On a clear night, a person with normal vision should be able to easily see a second, fainter star very close to the main one; that's the test the Indians used.

"And the ancient Greeks used the Seven Sisters of the Pleiades star cluster in Taurus the Bull as an eye test—could you see all seven? Well, today, even with normal vision, only six are clearly visible—one of the Pleiades stars has dimmed over the millennia. But the fact that ancient peoples had eye tests proves that poor vision is hardly something new."

Dale glanced at the jury, then looked back at the Canadian scientist. "Still, Dr. Smathers, surely the question of focus is a minor one. Surely, in its overall design, the perfection of the eye demonstrates the existence of a divine creator?"

"No, it does not," said Smathers. "The eye, in fact, is *incompetently* designed. No engineer would ever do it that way. Remember I mentioned three fundamental components—the lens, the retina, and the optic nerve? Well, a sensible design would have the retina connected to the optic nerve at the back—so that the optic nerve doesn't obscure the light coming from the lens to the retina.

"But our eye is wired up ass-backward—forgive me, Your Honor—with the optic nerve connecting to the retina in the front. Our vision would be sharper if the light coming through the lens didn't have to pass through layers of neural tissue before reaching the retina. It's degraded further by the fact that there's also a network of blood vessels on top of the retina to service that neural tissue.

"And, if all that weren't bad enough, the nerve tissue has to make a channel through the retina to come out at the back of the eye and head on to the brain. That channel causes a blind spot in each eye. We're not normally aware of it, because our brain fills in the missing visual information with an extrapolated picture, but I'm sure many people in this court have done the easy experiments that let you demonstrate that you *do* have a blind spot in your vision. The loss of image quality I mentioned earlier and the blind spot simply would not be necessary if our eyes had been designed logically, with the neural wiring behind, rather than in front, of the retina."

Ziegler rose again. "Really, Your Honor, I must renew my objection. Where is all this going?"

"The Court is baffled, Mr. Rice," said Pringle.

"I need but a moment more to finish with this witness, Your Honor."

"Very well, Mr. Rice. But no more than that."

"Thank you." Dale looked at Smathers. "You were talking about the loss of image quality due to the backward wiring of the human eye. But surely, Professor, what you're really saying is simply that you haven't perceived the wisdom of God's design. We can't build an artificial eye yet, after all. Perhaps there's something fundamental that we're unaware of that requires the apparently incompetent design you've mentioned."

"No, there's not. It's true that *we* can't build eyes yet, but nature builds them all the time. And because nature operates by trial and error through evolution, sometimes she gets it wrong, as in our eyes, but other times she gets it right. It's often said that octopuses and squids have eyes very similar to human eyes, and they do. But theirs evolved independently of ours, and are wired properly, with all the neural tissue behind the retina. Neither an octopus nor a squid has blood vessels or neural tissue diffusing the light falling on its retina, and neither of them has blind spots. Far from being proof of divine creation, Mr. Rice, the human eye is one of the best proofs of the fact of evolution."

THIRTY-TWO

"On the record now, in *California* v. *Hask.* The jury is not present. All right, Mr. Rice, you may proceed."

"Your Honor, I'd like to speak in support of the two defense motions Ms. Katayama filed yesterday."

"Go ahead."

"First, on the matter of our new witness—"

"I don't like new witnesses this late in the game, counselor," said Pringle.

"Nor do I. But this is a special instance. The witness is Dr. Carla Hernandez, who assisted in the surgery on Hask. Obviously, she had no involvement with Hask until he was shot, so there was no way she could have been deposed earlier."

"Your Honor," said Linda Ziegler, "this case is about the murder of Cletus Calhoun. Anything that might have happened *after* that murder is irrelevant to the proceedings at hand."

"Dr. Hernandez's testimony *does* relate to matters that occurred before the murder," said Dale.

"Very well," said Pringle. "I'll allow it."

"Thank you, Your Honor. Now, about my motion that the other Tosoks be barred from the courtroom during Dr. Hernandez's testimony—"

"I can see barring the Tosoks on the witness list, if what Hernandez is going to say might influence their testimony, but that only applies to Kelkad, Stant, Ged, and Dodnaskak."

"As you can see in my brief," said Dale, "I may wish to expand the witness list, as a direct result of Dr. Hernandez's testimony."

"All right," said Pringle. "I'll order all of them out of the room, and I'll ask them to avoid the media coverage of Hernandez's testimony."

"Thank you, Your Honor. Now, to my other request—that the lawyers and the jury be allowed to tour the Tosok mothership."

Linda Ziegler spread her arms in an appeal for basic common sense. "The People strenuously object to this bit of theater, Your Honor. The murder took place on Earth. Now, if Mr. Rice felt there was a need for the jury to tour the crime scene at the University of Southern California, the People might indeed support him in such a motion. But the only reason for wanting the jury to see the alien ship is so that they can be awed by it."

"The Court is inclined to agree," said Pringle. "Mr. Rice, I see nothing in your brief that makes me want to grant your request. Besides, you had your chance during the discovery phase to request any evidence you thought was necessary."

"Your Honor," said Dale, "the defense believes that Dr. Hernandez's testimony will suggest a further line of inquiry that can only be accommodated aboard the mothership." He turned to Ziegler. "The police should have searched the accused's home, as a matter of course. That no search was done is surely the People's fault, and we should be entitled to a wide-ranging remedy for that oversight."

Ziegler spread her arms again. "Your Honor, for Pete's sake, the Tosok mothership is hardly located within the jurisdiction of the LAPD. It's not in *anyone's* jurisdiction. No one can issue a valid search warrant for it."

"But if Captain Kelkad agrees to let the jury—"

"No," said Judge Pringle, shaking her head. "No, even if he agrees, it doesn't matter. There are all kinds of liability issues here. If one of the jurors were to be injured, the lawsuits would be incredible."

"We could ask the jurors to sign waivers," said Dale.

"And if even one of them chooses not to?" said Pringle. "Then we're looking at a mistrial."

"There are alternates—"

"I'm not going to manufacture a situation in which we have to dip into the alternate pool again. No, Mr. Rice, if you think there's evidence aboard the mothership, find a way to present it in my courtroom. Now let's get the jury in here, and get back to work."

Dale glanced at the double row of empty Tosok chairs, then turned back to face the judge's bench. "The defense calls Dr. Carla Hernandez," he said.

The woman was sworn in and took her place in the witness box.

"Dr. Hernandez," said Dale, "what's your job title?"

"I'm chief of surgery at the Los Angeles County-University of Southern California Medial Center."

"And in that capacity, did you have an opportunity to assist in surgery on a Tosok patient?"

"I did."

"Please describe the circumstances of that."

"The defendant Hask was shot on May eighteenth. He

required immediate surgery to remove a bullet still lodged in his chest. Another Tosok named Stant performed the surgery, and it was my privilege to provide assistance to Stant while this was being done."

"When surgery is performed on a human, is the human normally fully clothed?"

Hernandez smiled. "No."

"In fact, the area in which the surgery is being performed is usually naked, correct?"

"Yes."

"Were Hask's clothes removed before the surgery was performed on him?"

"I removed his tunic, yes, then covered most of the torso with sterile sheets so that only the entrance wound was exposed."

"Did you do this before or after Stant entered the operating theater?"

"Before. Stant was receiving hurried instruction on using our operating instruments in the adjacent, identical theater."

"So only you saw Hask's naked torso in its entirety that day."

"No, three nurses also saw it."

"But Stant never actually saw it?"

"That's correct. Stant had me close the wound once the bullet was removed. Stant had left the operating theater by the time the sheets were taken off Hask's body."

"When you saw Hask's naked torso, did you notice anything unusual?"

"Well, *everything* about Tosok anatomy is unusual. As a doctor, I was fascinated by every aspect of it."

"Of course, of course," said Dale. "What I meant was this: was the bullet entrance wound the only sign of recent injury to Hask's torso?"

"No."

"What other signs were there?"

"I saw three raised, dark-purple lines on his torso."

"Did these lines remind you of anything you'd seen before?"

"Yes."

"And what would that be?"

"Well, except for the color, they looked like recent scars."

"What kind of scars?"

"Well, normally I'd say they were untreated injury scars, but . . ."

"What do you mean by 'normally'?"

"Well, a surgical scar will usually be flanked left and right by small dots of scar tissue, caused by the sutures used to seal the wound."

"So these weren't surgical scars?"

"On the contrary, I think they were indeed. Stant told me that his people don't use suture—at least not anymore—to close wounds. But a wound *has* to be closed somehow; otherwise, it simply gapes open. These were very neat, very precise lines—the kind one gets with a scalpel. And they clearly had been closed somehow."

Dale reached into a bag on his desk and pulled out a Tosok doll; Mattel had rushed them to market shortly after the aliens had arrived on Earth. "Dr. Hernandez, using this doll, would you indicate where you recollect the scars being?"

"Certainly." She started to leave the box, but Dale motioned for her to stay there. He walked through the well and handed her the doll and a purple Magic Marker.

"The first one was here," she said, drawing a line vertically between the front arm and the left leg near the bottom of the torso.

"The second was here," she said, drawing a horizontal line well below the left-front breathing orifice.

"And the third was here," she said, making a diagonal line behind and just to the left of the front arm. "There could have been other scars, as well; I never saw Hask's back."

"Now, Dr. Hernandez," said Dale, "you are the only human ever to assist in a surgical procedure on a Tosok, correct?"

"Yes."

"And have you followed the revelations that have been made during this trial and elsewhere about Tosok anatomy?"

"Yes. As you know, the Tosoks are not at all forthcoming about such matters, but there's an Internet newsgroup devoted to what we've been able to glean about Tosok physiology; I've been on that from the day it started."

"If these scars were left behind from surgical incisions, what areas of Tosok anatomy would the surgery likely have concentrated on?"

"One of the four Tosok hearts, one of the four Tosok lungs, and one of the four organs that we've gathered serves a combined function similar to what our separate kidneys and spleen perform."

"Thank you, Dr. Hernandez. Your witness, counselor."

Ziegler rose warily. She clearly had no idea what Dale was getting at. Still, her natural instinct was to discredit anything the defense tried to enter into evidence. "Dr. Hernandez, have you examined Hask since you closed the bullet entrance wound on him?"

"No."

"Does he still have the stitches you put in him?"

"No."

"What happened to them?"

"Stant removed them, I'm told."

Ziegler paused for breath, presumably expecting a "Hearsay!" objection from Dale, but it didn't come. She pressed on. "But you put in the stitches yourself."

"Well, putting stitches in requires a certain skill. Taking them out is easy—you just snip the suture with scissors, then pull the threads out. Stant had asked me how it was done, and I told him; he said he was sure he could manage it himself."

"So you've never actually seen Tosok scar tissue, correct?"

"I believe I have, yes, in the three places I indicated on the doll."

"But you've never seen what you were *sure* was Tosok scar tissue."

"Not a hundred percent sure, no, but in my best expert medical judgment, that's what it was."

"But, Dr. Hernandez, we all know that Tosoks shed their skin—we even saw it happen in this courtroom. Surely any old scars are discarded with the old skin."

"Human beings replace all their skin cells over a seven-year period, Ms. Ziegler. And yet I've got scars I've had since childhood. My judgment from having seen the bullet wound on Hask is that the Tosok body covering is multilayered, and that the so-called new skin revealed when old skin is shed is already many years old, but simply never has been exposed at the surface before. Indeed, it would have to be thus if we're to believe that shedding of the old skin can be induced at any time. If you carved right through all the layers of skin, into the organ cavity, I'm sure you would leave scars that *would* survive the shedding of the outer skin."

"But what about the Tosok recuperative powers? We heard earlier in testimony from Captain Kelkad that Tosoks can regenerate damaged organs. Surely beings that can do that would not have scars that persisted for long?"

"One has nothing to do with the other," said Hernandez. "Scar tissue isn't a replacement for the skin that's normally there—it's a supplement, a natural attempt to help close the injury site and protect if from being damaged again. No one knows for sure, of course, but it's my expert opinion that the scars on Hask's body are of relatively recent origin, but predate his most recent skin shedding."

During the lunch break, Frank and Dale went for a walk.
First, of course, they had to push through the crowd of
reporters and onlookers, but once that was done, they made
their way onto Broadway. It was a bright day, and as they
left the courtroom Dale put on his sunglasses. Frank, meanwhile, took a pair of clip-ons out of his jacket pocket and
affixed them to his normal glasses.

And then he stopped dead in his tracks. "*That's* what's
been bothering me!"

"Pardon?" said Dale.

"Alpha Centauri—the Tosoks. Something just hasn't
quite added up about them." Frank started walking again,
and Dale fell in next to him. "I even went over to the PBS
studios to look at Clete's old show on Alpha Centauri. What
do you know about Alpha Centauri?"

"That's where the Robinsons were headed in *Lost in
Space,*" said Dale.

"Anything else?"

Dale shook his head.

"Well, as you heard in the courtroom, Alpha Centauri
isn't really one star—it's actually three stars very close
together. We call the three parts Alpha Centauri A, B, and
C, in descending order of brightness. The Tosoks claim they
come from a planet orbiting Alpha Centauri A, and I'm
inclined to believe that. If they came from B, the principal
lighting aboard their mothership would be orange instead
of yellow."

"Okay."

"Well, Centauri A is almost a twin for our sun. It's what
we call a G2V star, precisely the same spectral class as Sol,
and—"

"Sol?"

Frank smiled. "Sorry. The word 'sun' is actually a

generic term. Any star that has planets is a sun. Our sun's proper name is Sol, after the Roman god of the sun."

Dale nodded.

"So, as I was saying," continued Frank, "Alpha Centauri A is actually damn near a twin for our own sun, Sol. It's the same color, the same temperature, and so on. And it's about the same age—actually, a little older. But there's one significant way in which Centauri A differs from Sol."

"And what's that?"

"Its brightness. Centauri A is an inherently brighter star—fifty-four percent brighter than our sun."

"So?"

"So even on cloudy days here, all the Tosoks wear those pop-in sunglasses. If they're from a world of a brighter star, our dimmer sun shouldn't bother them."

"Maybe they have a different atmosphere from us; maybe it's not transparent like ours is."

Frank nodded, impressed. "That would be an excellent explanation, except for one thing: the Tosoks breathe our air without any difficulty, and when Clete went aboard their mothership, he breathed their air without trouble, too—and you saw in those videotapes that it was crystal clear."

"Well, then, maybe they orbit their sun farther out than we orbit ours."

They had come to a park bench. Dale motioned for them to sit down.

"Exactly," said Frank, lowering himself to the bench. "In fact, when I was talking to Kelkad about how long it would take to build replacement parts for the mothership, he got upset when I said two years—but he calmed down when Hask explained I meant two *Earth* years. The Tosok year is obviously much longer, and since Alpha Centauri A is about the same mass and size as Sol, to have a substantially longer year, the Tosok home world must orbit much farther out from it than we do from our sun."

"I don't know anything about astronomy," said Dale, "but that sounds reasonable."

"Well, it is—sort of. Remember, Centauri A is the same size, but 1.54 times as bright as our sun. A planet orbiting the same distance from Centauri A as Earth is from Sol would therefore get 1.54 times as much light from it."

"Okay."

"But if you double the distance, you only get one quarter of the sunlight. So, a planet orbiting Centauri A at a distance of two AUs—two times the distance between Earth and Sol—would get one quarter of 1.54 times Sol's light as seen from Earth. That works out to—let me think—something like forty percent of what we get."

"Well, that would explain why they always need sunglasses, even on cloudy days. But wouldn't that also make their world much cooler than ours?"

Frank smiled. "For someone who doesn't know anything about astronomy, you ask all the right questions. Certainly, Clete said the mothership's air temperature, even outside the hibernation room, was only about fifty degrees Fahrenheit. But how far away from a G2V star can a planet be and still have a fifty-degree surface temperature? Well, the answer depends on how much carbon dioxide, water vapor, and methane there is in the atmosphere of the Tosok home world. See, those gases trap heat. You've heard of the greenhouse effect? It's caused by excess amounts of them, all of which are clear, colorless gases. They're the wild card in planetary positions. If you've got enough of a greenhouse effect, you could be much farther from our sun and still have surface temperatures comparable to those on Earth—in theory, there could be an Earth-like planet out in the orbit of Jupiter as long as it had enough greenhouse gases to trap sufficient heat."

"So there's your answer," said Dale. "The Tosoks come from a planet that orbits much farther from its star than we do from ours."

"Ah, but you're forgetting something when you say 'its star,' singular. Alpha Centauri is a multiple-star system. When Centauri A and B are at their closest to each other, they're only eleven AUs apart—just about one billion miles."

Dale frowned. "So you're saying the light from Centauri B would make things bright, even if the Tosok world orbited a long way from Centauri A?"

"No, no. Even at its closest approach, Centauri B would only appear about one percent as bright as our sun. That's still thousands of times brighter than our full moon— meaning nights on the Tosok home world when A has set but B is still up are probably reasonably bright, but surely no brighter than our streetlights make our streets."

"Oh."

"No, the problem isn't Alpha Centauri B's light—it's its gravity. Clete explained all this in his show. According to celestial mechanics, planetary orbits in a double-star system are stable out to a distance of one fifth the closest approach between the two stars. Since the closest A ever gets to B is eleven AUs, then planetary orbits around A are stable out to just over two AUs—just over twice as far out as Earth is from our sun."

"But farther out than that, they're unstable?"

Frank nodded. "And an unstable orbit could be threatening them with extinction. In which case, it's possible that they're not just here for a visit. The Tosok race may be looking for a new home."

"You mean, as in invading ours?"

Frank shrugged. "It's possible."

"God."

"Exactly," said Frank. "And think about the missing body parts: the eyes are clearly one of our most fragile components. And the throat—you heard what Professor Wills said: the design makes it easy to choke to death. And the appendix, a part that can be made to burst, causing death if not treated immediately." He paused, and looked at the old lawyer. "You know what Linda Ziegler's got Packwood Smathers doing: looking for a way to kill a Tosok, should the jury hand down a death sentence. Perhaps the Tosoks were doing something similar: looking for a way to wipe us out, to make room for them to come here."

THIRTY-THREE

The video monitors in Judge Pringle's courtroom flickered into life again with a view aboard the alien mothership. But this time the images weren't old tapes—this time, they were a live broadcast . . .

Francis Antonio Nobilio floated down the dim corridor of the alien ship. It was exhilarating! He felt ten years younger. There had been a hint of nausea at first, but his body had quickly gotten used to the lack of gravity, and now he was enjoying himself thoroughly. The air had a slightly salty taste, as though he were at seaside, and there were several other faint smells. Frank had never noticed a Tosok body odor before, but over the centuries the beings had spent aboard this ship, whatever normally undetectable scent they gave off had been magnified past the threshold of discernibility.

There were lots of sounds. A low-pitched electrical hum, the occasional sloshing of water or other liquids moving through pipes, and a *tick-tick-ticking* that Kelkad, who was accompanying Frank, said was caused by uneven heating of the ship's hull as its orbit moved it out of the Earth's shadow and into direct sunlight.

Frank was carrying a video camera, on loan from Court TV. He also had a radio microphone and earpiece. Kelkad, who was wearing a headset that had been specially adapted for him, had arranged for the signals to be broadcast directly from the ship to the courthouse; the problems that had prevented Calhoun from broadcasting during his original impromptu visit had proven trivial to overcome. Doubtless over a billion people the world over were watching the live broadcast—but the only audience Frank was really interested in consisted of six women and six men in the Los Angeles County Criminal Courts Building. Judge Pringle had told Dale Rice to find a way to bring the evidence there, and Dale had done precisely that.

"Dr. Nobilio," said Dale's voice over the radio, "can you hear me?"

Frank reached a hand up to adjust his headset. "Yes."

"All right," said Dale's voice. "The jury is present, and we would like to now continue with the testimony. Captain Kelkad, will you please escort Dr. Nobilio into the Tosok medical facilities?"

"Certainly," said Kelkad. He gave an expert kick off a wall and headed down the corridor. From underneath, the alien looked a bit like an amputee squid, with his four evenly spaced limbs dangling straight behind his body. Frank struggled to keep the camera steady as he, too, pushed off the wall and tried to head in the same direction. Kelkad managed a pretty straight path down the corridor, but Frank ended up bouncing off of both walls as well as the ceiling and floor. At one point the camera lens ended up jammed directly into one of the circular yellow lights set into the ceiling. Frank mumbled an apology to the people watching back on Earth.

Finally they came to the starship's sick bay—a room no

human had ever seen before, but that the Tosok biochemist
Stant had described to Dale during his deposition. In its
center was a wide operating pallet, with a trough down its
long axis to accommodate an arm. The ceiling sported a
mechanical octopus of surgical tools attached to articulated
arms—they apparently could be pulled down as required
to aid the surgeon. Along the walls were interlocking storage
units with hexagonal openings, each about eighty centimeters in diameter. The color scheme was mostly light blue,
with silver and red highlights. Rather than the usual ceiling
lighting disks, the whole roof seemed to be one giant lumi-
nescent panel that glowed yellowish white.

"Thank you," said Dale's voice. "Now, Kelkad, I am
informed that this is the room in which Hask would have
performed the organ harvesting of Seltar, the member of
your crew who was accidentally killed, correct?"

Kelkad was floating midway between the floor and ceiling, keeping himself in place with his front hand lightly
gripping the operating pallet. His cranial tuft waved forward. "That is correct."

"Dr. Nobilio," said Dale, "please pan the camera around
the room, and while you do so please describe the room's
level of neatness or disarray."

Frank moved the camera over the walls and floor, and
did a long, slow pan up the length of the operating pallet.
"Everything seems immaculate to me," he said. "There's no
sign of messiness."

"No blood splatters?" said Dale's voice. "No evidence of
carnage?"

"None."

"Now, Dr. Nobilio, please show us the storage units
mounted in the wall." Frank complied. "I would like you to
zoom in on the labels on each one, and, Kelkad, I would
like you to translate those labels for us."

Ziegler's voice over the headsets now: "Objection, Your
Honor. Sidebar?"

"You may ap—" Judge Pringle must have killed the microphones; her voice was cut off in mid-word. Frank, still floating, tried to shrug in Kelkad's direction. "Sorry about this," he said.

Kelkad's topknot rippled. "Your courts do seem to spend an inordinate amount of time on procedural issues."

"You should try working in government," said Frank ruefully. "It seems all we do is argue."

"I thought Mr. Rice said you were an idealist?"

"Compared to Dale, I certainly am. But I'm an idealist in the sense that I believe the ideal is attainable, whether it's efficient courts or efficient government. And besides—"

"—stand back." Judge Pringle's voice again. Whatever legal issue had been raised had apparently now been sorted out. "Mr. Rice, proceed."

"Thank you, Your Honor. Dr. Nobilio, you were showing us the wall storage units."

"Oh, sorry." Frank re-aimed the camera. "How's that?"

"Fine," said Dale's voice. "Captain Kelkad, would you translate?"

Frank realized Kelkad was looking at the upper right unit, while the camera was focused on the upper left—one of those little cultural differences. "This one says—"

"No, Kelkad," said Frank. "Please start at the upper left."

"Oh, sorry." The Tosok used his front hand to push himself along the wall. "This one says 'surgical'—well, you would call it 'supplies,' but the word is more general. 'Surgical stuff.'"

"Miscellaneous surgical equipment?" offered Dale's voice.

"That's correct."

"And the next one?"

"Horizontally or vertically?" asked Kelkad.

"Horizontally," said Dale. "The next one to the right."

"'Bandages and gauze.'"

"And the next one?"

"'Artificial joints.'"

"By which you mean mechanical elbows, knees, and so on, correct?" said Dale.

Kelkad's tuft moved forward in agreement. "Yes."

"And the next one?"

"That green mark is not a word; rather, it is a symbol we use to indicate cold storage."

"As in refrigeration, correct?" said Dale.

"Yes."

"So the contents of that unit are kept at low temperatures?"

"That is right."

"Beneath the symbol, there's some more writing. What does it say?"

"The first column says 'organs for transplant.' The second column says 'hearts.'"

"Now, Kelkad, the words that you are referring to look fundamentally different from the writing on the previous units you showed us. Why is that?"

"The writing on the previous units was machine-produced. This is handwriting."

"Tosok longhand, correct?"

"Yes."

"Do you recognize the handwriting?" asked Dale.

"Objection!" Ziegler's voice. "Kelkad has not been established as an expert in Tosok graphology."

"Overruled." Judge Pringle's voice. "You may answer the question."

"That is Hask's handwriting," said Kelkad. "It is quite distinctive—and rather sloppy."

Frank could hear a small amount of laughter in his earpiece.

"So is it fair to say that this compartment was labeled after the commencement of your voyage from Alpha Centauri?" asked Dale.

"Unquestionably. We had no organs for transplant in inventory when we left."

"Where did these organs come from?"

"From Seltar, the deceased member of my crew."

"I know Tosoks are sensitive to cold," said Dale's voice. "Is it safe for you to open a refrigerated compartment?"

"Yes."

"Doing so won't trigger your hibernation reflex?"

"No."

"Will you do so?"

"I must protest," said Kelkad. "Internal organs are not to be displayed for nonmedical reasons."

"I understand," said Dale. His voice seemed to go off the microphone. "Perhaps the other Tosoks would like to leave the courtroom?"

There was some muffled commotion as they did so.

"There are no other Tosoks viewing this now," said Dale. "Will you please continue?"

"If I must," said Kelkad. Just above the bottommost edge of the hexagonal door were four circular indentations. He slipped the four fingers of his front hand into these. Frank zoomed the camera in to show the action. Kelkad's knuckles flexed, and there was a clicking sound. The alien pulled the hatchway toward him, and a transparent hexagonal module, like a giant quartz crystal, pulled out of the wall. He brought it out about eighty centimeters, making the exposed part equal in length and width. Cold air drifted toward Frank, propelled by the gentle currents of the mothership's air-circulation system. Through the viewfinder of his camera, he could see the image briefly fog then clear.

"Dr. Nobilio," said Dale's voice, "can you get us a good shot inside the chamber?"

Frank flailed about trying to comply. Kelkad reached out, offering his back hand to Frank. Frank took it, and managed to haul himself into position. "How's that?"

"Fine," said Dale. "Now, Kelkad, can you identify the object we're seeing?"

The chamber contained a pink mass about the size of a

clenched fist, apparently wrapped with a clear film of plastic and packed around with ice chips. "Certainly. It is a Tosok heart."

"Which one?"

Kelkad peered closer, then moved his front arm vaguely in the air, as if working it out for himself. "The right-front heart, I believe."

"Very good," said Dale. "Is that the only thing in the chamber?"

Kelkad gripped the four holes on the front panel and pulled the transparent drawer out farther. A second Tosok heart, packed in ice, was revealed.

"No," said Kelkad. "Here is another one—the left front, it looks like." He continued to pull out the drawer. "And a third one—right rear," he said. He pulled on the drawer again. "And a fourth—the left rear."

"Are you sure it's the left rear," asked Dale. "Or are you just anticipating that?"

Kelkad's front eyes compressed from the sides—a Tosok squint. "No, it is indeed the left rear."

"Anything else in there?" asked Dale.

Kelkad yanked on the handle some more. There were two additional compartments in the drawer, but both were empty. "No."

"So, just to be clear for the jury, there are four hearts there, correct?"

"Yes."

"And a normal Tosok has four discrete, individual hearts."

"That is right."

"And those four hearts are each distinct in shape."

"The overall shape is pretty much the same, but the positioning of the valves is unique on each one."

"Thank you. Let's move on to the next compartment."

Frank pushed lightly off the wall and repositioned himself, with his hand flat against the cool, glowing ceiling.

"This one is also a refrigerated compartment," said Kelkad. "And it is also labeled in Hask's handwriting. It says 'organs for transplant—lungs.'" His finger traced out the words as he pointed to them.

"Please open the compartment."

Kelkad did so.

"Please pull it out all the way," said Dale's voice.

The captain gave a healthy yank. As soon as he let go of the four-holed handle, he began sailing under inertia across the room. Frank jockeyed for position. Inside the drawer were four blue semicircular masses.

"What is inside the compartment?" asked Dale from Earth.

"Four Tosok lungs," replied Kelkad, having now floated back.

"The normal number found in a Tosok body, correct?"

"Correct."

"Is there any way to distinguish a right-front lung, say, from a right-rear lung?" asked Dale.

"Not without doing a dissection or tissue scan," said Kelkad. "Indeed, they are essentially interchangeable—you can successfully transplant a lung from any position into any other position."

"And these four lungs, they were not in storage either when you left your home world?"

"No. As I said, we had no organs of any kind in storage. These would have been harvested from Seltar at the same time her hearts were taken out."

"And the next chamber over, what does that contain?"

"The label says it contains *gebarda*—the cleansing organs that serve the same function as your kidneys and spleen."

"Please pull that drawer all the way open," said Dale.

Kelkad did so, this time managing to keep his position near Frank.

"Are there four organs in there?"

Kelkad's tuft moved forward in assent. "Yes."

"Thank you," said Dale. "Now, being mindful of the Court's time, perhaps rather than searching methodically, we can have you simply go straight to whatever drawer might contain Seltar's *kivart.*"

Kelkad closed the hexagonal drawer containing the four *gebarda,* then scanned the rest of the doors.

"We're waiting, Kelkad," said Dale's voice.

"I am looking for it."

"I do have the term correct, don't I?" said Dale. "The *kivart* is the single organ in the Tosok body responsible for producing free-floating nerve bundles?"

"Yes," said Kelkad. "But I do not see it here."

"The *kivart* can be harvested for transplant, can't it?"

"Yes."

"In fact, as an organ that a Tosok has only one of, it's one of the most important ones to harvest, isn't it?"

"Yes."

"Indeed, a Tosok can get by for extended periods with only three lungs, no?"

"In fact," said Kelkad, "in the elderly, the strain of transplanting a fourth lung outweighs the benefits of having it in most cases."

"Indeed, you can get by, as long as you don't exert yourself, for an extended period with just two lungs, correct?"

"That is right."

"And, again so long as one doesn't exert oneself, three hearts, or even just two, would be enough to allow life to continue, no?"

"That is right."

"But the *kivart*—well, if the *kivart* goes, severe motor-control problems develop almost at once, isn't that so?"

"Yes," said Kelkad.

"Indeed, without his or her one and only *kivart,* a Tosok would die quickly, no?"

"That is correct."

"And so," said Dale, "Hask would doubtless have harvested Seltar's *kivart,* which, in many ways, is the most crucial of all the organs to recover, and—"

A muffled sound, then Judge Pringle's voice: "Mr. Rice, caution your client. I will not tolerate outbursts in my courtroom."

"I'm sorry, Your Honor. Hask, be quiet—"

Hask's untranslated voice, plus the near-simultaneous translation, both somewhat murky, as if being picked up by a microphone some distance away: "Do not pursue this line of questioning."

"I'm sorry, Hask." Dale's voice. "It's my job to defend you."

"I do not wish this defense."

"Mr. Rice." Judge Pringle again. "Mr. Rice."

"A moment, Your Honor."

"Mr. Rice, the Court is waiting."

"Hask." Dale's voice. "Hask, I'm going to finish."

"But—"

Judge Pringle: *"Mr. Rice—"*

"Kelkad," said Dale, "it *is* true that the *kivart* is a crucial organ, yes?"

"Most definitely."

"And yet it is missing from the collection of harvested body parts, no?"

"Apparently."

"Hask would have known to harvest it, no?"

"Doubtless. And, regardless, he would have consulted the procedures manual when confronted with Seltar's accidental death; that would have reminded him."

"So expected body parts are missing here, too, aren't they?" said Dale. "Just as they were from Dr. Calhoun's body?"

"I—I suppose that is true," said Kelkad.

"Thank you," said Dale. "Your witness, Ms. Ziegler."

"Umm, no questions," said a muffled voice. Ziegler sounded perplexed—and Frank didn't blame her. It seemed as if Dale was arguing Ziegler's own case: that Hask had first practiced his aberrant behavior on one of his own before trying it on a human being.

THIRTY-FOUR

The camera had been shut off. Frank floated in the starship's sickbay, looking at Kelkad. They were more alone than any two people in the solar system right now; even *Mir* currently had more people aboard, as well as constant contact with the ground crew in Kaliningrad.

"We should return to the planet," said Kelkad.

The planet. Not "to Earth." Not "home." The planet. The gulf between them was gigantic.

And yet Frank knew he would never have another chance like this one—away from the other Tosoks, away from the media, away from the rest of the scientific entourage, away from the court.

"Kelkad," said Frank, "privately, just between you and me, do you think Hask killed Clete?"

Kelkad did not hesitate. "Yes."

The word surprised Frank. He'd expected a denial—but perhaps denial was a human failing.

"But why? Why would he commit murder? Is he—is he crazy?"

Kelkad's tuft moved backward in negation. "No more than any of us."

"Then why would he do it?"

Kelkad pushed gently off the wall. "We should leave."

"No, please. Just between you and me. I have to know."

"You would not understand."

Frank thought about that. It had always been a possibility—that the aliens' psychology would prove so different, so bizarre, that none of their actions would ever make sense to a human. "Try me," he said simply.

Kelkad had reached the far side of the room. He stuck out his front hand to brake himself. Once he'd touched the wall, he began to drift slowly back in the other direction. He seemed to be thinking, as if deciding how to possibly put the idea into words the human might understand. "Like you," he said at last, "we believed we were created in God's own image—and that meant we must be perfect beings, divinely designed and flawlessly executed. It gave us great comfort knowing this—how much easier the problems of life are to bear when you know you are a child of God!"

Frank thought about his own Catholic upbringing. He nodded slightly.

"But then," said Kelkad, "like you, we discovered the principles of evolution." He had reached the near wall again. This time he grabbed onto one of the storage-unit handles to anchor himself.

"In our case, it was different," continued Kelkad. "You humans have a world that is mostly water, with landmasses isolated one from the other, creating discrete habitats in which evolution can proceed separately. Indeed, it astounds us that your race has only so recently learned of evolution, for it should have been obvious many hundreds of years ago.

"We Tosoks may be forgiven, I think, for taking longer to puzzle it out. Our world is about twenty percent water, and there are no isolated landmasses. Many species roam the entire globe. Still, there is the fossil record—again, on a drier world, such as ours, sedimentation and therefore fossilization take place less rapidly; our fossil record is spotty, although it is supplemented to a degree by naturally mummified remains. But its analysis nonetheless hinted at a sequence of steps between ancient lifeforms and modern ones.

"Still, the proof of evolution came not, as it did on your world, from observing isolated populations showing specialized adaptations, but later in our intellectual development through biochemistry, through analyzing the divergence in genetic material between related species."

"We do similar things here," said Frank. "Although the fossil record of primate evolution is scanty, we know, for instance, that apes and humans split five million years ago, based on analyses of the degree of difference between our DNA and theirs."

"Exactly: what for you has been a subsequent corroborating proof of evolution was for us its principal evidence. But no matter which route one takes to that knowledge, the conclusion is inescapable: both you and I are the products of natural selection, not divine engineering."

"I suspect that's as universal a truth as the law of gravity," said Frank.

"You speak sacrilege!" said Kelkad, angry enough to let go of the handle. He was now floating freely a meter from the human.

"I—I beg your pardon?" said Frank.

"To our everlasting shame, it is true that the Tosoks, and all life on our world, evolved. And, as we have learned, it is true that life here on Earth evolved, too. But somewhere— *somewhere*—in this vast universe, there must be true children of God, created in her perfect image."

The words were out before Frank realized how impolitic they were: "Really, Kelkad, you can't believe that."

"I believe it with every fiber of my being," said Kelkad. His tuft was moving excitedly. "God *must* exist, or the universe is without meaning and purpose. Since the latter premise is unacceptable, the former—the existence of a divine being—must be true."

Frank was struggling to understand. "And so having discovered that *you* weren't the products of divine engineering, you came to Earth looking to see if *we* were the products of it?"

"That was part of our mission, yes."

"And what makes you think we're not?" asked Frank.

Kelkad's topknot split in a shrug. "At first we thought you might indeed be—you were so different from us! Evolution produced the Tosok form, and we had assumed it was a sort of generalized product of random chance—not perfect, you understand, but we felt that the basic fourfold symmetry, with arms front and back and legs left and right, would be a model that evolution would tend toward. But your form—twofold symmetry, arms above and legs below—was so bizarre that we thought perhaps we might be staring at a miniature form of God, that in you we saw the true form of the creator. But then . . ."

"Then?"

Kelkad seemed reluctant to go on, but after a moment he did. "Once we discovered the biochemical fact of evolution, we could not help but look at ourselves, and the other forms of life on our world, in a different light. Far from being the optimized form we had always assumed, we began to realize that there were many basic flaws in the Tosok body plan. Our hearts, for instance, allow oxygenated and unoxygenated blood to mix."

"Reptilian hearts here on Earth do that," said Frank. "They have three-chambered hearts; humans have four-chambered ones that keep used blood separate from freshly oxygenated blood."

"A fine design," said Kelkad.

"Well, it's better than the reptilian one," agreed Frank. "But, then, reptiles are cold-blooded. They don't have to support a high level of metabolism. But the warm-blooded forms on Earth—mammals and birds—each independently evolved a more efficient four-chamber heart."

"They are fortunate," said Kelkad. "We do not have such things. Oh, we manage a high level of metabolism, but that is attributable in part to having four hearts working in unison, rather than to a basic efficiency of the Tosok cardiac design. Such flaws prove our lack of divine origin—just as such flaws prove the same about yourselves."

"What flaws?" said Frank.

"Your throats, for instance. Food can block your own air passageway, and—"

"And—my God!" said Frank, heart pounding. "My God! And our eyes—our eyes are wired backward. And our guts contain an appendix that does nothing useful at all. When Hask dissected Calhoun, he was looking for design flaws, for things that would prove we had not been created from an intelligently designed blueprint."

"In fact," said Kelkad, "I suspect he was looking for the opposite—for proof that you were divine, that we had found God's true children in our own backyard. His disappointment must have been profound at discovering that you, too, had evolved inefficiently through trial and error."

"Wait a minute," said Frank. "If Hask thought we were God's children, what would move him to kill one of us in the first place? Surely he must have thought that God would frown on murdering one of his creations?"

"Hask did not intend to kill Calhoun."

"Oh, come on! I don't care where it evolved, no lifeform could have survived that kind of dissection."

"The dissection was done *after* Calhoun was dead, of course."

"But to sever a limb!"

"Hask cut off Calhoun's leg," the alien captain said in agreement. "Doubtless to Hask's astonishment, Calhoun bled to death."

"A clean cut like that, right through the femoral artery? *Of course* he bled to death!"

"That was likely Hask's first clue that the human design was inefficient."

"Well, what the hell would happen if I cut off *your* leg?"

"I would be unable to walk, until the leg regenerated or was reattached."

"What about blood loss? We've seen Tosoks bleed."

"A small amount of blood would escape, but valves in our arteries would close, preventing any significant loss."

"We don't have valves in our arteries," said Frank.

"Imagine Hask's shock when he discovered that."

"Christ," said Frank. "Jesus Christ." He closed his eyes. Humans do have valves in their veins—which carry used blood back to the heart—but not in their arteries, which carry freshly oxygenated blood away from the heart. When venous valves fail to function properly, the result is varicose veins. "Dammit, dammit, dammit," said Frank, getting it. "The human heart is located near the top of the body; fresh blood going down into the legs needs no help—gravity causes it to flow down anyway. It's only blood coming back up, climbing four, five, or even six feet from our feet to our heart that's in danger of slipping backward; that's why we have valves that close when it does so. But the four Tosok hearts—Stant testified in court that they're located near the bottom of the torso. So, in you, blood going from the heart up to the head is also prone to slipping back. Of course you'd have valves in both your arteries and in your veins." He shook his head, angry with himself for not having seen it earlier. "But why would Hask cut off Clete's leg in the first place?"

"Leg amputation is a standard method of prisoner restraint on our world."

"Prisoner!" said Frank.

"Yes. Clearly Hask needed to keep Calhoun from getting away while he went to do something—presumably summoning me, his commanding officer. He had no bonding equipment with him, but he *did* have his monofilament cutting tool."

"But why would he need to restrain Calhoun?"

"Of that," said Kelkad, "I have no idea."

THIRTY-FIVE

As soon as Frank returned to Earth, Hask demanded a chance to consult privately with him and Dale Rice. The two of them drove out to Valcour Hall at the University of Southern California, and met with Hask in his room.

"I wish to change my plea," said Hask.

Dale kept his face impassive. "Do you, now?"

"That is my option, no? I wish to change to a plea of guilty."

Dale looked over at Frank, whose eyebrows were high on his forehead. "You realize," said Dale, looking back at Hask, "that if you plead guilty, the presentation of evidence will end, and Judge Pringle will charge the jury with sentencing you."

"Yes."

"And," said Dale, "the sentence they will likely call for is execution. Often, the death penalty is not invoked even when applicable to the crime if there's still a shadow of a doubt. A jury might feel comfortable sentencing you to life imprisonment, but generally will want to be convinced to a higher degree before calling for execution. But if you admit your guilt, any remaining doubt in the jury's mind is eliminated."

"I am prepared for the consequences."

Dale shrugged. "It is, as you say, your prerogative. As your lawyer, I should inform you that a better option would be for you to simply dispatch me to Linda Ziegler's office and tell her that we might be receptive to a deal. We could plea-bargain this down from murder one to manslaughter— you'll certainly not be executed, and probably get off with five years or so."

"Whatever," said Hask. "Just so long as the presentation of evidence ends."

"All right," said Dale. "But, look, I've gone to a lot of trouble preparing my summation and argument. You really owe me a chance to present it—at least to you and Frank."

Hask's tuft waved in confusion. "I hardly see the point of that."

"Humor me," said Dale.

"There is no reason to—"

"I think there is," said Dale. "Please."

Hask made a very human-sounding sigh. "Very well."

"Thank you," said Dale, standing up in the small dorm room. He hooked his thumbs into his suspenders and turned to face a nonexistent jury. "Ladies and gentlemen of the jury, I'd like to thank you for your attention during this very difficult trial. It's been a case like no other, with issues that range far beyond this courthouse—" He paused, interrupting himself. "That's where Linda would jump up and object," he said, smiling. "Can't urge the jury to take anything into account other than the facts of the case, as presented during the trial." He switched back into courtroom mode. "Anyway, ladies and gentlemen, let us review the evidence.

"We've heard from Captain Kelkad that his crew originally consisted of eight Tosoks, including himself. We heard, too, that one of those Tosoks, named Seltar, died during the flight to Earth, and the defendant, Hask, performed a harvesting of her organs, which was the normal, proper procedure should someone die during the mission.

"Now, the People would have you believe that this unforeseen event—the need to carve up a corpse—turned out to be unexpectedly titillating to Hask, so much so that he found himself overcome by an irresistible urge to have a similar experience again. And, when the opportunity presented itself, according to the People, Hask did indeed repeat the experience, killing and brutally dissecting the body of Cletus Robert Calhoun.

"We also heard that Tosok blood was found at the crime scene—but no evidence has been presented conclusively linking that blood to Hask. Also at the scene was a bloody mark that might be a Tosok footprint, but, again, the People utterly failed to demonstrate that this footprint belonged to Hask.

"Now, it is true that my client did indeed shed his skin at approximately the same time that Cletus Calhoun was killed. The People have stressed this fact, suggesting that Hask induced this shedding because he had ended up covered in Dr. Calhoun's blood.

"Apparently corroborating that the shedding was induced was the testimony of Stant, another Tosok—who turned out to be Hask's half brother. And it was revealed that, as was required by the peculiarities of Tosok biology, Hask and Stant must have been born within days of each other, and that their shedding schedules should have been closely synchronized. But, as we all saw in this courtroom" (Dale winked here, acknowledging to Hask and Frank that he wasn't completely caught up in this fantasy closing argument) "Stant himself shed his skin without any apparent inducement some five months *after* Hask did.

"Now, as this trial progressed a horrible thing happened. A deranged human being shot the defendant. Judge Pringle will doubtless instruct you, quite rightly, that your verdict should not be influenced one way or the other by this event *per se.* That one individual saw fit to shoot Hask does not make him guilty. Neither, of course, should sympathy over his wound lead you to find him innocent. Indeed, you should probably ignore the incident altogether.

"But one person who could not ignore it was Dr. Carla Hernandez, the human surgeon who aided the Tosok named Stant in removing the bullet from Hask. Dr. Hernandez helped prepare Hask's body for surgery, and in so doing, she saw on his body what she clearly recognized as scar tissue—scar tissue left behind by previous incisions.

"We've heard much about the Tosok powers of recuperation, of course. Why, we've even heard testimony that they can regenerate not just damaged limbs, but damaged organs as well. So, it goes without saying that any prominent, fresh-looking scars on Hask's body must be of quite recent origin—given enough time, they would have disappeared completely.

"But what would have caused such scars? The answer, ladies and gentlemen of the jury, is obvious—they were caused by the surgical removal of organs from Hask's *own* body.

"When Dr. Nobilio and Captain Kelkad returned to the Tosok mothership, they confirmed what I'd come to suspect myself: that several organs one would have expected Hask to have harvested from Seltar's body were also missing.

"Now, is Hask some sort of interstellar monster, so hungry for body parts that not only did he devour some of his dead colleague's ones, and some of Dr. Calhoun's, but that he also went so far as to remove some of his own organs for that purpose?" Dale paused, looking first at Frank, then at Hask. "Of course not. What a ridiculous notion! After all, that arm in his back might give Hask certain advantages at manual tasks over humans, but surely those advantages don't extend to performing surgery on himself.

"And *that,* ladies and gentlemen, means that the surgical scars on Hask's own body were inflicted by somebody else.

Now, who could that have been? Surely if it were a human being, Hask would simply tell us who it was—what an irony that would have been for our UFO-nut friends! Aliens come to Earth, and humans take out their organs, instead of the other way around! But that is *not* what happened here. No, clearly Hask was operated on by another Tosok—the fact that the incisions were closed with something other than suture proves that. But why? And which of the remaining six members of the starship's crew did it?

"Well, of course, we've seen that Stant is also highly skilled in surgical matters—it was he, after all, who removed the bullet from Hask at the LAC-USC Medical Center. And indeed Stant invoked the Fifth Amendment over the question of whether an individual Tosok's blood could be identified by chemical analysis."

Dale lowered his voice conspiratorially. "Linda would object strongly here, too—I'm really not allowed to touch on the motive of a witness for taking the Fifth." He hooked his thumbs in his suspenders again, readopting his court-room persona. "The obvious initial conclusion, of course, is that Stant believed his own half brother, Hask, to be guilty, but knew that, as close relatives, their blood types would be similar, and that any blood evidence that tended to convict Hask would also serve as evidence against Stant.

"A more direct interpretation is that the Tosok blood found at the crime scene was Stant's own—which, of course, is why he wouldn't want to testify that it could be identified as such. But I favor the first interpretation, that Stant feels Hask is guilty, but knew the blood evidence could as easily point to Stant himself as to Hask. Yes, I'm sure Stant believes Hask did it—but, ladies and gentlemen, I myself do not believe this.

"I do not believe that Hask killed Cletus Calhoun, and I do not believe that the shedding of his skin was induced. Rather, I believe Hask shed his skin at precisely the natural time for it to be shed. It happened five months prior to his half brother's shedding because Hask was out of hibernation not for the few days that dealing with the impact in our solar system's Kuiper belt would have required—but rather because he was out of hibernation for almost half a year!"

Frank Nobilio sat up straight in his chair. "God!"

"And why," continued Dale, "would he have stayed out of hibernation so much longer than he had claimed? The answer is simple: so that organs surgically removed from his body could regenerate internally.

"We have heard, ladies and gentlemen, that a Tosok can live for extended periods with only two hearts, instead of four, and only two lungs, instead of four—and the scars Dr. Hernandez noticed on Hask's left side indicate that his original two left hearts and his two left lungs had indeed been surgically removed, along with his left-side *gebarda* organs.

"Now, Dr. Nobilio found in the Tosok sickbay four Tosok hearts, four Tosok lungs, and four Tosok *gebardas*—but none of the organs of which Tosoks have only one apiece. And, I have no doubt, ladies and gentlemen, that if genetic tests were performed on the right hearts and right lungs found there they would indeed be proven to be those of Seltar. But I submit to you that the left lungs and left hearts are not Seltar's, but Hask's own.

"The truth of the matter, ladies and gentlemen of the jury, is that Seltar did *not* die during the Kuiper-belt accident, but, in collusion with Hask, her death was faked. He removed two of her hearts, two of her lungs, and two of her *gebardas,* and she removed two each of his. Then she and he stayed out of hibernation, letting replacements grow within them. A cursory check would have shown roughly enough body parts to corroborate Hask's story that Seltar was dead, but in fact she is not. She hid aboard the Tosok mothership, and while Hask came to Earth with great fanfare, streaking across the skies of the world and ostentatiously splashing down in the Atlantic, Seltar made a more stealthful landing somewhere else, using the landing craft that Hask told us and his shipmates had been lost during the collision. It is she who killed Cletus Robert Calhoun, and, for reasons of his own, Hask has chosen to cover for her.

"I urge you, ladies and gentlemen of the jury, to find the only just verdict possible: acquit Hask of this crime that he most assuredly did not commit, and let us now begin a search for the real murderer—wherever she may be."

THIRTY-SIX

Dale heaved his massive bulk back into a chair in Hask's dorm room. "Well?" he said.

"God," said Frank, again. "God. Hask, is it true?"

Hask's tuft was moving in ways Dale had never seen before.

"Hask," said Frank again, "is it true? Is Seltar still alive?"

"There are issues here," said Hask slowly, "of which neither of you are aware. Do not mention your speculation anywhere else, Dale."

"This is the trial of the century," said Dale. "I'm not going to lose it."

Hask's tuft swayed in negation. "It is the trial of the *millennium*," he said. "It is the trial of all time—and it is not being played out in the tiny confines of Judge Pringle's courtroom. I beseech you, Dale, do not pursue this."

"Why, Hask? I need a reason."

Hask was silent for a time, then: "Frank, you are a powerful person on this world, no?"

"It would be more correct to say I work for a powerful person," said Frank.

"Regardless of the subtleties, you have access to extraordinary resources. If I asked you to take me somewhere, you could arrange the trip in such a way as to attract no public attention, yes?"

"Are you asking for asylum?" asked Frank.

"No. But if I am to answer Dale's question, it cannot be done here. We must go somewhere else."

"Where?"

"Northern Canada."

"Why?"

"Arrange the passage. I will take you and Dale there, and then, I promise, we shall return to Los Angeles, and I will face justice."

Dale sent Michiko Katayama to court the next day, to beg off, saying that Hask had suffered a relapse from his gunshot injury. Frank arranged for Hask to be smuggled out of the USC residence in a laundry container, which was driven to March Air Force Base, nine miles southeast of Riverside. From there, a US military jet flew Frank, Dale, and Hask to a Canadian Forces Base in Cold Lake, Alberta. They transferred to a Canadian plane, which took them into the Northwest Territories.

Frank didn't particularly like to fly, especially in small planes. He kept his equilibrium by thinking about his daughter, Maria, conjuring up her beautiful, wide-eyed, twelve-year-old face. So much had happened—and, it seemed, so much more was still going to happen. All his life, he'd been trying to make the world a better place, but never for himself. It had always been for her, for the children, for the future. What effect would the outcome of this trial have on humanity's relations with the Tosoks? What kind of world would be left for Maria once the verdict was handed down? He shivered in the plane's small cabin, and not just from the cold.

The Canadian pilot almost missed the ship. Hask's lander had amply demonstrated its ability to change color by cycling through red, orange, yellow, green, blue, indigo, and violet while bobbing on the Atlantic. This lander, too, had changed color, to precisely match the lichen-covered rocks of the tundra. But once Hask had pointed it out, its shield shape was obvious. The plane had pontoons; the Canadian pilot put it down in a lake about a quarter mile from the alien craft. Finding a parka big enough to accommodate Dale had been a challenge, but they'd managed it. Hask was actually wearing a Tosok space suit, brought from one of the Tosok landing craft at USC. It was pale green in color and hugged his form snugly—but, he said, provided more than enough insulation to keep out the subzero cold.

They made their way ashore in an inflatable rubber boat and walked the short distance across the barren landscape to the lander, their breath escaping in clouds of condensation. A radio in his space suit allowed Hask to communicate with the lander's occupant; when they arrived, the outer air-lock door opened for them.

They cycled through the air lock—and there she was.

Seltar.

Her hide was purplish gray, and her eyes were pink and orange and ebony and navy blue. She was slightly shorter and slightly broader than Hask.

Hask touched controls on his space suit and it fell away, like a shed skin. He rushed to Seltar. His front arm came up, as did hers, and they intertwined their eight fingers. Meanwhile his back hand came up and reached over his head to touch Seltar's tuft; Seltar, meanwhile reached over with her back hand to stroke Hask's tuft.

"God, it has been *so* long—" said Hask. He realized his translator was still on, and disengaged his front hand from Seltar's long enough to deactivate it. They continued to embrace, and to chatter to each other for several minutes. Frank looked at Dale, slightly embarrassed.

At last the embrace ended, and Hask turned to look at the two humans. He was still holding front hands with Seltar, but he reactivated his translator with his back hand.

"Forgive us," said Hask. "Did I mention that Seltar is my mate?"

Frank grinned. "No, you didn't."

"Well, she is. In fact, she is my four-mate—we have agreed, when the time comes, that I shall impregnate all four of her wombs."

"You kinky devil," said Dale, with a smile.

When Hask had spoken all those months ago of the female Tosok God, Frank thought he'd heard Hask call her the "foremother" of the race, a feminine version of "forefather." He realized now that what Hask had probably really said, though, was "four-mother."

"Please," said Hask, "let me make proper introductions. Seltar, this is Dale Rice, a human attorney. And this is Frank Nobilio, a human scientist and government official. They are good people, and they are my friends."

"How do you do, Seltar?" said Frank.

Her translated voice was identical to Hask's—presumably Hask had simply copied the translation program from his portable computer to hers. "I do very well, thank you," she said.

"You've been here all this time?" asked Dale.

"Yes," she said.

"But why here? Isn't it too cold for you?"

"My space suit provides adequate protection when I feel the urge to get outside of this lander," said Seltar, "but when I do go outside, the light is agreeably dim. The sun does not get far above the horizon this far north."

"Amazing," said Dale. "And the others all think you're dead?"

"They do," said Seltar. "And we must keep it that way."

"Why?"

"I am your only hope."

"To clear Hask, you mean?"

Her tuft split in the now familiar Tosok shrug. "Your language lacks sufficient pronouns. I am *your* only hope. I am the only hope of you."

"Pardon?"

Hask stepped forward. "As Cletus might have put it, 'I am the only hope of y'all.' She means she is the last hope of the human race."

"What?" Frank felt his eyebrows climbing.

"The things we shall tell you must remain secret," said Seltar. "You cannot divulge them to anyone without my permission."

"We promise not to say anything," said Dale.

Hask turned to Seltar. "He is speaking the truth."

"Then tell them," said Seltar.

Hask turned back to the humans. "Seltar and I belong to what you might call a different religion than the other six Tosoks, although perhaps a different philosophical school would be a better description." He looked at Frank, then at Dale. "The crossbreeding that is the norm among Tosoks— four males and one female involved in most unions—has led to a substantial degree of interrelation among the Tosok people. The result is that we tend to think of the survival of our race as more important than the survival of any one individual. The school Seltar and I belong to abjures that; we have seen the damage it can do. That is why we are mating exclusively with each other."

"I don't understand," said Frank. "Surely such interrelation would have all kinds of benefits. I bet you have fewer wars than we do."

"We in fact have no wars," said Hask. "I was amazed to learn of the human propensity for them. But on the question of interrelation, as in all questions, one side always has more power, and in this one, the negative aspects of protecting the species at all costs are greater than the benefit." He paused, as if thinking about how to express himself. "Dale, during this case we encountered at least one juror who would say and do anything to get accepted, presumably in order to ensure a particular outcome. Well, Seltar and I did everything we could to get appointed to one of the star missions." His two front eyes blinked. "The tragedy is that several missions did get away without any of us among the crew."

Dale sounded confused. "What are you talking about?"

"What do you think the purpose of the Tosok expedition to your solar system is?" asked Hask.

"Exploration, no?" said Dale. "To see what was here?"

"No. The purpose of the mission was survival—survival of the Tosok race."

Frank nodded, his worst fears confirmed. "So you did come to invade Earth."

"Invade?" Hask's tuft waved backward. "No. We certainly would not want to live here. Your sun is so bright and large, your air smells, and all those annoying insects! No, no, the Tosoks are quite content with our home."

"Then what did you mean by saying your mission is survival?"

"We come from a world currently orbiting Alpha Centauri A at a distance much greater than your world orbits your sun. In fact, we orbit so far out from Centauri A that we are just on the outermost edge of orbital stability—any farther out, and the gravitational effects of Centauri B would be significant."

"So your planet *is* at risk," said Frank.

"At risk? No, not at all."

"Then what's the problem?"

"There is a third star in our system—Centauri C. Centauri C orbits the center of mass of the A-B system in a hugely eccentric path. Approximately every four hundred thousand Earth years it passes very close to us. When it last approached us, Centauri A was positioned between Centauri C and the center of mass of the A-B system; when it next approaches us, Centauri B will be between C and the center of mass.

Indeed, since the orbital period of C is a precise multiple of the A-B orbital period, there is a perfect alternation: on one pass, A will be between C and the center of mass; on the next pass, B will be between C and the center of mass, and so on."

"So?" said Frank.

"So mass curves space, of course, and at each near passage of C, that curvature becomes sufficient that my home world slips from orbiting around A to orbiting around B, or vice versa. We call this transfer 'the handoff.' Of course, there is a period of instability during the handoff. Still, when orbiting A, we ultimately settle in at a comfortably warm two AUs or so from that star. But when orbiting B, although we also settle into an orbit not much greater than two AUs from B, things are much colder, for B is a much fainter star. Our climate is temperate when we orbit A, but when we orbit B, our surface temperature drops to"—he paused, and worked controls on his pocket computer—"eighty degrees below zero Celsius."

"My God!" said Frank. "That's below the freezing point for carbon dioxide. It must kill everything."

"It does not. Those lifeforms that have persisted on our world have developed a natural ability to hibernate during these times. Everything simply pauses for four hundred thousand years, until Proxima swings by again, causing a reverse handoff, bringing us back into orbit around Alpha Centauri A. Temperatures rise, the long sleep ends, and we continue on."

"That's incredible," said Dale. "I mean, wouldn't it require enormous luck for a world to exist in a stable configuration like that?"

"Incredible? No. Unlikely perhaps, but, then again, no more unlikely than the coincidences of sizes and orbits that makes possible the kind of perfect total solar eclipse we observed from Earth's surface. Of all the inhabited planets in the entire universe, Earth may be the only one that enjoys such a spectacle."

"I suppose," said Dale, "but—"

"And, of course, there usually are such harmonics to orbital mechanics. Orbits of bodies around each other are often in perfect ratios: two-to-three, one-to-two, and so on. Your innermost planet, Mercury, for instance, revolves round your sun exactly two times for every three times that Mercury rotates around its own axis; its day is precisely two-thirds the length of its year." Hask's tuft split in the center. "No, our configuration may be as unique as the perfectly eclipsing combination of your Earth, your giant moon, and your sun, but it *is* possible, and although it may not always have been this way, nor may it always be this way, it has indeed been stable for millions of years."

"Doesn't the handoff cause a lot of earthquakes?" asked Dale.

"The Tosok home world has no moon," said Hask. "It probably did once, or else our world would have an even greater greenhouse effect than it does now; Clete told me that without the moon, Earth's atmosphere would resemble Venus's—a thick blanket covering the world. Our old moon's gravity doubtless skimmed off some of our original atmosphere, but that moon must have been lost during one of the handoffs. Anyway, without your own moon churning up Earth's interior through its tidal effects, you would not have any plate tectonics; Earth is, after all, unique among the planets in your solar system in having such things. Without crustal plates, you do not get earthquakes; they are unknown on our world. Except for the impact on our climate, the handoffs proceed quite smoothly."

"But if handoffs occur only every four hundred thousand years," said Frank, "your race can't have known one yet. I mean, you guys are advanced beyond us, but by hundreds of years, not by hundreds of centuries."

"True," said Hask. He paused. "Our fossil record is scantier in many ways than is yours. But since we have no plate tectonics, no portion of our crust is ever subducted and

destroyed through the passage of time; although there are
fewer fossils, our record is contiguous in a way that yours is
not. We were astounded when our geologists found proof in
core samples of the huge periodic temperature changes our
world had undergone for at least many tens of millions of
your years. But although the fossil record shows that a few
species die out at each great freezing, most simply continue
on immediately after the thaw. Life on our world has evolved
to deal with the handoffs—or, more precisely, only those
lifeforms that had an ability to survive freezing survived the
first handoff, and all current lifeforms are descended from
them." He paused. "Perhaps it is not coincidental that our
hearts are primitive compared to yours; I understand many
Earthly fish and amphibians—creatures with similar
hearts—can also survive periods of freezing."

"That's why there was no hibernation equipment aboard
your ship," said Dale.

"Exactly. Simple cold temperatures are enough to induce
hibernation. The two centuries of sleep required for the
journey from our planet to here were insignificant; we could
as easily have gone many hundreds of thousands of years."

"All of that is fine," said Frank, "but then what did you
mean when you said your starflight was about survival?"

Hask's tuft danced in agitation. It was a moment before
he replied. "Our race sent starships to all the worlds neighboring ours to see if there was any life there. Actually,
although Sol is our closest neighbor, we dispatched much
faster ships to several more-distant stars, including the ones
you call Epsilon Indi and Epsilon Eridani, from whom we
had already detected radio signals. As you may have noticed,
we make much less use of metal than you do; again, the lack
of lunar churning has kept most of our world's metals deep
beneath the crust. We simply did not have the resources to
send equally sophisticated ships to all possible destinations.
When we left Alpha Centauri, two hundred of your years

ago, you had not yet begun to broadcast by radio, of course, and so you were not a high-priority target.

"Still, we were not just looking for intelligent life, you understand, but also for *potentially* intelligent life. Four hundred thousand years ago, after all, your own species did not exist—but its forebears did. These missions were sent to ascertain if any intelligent life was present now on neighboring worlds, or if any might arise by the time the next long sleep was over. For eons, life on our world has passed peacefully through the periodic sleeps—after all, the entire ecosystem shuts down during them, so we have no fear of indigenous predators. But what about predators from the stars? What about hostile worlds bent on conquest? No aliens had yet visited our world, so we assumed we were the most advanced form of life in the local universe. But if we were to stop evolving for four hundred thousand years, who knows what now primitive lifeforms from other worlds would—what was the word you used, Frank?—would leapfrog past us during that time? Who knows what threat they might pose to us when we reawaken? Who knows if they would even allow us to reawaken, or would kill us all while we slept?"

"God," said Dale. "You came here to wipe out all the life on Earth."

"Not all the life, Dale—I doubt we could do that, anyway. But we certainly intended to wipe out all the vertebrates, just to be on the safe side."

Frank felt his jaw go slack. *All the vertebrates.* Jesus Christ. It was so big, so massive—and then, all of a sudden, it had a human face. Maria. They would kill her, along with everything else. "That's—that's monstrous," said Frank, his voice quaking with rage. "That's downright evil. What gives you the right to go around the galaxy, wiping out whole planets?"

"A very good question," said Hask. He looked at Seltar,

then continued. "We used to think we were the divinely created children of God—and that, of course, would be sufficient to give us the right to do whatever we deemed necessary; if God did not want us to do it, after all, she would thwart our attempt. But when we discovered that that is not true, that we are merely products of evolution, well, then, the question of having the right to do something no longer enters into it. Survival of the fittest, no? The struggle for life, no? Competition, no? If we can advantage our species, then we have the right and the obligation to do so."

"Jesus," said Dale.

"I agree," said Hask.

"Pardon?"

"Do I misunderstand you? When you invoke the name of your putative savior in that tone of voice, you are expressing disgust, no?"

"Well—yes."

"Then we do agree. I share your disgust, and so does Seltar. But we are a tiny minority. Our hope was that once the others met you, they would realize that it would be inappropriate to wipe your planet clean of life. But they have not wavered in their plan. Indeed, if it had not been for the accident in your Kuiper belt, they would have already completed that task: our mothership is equipped with a high-powered wide-angle particle-beam weapon, which we would have trained on your world from orbit. In short order, we would have irradiated the entire surface of your planet. Indeed, the other Tosoks still intend to do that, once the repairs are complete."

Dale's deep voice: "Do the other Tosoks know that you're a . . . a . . ."

"A traitor?" Hask lifted his front and back shoulders, an acquired human gesture. "Do not hesitate to say it; I am comfortable with the term. No, they do not. We had two possible hopes. The first was to prove that your race was divinely created—if we could show that you were the true children of God, our people would never have harmed you. But your form is as imperfect as ours."

"And the other hope?"

"Seltar. If the mothership was repaired, and the attack on Earth imminent, then Seltar would sabotage the ship— something she could only do if no one suspected her existence. The eight of us would have been marooned here, but that would be—what is your metaphor?—a small price to pay."

"If you woke up first, why not just disable the ship then?" asked Dale.

"I do wish to return home, counselor."

"You could have killed the other Tosoks in their sleep," said Frank.

"God did not move me to do that; despite what happened to Clete, I am no murderer."

Frank's voice was hard. "And what, precisely, *did* happen to Clete?"

"He discovered that Seltar was still alive. I had been careless. While the others were off at the lecture by that paleontologist, I took the opportunity to contact Seltar by radio; I missed her so much, I could not bear not to speak with her. Although my translator was off, Clete overheard me—I had not realized that he, too, had demurred from attending the lecture to work on his script, and he had the habit of pacing the halls as he thought of what he wanted to write. Clete realized that I was speaking to a Tosok other than the ones at the lecture—and doing so in realtime. I chased him back to his quarters and tried to explain to him the necessity of keeping the secret. He said he would not tell anyone—but I could tell he was lying; his face had grown brighter."

"What?" said Dale.

"His face grew brighter—all your faces do that when you lie; I noted the correlation within days of arriving on Earth."

"You mean you saw him blush?" asked Dale.

"No—blush is to change color, is it not? No, I said brighten."

"Oh, Christ," said Frank. "We suspected you guys could see into the infrared, but . . ."

"What?" said Dale.

Frank looked at the lawyer. "He sees infrared—he sees heat. Even if a person isn't visibly blushing, capillaries do dilate in the cheeks, causing the cheeks to warm. Hask here is a walking lie detector."

"As you say," said Hask. "I had no doubt of Clete's intentions. The moment I left, he was going to rush off to the lecture hall to tell you, Dr. Nobilio. I could not allow that—I could not risk that you, or someone you would tell, would reveal the information to Kelkad and the others. Remember, the other Tosoks all knew when you were lying, too." He paused. "I—I just wanted to restrain Clete long enough to bring him proof of what the other Tosoks were going to do, in hopes that he would make a sincere promise of silence . . . so I encircled his leg with the monofilament. I *told* him that if he struggled at all it would cut through him, but . . . but he *did* struggle." Hask paused, and his tuft waved in sadness. "I am so sorry. I meant only to detain him. But he kept bleeding and bleeding. I have never seen so much blood in my life."

"So, with him dead, you decided to dissect the body," said Frank.

"Yes. Do you not see? I was looking for proof of perfection in its design. I wanted so much to find proof of that—it would have saved your race. But instead I found design flaw after design flaw. I could not dispose of the corpse, but I did manage to steal at least some of the most egregiously obvious evidence of evolution rather than inspired design. The bad design of the throat was obvious at a glance, especially since I had already seen you choke on some water, Frank. The eye was harder—but my pocket computer allowed me to do a decent scan of its structure. And as I traced your digestive system—messy thing that it is—I found that closed tube that seemed to do nothing at all. By wrapping them up and tossing them in the trash, I had hoped to delay the others discovering that your race is not divine."

"But why didn't you just come forward and tell the world the truth?" asked Dale. "For God's sake, you were interviewed by Barbara Walters. You could have simply said, while the cameras were rolling, that your people have come to destroy us. Then we would have apprehended all the other Tosoks. End of problem."

"Counselor," said Hask, "surely you do not think all of us would have come down to Earth's surface without some way to control and operate our mothership remotely? Yes, our main engine is damaged, but the fusion reactor still functions, and the particle-beam weapon is in working order. Kelkad has surgically implanted in his person a device that can activate the weapon from the ground. True, using it while he is still on the surface would kill him and the rest of the Tosoks, but he would view that as proper fulfillment of his destiny, and it would accomplish the primary mission: sterilizing the surface of your planet. If any attempt is made to arrest him, I have no doubt that Kelkad will trigger the weapon."

"Well, then," said Dale, "our military could simply shoot Kelkad dead."

"The same device monitors his vital signs. If he dies, the weapon will be fired automatically."

"Christ," said Frank.

"Exactly."

"So, what do we do now?"

"I am not sure," said Hask. "But there is much more to this court case than simply my fate. The fate of your world hangs in the balance."

"What if the particle-beam device were disabled?" asked Frank.

"Neither Seltar nor I have the expertise to do that; it had

automatically locked onto your world from the moment we entered your solar system, and we were terrified that if we meddled with its workings, we would accidentally activate it."

"You may not have the expertise," said Frank, "but my government's military has many people in its employ who specialize in high-tech weaponry—and most of them haven't had much to do these last few years . . ."

THIRTY-SEVEN

Detective Lieutenant Jesus Perez came out of the eleva-tor into the sixth-floor lounge at Valcour Hall, accompanied by five uniformed LAPD officers. Six Tosoks—Kelkad, Rendo, Torbat, Dodnaskak, Stant, and Ged—were seated in the lounge, watching a taped movie on the TV there.

"Which one of you is Kelkad?" said Perez.

The alien captain touched a control on his translator. "I am Kelkad."

"Kelkad," said Perez, "you are under arrest."

Kelkad's tuft flattened in disgust as he rose to his feet. "So this is human justice! Your case against Hask is failing, so now you are going to put me on trial?"

"You have the right to remain silent," said Perez, reading from a card. "If you give up the right to remain silent, anything you say can and will be used against you in a court of law. If you desire an attorney and cannot afford one, one will be appointed for you without charge. Do you understand these rights as I've explained them to you?"

"This is an outrage!" said Kelkad.

"Do you understand these rights?"

"Yes, but—"

"Fine. Which of you is Rendo?"

"I am she."

"Rendo, you are under arrest. You have the right to—"

"What are you going to do?" asked Kelkad. "Arrest *all* of us?"

"That is correct," said Perez.

"But that is insane," said Kelkad. "I have learned about your laws. You cannot arrest multiple suspects simultaneously for a crime that clearly only has one perpetrator. None of us were involved in the murder of Dr. Calhoun."

"Who said anything about Dr. Calhoun?" said Perez. "You are being charged with conspiracy to commit murder."

"Whose murder?" demanded Kelkad.

"Everyone's murder," said Perez.

"This is preposterous! We are your guests. We have done nothing wrong."

"Once your fusion engine is repaired, you plan to turn a particle-beam weapon onto the Earth."

Kelkad was silent for a moment. "Where did you get a wild idea like that?"

"You will have a chance to face your accuser during your trial."

"But who could—" Kelkad clapped his front and back hands together at his right side. "Hask! Hask has told you this. What kind of system of justice is this? Hask is an accused murderer—he would say anything to deflect attention from himself."

"Until now, you were insisting publicly that Hask is innocent."

"Innocent? No, he is clearly a killer. Clearly insane. You heard the testimony—he is unbalanced by the standards of your people. I tell you now that he is unbalanced by the standards of mine as well."

"Hask is the only decent Tosok I've met." Perez paused. "Well, one of the two decent ones, anyway."

Kelkad rotated his torso so that his eyes fell on each of his companions in turn. "So one of you is in league with Hask?" he said.

"Oh, it's not one of them, Kelkad," said Perez. "Michaelson, do you have that tape?"

"Right here, sir."

"Play it."

Michaelson moved toward the VCR, ejected the tape the Tosoks had been watching—*Star Trek II: The Wrath of Khan*—and inserted the one he'd brought with him.

"This was recorded about an hour ago," Michaelson said, hitting the play button.

It took a second for the picture to stabilize. When it did, it showed a view inside the Tosok mothership, obviously taken by a camera mounted on a Tosok's torso; periodically a hand or part of a U-shaped foot was visible in the field of view. The Tosok was floating down a ship's corridor, large yellow lighting disks—simulating the sunlight from Alpha Centauri A—alternating with smaller orange ones, simulating Centauri B's rays.

The corridor ended at a square door, which slid aside. Standing next to Perez, Kelkad made a sound that was untranslated, but Perez assumed it was shock at which door was being entered.

The image bounced around as the Tosok with the camera kicked off walls and the ceiling. The voice narrating the tape was the translator's; it was almost impossible to hear the actual Tosok voice underneath. "All right," it said, "I am at the main control unit for the particle-beam weapon. Now, give me a moment . . ." Hands reached into the picture, pulling a panel off one of the instrumentation banks. "There it is," said the voice. "See that red unit in the center? That's the circuitry controlled by Kelkad's transmitter." The image bounced some more, and the red unit slid out of view as the Tosok jockeyed for position. "There are three lines going into it."

A female human voice, crackling with static over a radio: "Just as I thought. Nothing complex—the designers obviously assumed Kelkad's deadman switch wouldn't ever be under attack from this end. Now, use the voltmeter I gave you—"

The human and the Tosok consulted for about ten minutes. Finally, the human said, "Okay, you'll want to cut the blue one."

The Tosok hesitated. "Of course," said the translated voice, "there is a small chance that I will trigger the weapon when I interrupt the feed. I suppose some last words are in order, in case that happens." A pause. "How about, 'You can choose your friends, but you can't choose your neighbors'?"

Hands appeared in the picture again—this time, holding small tools—and the image bounced back to show the red unit. "Here we go . . ." One of the tools snipped what looked like a fiber-optic cable leading into the unit.

"The weapon did not discharge," said the Tosok voice.

"The deadman switch should be deactivated now," said the human voice.

In the sixth-floor lounge, Torbat said, "Hask will die for his treachery."

As if on cue, the recorded voice said, "As you humans would say, this is one for the history books, so I suppose I should get a decent shot of myself." The image went dark as a hand reached toward the camera, and there was a clicking sound as it was disengaged from the suit. The view spun wildly as the camera was swung around, showing the Tosok—

"Seltar!" said Kelkad, the word sounding somewhat different when untranslated. *"Kestadt pastalk ge-tongk!"*

"If that's 'I thought you were dead!'" said Perez, with relish, "then you've got another think coming."

"That should take care of everything," said Seltar, on the tape. "You can go ahead and apprehend the others now."

Michaelson moved in and clicked off the VCR. The TV came on in its place, showing *Wheel of Fortune*.

"Now," said Perez. "Which of you is Dodnaskak?"

A front hand went up meekly.

"Dodnaskak, you have the right to remain silent—"

"Where is Hask?" said Kelkad.

"Don't worry about that," said Perez.

"He is here, no?"

"That's not important," said Perez. "I advise you again to say nothing until you've consulted with an attorney."

"He *is* here," said Kelkad. His breathing orifices were dilating. "I can *smell* him."

"Stay where you are, Kelkad." Perez gestured at one of the officers, who put a hand on his holster.

"Do not threaten me, human."

"I can't allow you to leave," said Perez.

"We have submitted to enough of your primitive foolishness," said Kelkad. He began to walk backward, front eyes still on Perez.

"Stop, Kelkad!" shouted Perez. Michaelson removed his gun from his holster. A moment later the other four officers did the same thing. "Stop, or we'll shoot!"

"You will not kill an ambassador," said Kelkad, whose long strides had already taken him most of the way to the elevator.

"We are allowed to use force to subdue those resisting arrest," said Perez.

Michaelson had his gun trained on Kelkad; the other four officers had theirs aimed at the remaining five Tosoks, who were standing perfectly still, except for their tufts, which were waving like wheat in a high wind.

"I know Hask is in this building," said Kelkad, "and he is going to answer to me."

"Don't take another step," said Perez.

Michaelson shifted his aim slightly, taking a bead on the controls for calling the elevator. He fired a single shot. The sound was loud, and a lick of flame emerged from the gun's barrel. The elevator controls exploded in a shower of sparks.

"You're next," said Michaelson, re-aiming at the alien captain.

"Very well," said Kelkad. He stopped moving, and began reaching his front hand up toward the ceiling. His back hand, hidden by his torso, must have been rising, too, and when it cleared the top of his dome-shaped head, Perez suddenly realized that there was something shiny and white in its four-fingered grasp.

There was a flash of light in Kelkad's palm, and a loud sound like sheet metal being warped. Michaelson was knocked backward against the wall. Perez wheeled around. A neat hole, perhaps an inch wide, had been burned through the center of the man's chest. His corpse was now slumping to the floor, leaving a long smear of blood on the wall behind him.

Four more quick flashes of light, four claps of aluminum thunder, and the remaining uniformed cops were all dead as well. "Do not make me kill you, too, Detective Perez," said Kelkad. "Did you think that after the attack on Hask, I would walk around unarmed?"

Perez immediately bent down to pick up Michaelson's gun, now lying on the floor. By the time he got it, Kelkad had already disappeared down the right-hand wing of the building. Perez crabbed sideways, keeping the gun trained on the remaining five Tosoks, who seemed to be unarmed. He picked up a second officer's gun. But another one of the guns had ended up quite near one of the other Tosoks. Perez couldn't get at it without exposing himself to physical assault, and he couldn't run off after Kelkad without the other Tosoks grabbing it, as well as the remaining two revolvers. Perez tucked one gun into his pants' waist and, keeping the other one aimed at the Tosoks, used his left hand to get his cellular phone out of his jacket pocket to call for reinforcements.

Hask was in his dorm room on the second floor of Val-cour Hall, clearing out his personal belongings. What with the other six Tosoks being taken away to jail, there was little point in him continuing to reside in this giant residence, which, after all, USC *did* have other uses for.

It was bad enough being a traitor to his own people, and knowing that he would never see the stars of home again, but at least his few possessions would help him remember his old life. Hask picked up the *lostartd* disk that had decorated his dorm room. The crack in it where the two halves had been joined together was only visible if he held the disk obliquely to the light. He carefully packed it in the suitcase Frank had given him, wrapping it in two of his tunics for protection.

Suddenly the sound of a gunshot split the air. It had come from upstairs. Hask felt all four of his hearts pounding out of synchronization—the sound reminded him of the shot that had dug into his own chest on the lawn outside this very building. Moments later he heard the sound of five Tosok blaster discharges. By the absent God—one of them must have brought a blaster along on the journey! Hask hadn't thought any handheld weapons had been among the mothership's supplies; no direct contact, after all, had ever been intended with aliens.

The sounds fell into place in his mind—the other Tosoks were resisting arrest. Another sound, faint and distant, came to his sensitive ears—the echoing slaps of Tosok feet on concrete. One of the Tosoks was coming down the stairs.

There had been five blaster discharges—presumably five humans now lay dead. And the Tosok with the blaster might very well be coming to get him.

Valcour Hall was large. If Kelkad—who but the captain

would have brought a hand weapon on the journey?—had been up in the sixth-floor lounge, he'd have to come down four flights of stairs. The sound was clearly coming from the stairwell at the end of the other wing; that meant he'd also have to run the length of both wings to reach Hask's room, which was at the opposite end of the building.

Hask thought about making his own escape, smashing his dorm-room window and jumping to the ground below. Earth's gravity was less than that of the home world; it was a significant fall, but probably one that he could survive. Hask would then have to try to escape by running across the campus. But the blaster had a range of several hundred meters—Kelkad could probably pick him off with ease. No—no, he would make his stand here.

Hask understood much of human law now: he was about to be attacked with a high-energy weapon and he honestly believed his life was in danger. He *was* entitled to respond with deadly force.

If only he had a weapon of his own . . .

Captain Kelkad rounded one stairwell and then another. He almost lost his balance several times; human steps weren't deep enough for him, and the hand railings were unusable. But he continued down, passing landing after landing, until he'd reached the second floor. He leaned his front arm against the horizontal bar that operated the door mechanism, clicking the locking bolt aside. He then took a step back and swung the door open, while remaining shielded behind it. He peered around it: no sign of Hask, or anyone else. He paused for a moment. His breathing orifices were spasming, gulping air—but they were also gulping aromas. He could smell Hask's phero-mones wafting this way; Hask must be in his room at the far end of this floor.

A fitting place for the traitor to die.

_____

It had taken a minute to get ready, but Hask was pre-pared now. He could hear the pounding of Kelkad's feet coming down the perpendicular corridor. Hask looked out his door, down his own stretch of hallway. Ten meters away was one of the glass-and-metal doorways that normally served to muffle sounds; when Valcour Hall was eventually filled with students, anything that helped keep sound down would be welcome. That doorway had been left open for most of the time the Tosoks had been using the facility; a wooden wedge was jammed underneath the door to keep it open.

Kelkad surely knew that Hask had no handgun; judging by the sound, Kelkad was running down the adjoining corridor at top speed. But Hask knew his captain well: Kelkad wouldn't open fire at once. First he would want to confront Hask, cursing him as a traitor—

Suddenly Kelkad appeared in the lobby between the two wings. Hask ducked mostly behind the wall of his room, only his head sneaking out of the doorway to watch. Kelkad lost some speed as he changed directions, but soon was charging down the corridor, knowing that he didn't have much time, knowing that more human police officers were doubtless rushing to the campus.

"Hask," screamed Kelkad. One advantage of having separate channels for the mouths and the respiratory system was that he could still speak clearly while gulping for breath. "You treasonous *distalb!* You complete—"

And then he hit the open doorway in the middle of the hall—

And suddenly the words stopped.

Kelkad's momentum—all that angry inertia, all that speed, all his mass—carried him through the doorway.

He continued on, mostly as a single unit, for a meter or so past the threshold, and then he began to topple—

—and pieces of him began to fall this way and that, like a child's creation made out of blocks—

—cubic hunks of flesh and bone and muscle, their newly exposed faces slick with pink Tosok blood, tumbling to the floor, some bouncing as they hit—

Hask came out of his room and moved toward the carved-up blocks, each about a foot on a side, that had once been his captain. Some parts were twitching, but most lay completely still.

Of course, there wasn't much blood; the valves in the arteries and veins still worked, even in death.

Hask reached up with his back hand to his own tuft, feeling it as it waved in relief. He looked at the door frame, and at the carving tool stuck to it with Krazy Glue on the left side of the jamb about four feet off the floor. Also visible were twelve of the blue beads glued to the side of the jamb, and to the lintel, and to the metal piece across the bottom of the doorway. What he could not see was the monofilament itself, stretched out in a grid of horizontal and vertical lines across the opening.

The words of his dear departed friend Cletus Calhoun came back to Hask. "It slices!" Clete had said. "It dices!"

Indeed it did.

Hask looked down at his own front hand. One of his fingers had been severed; he'd been in such a hurry setting up his trap that the digit had gotten in the way of the monofilament. But it would grow back in time.

New noises came to Hask's ears: the sound of approaching sirens. Soon, the police would be here.

For this crime, at least, Hask knew he'd get off.

THIRTY-EIGHT

There was still the matter of *The People of the State of California* v. *Hask*. After the arrest of the other Tosoks, Hask and Seltar had gone public with their story, and Hask retook the witness stand to tell it all. There was no doubt now that he had indeed killed Cletus Calhoun—Dale had been wrong in assuming Seltar had been directly involved.

Linda Ziegler made her closing argument, Dale followed with a passionate plea for leniency in his summation and argument, then—as California law allowed—Ziegler got the final word, presenting a summation that reminded the jurors that Cletus Calhoun was dead, and regardless of everything else, someone had to answer for that crime.

Finally, Judge Pringle took the jury through CALJIC: the California Jury Instructions—Criminal. "Ladies and gentlemen of the jury," she began, "you have heard all the arguments of the attorneys, and now it is my duty to instruct you on the law as it applies to this case. You will have these instructions in written form in the jury room to refer to during your deliberations. You must base your decision on the facts and the law.

"You have two duties to perform. First, you must determine the facts from the evidence received in the trial and not from any other sources. A 'fact' is something proved directly or circumstantially by the evidence or by stipulation. A stipulation is an agreement between attorneys regarding the facts.

"Second, you must apply the law as I state it to you to the facts, as you determine them, and in this way arrive at your verdict.

"Note this well: you must accept and follow the law *as I state it to you,* whether or not you agree with the law. If anything concerning the law said by the attorneys in their arguments or at any other time during the trial conflicts with my explanation of the law, you must follow my directions . . ."

The jury instructions took most of the afternoon, but finally they came to an end:

"You shall now retire," said Drucilla Pringle, her voice noticeably hoarse by this point, "and select one of your number to act as foreperson. He or she will preside over your deliberations. In order to reach verdicts, all twelve jurors must agree to the decision. As soon as all of you have agreed upon the verdicts, so that when polled, each may state truthfully that the verdicts express his or her vote, have the forms dated and signed by your foreperson and then return with them to this courtroom."

"What if the jury brings in a conviction?" asked Dale. He and Frank had returned to Dale's office; there was no telling how many hours or days the jury would spend deliberating. Hask was off spending what might be his final few hours of freedom with Seltar.

"Then we appeal, no?" said Frank.

Dale sighed. "Everyone says that. But, you know, we can't appeal a jury verdict *per se.* They're not subject to any kind of review. You can only get an appeal if the *judge* has made a mistake. In this kind of case, it has to be a mistake in law. If Pringle sustained objections she should have over-ruled, if she disallowed evidence she should have allowed, or if her instructions to the jury were flawed, then we can get an appeal hearing—but that's no guarantee that the verdict will be overturned."

"Oh," said Frank. "You always hear about appeals. I thought we automatically got another shot."

"No. Which is why I asked the question: what do we do if the verdict *is* guilty?"

"I don't know," said Frank. "Any ideas?"

"Yes. Have a word with your boss."

"Excuse me?"

"There are only two people in this world who are more powerful than that jury. One is the governor of California, and the other is the president of the United States."

Frank nodded. "An executive pardon."

"Exactly. There's no way the governor is going to go against Monty Ajax when he knows that Ajax is going to be running in the next gubernatorial race—so that leaves the president."

"Christ, I don't know. He hates stuff like this, especially in an election year."

"We have a client who did indeed kill a human being," said Dale. "This may be Hask's only hope, and—"

Dale's intercom buzzed. He pounded the button. "Yes, Karen?"

"The courthouse just called. The jury has a verdict."

Frank jumped to his feet, and even old Dale Rice managed to move his vast bulk quickly.

"Ladies and gentlemen of the jury, have you reached a verdict?" asked Judge Pringle.

Frank was seated behind Dale and Michiko. Hask had also returned; his tuft was moving in agitation. His front eyes were locked on the jury box; his back eyes were locked on Seltar, who was sitting alone in the bank of six Tosok chairs at the side of the courtroom. There was a hush over the room; every spectator and every reporter was leaning forward.

The foreperson, a thin black man in his early thirties, rose. "We have, Your Honor."

"Please hand it to the clerk." The paper was passed to the clerk, who carried the sheet to the judge's bench. Drucilla Pringle unfolded the page and read the verdict. Judges were supposed to be stone-faced—they knew every eye in the court was on them at such moments. But Pringle was unable to prevent one of her eyebrows from climbing her forehead. She refolded the verdict and handed it back to the clerk.

"You may read the verdict, Mr. Ortiz."

The clerk cleared his throat, then: "We, the jury in the above entitled case, find the defendant, Hask, not guilty of the crime of first-degree murder of Cletus Robert Calhoun, in violation of Penal Code section 187, as charged in count one of the information.

"And we further find that the defendant did not use a deadly weapon, to wit an alien cutting device, in the commission of this crime.

"And we further find that in the commission and attempted commission of the above offense the defendant, Hask, did not personally inflict great bodily injury upon Cletus Robert Calhoun, and was not an accomplice to the above offense, within the meaning of Penal Code section 12022.7."

Frank let out a great cheer and reached over the wooden fence to thump Dale on the back. Michiko Katayama had thrown her arms as far around her boss as they would go and was hugging him. Seltar rushed over to embrace Hask across the wooden barrier between the audience section and the defense table.

For her part, Linda Ziegler was absolutely stunned, her

eyes wide, her mouth hanging open a bit. Next to her, her second chair, Trina Diamond, just kept blinking.

"This is your verdict, so say you one, so say you all?" asked Judge Pringle, facing the jury.

The jurors nodded. "Yes," they replied in unison.

"Counsel, do you wish the jurors polled?"

"No, ma'am," said Dale, grinning from ear to ear.

"The People?" said the judge.

"Ah, no," said Ziegler, after a moment. "No, Your Honor."

"Ladies and gentlemen of the jury, do you wish to address the lawyers?"

The jurors looked at each other. They certainly were under no obligation to do so, but California law permitted them this opportunity. The foreperson turned to Pringle. "Nothing we say now can weaken the power of our verdict?" he asked.

"That's correct," said Pringle. "What's done is done."

The foreperson nodded. "Then, yes, we would like to say something to the lawyers."

"Go ahead, Mr. Foreperson."

The man took a deep breath, then looked at Ziegler. "I'm sorry, Ms. Ziegler. You should have won. You had him dead to rights. I mean, we all agreed that he *did* do it. He did kill Mr. Calhoun."

Ziegler's eyes went even wider. "Jury nullification," she said.

The foreperson looked at Pringle. "Your Honor, you instructed us in the law. But, well, we couldn't bring ourselves to apply it." He looked to Ziegler again. "Hask didn't mean to kill Calhoun, so it wasn't premeditated. Still, we could have found him guilty of a lesser charge, like involuntary manslaughter. But if we'd found him guilty, there might have been an appeal—the defense can appeal guilty verdicts, but the prosecution can't appeal innocent ones, isn't that right, judge?"

Pringle nodded. "In most cases, that's essentially correct."

"So we let him go. We let him go so he wouldn't be jailed; after all, we all agreed he presented no threat to anyone else." The foreperson looked at the other jury members, then turned back to the judge. He shrugged a little. "Yes, the rest of the crew are now in prison—but Kelkad did send a message to his home world, and other Tosoks will be coming to Earth at some point. Who knows what changes there have been in Tosok society in two hundred years? We thought that if these new Tosoks saw that we are a reasonable, compassionate, and forgiving people, then maybe, just maybe, they wouldn't wipe our planet clean of life."

"I don't understand," said Frank. He stopped the grinning Dale before the lawyer stepped out of the courtroom into the crowd of waiting reporters. "What is—what did Ziegler call it?—'jury nullification'? What's that?"

"The jury is the conscience of the community," said Dale. "They can do whatever they damn well please."

"But the judge said they had to follow the law, whether they agreed with it or not."

Dale shrugged. "Judges always say that—but, in fact, there's no legislation to that effect, and plenty of precedent to the contrary. The jury never has to explain or justify its decision to anyone, and there's no mechanism for punishing jurors for making a verdict that goes against the evidence. If they want to let someone go free, they're entitled to do that."

"Thank God for juries," said Frank.

"For once," said Dale, still grinning from ear to ear, "I agree with you."

THIRTY-NINE

No one expected to see another Tosok ship anytime soon. After all, the message Kelkad had sent from Earth to Alpha Centauri had to take 4.3 years to get to its destination, and the fastest any reply—whether a ship, or simply another message—could arrive was another 4.3 years later.

Or so people had thought.

But in the intervening two hundred years, the Tosoks had apparently discovered a way to outwit Einstein. The new vessel appeared without warning in orbit near the Tosok mothership just four and a half years after Kelkad had sent his message. Some astronomers declared they had detected a flash of Cerenkov radiation just as the ship appeared, and others were muttering things about hyperspace and tardyon/tachyon translations.

The new arrival was eighty meters long, and there were no right angles anywhere in its construction. Its hull was smooth—no vents, no projections, no apparent windows— and a mural had been painted on it. It was abstract, and no one was quite sure at first what it depicted. Only when it was imaged with cameras that saw well into the ultraviolet did the image become apparent.

The starboard side of the ship depicted a landscape of crystal mountains, what might have been treelike things with trunks made of chains of spheres, and a lake with either a giant floating city or boat in it, or an island every centimeter of which was covered by majestic spires and towers.

The port side showed what was obviously the Milky Way galaxy, as well as Andromeda, and the two Magellanic Clouds.

The alien ship simply orbited Earth for two days, but finally a small translucent sphere bubbled up out of its surface, then separated from it. The sphere simply dropped to the Earth at a speed of about five hundred kilometers an hour—fast, but not nearly fast enough to make for a fiery passage through the atmosphere. It slowed when it was about three kilometers up, and settled gently as a feather in the United Nations plaza, next to one of the Tosok landers; Hask and Seltar spent much time at the UN these days. Whether the new arrivals were aware of the significance of the UN, or had simply located the Tosok lander with some sort of scanner, no one could say for sure.

UN and U.S. troops were waiting for the spherical craft. Tanks and bazookas were trained on it. It was unlikely that either could destroy the ship, but if more Tosoks came out, Earth would not go down without a fight.

The current U.S. president was in the underground command center in Virginia, built for use in case of nuclear war. Frank Nobilio was with him. They were in contact with the troops in New York via communications satellite, and were watching the live video feed being provided by CNN.

The alien ship was on the ground for about ten minutes before a door materialized in its side. One second, the curving wall was absolutely smooth; the next, a square hatch had appeared in it. The hatch dropped open, its curving doorway forming a ramp. The picture went wild for a moment as

CNN's camera operator tried to get a close-up of whatever was in the chamber.

It was not a Tosok.

The creature stood about 1.2 meters tall. It had radial symmetry, like a starfish. Six legs dropped down to the ground. Interspersed between them were six arms or tentacles that, incredibly, were lifted up above the creature's torso, as if in surrender.

"Is that a lifeform?" said the president. "Or could it be a robot?"

Frank was science advisor to this president, as he had been to his predecessor. The camera operator was several hundred feet away, and every small jiggle of his equipment caused the zoomed-in image to bounce wildly. Frank nodded at the president. "It does look metallic . . ."

The thing stepped forward, onto the ramp. CNN cut for a second to a shot of the troops. Every weapon was trained on the starfish. It started down the ramp. Frank peered at the screen some more. "No—no, it's not a robot. It's wearing a space suit. See?" He pointed at the creature's legs. Strapped to each one was a thin cylinder, presumably containing whatever gases the creature breathed.

"But Tosoks can breathe Earth air . . ." said the president.

Frank nodded. "Meaning not only is that not a Tosok, it's not even from the same *planet* . . ."

"Why are its arms up in the air like that?"

Frank shrugged. "To show it's not carrying any weapons?" A pause. "Mr. President, if it's not a Tosok, and it's not armed, you should get the troops to stand down."

The president looked at one of the generals seated near him. "We still don't know what it is," said the soldier.

"For God's sake, Karl," said Frank to the general, "you saw its mothership—if it wanted to kill us, it could have done so from orbit."

The president spoke into a telephone handset. "It's our

recommendation to the UN commander that the military forces assume an at-ease posture."

The alien continued to move forward.

"Frank," said the president. "We need to talk to that thing. Can we communicate with it the way we did with the Tosoks?"

Frank shrugged. "I don't know. I mean, eventually, sure, at least about some basic math and science, but—" His eyebrows went up. "It may not be a Tosok, but I bet it knows how to speak the Tosok language. After all, it presumably came in response to Kelkad's message."

"So?"

"So send Hask out to greet it."

FORTY

On second thought, it was deemed better to send a human out to make first contact. There were those who still didn't trust Hask or Seltar, and the two Tosoks might also be in danger from this new alien: they were, after all, traitors to their own people.

Since Frank Nobilio was the only living person with direct experience at first contact, the job fell to him. He was flown from the Virginia command center to the UN aboard a two-seater Marine Corps Harrier TAV-8B VTOL jet, dispatched from a training squadron at Cherry Point, North Carolina.

Once he'd arrived in New York, Hask and Seltar greeted Frank in an office inside the looming monolith of the Secretariat building.

"It is good to see you, friend Frank," said Hask.

"You, too," said Frank. "You recognize that ship?" The alien vessel was visible through the mirrored office window.

"No," said Hask. "But that is meaningless. So much may have changed in the intervening centuries since our departure." The male Tosok's tuft waved. "Whatever happens now, Frank—to you, and to your world—I thank you for your previous help, and ask you to remember that humanity had at least a few friends beyond this planet."

Frank nodded. "I will."

Seltar raised her front hand, bringing it tentatively toward Frank's head. "May I?" she said.

Frank was momentarily taken aback, but then paused and smiled. Seltar's four flat-tipped fingers tousled Frank's hair, which was now mostly gray. When she was done, Frank used his right hand to briefly stroke Seltar's tuft, and then, in a move that clearly surprised the male Tosok, he reached over and mussed Hask's tuft as well.

"I have to go," said Frank. "Can't keep our new visitors waiting."

Hask took his portable computer, with its cross-shaped keypad, from its pouch on his tunic and handed it to Frank. Frank took the elevator down to the ground floor and walked slowly across the United Nations parking lot, toward the spherical ship. The twelve-limbed alien had retreated into its lander some time ago. Frank was afraid he was going to have to go right up to the landing craft and knock on its hull, but when he got within about fifteen meters of the lander, the door appeared again and the alien—or another one just like it—came out.

Frank held up the portable computer, hoping the alien would recognize it, and know what to do with it. It was a gamble: Frank certainly wouldn't recognize a specialized Italian farm implement from A.D. 1800, let alone one from a culture that wasn't his own; there was no real reason to think that the newcomer would recognize a two-century-old Tosok computer.

The alien reached out with one of its long arms—from the way it moved, it appeared to be jointed every twenty-five centimeters or so, rather than being a tentacle of pure muscle. Frank took a deep breath and continued to close the distance between them. The alien was indeed wearing some sort of space suit, made of a silvery fabric. There was a clear strip, though, near where each leg joined the torso, and through it Frank could see the creature's real skin, a scaly yellowish gold. The clear strips were meant to allow the alien's eyes to peer out—Frank could see two oval-shaped eyes, one atop the other, on each leg. The eyes had lids that closed from left to right, but no two eyes on the same leg ever seemed to shut simultaneously. The tanks of gas on the legs joined directly to the suit at the base of each leg; presumably that's where the creature's six breathing orifices were located.

Frank continued to hold the computer out in front of him. Because of the alien's short height, he could look right down on it from above. It really did seem to be perfectly radially symmetrical; if it had a preferred front side, Frank could see no indication of it. One of the six arms reached out to Frank. Although its tip was gloved in the same silvery material, Frank could see that it was bifurcated. The two branches easily plucked the computer from Frank's hand. The suit had been warm to the touch; it was radiating excess heat— the alien perhaps came from a cooler world than this one.

The alien folded its arm back, bringing the computer up to one of its vertical pairs of eyes. It turned it around, apparently unsure how to hold it. Frank's heart fell—they'd have to start over from scratch, apparently, trying to learn to communicate.

Suddenly a second starfish alien emerged from the spherical lander. It came toward Frank quickly, its body rotating as it did so. When it got close, Frank saw that it had something in one of its hands—a device that ended in precisely the same sort of tripronged connector he'd come to associate with Tosok technology. The second alien took Hask's computer from the first alien and plugged it into the device it had brought along. Lights began flashing on both devices.

Frank was aware of a high pitched buzzing sound, barely audible. At first he thought it was coming from Hask's computer, but his ears soon focused better on the source. The two aliens were apparently conversing, using mostly ultrasonics. The buzz alternately came from one of them, then the other.

The lights stopped flashing on Hask's computer. The second alien disengaged it from the device he'd brought, and proffered it to Frank. Frank was surprised, but took it back. The alien handed the other device to the first alien, then twirled back a dozen meters.

The buzzing started again from the first alien, and within seconds, the synthesized voice Frank had come to associate with Hask was emerging from the device the starfish creature was now holding. "Do you understand me?" said the voice.

"Yes," said Frank, his heart pounding with excitement.

"There is no accepted way to render my own individual name in the subset of the Tosok vocal range that you apparently communicate with. Please assign to me a name whose sound you can replicate."

Frank was momentarily lost. "Umm—Tony. I'll call you Tony."

"Tony. And you are?"

"Frank."

"We came as soon as we received the Tosok message. I saw from orbit that we were not too late."

"Too late?"

"To keep your planet from being wiped clean of life."

"You came to prevent that?"

"We did. The Tosoks tried to extinguish us as well. We are . . . resilient. They have been subdued."

Frank felt his features spreading into a broad grin. "Welcome to Earth, friend."

The new aliens—already dubbed Twirlers by CNN's correspondent—were originally from the star humans called Epsilon Indi, which, although it was eleven light-years from Earth, was only nine from Alpha Centauri. The Twirlers had begun using radio centuries before humanity had, and so a high-speed Tosok mothership had been dispatched to that star, arriving there thirty-odd years ago. Although it took decades, the Twirlers had managed to defeat the Tosoks.

There were twenty-six Twirlers aboard their beautiful mothership, but it was Tony who served as the sole communicator with humanity. And today, Tony was addressing the General Assembly of the United Nations. He stood at the same lectern Kelkad had used five years before, the great seal of the planet he'd so recently arrived upon spread out behind him, embraced by olive leaves.

Tony no longer used Hask's voice; once that had been explained to him, he asked for a sample of a new voice so that he could adopt it as his own. Frank had mulled it over, then sent an aide to Blockbuster Video to rent *To Kill a Mockingbird;* Tony now spoke with the voice of Gregory Peck's Atticus Finch.

"People of the Earth," said Tony. "My government sends its greetings. We are pleased that the Tosok plan has been averted, and that you are safe. But other worlds have not been so fortunate. We have found three that have been wiped clean by the Tosoks, and two continents on my own home world were rendered uninhabitable during our conflict with them. You have a grievance, no doubt, against the Tosoks who came here—but I hope you realize that they in fact have done nothing against Earth beyond the killing of a handful of individuals. In concert with races from two other worlds that the Tosoks had threatened, my people are planning to try the few surviving Tosoks for genocide and attempted genocide—including the five surviving ones here on Earth who were involved in the plot. We invite you to participate in this undertaking if you wish, or to leave it to us. But we do now formally request the extradition of the Tosoks known as Rendo, Torbat, Dodnaskak, Stant, and Ged. We assure you, they will pay for their crimes.

"I stand here, in your United Nations, whose brief, and—I hope you will forgive me for saying—troubled history has been explained to me. The UN, with whatever problems it has, represents an ideal—an abstraction made concrete, a belief that by all working together, peace can be assured. It hasn't always worked, and it may not always work in the future, but the ideal—the promise, the hope, the concept—is one that my people share, as do those of the other two inhabited worlds I mentioned.

"Our three worlds have already begun creating a—well, let me translate it in a parallel way—a United Planets, an organization representing all of our interests, designed to ensure that never again will war rage between the stars.

"Your planet is, frankly, primitive compared to the existing members of the United Planets. But I see here that the United Nations has long been involved in upgrading the standards of its less affluent, and less developed, members. This, too, is an ideal shared by the United Planets, and I stand before you all, as representatives both individually of your nations and collectively of your world, to invite Earth to join us." Tony paused, looking out at the faces of humans black and white and yellow and red. "My friends," he said, "we offer you the stars."

EPILOGUE

The next time he was in L.A., Frank Nobilio stopped by the offices of Rice and Associates to say hello. To his astonishment, he found Dale Rice in the process of packing up his diplomas, books, and framed jigsaw puzzles.

"What are you doing?" said Frank. "They can't fire you; you're the boss."

"I'm leaving," said Dale. "I'm finished."

"Mr. Rice exits a winner," said Frank, nodding. "Are you going to that Georgia cabin you'd always talked about?"

"Not Georgia," said Dale. "And I'm not retiring. Seventy-two is *young*, son."

"Then what?"

Dale pointed a finger upward.

"You're becoming a judge?"

He laughed. "No. I'm going up."

"Up?" And then realization dawned. "You're going with the Twirlers?"

"Yes."

"But why?"

Dale shrugged. "Maybe some of your idealism has

rubbed off on me. Or if not yours, maybe some of Atticus Finch's. Maybe, down deep, even after all these years, I *do* believe in the ideals of justice. And that means, whether they're guilty or innocent, that the Tosoks deserve the best damned defense they can get."

Frank's mouth dropped open. "My God—you're going to defend the Tosoks!"

Dale smiled. "I went by the Tosok section of the L.A. County Jail yesterday and spoke with Dodnaskak, who has succeeded Kelkad as their captain. She's pleased to have me as lead counsel. So, yes, the Twirlers are going to take me with them when they return home."

"Incredible," said Frank. "But good luck. I have a feeling you're going to need it."

There was quiet between them for a time. "You know, the trials are going to be like Nuremberg," said Dale. "There'll be judges from each of the worlds the Tosoks threatened, but Tony says the judges don't have to be legal types; after all, there are widely different judicial concepts among the various races. Maybe you should put your name in for being one of the Earth judges."

Frank's eyebrows went up. "Me? No, no—not me. It wouldn't be right. I've already made up my mind what the verdict should be."

Dale looked at him. "You darned idealist, you. You'd let them off."

Frank just smiled.

ABOUT THE AUTHOR

Robert J. Sawyer is one of only eight writers in history to win all three of the world's top awards for best science-fiction novel of the year: the Hugo (which he won for *Hominids),* the Nebula (which he won for *The Terminal Experiment),* and the John W. Campbell Memorial Award (which he won for *Mindscan).* The ABC television series *FlashForward* was based on his novel. His latest novels are *WWW: Wake, WWW: Watch,* and *WWW: Wonder,* a trilogy.

In total, Rob has won forty-five national and international awards for his fiction, including eleven Canadian Science Fiction and Fantasy Awards ("Auroras") and the Toronto Public Library Celebrates Reading Award, one of Canada's most significant literary honors. He's also won the Crime Writers of Canada's Arthur Ellis Award, *Analog* magazine's Analytical Laboratory Award, and the *Science Fiction Chronicle* Reader Award, all for best short story of the year, as well as the Collectors Award for Most Collectable Author of the Year, as selected by the clientele of Barry R. Levin Science Fiction & Fantasy Literature, the world's leading SF rare-book dealer.

Rob has won the world's largest cash prize for SF writing, Spain's 6,000-euro Premio UPC de Ciencia Ficción, an unprecedented three times. He's also won a trio of Japanese Seiun awards for best foreign novel of the year (including for this book, *Illegal Alien),* as well as China's Galaxy Award for Most Popular Foreign Author. In addition, he's received an honorary doctorate from Laurentian University and the Alumni Award of Distinction from Ryerson University.

Rob's books are national mainstream bestsellers in Canada and have hit number one on the bestsellers list published by *Locus,* the trade journal of the SF field. He's a frequent TV guest, with more than three hundred appearances to his credit, and has been the keynote speaker at many science, technology, and business conferences.

Born in Ottawa in 1960, Rob now lives in Mississauga, Ontario, with poet Carolyn Clink, his wife of twenty-seven years.

For more information about Rob and access to his blog, visit his World Wide Web site, which contains more than one million words of material, including a book-club discussion guide for this novel. You'll find it at **sfwriter.com**.

New from Hugo and Nebula award–winning author

ROBERT J. SAWYER

The final book in the WWW trilogy

0001110010101010000000010111111101010000000010100010101000000010111010100101010

W W W : W O N D E R

0001110010101010000000010111111101010000000010100010101000000010111010100101010

The advent of Webmind—a vast consciousness that spontaneously emerged from the infrastructure of the World Wide Web—is changing *everything*. From curing cancer to easing international tensions, Webmind seems a boon to humanity.

But Colonel Peyton Hume, the Pentagon's top expert on artificial intelligence, is convinced Webmind is a threat. He turns to the hacker underground to help him bring Webmind down. But soon hackers start mysteriously vanishing. Is Webmind killing them before they can mount an attack?

Caitlin Decter—the once-blind sixteen-year-old math genius who discovered Webmind—desperately tries to protect her friend. Can this new world of wonder survive—or will everything, Webmind included, come crashing down?

penguin.com

New in hardcover from award-winning author

ROBERT J. SAWYER

000111001010101000000001011111110101000000010100010101000000010111010100101010

WWW:WATCH

000111001010101000000001011111110101000000010100010101000000010111010100101010

Webmind is an emerging consciousness that has befriended Caitlin Decter and grown eager to learn about her world. But Webmind has also come to the attention of WATCH—the secret government agency that monitors the Internet for any threat to the United States—and the agents are fully aware of Caitlin's involvement in its awakening.

WATCH is convinced that Webmind represents a risk to national security and wants it purged from cyberspace. But Caitlin believes in Webmind's capacity for compassion—and she will do anything and everything necessary to protect her friend.

M603T1109

Don't miss the first book in the WWW trilogy
from Hugo and Nebula award-winning author

ROBERT J. SAWYER

000111001010101000000001011111110101000000001010001010100000001011101010010101010

WWW:WAKE

000111001010101000000001011111110101000000001010001010100000001011101010010101010

Caitlin Decter is young, pretty, feisty, a genius at
math—and blind. Still, she can surf the net with the
best of them, following its complex paths clearly
in her mind. When a Japanese researcher develops
a new signal-processing implant that may give her
sight, she jumps at the chance, flying to Tokyo for the
operation. But Caitlin's brain long ago co-opted her
primary visual cortex to help her navigate online.
Once the implant is activated, instead of seeing reality, the landscape of the World Wide Web explodes
into her consciousness, spreading out all around
her in a riot of colors and shapes. While exploring
this amazing realm, she discovers something—some
other—lurking in the background. And it's getting
smarter . . .

penguin.com

THE ULTIMATE WRITERS OF
SCIENCE FICTION

John Barnes	Jack McDevitt
William C. Dietz	Alastair Reynolds
Simon R. Green	Allen Steele
Joe Haldeman	S. M. Stirling
Robert Heinlein	Charles Stross
Frank Herbert	Harry Turtledove
E. E. Knight	John Varley

penguin.com/scififantasy

ACE RoC